Raised in New England, with degrees in literature and writing from the University of New Hampshire and the University of Iowa Writer's Workshop, Richard Duggin spent 55 years teaching fiction writing at the University of Nebraska at Omaha, where he founded a four-year Bachelor of Fine Arts degree program in creative writing, and a two-year low residency Master of Fine Arts in Writing program. He is still teaching and writing.

His published books include the novel, *The Music Box Treaty*; a short story collection, *Why Won't You Talk to Me*; and this novel, *Woman Refusing to Leave*. A new novel recently completed, *The Snipe Hunters: Boys in Exile*, is yet due to be published. Other stories of his have appeared in periodicals such as *Playboy, American Literary Journal, Beloit Fiction Journal, Laurel Review, Kansas Quarterly, The Sun,* and elsewhere.

For Cynthia
My wife
My lifelong companion
My literary provocateur

Richard Duggin

WOMAN REFUSING TO LEAVE

AUSTIN MACAULEY PUBLISHERS™

LONDON • CAMBRIDGE • NEW YORK • SHARJAH

Ordering Information:
Quantity sales: special discounts are available on quantity purchases by corporations, associations, and others. For details, contact the publisher at the address below.

Publisher's Cataloging-in-Publication data
Duggin , Richard
Woman Refusing to Leave

ISBN 9781643786452 (Paperback)
ISBN 9781643786469 (Hardback)
ISBN 9781645364764 (ePub e-book)

Library of Congress Control Number: 2019920973

www.austinmacauley.com/us

First Published (2020)
Austin Macauley Publishers LLC
40 Wall Street, 28th Floor
New York, NY 10005
USA

mail-usa@austinmacauley.com

+1 (646) 5125767

I am truly grateful to the following for their invaluable and gracious support of my need for cloister while I am in the solitary labor of writing:
Anderson Center for Interdisciplinary Studies
The University of Nebraska at Omaha Research and Grants Committee
The Nebraska Arts Council
The National Endowment for the Arts
Ragdale Foundation Residency for Artists
Yaddo Corporation Residency for Artists

Part I
Thursday Evening

Chapter 1

The cold front swept down through Wyoming, gathering momentum as it entered Nebraska in squall lines of thunderstorms that lit up the insides of dense clouds with stroboscopic flashes of lightning. With each spectacular explosion of light, the gray underbellies of the clouds glowed, as if they were loosely woven duffels stuffed with light itself. But instead of pouring down rain, it snowed. It fell in flakes the size of pillow feathers. Behind the first violence of the passing front that drove temperatures down from the morning high of 65 to 32 by early evening, the clouds stretched out low and flat, settling like slate on Platte City.

Catherine Harper's fifteen-year-old daughter, Holly, was exultant when after the first hour it seemed the snow was going to stick to the ground instead of watering in. "Bet there's no school tomorrow!" She was kneeling on the sofa in the living room, leaning over its back to peer through the parted drapes over the bow window. "It's still snowing like mad out there!" There was a tinge of admiration in her voice for the craziness of the event.

Catherine scowled. "It can't possibly last this late in the season. It'll melt by morning."

"But, Mom, check it out." Already, the snow was lacing the edges of the mullions. "It's piling up big time."

"You're going to school tomorrow. They will *not* close school," Catherine said firmly, as if Holly's observation was a matter of poor mental discipline.

It was already the fourth week in April. Thursday morning had started out warm and cloudless, with no more warning of change than what last evening's weather report on the 10:00 news had mentioned as a *possibility* of a thunderstorm later in the afternoon, associated with an incoming front out of the Rockies. But even with a Nebraskan's wait-and-see tolerance for unpredictable weather, Catherine, who was keenly sensitive to change and instability in her life lately, never in the world would have expected this. It wasn't just a fluke of nature, it was an aberration. It had begun as one thing and had become another—a spring rain turned to snow, spring itself snatched back into winter with a cat's deadly play.

"Let's see if there's anything on the radio that'll tell us what's happening," she said.

"Bet they say it's a blizzard," Holly said. "I hope there's three feet of snow coming."

Catherine opened the wood cabinet doors in the living room that housed the components of her old stereo system, a relic of her college days. She tuned the radio away from Holly's rock music station to KPLC, the local Platte City talk and news station. There was a commercial in progress for an agricultural herbicide. *"Bigfoot is coming, and he packs a wallop,"* the sonorous male voice boomed from twin floor speakers.

She had caught the beginning of *Speak Out,* the local call-in talk show. This night's topic was: *"The rise of gun-related deaths in Nebraska. Will the ease of purchasing guns keep us as safe in our homes as we once were?"* Catherine dismissed any interest in the topic, but the moderator began the broadcast with an acknowledgment of the dangerous weather out there. *"If you're out on the streets driving, take it very carefully. Conditions are hazardous, with slippery roads and low visibility. If you don't have to be out there in your car, good people, stay put at home. Light a fire and spend the next two hours with us speaking out on gun ownership…"*

Catherine switched the radio off. She would not even allow a gun in her house. Early in their marriage, Donald had got the wild idea that he would teach their son to shoot a gun when he was old enough to go hunting with him during pheasant and deer season. He bought a big, ugly shotgun the size of a piece of field artillery, with a deer hide scabbard to carry it in. "It's supposed to help disguise the smell of the gun," Donald said.

"But the skin of a *deer*!" Catherine had decried.

His only defense was, "You wear shoes made from the skin of a cow." As if it were the same thing. As if two wrongs made it right. At her insistence, he'd hung the gun on the pegboard over the tool bench out in the garage. "In deference to your phobia," he'd told her. As it turned out, by the time Donald Jr. was of an age where other sporty fathers would have taken their sons on first fishing trips or out to target practice, Donald's brother William had already borrowed the shotgun and never returned it.

"I don't think we're going to hear much more until the ten o'clock news," she said to Holly, who by this time had stretched out on the sofa with a recent issue of Catherine's *Self.*

"Doesn't matter," Holly said. "I know already what's going to happen."

"Oh, well. Good for you then. Apparently, you're clairvoyant," Catherine said. "You must have inherited that from me."

"From Dad," Holly said.

12

"Not likely," Catherine replied.

"Sometimes he knows things that are going to happen. He can tell sometimes when there's going to be a big fire or when there's going to be a bunch of accidents and people hurt. 'They come in threes,' he says."

"That's just statistical data he reads in his firemen's magazines," Catherine said. She didn't want to pursue it, even in banter. Her ex-husband's obsession as a firefighter with other people's crises and his long shifts on duty away from home had been the wedge driven in their marriage that finally split them apart when their son Donny died. *Ten years old!* she thought as the unexpected reminder erupted in a painful catch in her throat. Their son's life had bled away on the emergency room table, while she was unable to reach his father to be at her side because he was across town attending to someone else's lesser troubles. Now, being reminded of her former marriage was somewhere she didn't want to be, especially while her own black premonitions about her court hearing tomorrow were still crawling like ants beneath her skin.

At this same moment, Donna, her eight-year-old, was coming downstairs from her room. She'd been up there since right after supper, leaving most of her meal on her plate. Catherine was not sure if she were ill or if it was a protest over another night of frozen dinners. She had let Donna leave the table without questioning her because she was in no mood herself to either sympathize with or explain to an eight-year-old why her mother was behaving so…*un*motherly. Steven had been gone from their home for almost three months already, and her eccentric behavior probably seemed almost normal to her children by now.

Holly looked up from her reading and said, "Look outside, Donna-Bonna, it's a blizzard."

"Big deal," Donna said.

"There's probably no school tomorrow," Holly replied.

"So? I want to go to school. I don't wanna stay home all the stupid day," Donna said and slouched off to the kitchen. But it struck Catherine like an inspiration that if, indeed, schools were canceled due to snow, government offices might be closed. The courts would have to postpone the day's docket. It could take another month to reschedule everything. And if things were postponed—if the unnatural snow were actually a good thing and not simply another dismal omen piled on top of all the others that had beset her—then anything could happen in the ensuing month of reprieve. With just a little more time to appeal to Steven, she felt almost certain she could make him listen to reason and come back home to make her life right again.

"Maybe there won't be school," she said. "Wouldn't that be something."

She could hear Donna in the kitchen dragging the stepstool from underneath the wall phone by the whiteboard. She heard her opening cupboard doors and pulling things down—peanut butter, no doubt, and the box of Club Crackers. Leaving Holly to her reading, Catherine went to the kitchen to investigate.

She found her youngest at work on a countertop, spreading peanut butter on the thin wheat crackers, and she paused to observe, touched suddenly by the frown of concentration on her daughter's face as she dipped the knife into the jar and then spread a gloppy dollop on a cracker held between her thumb and forefinger. Meticulously, Donna had begun to arrange each cracker in a ring around the edge of the plate.

"I'm sorry, Donna Joanne, that your supper, which you didn't even finish, wasn't enough to fill you up."

Donna set the cracker on the plate, licked her thumb and finger clean of the overspread, and began again. "That wasn't even supper," she said. "I hate pot pies. They're mushy."

"Well, maybe you'd like to plan the menu for tomorrow night. *And* do the cooking."

"I could make better stuff than pot pies," Donna said.

"You should be grateful your sister made any dinner at all for us. I'm not feeling well today."

"Like, not just today," Donna replied and bit into a peanut butter frosted cracker.

The sarcasm prickled. But she deserved her daughter's scorn. This wasn't the way she normally spoke to her children, by innuendo or pointed irony. It was the way Steven had dealt with them. Catherine had too often let him take charge of their moments of unrest. He would use his facility with language to twist and manipulate, although the girls responded well enough, matching him, sometimes, jibe for jibe, slight for slight. It seemed to bring them alive for the brief and tumultuous time their stepfather had lived with them. For a while, he'd animated all their lives.

Avoiding further confrontation, Catherine left Donna to her self-pity and retreated to the family room beyond the kitchen on the opposite side of the house from the living room.

She stood at the sliding glass door looking out over the deck and backyard beyond, where she could see the snow falling steadily, silently, covering everything, filling even the dark cracks between the planks of the deck that Donald had made during the last summer they were together. In the middle of the deck, light from the kitchen through the family room etched an elongated parallelogram on the snow.

She unlatched the patio door and slid it aside. A small avalanche of snow, from a low drift against the bottom of the door, cascaded inward onto the carpet, and she leaned out through the opening. The cold air was an astringent on her face, and she sucked it in sharply, freshening her lungs. The snow hissed as it struck.

"The snow falling faintly through the universe and faintly falling like the descent of their last end upon all the living and the dead," she whispered, and was both surprised and pleased the line came back to her unbidden. It was the last line from a James Joyce story Steven had introduced to the class when she was a student of his in a creative writing course. She had signed up on her therapist's advice to help "regenerate her creative energies," enough to find her way back to her painting again by exploring another art form. It had worked far better than she could have imagined.

Because Steven was a colleague of Martin Stuart, the chair of the Art Department where Catherine taught drawing and art history courses part-time, he had "taken her under wing," inviting her to his office after class for individual conferences over her writing, then to coffee at the student union, helping her to craft into language that awful passage of her life, from the once-manageable contentment in her province as mother and wife to the unbearable loss of her son that had emptied her of all desire. A burned-out tree stump was the image of her body and spirit she saw in her head all through her hospitalization and eventual return to her ashen life at home.

Through his solicitous care for her need to put into language the shapes and colors of her despair and anger, Steven had raised her from the doldrums of a bleak marriage into a radiance of renewed creative spirit. So of course, she would feel in the gifts of his attention what she perceived must have stemmed from his craving for her. She was convinced they had both been waiting years for each other. When, inevitably, he took her to his bed, her own awakened hunger to feel passion for life again had miraculously brought on her first-ever epiphanic orgasm before she could even give name to what she was experiencing. When it happened, she believed she was going crazy again. Her mind exploded in vivid colors—red, orange, blue—and she could hear her blood pumping through her ears, feel her nerves along her spine and hips firing with electrical spasms that arched her back. When she came back from it, she found Steven raised on stiffened arms above her, smiling down in wonder. "*Mein Gott*, Dr. Frankenstein," he'd quipped. "She's alive! She lives!"

Catherine had only just eased onto the sofa in the shadows across the family room, sinking into a huge throw cushion propped against one end away from the slant of light from the kitchen window when Donna shrieked from the kitchen, "No! Get out of here!"

"Just one," Holly said in a hushed voice meant for Catherine not to hear.

"No! Get out of here, now! Mo-*om*!"

"Don't be so stingy," Holly said with louder retort.

"Give it back," Donna cried. "Brat."

"*Brat*," Holly mimicked, mincing the word.

Catherine saw in her mind the nasty twists of her daughters' faces. Their strident voices shattered the safe darkness of the family room, pushing her deeper into her cushion.

There was the sound of skin on skin, a sharp slap.

"You little *shit*," Holly hissed, but not low enough to avoid Catherine's hearing.

"Mom!"

Another slap. Now Donna was screeching in rage.

"You hit me first, you little shit!"

There was no escape. Their voices became even shriller—Donna screaming for her attention, Holly alternately taunting and beseeching, "Big baby. Shut up, now. *Shh*, quiet. Leave Mom alone! You little pissant."

All at once, in the grating sound of their voices piercing her thoughts, Catherine felt the familiar bands tightening around her head, compressing her skull, tightening with a snake's squeezing coils. And then, just as suddenly, she saw them vividly in her mind—steel bands, the kind men cinched around stacks of lumber and wooden shipping crates, cutting into the skin of her forehead and temples until the metal sang with tension.

Then it was Donna, rushing into the family room. "Mom, Holly *hit* me!"

"I heard," Catherine rasped, squeezing air from her lungs to sound the words. The pain in her head and now a crushing weight on her chest made even speech a labor, and she could feel her heart pounding at the onset of another panic.

Donna was crying, great sobs of outrage. "I made them for myself, she can make her own…such a brat…I hate her."

Catherine shook herself upright, driving away the images by focusing on the glass doors to the deck, the snow falling, falling. "I can't deal with this," she said. She was woozy, sick to her stomach. She could hear Donna gulp in mouthfuls of air and push them out again to control her tears.

"I'm sorry, you'll have to settle it for yourselves," Catherine said, her voice sounding distant to herself. She could not feel her mouth shaping the words. Her lips had gone numb.

"Mom, it's not fair!" Donna tried once more.

"Go to your room," Catherine replied, waving the air abstractedly with a hand, motioning her daughter away. "Go on, go up to your room. I don't want to hear any more of this. I don't feel well. Please. Go play, go to bed, go read a book. Just stay away from Holly."

"But I didn't *do* anything." Donna did a spin on one foot and ran from the room. Her footsteps on the carpeted stairs to the second floor sounded like hammer blows as she kicked each riser with her toes on the way up. Her door slammed shut, and blessedly, their voices were silent again.

For a time, there was nothing more than the normal hums and clicks of the house breathing. She could hear the refrigerator motor kick on, the sound of wind along the eaves outside the family room door. But she sensed there was something incomplete, something still about to happen, although she couldn't say just what. Her heart drummed in her chest and her breaths were shallow and quick. Her fingertips tingled. She felt a compelling urge to rise, to get up and move before she was pulled down into unconsciousness, but she could not lift even an arm against the oppressive weight. The panic was spreading like waves breaking over sand.

There was movement in her peripheral vision, a shadow on the carpet, and her body was iceshot by an electric pulse to her heart.

"Mom?" Holly stood at the entrance to the dining el. "Are you all right?

"Yes," Catherine said, vexed by the fright her daughter had given her. But the adrenalin in the sudden startle had shocked her enough to revive her. The tingling under her skin, the great commotion in her head, ebbed.

"Should I bring these to her?" Holly said. "She left them." She was holding the plate of crackers and peanut butter, all jumbled helter-skelter now.

"Leave her alone, Holly. Just don't go near her. You ought to know better than to antagonize her like that. She's eight years old. You're fifteen."

"I didn't do anything. Geez."

"I don't know what to tell you right now. Go on upstairs," Catherine said. "Please, go to your room. I'm having a bad time here. I can't handle any more stress right now."

Holly looked dumbly at the plate in her hand for a moment, then shrugged her shoulders. "Do you want me to get you something, or call Aunt Charly or someone?"

"No, I'll be fine. Go upstairs now."

"I could call Dad," Holly said in a quieter, tiptoe voice.

That had become Holly's stock answer after Steven had left and Mom couldn't fix, find, or cope. "For what?" Catherine said. "He's probably on duty. I'll be fine if you'll just leave me alone for a while. I've got a wicked headache, is all. And I'm upset."

"Why?" Holly said.

"Why? Do you not remember what's happening tomorrow?" Catherine said.

Her daughter was quiet a moment. Then, "Are you…you know…having a breakdown again?"

Catherine sucked in her breath, gritting her teeth. She was about to answer her with anger. But then she let the breath out. "Holly, you *know* what is going to happen to me—to *us* tomorrow—don't you?"

Holly shrugged.

"I am going to court. I am going to be *divorced* in the afternoon from your stepfather. Before a judge. In a court of law."

"Well, sure, I know that," Holly replied in a tone that carried its own dismissive shrug. "But you've done it before. You're not going to jail or anything, right?"

A single startled laugh erupted from Catherine's throat like a hiccup. She leaned back again, waving Holly away with a flaccid arm. "Oh, sweetheart. Just go. I'll be fine if I can have a little peace and quiet to collect my thoughts."

"Okay, Mom." There was a note of resignation in Holly's manner. Was it disappointment in her mother's behavior? Catherine had ample reason for the way she was feeling, but she couldn't explain herself just then. Pressed down as she had been all day, first by suffocating anxiety, then alternately drained by debilitating lethargy, it was as if a watersodden net had been cast over her and her brain was nested in kelp, her thoughts barely able to bubble up through dense brown seaweed.

She shook off the image before it became real. She *would no*t go through that again.

In another few minutes, she rose from the sofa and left the family room. In the dining el, the table was littered still with the girls' supper dishes. Donna's potpie was a glutinous mess mashed about her plate. Catherine stacked the dirty plates from the table, one on top of the other, and took them to the sink, scraping the residue into the open maw of the InSinkErator.

On a counter beside the sink sat the plate of crackers. She left the crusted dishes and silverware in the sink, unrinsed, and turned quickly away. The stepstool was still out where Donna had dragged it to reach into the cupboards above the countertop, and she slid it across the floor and set it beneath the whiteboard and wall phone.

On the board in the upper left corner was printed in heavy black marker lines:

Don't Wait Until Tomorrow
DO IT—TODAY!

Steven had put it there, his euphemistic admonishment against procrastination, when he first moved into their house, and it remained the only message never erased. Even after he'd left, Catherine had kept it, although she never heeded the advice.

She turned off the lights in the kitchen and climbed the stairs to her bedroom where she entered her bed, sliding between the limp sheets, dank after a week without change.

For a time, she lay flat on her back, her arms pressed into the mattress, trying to will her body and mind to come to rest and welcome sleep to overtake her again. She took deep, slow breaths, the way Nancy, her therapist, had taught her as a way to remove stress from the body and prepare her mind for more creative work. "Now you're lying on a warm beach next to the ocean," she'd offered the image for Catherine.

This was when Catherine was afflicted again with terrible panics after the loss, last August, of her teaching job at the college followed shortly by Steven's unfathomable separation from her. It had seemed in the collapse of the two pillars of her stability—purpose and love—that both events were linked causally by more than their rapid chronology. Nancy had listened to her while she alternately sobbed and raged, and finally, she had made Catherine lie down on a yoga mat on the floor in her office, and she sat down on the floor beside her and intoned instructions in a voice Catherine supposed her therapist believed would soothe her. "The sun is shining down warm on the top of your head, warm and radiant, and with each breath you take in, you feel the warmth entering through the top of your head, pushing the stress out of your mind, out your head, across your chest, and down your arms through your fingertips, and with each breath you let out, you can feel that warm, radiant sunlight seeping in to fill all the hollow places."

But now, as Catherine lay still, breathing in, breathing out, she was only becoming lightheaded. There was no hole in her skull for sunshine to enter. Her heart was not so much beating as vibrating in surges, sending electric tingles to her fingertips.

She bolted upright and drew her knees to her chin, wrapping her arms tightly about her shins. From within the swamp of images and colors roiling in her head, she sensed another movement, a hand—a groping hand—reaching up and out through the front of her skull. It was a strong hand, veined, masculine. It stretched out of her, and she could see the whole hand and its wrist slip through her brain like an arm through a sleeve. The fingers, the palm, the wrist stretched from her skull, reaching toward something—*what?* It protruded from her forehead like a horn. *God's hand?*

All at once, she was desperate to call Steven. He could tell her everything was going to be all right. If she heard his voice, its deep vibrations resonating along her nerves, she would be able to calm herself again.

Fumbling with the phone on her bedside table, she mistook the numbers on the keypad, then mistook them again. It was as if her hands were foreign to her arms and her will to make them work. Her fingers seemed dead things, functioning autonomically—helpless to hold, to make, to fix on their own—but operating thoughtlessly all the same. Twice she almost dropped the receiver in her weak grip. Her head throbbed at the point near the crown as the hand groped the air.

Finally, on her fourth try, stabbing buttons with her index finger, she made the connection. She waited, listened to his cell phone ringing, and waited longer for Steven's hand on the other end to pick up and touch her through the air. It rang five, six times before a recorded message interrupted, informing her in a tinny female voice that a voice mailbox had not yet been set up for that number. She was confused by the message. She'd not heard it before because he had always answered by the third or fourth ring when she needed to talk to him. Certainly, he would be home tonight, of all nights. The snowstorm would have kept him in.

Something was wrong. Something must have happened to him. She saw blood.

Instantly she was out of bed, wide-awake and shot full of adrenaline. She rushed from the bedroom to the bathroom and back, looking for something, but she could not bring to mind what.

"What am I doing? What am I *doing*?" she said to no one. Her ears were full of buzzing insects on the wing.

In a flash of inspiration, she was certain now that it had been intended she call him. The hand in her head—the vision was *real*—a desperate summons from him. It was he who needed help, not her. He needed *her* help.

Back in her bedroom, she threw on the first clothes she could find—the same patio dress and slip-on sandals she had worn yesterday and discarded on the cedar chest at the foot of the bed when she'd returned home from the store before the storm. She rushed down the stairs into the darkened living room, then down the shorter flight to the front hall, arguing with herself the whole way. *What are you doing? This is crazy.* Nonetheless, she snatched her winter parka from a hanger in the small closet by the front door and then hurried to her car in the garage, finally with a sense of purpose.

Chapter 2

Donald Sparta, in jeans and sweatshirt, stood at his bedroom window staring out at the snow falling on the parking lot behind his condominium building. It was falling steadily, mounding on the roofs and hoods of the cars that had not been moved since the storm began earlier in the evening. On the ground, it lay deep enough to crest half way up their wheels, and around pickup trucks or vans it had formed levees, leaving black areas of bare asphalt visible beneath each vehicle.

He had been pondering what lay ahead for him tomorrow on his company's first day back from their monthly six-day rotation off duty. For several days now, he'd been dogged by an uncharacteristic worry over a backlash he feared was coming from his crew because of the new assignments of the recently graduated fire department recruit class. It had been in the papers for the past six months, from the opening headlines back in late October—*First Females Pass PCFD Physical. Will Women Firefighters Fill Men's Boots?*—to the recent announcement of the graduation of the latest recruit class from the fire academy. Rumors had been flying for the ten weeks; it had been known that two women had passed the department's qualifying test for the first time. But finally, the orders had come down from the Chief's office last Thursday, the day before C-Shift, Donald's shift, went on rotation, and they had learned that one of them, Deborah Gallant, had been assigned to Engine 55. She would begin her first shift with them when they returned to the station tomorrow morning at 0700.

Donald had received the news in a visit from his district chief, Kyle Thorpe. It was the beginning of a new order of things in Platte City fire service. "A new fire service culture," was how Chief Thorpe put it, and he warned Donald that the dubious honor had befallen him "to see to it there's no flak, no scandal, no bitchin' to the press by anyone—not the veterans or the rookie. There's probably going to be all kinds of newspaper people and TV people wanting to do interviews, and city hall doesn't want any static over this thing."

"What do I say when they want to interview her?" Donald wanted to know.

"Show 'em around the station, be helpful as you can, but make it clear they've got to stay the hell out of your way. This is a fire station, and you're all at work. And nobody comes in to do a story that hasn't first got clearance from the Chief's or the Mayor's office, and then you'll get a call from downtown first before they get here. Most important, though, is that, on the inside, you babysit your people and make sure you cool down any friction before it gets hot. There's no turning this thing around, so the guys have just got to suck it up and get on with their jobs. This is the fire department, and these new cadets are firefighters."

Donald had reacted as he felt any other captain would have: he showed the chief around the station on inspection, offered him a cup of coffee which was politely refused, and then, when the chief had left, Donald posted the order on the fire station bulletin board. His inner reaction was that his boat was being rocked. And the waves began stirring almost immediately in the responses of his men.

They argued in the histrionic manner of those used to speaking before they thought. The crew of Aerial 53—the companion apparatus to Engine 55 in the station—ribbed those on the engine company over their bad luck. Among Donald's crew, there were threats of resignation, walkouts, and transfer, and there were obscene jokes from the truckmen of the aerial company. The only one who seemed to take it in stride was Charlie Wesson.

Wesson was the oldest firefighter in the department and still a smoke-eater with forty-two ambitionless years of service at the lowest rank. He refused in all his years of duty to wear an air mask into a fire. He was an emphysematic, had high blood pressure, and was at mandatory retirement age of sixty-two, but he was too cantankerous to quit until they kicked him out. That would happen at the end of this month. It was to replace Wesson that Deborah Gallant was being assigned to Engine 55. "The Old Man is giving me an early retirement present, is all," he said of the new development. "The onliest reason she's comin' to Fifty-Five's is to give me a bunkmate so's I don't have to diddle myself no more."

"That's just the kind of bullshit that'll be going around, too," Gene Metzger said. He was the young driver-engineer of Engine 55. "My wife's jealous enough as it is, but when she finds out we've got a woman bunking in with us, I might as well pack up and leave home."

"Nothin' to worry about there," Wesson said. "She ain't no woman. She's a firefighter. She's a fire*person.* Federal Government says so. The Public Safety Director and the Fire Chief says so, and I suspect shortly, when they start deducting her dues, our exalted International Brotherhood of Firefighters will say so." Even though he was a union member, Wesson had little respect for politics in the fire service.

Al Czernecky, the fourth member of Engine 55, speculated the new rookie was no woman at all, but probably she and the other one who had made it through the academy were dykes.

Donald had been nettled more than usual by their pettiness. It was always something with them: wages, callback policy, new operating procedures. Now this. Only he wasn't in the mood to listen to them this time. "There's an order down and it stands," he spoke up finally. "You've got six days to get used to the idea that you're going to be working with a new man…or person. Whatever." He flushed at his slip, annoyed he couldn't even handle the simplest authoritative transaction.

"See, you don't even know what to call her," Metzger said. "But I don't give a shit. I'm gonna lodge a complaint through the union for discrimination if I come back here Friday and find the City's given her a special bedroom or a private shower, or done anything at all that shows this chick's gonna get treated different because she wipes herself when she pees."

Donald had tried to mollify them. "Look, she's passed all the same application tests you did. Now she's passed the coursework in the academy. She's a firefighter. You can't keep her off the department, so I'd suggest, you treat her with the same consideration you all got when you came on shiny-faced and scared shitless as rookies. Let her do her job."

But that only led to more argument, more complaint. Someone wanted to know what they had done wrong to draw the attention of the administration to them this way. Who knew why the administration did anything? Donald offered. "We're in a quiet house. It's a good place for a rookie to learn the business, and we've got an opening—or will have by the end of the month when Leather Lungs, here, retires." He indicated Wesson. The others sneered at this. No one in the entire station had ever spent his probation time in a quiet house, they reminded each other. They'd all spent their first year either at Station 1 downtown, or else at Station 2 and 3 in the warehouse and riverside districts of Corinth.

"What happened to the other one?" Metzger asked. "Where did she get stationed?"

"She's the Chief's aide." Donald said. "She's down at Station 1, driving car for The Man."

"Jesus Christ!" Wesson had rasped. "We got the ugly one!"

For most of his rotation days off, Donald had kept himself from thinking further about it. The griping among his crew had fizzled out when it was time to leave at end of shift, and they would have had six days to calm down. But with tomorrow morning fewer than eight hours away, he found himself in an uncharacteristic state of anxiousness over what he feared might happen that would create more friction in house between the men, Cadet Gallant, and himself.

Now his bedside phone was ringing, and when he picked up the receiver, it was his daughter Holly's voice on the other end.

"Dad?"

"Hey you," he said.

"Did I wake you?"

"No, the phone did." It was an old joke he'd taught her years ago. "What time is it?"

"I dunno. Around quarter to twelve, I think," she said.

He looked at his watch and registered the late hour. "What's up? Why aren't you in bed?"

"I was. I've been asleep for hours. Mom sent us to bed early tonight."

"Oh?"

"Mom sent us to our rooms. Donna and me…well, you know…. It's not all that important, Dad," Holly said wearily.

He was wary suddenly that she was calling for something bigger. "What happened?"

"Nothing. She was being crabby and threw this major hissy fit because I took a peanut butter cracker she made. No biggie. I just woke up a few minutes ago to go the bathroom, and…well, Mom's not home."

"What do you mean she's not home?" He looked at his watch again.

"I can't find her. When I went to bed, she was in the family room on the couch. She was having one of her bad headaches again. And then when I got up, she was gone."

"Have you checked her studio?" Early in their marriage, he had built Catherine a room over the garage, complete with a skylight in the north slope of the roof, where she could shut herself away with her easels and paints.

"I looked there. I checked all over. And her car's not even in the garage."

"Her car's gone?" he said. He'd registered Holly's dismissive "one of her bad headaches." He was alert now to signs from the past.

"What did she say to you about her headache? How was she talking?"

"She just said she wasn't feeling well, and she had a real bad headache. And she said she was upset about tomorrow."

"Tomorrow. Why tomorrow?"

"She has to go to court. She and Steven get divorced tomorrow."

"Oh, sure," Donald said. He had known about that. Catherine had informed him of her court date when he had picked up the girls last Friday, his first

24

rotation day off. In the distraction of his recent problems at work, he'd forgotten it was coming up this soon. And, frankly, other than a brief vindictive satisfaction he'd enjoyed a couple months ago when she separated from Harper, he had suppressed any interest in the details of her marital trouble that didn't affect the girls. But the news had gratified him, nonetheless. More than that, even: for the first time since she had abandoned him three years ago, Donald felt heartened without daring to give name to why.

"Did she leave a message for you anywhere?"

"No, uh-uh. I looked," Holly said. "I'm standing right here by the board in the kitchen, looking at it. No message, except the dumb 'Do It Today.'"

His daughters had told him about their stepfather's silly slogan on the whiteboard alongside the phone. It was another of the man's pomposities, like the irritating voice message he had put on Catherine's home phone: *"You've reached the Harpers. We are absent or otherwise incommunicado and powerless to answer your call…."* Such a pretentious asshole.

"I'm sure she'll be right back," Donald said, but without conviction. "I'll come out to the house and stay with you until she gets back. Just leave the front door unlocked so I can get in, and you can go back to bed."

"No, Dad. No, it's all right. I'm not afraid or anything. I can take care of things here. I've done it plenty of times when Mom and Steven went out for a night together. It's just that she would call if she was going to be late coming home."

He took an even breath to calm himself. "All right, then. I trust you're old enough to handle things." In fact, he was grateful that she told him not to come. He did not feel at all comfortable in that house, hadn't for a long time. It was alien to him now with the other man's aura about it. "Now listen. You have her call me just as soon as she gets in tonight, okay? Write a note for her on the board where she can find it. I don't care what time it is, she should call me."

"Okay."

"She's probably gone to the store for something. But if she's not and you get worried or need something, call me, okay? I'll be here until I have to go on duty at seven tomorrow morning. You call if you need me to come over for anything. Anything at all."

"I'm not worried. I just wanted to see if…you know, if you might know where she went or anything," Holly said. And then in a brighter voice, "Do you think there's gonna be any school tomorrow?"

"Probably not. The snow's still coming down pretty heavy. Now, don't forget to leave a note for Mom, okay? Do it right now, when you hang up," he said.

When he'd hung up, Donald stared at the phone. Catherine was not home on such a night…. As sure as hell, she hadn't just slipped out for a bit to go to the store, the way people do when it starts to snow and there's the possibility of being housebound by the weather. He was concerned now that it had to do with the way she got when she was having "one of her bad headaches," as Holly put it. He suspected that her call was not to ask if he knew where Catherine had gone, but to alert him that her mother could be on the verge of going off the rails again where she experienced the hysteria and delusional hauntings that had hospitalized her after their son had died.

His first thoughts were how he might find out where she was and if she was safe. With that in mind, he dialed the fire department dispatch line. "Captain Sparta," he said to the voice that answered. "Just checking if there have been any vehicle accidents in the area tonight."

"No, captain. Not yet anyway," the dispatcher said. "Looks like all the crazies stayed home tonight for a change."

Not all, Donald thought.

If Catherine was falling apart, as Holly seemed to intimate, then she could well end up in the hospital again, as she had when she had landed in St. James Hospital in Lincoln after Donny's death. And if she did need that kind of intervention, it would be worse for her this time because the son of a bitch she was divorcing now wouldn't be there to look after things, to keep the house going for Holly and Donna and be Catherine's contact with the world outside. Harper would be safely out of it after today. Who, then, was there to stand in and look after her?

He already knew the answer and strangely, the prospects of stepping up didn't disturb him the way he had once imagined it might.

He remembered how it was for him the first time, how distressed he was by the startling change in her behavior, and he was assailed again by that pitiable image of Catherine. Why, after all this time, it still affected him with such pangs of sadness and insult, he didn't know.

He had come home from duty one morning in late June to find her in bed unable to move. "My muscles don't want to work," she said, in a voice timid as a child's. "I don't have any strength in them at all." She had been crying for most of the time he was gone on shift, she'd told him, and she'd "run out of tears."

Donald had helped her dress and led her downstairs to the car, supporting her as he would do with someone taking her first tentative steps after major surgery. Dr. Nelson, their local family physician, could offer no conclusions after examining her except that Catherine was suffering an "emotional event," a condition he was not confident in his ability to treat beyond prescribing a tranquilizer. She needed hospitalization, he advised. He recommended one of the hospitals in Lincoln fifty miles away for complete assessment and bed rest.

It took a week and a half to get Catherine a room at St. James and to make arrangements with the psychiatrist recommended by Dr. Nelson to evaluate and treat her. During that time, she maintained the same docile air of profound fatigue she had shown Donald when he found her that first morning. She stayed to her bed most of the time. She wept frequently. But what unnerved him most was the way she spoke with a spiritless childlike simper and acquiesced to almost anything anyone asked of her. She seemed helpless to decide things for herself. "I have no will of my own," she told him, almost dreamily. "I can't make a decision about anything. Isn't that funny?"

"It's understandable," he'd tried to reassure her. "We've been through an awful lot." He meant losing their son, of course. But he suspected something deeper and suppressed in Catherine that Donny's death had uncapped and had come seeping up like oil through the earth's crust until it became a gusher. That was the metaphor *he* had used to describe to the doctor what he'd observed in her behavior.

Dr. Arbuthnot—a wiry-haired, bespectacled man with dark complexion and a tangled black beard—reinforced Donald's suspicions that it was not their son's death alone that had created the problem she was experiencing. It simply had been the catalyst to hasten her "unfolding." This was the delicate way he put it. The problem was rooted in messages from an emotionally volatile childhood. But, as the doctor surmised, her condition was perhaps inherent in a genetically errant chemistry in her brain. Both conditions had been waiting for just the proper circumstances to create an emotional collision.

Donald knew about Catherine's childhood, knew the stories she had told him about her father's rages, her mother's spitefulness—everyone had a childhood they were recovering from, was the way he looked at it. But none of that seemed to explain to him the startling change in her personality. Was it a metamorphosis, or an unmasking of what had always been there?

When he checked Catherine in at St. James hospital in Lincoln, in the Acute Care Unit, Donald was told by her doctor not to visit her until she had "stabilized."

The first time he came down from Platte City to see her, he'd found her in a glassed-in activities room with a group of six or seven heavily sedated patients seated around a long table, busy potting little flowers—violets, pansies, and marigolds with fragile yellow and purple and red blooms—transplanting them from hives of little plastic nursery pots to round bowls cut from the green bottoms of 7-Up bottles. It was some sort of arts and crafts session conducted by a visiting recreational therapist—a young woman, wearing a canvas gardener's apron, who spoke in an encouraging voice to the table of drugged adults as if she were dealing with six-year-olds away from home at day camp. Donald had been directed by a ward nurse to wait on a vinyl couch in the reception area down the hall until this planned portion of Catherine's day was ended. Instead, he had stood in the hall outside the room, watching. Catherine had spotted him and started to rise from her chair to come greet him, but she was quickly admonished by the woman. "No, no, Catherine. Let's finish our task. Our plants need to be put into their new earth so they can grow." The therapist had looked reprovingly at Donald while she spoke. Catherine returned meekly to her seat and took up her plastic pot. She sat at one corner of the table, a smile on her face, her fingers grimy with potting soil, and concentrated on her task without another glance at Donald.

The others on either side of her—a bald man in his forties, wearing a bright coral terry cloth robe, and a skinny adolescent girl in jeans and black T-shirt, with huge dark raccoon rings around her sunken eyes—worked along on their own pots of drooping flowers. All the while the woman patrolled around and around the table behind them, cooing and lisping praise and instruction.

"She's like a zombie," he'd protested on his third visit to Lincoln, when he had found Catherine had become even more listless and malleable.

"Some of it's the medication we've prescribed for her. Until we can adjust the dosage, she may seem more subdued," the doctor assured him. "But that's necessary, as well, to intervene in the progression of her particular psychosis. We can't begin adequately to address it until we've halted its downward spiral."

"Are you saying she's psychotic?" he asked.

"Not the way the layman usually thinks of it. She's not going to take a butcher knife to you in the middle of the night, if that's what you mean."

The man was patronizing. If there was anyone Donald distrusted even more than lawyers, it was psychiatrists. But he did not want to show it in the doctor's own domain. "I'm not worried about her being violent," he said. "I was simply asking if having a psychosis meant someone is psychotic."

"She has had a psychotic *episode* in the sense that her symptoms clearly had no physical cause. And the images she uses to describe what is happening to her border on the hallucinatory. These are manifestations of a hysterical reaction."

"Well, the cure seems worse than the problem," Donald said. "I mean, she's an artist. She works in images all the time. She has a unique way of looking at the world. Now she acts like one of the Stepford Wives."

Dr. Arbuthnot had nodded paternally, but Donald detected a knotting of the muscles along his lower jaw. Which pleased him. He'd been angered by the glossy superciliousness with which some doctors and the nurses at St. James seemed to treat everyone—patients and family alike—who entered their ward: that somber unctuousness he associated with undertakers who believed their role was to fabricate a veneer of calm over an emotionally extraordinary moment.

"What does it feel like to you, with the medication?" he asked Catherine, hoping to gather her support against the doctor's prematurely resorting to chemicals rather than counseling. From what Donald could gather, Arbuthnot spent only cursory time with her, nothing resembling the more intense personal session Donald expected of psychotherapy.

"Feel like? I don't know. It feels like…nothing," she said, as perplexed as if she were trying to remember the meaning of the word "feeling" itself. "Everything feels like yesterday, like it's already over with."

When he had tried to tell her about how things were going at home in her absence, she seemed distant, only mildly interested. "We got to go on a 'field trip' yesterday," she said. "They took us for a hike through the neighborhood to look at the leaves on trees and see how other people live. Lincoln is a lot dirtier and more rundown than Platte City. At least, this part of Lincoln is. Don't you think that's strange for our capitol city?"

Over the next two weeks of her confinement, Arbuthnot, true to his word, made adjustments in the dosage levels of Catherine's medication, and when she was finally released—with tearful good-byes and promises to stay "connected" with friends she'd made among patients and staff—she did seem more like her old self—more stable—Donald would agree, and emotionally stronger in many ways, although less spirited than before. She continued faithfully to take her "meds" daily for several more weeks.

Then, abruptly, she stopped taking anything other than vitamins, and she never went back to the pills that Arbuthnot had prescribed for her. "I won't be a drugged-up mother trying to raise my children," she said vehemently the one and only time Donald had asked if she intended to continue her therapy.

Three weeks later, she had filed for divorce.

Now, Donald sucked in a long and dreary breath, held in for a time before letting it escape again with a sound like a deflating balloon. His thoughts were pinballing in his head, worked up over his job, his anger at the politics of correctness that would test his mettle as an officer; over Catherine's unstable behavior, waiting for her to call to say she was safe or to ask for his help; waiting for Holly to call again, needing his assurances, delivering bad news. It was useless for him to even try to get some sleep yet tonight.

He decided on a shower, hoping to alert his mind for the rest of the night ahead. In the tiny bathroom stall, he tilted his face toward the showerhead and let the spray massage his forehead and cheekbones and warm his sinuses. With each breath, he blew a fine mist of water away from his mouth.

While he toweled off before the ghostly image of himself in the steamed-over mirror above the sink, he appraised the shock of dark blond hair on his head, threaded with silver but still thick. His eyes were pouched from too many years of smoke, from inhaling the toxins of the hundreds of fires he had fought, and his lips were stretched thin. He looked plain haggard, his age struck in *bas relief* in the flesh of his face; and beneath his skin, he felt a fluttering pulse of apprehension that there was something yet to come that would mark him even more before he could sleep again.

Chapter 3

Steven Harper lay naked in bed, his head cupped in the saddle of his laced hands, arms splayed open like plucked turkey wings while he stared thoughtfully at the ceiling of Saundra Bourcek's bedroom.

"Marriage is an affliction of mutual habits, wherein two people swap their neuroses. Prolonged marriage will produce very neurotic behavior," he was explaining to Saundra.

Beside him, Saundra chuckled. "You're such a strange man," she said. "Everything serious you turn away with humor."

"Humor *is* serious," Steven replied with feigned indignation. "It's a serious prophylactic against boredom, even insanity."

"Anyway," Saundra said, "you've never been in a prolonged marriage, according to you."

"And how would you know that?" he replied, turning his head to look at her. Sex-sated and sober for the moment, his defenses were sharpened again when Saundra pressed him for more details of his personal life.

"You told me you were married before, very young. At your apartment, you told me that you and your first wife were only married for a year and a half, maybe, and now this time it was just two years."

He propped up on one elbow to look down at her. "Huh. I told you that? I don't remember a lot about that night. Are you sure you were there?"

Saundra poked him in the ribs, and he snorted a startled laugh, rising up to grin at her.

"Don't you remember anything you tell people about yourself?" she said.

He lay back again, looking at the ceiling. "There's a lot I don't remember about myself, unless someone triggers the memory. I've spent my life dedicated to forgetting my mistakes."

She was right about his use of irony to turn away any serious discussion about himself with humor, sometimes flippant, sometimes cynical. Saundra was a student from Steven's American Literature survey class. They were in bed together for only the second time. The first, two weeks ago, she had simply lingered after a party for some of his students at his recently rented apartment, helping him wash glasses and put away leftover snacks after everyone else had left, then talking with him late into the night, until he was gin giddy and word weary. When she might have left, she had turned to him at the door and kissed him so warmly and urgently at the same time, it seemed natural that they go to bed together. In the only moment of doubt, to make certain of her intent, he'd asked, "Don't you have to get home to your family?"

"My husband's on the road. I left the kids with their grandma because I knew I'd probably be late coming home." The fact that she had made plans, had thought ahead to eventualities, was enough to arouse the *carpe diem* fool in Steven. She had decided for them, and he was a sucker for a woman who knew her mind and desired to include him in the hankerings of her body. His incapacity to resist had been his weakness since boyhood, at an age well before he'd learned that *carpe diem* would lead to his perpetual hunger to be wanted.

This evening, dusted in freshly falling snow, it was he who had come to her door to beg for "refuge from the storm, dear lady." He'd been drinking, he admitted, and he could not stay alone in that dreary monastic cell of his on the depressing eve of his divorce from his "crazy wife." He needed the distracting comfort of Saundra's company.

She'd made him a cup of coffee, then another, and they sat on the white sofa in her living room with her arm around his shoulder while he prattled on about the terrible mistake he'd made by marrying Catherine. Terrible for them both, he insisted.

"She was exciting, she was bright and she was pretty. I was in love with her," he insisted. "I'm pretty sure I was. But now I don't know if being in love means the same thing for other people who get married and live with each other for a dreadfully long time."

Saundra had nodded as he talked, and she stroked the nape of his neck.

"You never know until it's too late," Steven went on, rolling his neck in the yoke of her fingers. "Who it really is that you've bound yourself to. You think you know someone intimately and then you wake up one morning to discover she is fatally flawed."

"You're just learning that?" Saundra said and pinched the back of his neck playfully.

"She has these…well, *visions* she calls them. I think they're hallucinations. She sees things, grisly crazy things happening in her head. She describes them to me. She spent time in the cuckoo's nest once before, you know."

"No, I didn't know."

"Her previous marriage. Her son died in an accident when a car ran into him on his bicycle…or the other way around, I don't remember. I should have talked to her ex before I married her. He's a fireman in Platte City. I'll bet he could have told me a thing or two about her mental stability that would have given me pause." He shook his head dolefully. Then he smiled. "But oh my god, did she ever love to…you know." He made a finger-in-the-hole gesture with his hands.

He had gone no further talking about Catherine before Saundra had taken him upstairs—"Shh, now. My kids are asleep next door"—and administered to him in the one sure way he had learned that a woman could bring him comfort.

Now, lying next to him after an hour of lovemaking with splashy vigor up and down her bed, she was pressing him to tell her more. "So, your first wife, then. She was a mistake, too?" She lay fetal beside him now, her head beneath his left armpit.

He knew he had been stupid earlier, careless with his emotions in front of someone who was younger than him and married herself. His only contact with her as a confidante had been that night two weeks ago, sloppy with self-pity for the spartan condition of his start-over life at forty-nine.

He drew a breath, let it go evenly while he decided. Then, "She was seventeen, fresh out of high school, a barista behind the counter in a Duncan Donuts shop. I was nineteen, a freshman in college, addicted to coffee and donuts every morning before classes because it was the 'in thing' to do on campus at that time. Everything I knew about love, politics, human suffering— all of it was glandular. Long story short, we met, we dated, we got pregnant, so we got married. *Veni, vidi, vici.* What else was an honorably intentioned young man to do back then?"

How could he explain—why *should* he explain—to someone thirty-three years old who had admitted she'd slept with five different boyfriends before she married the sixth when she was just twenty-four, and who was now sleeping with a man sixteen years her senior while her husband was out of town—how could he make clear the moral obligations he often felt toward the women with whom he had sex? That even now he felt toward Saundra Bourcek for taking him in.

"In any event, my first wife, Janice, had two overpowering virtues, and they were compelling mitigations of any weaknesses to our compatibility," he said.

When he did not go on, she said, "Yes?"

Smiling because she'd bitten, he said, "She had the most exquisite set of hooters I'd ever seen in or out of a sweater."

Saundra yanked a hair on his chest. "You are so *bad.*"

He yelped, then chuckled, believing he was off the hook.

She lay quietly for a time, stroking his chest. Finally, she said, "So you had a child together?"

"Nearly. But no. The irony was, we never had the baby that coupled us. She miscarried in her sixth month."

"Ooh," she breathed. "I'm sorry."

"I was, too. But I think that's when I understood that we really had nothing more going for us as a couple other than we'd tapped into each other's itch," he said. "I confused that with a need, or a maybe it was an obligation, to be in love with the person who had been so willing to fuck me. It must have been all that sugar in the donuts."

"It's the same with women, you know. The itch, I mean," Saundra said. "But you don't need to be in love to have sex with someone you want to sleep with."

"You're preaching to the choir," he said flatly. "I learned that from an expert my very first experience, before I even understood what *that* was."

"Oh?" She rose on an elbow and looked down on him with an impish smile. "Was there a Mrs. Robinson in your life?"

Her assertion that a woman could want sex without love triggered the voice from his past that brought him up short: "*Making love is not the same as being in love, Stevie.*" He had accepted her aphorism as literally as a novitiate receives the gospel. The one who expressed it had nearly broken his heart with its simple truth.

"Who was she?"

He was not going to go into that. Except for the occasional reminders that erupted in unexpected moments like this, he had packed that away in the attic of his mind. Both the experience and the one who had taught him were enmeshed in the cobwebs of his psyche. She only returned to him in occasional dreams—more frequent now that he was living alone again—when he found himself yearning for something more to his life than what he had settled for here in Platte City in the bovine belly of the country. In his dreams, she was the same age she had been then, her same puckish self, her same lush body. But in each dream, he was always his aging self, drawing away from her.

"So?" Saundra coaxed.

"Some other time," was all he'd say.

Saundra became silent again. They lay shoulder to shoulder, thigh to thigh, their hands clasped. He had to take a leak now, but he was reluctant to get out of bed and use the little bathroom adjoining the bedroom. The configuration of furniture put the bed only a scant few feet from the bathroom door, and he was self-conscious about the sounds he might make pissing in the toilet water.

The opportunity came when she turned lazily on her side to look at him again.

"Anyway, do you like *my* breasts?"

He rolled his head toward her. She wiggled her torso to make her breasts sway. Steven appraised them. They were small and widely separated, her breastbone a washboard between them. They were pear-shaped and dropsical from the stretch of childbearing, and they rolled away from each other like shy children.

"Sure," he replied. "They're positively esculent. As are your lips, your inner thighs, and the sweet morass of your nether regions."

She smiled self-consciously and lay back again into the bed. "Must everything be simply wordplay?" It seemed more a statement of observation than judgment. "I don't know when to believe you and when not. Even when you teach class, I sometimes don't understand when you're serious or just putting everybody on."

Steven turned on his side to face her then. "What is it you wish to know, dear heart?"

"What I said. Do you wish I had big breasts like your first wife?"

"No."

She took his right hand and covered her left breast with it. "I mean, I don't mind, or anything, but you hardly touched them when we made love."

He chuckled and gave her a playful squeeze. "Not much to touch," he said, exaggerating the rhyme. It was his regret when he saw the wounded look she flashed him that all at once released him. He swung himself up and left the bed. "Be back in a jiffy," he said. "Nature calls."

The little bathroom off Saundra's bedroom contained only a stool, a shower stall, and a small sink. But everywhere there was clear evidence this was the comfort room used by Saundra's husband, Jack. On the narrow counter beside the sink were bottles of Brut and Old Spice, a plastic can of Mennen talc, a Gillette razor. In the sliver of counter between the faucets and the splashguard was a pummeled tube of Crest. The latest issue of *Sports Illustrated* draped the top of the toilet tank.

Rather than stand to the open stool, he lowered the toilet seat and sat on it to muffle the splash. Besides a mild embarrassment at being heard by Saundra, he was feeling the inevitable qualms from being in her house. He hoped the quieter he was about it, the gentler his unease would be.

The fact did not weigh lightly that her two children were asleep—he fervently hoped—in their rooms across the hall. Sitting on the stool in that tight little closet surrounded by the toiletries of the man with whom she had sex regularly when he was home—no doubt on that same bed in which they had just rutted and she had conceived children by him—the weight of this knowledge brought a queasiness of unpredictability.

Of late, there had been something else looming over him, eclipsing the initial buoyant freedom he had experienced when he had finally separated from Catherine. It was a sensation of something gravitational or tidal that he couldn't pull against any longer to float his hopeful spirits. It was that feeling which had compelled him to reach out to Saundra Bourcek tonight, like groping in rising water for a life ring. He was unmoored, uncertain of his heading, and it was a muddle totally foreign to him. It wasn't the same feeling of instability as the windless calms he'd experienced at other times in his career that made him want to stir the doldrums of his academic life into eddies of new complication. Nor was it just the bleak failure he felt in divorcing Catherine. She talked about omens and dark visions in her moments of panic or anger. It wasn't any of that bullshit he was experiencing. This new mental…*thing* had begun to muddy his ability to have any view beyond the unstable present of a future that held anything more life changing than tomorrow's concluding event in court.

When Steven returned from the bathroom, Saundra was asleep. She was on her stomach with her face turned to the wall away from him, legs spraddled like a runner's in full sprint—one stretched straight, the other turned out and lifted for the next stride, as if she were heading in two different directions at once, like a figure in an ancient Egyptian wall fresco. She lay under a twist of top sheet that draped the small of her back but left her legs and rear exposed.

Seeing her that way, corkscrewed in exhausted sleep, her buttocks bared and canted slightly up to him, Steven felt tenderness and that familiar gratitude in the warmth he experienced every time a woman offered to console him with sex. Saundra Bourcek was an agreeably attractive and direct young woman— bright and intelligent the way Catherine often was, but less fragile than Catherine and uncannily attuned to his cravings in the midst of his recent unease. He was extremely fortunate, really, to have discovered her; her timing had been almost providential.

Lying in the bed beside her, on the side in which her rear was exposed, Steven edged his body closer to hers, carefully so as not to wake her. Her face was turned away from him, but he was able to nestle up to her in a way that allowed him to settle his groin into her thigh. Slowly, he let his hand curl down the slope of buttock to cup the fine mat of pubic hair. She moved in adjustment to his presence against her, drawing her thighs closer together, clamping his fingertips between them. He lay perfectly still like this and listened to the hiss of the icy snow pelting the screens and siding of her house. He would wait out the storm here with Saundra Bourcek for a while longer before standing up to the day ahead.

Chapter 4

In spite of the snow, Catherine's little car crawled steadily along the streets. Last fall, Steven had insisted she buy new tires, and she was glad now she had heeded him. Once out of the side streets of her neighborhood onto the main street into the city where the plows had already gone through spewing salt and sand behind them, she was able to accelerate a bit more. The worst problem was not what was on the road, but what was coming at her against the windshield. Light refracted in the millions of crystal flakes rushing at her. While she could see what was immediately in front of her, the periphery of her vision was blurred and the beams from her headlights tunneled the snowflakes that swarmed like insects into the light. The confusion of light and the turbulence of snow rushing out of the dark at her windshield only aggravated her distress.

Steven lived in an old apartment building of yellow brick and limestone blocks at the corner of 42nd Street and Taylor near the College. His apartment was on the ground floor, one small bedroom, a living room with a dining alcove, a kitchenette and a bath. Catherine had been there several times in the early days of their separation to argue against the needless course they were on, to plead for his consideration to return home where he belonged. Each time, stubbornly, he insisted this place was now his home and sent her back to her house. But she was still able to entice him into making love to her before she left. As long as she could still exploit with her sex his need for reassurance, she believed there was time to coax him back to her where he had once agreed he belonged after too many years spent alone. He didn't know his own mind the way she did. He certainly had proven he didn't know his own feelings. For all his intelligence, he was still densely fearful of surrendering to the imperatives of his own heart.

The apartment he lived in seemed bleak and grainy, threadbare with its sparse furnishings. In the first month he'd slept on a mattress on the floor of the bedroom because he'd taken from their house only the remnants of furniture that were still left over from the other hovel he'd lived in before he married Catherine. Everything about his new apartment depressed her. It was so far away from their home in Westgate, so inconvenient and unnecessarily distant from her. There were lots of newer apartment complexes he could have chosen from in the western part of Platte City. Certainly, he could afford better on his salary as a tenured Professor, even with the support he was giving her until their divorce should be final. This place reminded her of where she had come from, the look and smell of diminished lives and fortunes; it was as if she were reverting, as well, beginning all over again in Corinth. But what depressed her even more than the image of her going through it again was the reality that she wasn't included in the romantic flavor of fresh beginnings, starting from scratch, cleaning the slate that Steven was experiencing without her. She hated his independence and envied his courage.

She pulled to the curb under the crumbling brick *porte cochere* in front of his building and stared intently at the two windows in the northeast corner of the first floor. They looked out from the living room and dining el of his apartment. There was no light warming them from within; behind the gauze of swirling snow, the rectangular panes were black embrasures. Almost all the other windows in the building were lit up, signs that people were at home and warm and awake during this terrible storm. She got out of her car and crossed the bare swath of pavement to the front stoop. On the panel next to the mailboxes she pushed the button that sounded the buzzer inside his apartment and waited for either his voice to come over the intercom or the front door lock to chatter open.

When there was no reply, she left the cover of the entrance porch and waded through the snow to the side of the building and his bedroom window where she reached up on tiptoes and rapped on the sill until her knuckles burned. Everything inside remained dark. She called his name as loudly as she could, in case he was really asleep and unable to hear her rapping. When that yielded no response, she continued on through the snow and around a back corner of the building to check the parking lot behind. His brown Taurus was not among the cluster of cars belonging to other tenants all safely and responsibly home on a night like this.

Defeated, she had to admit he truly was not there, that he was not injured or in need of her as she had taken the sign of the hand in her head to augur. The stupidity of what she had done settled on her.

To come out in such foul weather, drive over halfway across the city, impelled by what? She returned to her car, angry, cold, her feet soaking wet because she had worn only her sandals out in a snowstorm. *Worse than a child*, she reproached herself. *What were you thinking?* But, of course, that was the rhetorical point: she had not been thinking, incapable of any rational thought under the lash of the demons in her mind.

On the drive home, she passed by a giant fiberglass statue of a cowboy in the parking lot of Dalton Western Wear. His broad oafish grin under his huge snow-crusted hat, his arm raised in an exaggerated country salute to passing city dwellers, galled her with its caricature of masculine conceit. "Where the hell are you?" she cried out, the panic that had sent her rushing into the storm to help him burned away now by a rage at his betrayal. Was he out getting drunk on the eve of their divorce? How cliché was that?

At the intersection of 45th and Center, the snowflakes hurtled at her through the beams of her headlights, and her windshield wipers could not slap them away fast enough. Then, before her on Center Street, she saw through the gauze of white, an explosion of lights—a shimmering phalanx of white and blue and yellow beacons strobing the air—coming straight at her in the middle of the street! She stomped on her brake pedal and jerked the steering wheel abruptly to the right, sending the car into a blind sidelong skid against the near curb. An orange snowplow clattered by with a jingle-jangle of chained tires, going the opposite way. A wake of slush splashed along the length of the car, sloshing gritty slop across the windshield. In her rearview mirror, the truck continued on, a carnival ride of flashing lights receding up Center Street.

Catherine sat with her chest pressed against the steering wheel while the windshield wipers smeared an arc of grit across the glass. When she finally straightened up, she was looking up at a lighted billboard atop the building to the right of her. Through the blur of the muddy windshield, she saw the image of a giant young blonde in open-necked white blouse and cut-off jeans leaning against a pool table, with a cue stick at a jaunty angle in her hands. The girl leered down at her foamy glass of beer on the pool table rail beside her left haunch. "Game On Sports Bar" the sign proclaimed in blood red letters. It leapt to her mind in that moment, taunted by the girl's provocative pose, that Steven could be with another woman. No, he *was* with another woman. In her bed right now, yes? Using his subtle voice that was both narcotic and stimulant, talking to her, arousing her in the darkness with his seductive voice and searching fingers the way he used to do with Catherine.

Of course he would be with someone else. She was reasonably certain he had slept with other women—*girls* from school, probably—before he'd known her. How could she not have understood what he was like? "Cheating bastard," she said between gritted teeth. But the words groaned from her in a pang of lament, and she could not blink back the welling of tears. "Couldn't wait to be free to fuck someone new!"

When he had her any time he wanted—his companion, his admirer, his lover—he had told her last January out of the blue that he felt smothered by her attentions and burdened by her emotional needs. *Her* needs!

Jamming the gearshift into reverse, she stomped the gas pedal floorward until the back wheels spun and the steering wheel rocked, and her car lurched backward through the slush and into the center of the street.

Then momentarily, the car was fishtailing forward until it straightened itself in the path left by the plow, and she accelerated, her breathing short and labored beneath the hot crush of anger in her chest.

"There's nothing like a little jelly roll to sweeten the sourest mood," he'd joked that first time she had offered herself to what she knew he desired from her. "Out of darkness into light." And she'd been blinded by her own desire for someone, whom she believed was enough like herself, to imagine that he was somehow complimenting her.

Outside the city, she fought the road on Highway 30 with steering wheel and gas pedal, accelerating, slowing, twisting, and gripping to hold the car straight and steady on the icy crust on the road beneath her tires. Her heart pounded in her ears and her emotions skidded back and forth—anguish, anger, righteousness, despair. A pressure behind her eyes blurred her sight. Through the haze, she could no longer see where she was steering. At the wide intersection of highway and suburban road she turned off Highway 30 and onto 98th Street, suddenly fighting an unplowed stretch of county road. Less than a mile from her home, unable to discern the sides of the street from the center, she felt the front of her car lurch off the left shoulder, its rear end sliding to follow. She was on the opposite side of the road!

Tilting on its left side, the car slipped sidelong over the shoulder of the road and down a steep embankment toward the bottom of an obscured drainage ditch below, plowing a wall of snow ahead of it. Under the building resistance of the snow's own weight pressing back against it, the car came to a slow stop halfway down.

Catherine tromped the gas pedal, but the car only dug itself deeper into the snow, its tires spinning viciously. Her left fender and half the hood were buried, and the view from the driver's window had been blacked out by the wall of snow against its side. She turned the engine off and sat in the silence of the interior of the car, collecting her wits.

Through her windshield, she saw the small band of light from just one headlight pushing back the darkness ahead of her, beyond which lay a flat scrim of snow and black night. The road somewhere above her, over the rim of the embankment was no longer visible. The driver's side of her car was banked solidly in snow. The passenger side was tilted up and she felt the weight of her body pressing against the driver's door, her knees and left hip squashed against the arm rest.

If her car had not slid off the road, she'd be pulling in her driveway by now. Back in the safety of her house, the comfort of her children. Her own disbelief in her predicament left her drained of either anger or fear. It came to her then that she had left her cell phone at home in her rush to leave the house. *What a fool!*

It was clear to her that she had to get out. She had to get home. No one was going to help her here. No one would find her until morning if she stayed strapped into this dark snow-lidded coffin. And that realization, rather than panic her, brought a grim resolve. For the first time this night, she had the concrete resolve to save herself.

Releasing her seat belt, she squirmed to pull her legs up and slide on her belly over the console between seats where she could stretch her legs back to find footing against the driver's door. But when she reached the door handle on the passenger side and released the latch, she did not have enough strength in her arms or legs to lever the weight of the door upward high enough for her to shimmy through its opening.

Kneeling on the console, she pushed with all her might against the door's downward gravity, the crown of her head pressed against the glass of the window. Three times she tried, straining to raise the door, now as solid as a steel hatch cover, but it would not rise any more than a crack the width of her arm. Defeated, she drew back and rested in an awkward crouch over the console, breathing hard from her efforts. She propped herself awkwardly on stiffened arms against the passenger seat cushion to draw deeper breaths. No panic. But her anger rose again recalling the sudden image of the billboard girl with the lecherous grin, taunting. Then the memory of Steven's hand tearing through her brain, reaching not for her but for someone new. *Stupid fool!*

She would save herself without help from anyone. She was not witless about coping with danger. She was not without capacity for logic to recognize what was needed to survive the moment. She was not crazy. *Not!* And they were not going to send her back to that place while there was still an open window to escape through.

She raised herself up enough to stretch her arm back and down the steering column, enough to turn the key in the ignition to power the windows. Then she toggled the switch on the handle of the passenger door and the glass lowered in its panel, bringing in the cold night air and a slant of blowing snow.

Gathering herself once more, Catherine rolled onto her back and stretched her arms over her head and outside of the car through the open window. With her feet planted on the console, knees tight to her chest, she pushed off like a swimmer against the wall of the pool.

She rocked and twisted side to side to wriggle through the opening, and her hands groped upward, grasping for purchase on the car roof. The metal was glazed with ice. She had no grip. And now the open window was not wide enough to accommodate her shoulders and chest. Even with her feet and legs straining against the console to birth her from the dark cabin of the car into the snow-blown darkness beyond, she was losing all strength in her arms and legs needed to force her body through the narrow opening. Her head lolled back in the night air, unable to hold itself up, and she gasped for air. The snow blew onto her bared neck and upside-down face, melting as it hit the heat of her skin.

With an animal bleat of alarm, Catherine caved to the realization that she was stuck in the window frame: the weight of her head stretched her neck downward, arching her chest against the top of the window frame, and the cocoon of her parka wedged her shoulders tightly against the sides. She could not even marshal strength of muscle and resolve any longer to raise her head and torso back up parallel to the sill of the open window and retract herself within the safety of the car.

Her fingers, numbed at their tips, slid from the ice-glazed roof and her arms dropped like felled branches, increasing the weight of her head and arched neck straining her back and shoulders. She was so close to the snow below the side of her car that her hands now sank into its powdered surface, guy-wiring her to the earth below.

What have I done? Her mind was spiraling beneath darkening water. *What will they do without me?*

Chapter 5

There was another possible source of information for Donald that might have given him some insight into Catherine's whereabouts and possibly her state of mind. Reluctantly, he made the decision to enlist the help of his brother William's ex-wife Charlotte. If anyone would know what was up with Catherine, she would. They had always been close. They had probably become even closer now that both of them had divorced their Sparta husbands. They had grown up together in Corinth, and they seemed more like sisters sometimes than friends and in-laws. Even his daughters liked their "Aunt Charly," although Donald had never warmed to her, not even when she was still married to his brother. She was obtuse, undereducated, and from the way she had skinned his brother William in the divorce—exacting possession of that huge house, custody of his children, and a huge cash settlement in alimony and child support that added up to nearly half of his sizeable net worth as head of Sparta & Sons Enterprises, the mammoth structural engineering company that Donald's father had hoped both his sons would one day manage together. Charlotte was, by Donald's standards, a certifiable gold digger. But at the moment, she was the only person he could think of who might know what was going on with Catherine.

When Charlotte answered the phone, she was laughing, and Donald could hear other laughter, as well, shrill and unfettered, in the background.

"This is Donald, Charlotte," he said. "I don't mean to bother you, but—"

"Hey! What's up, little brother?" Charlotte said. "I haven't heard from you since Jesus was a baby." Her voice was burred the way he remembered it when she'd been drinking. She had taken to calling him "little brother" shortly after she married William, because that's what William had often called him. It had stuck, but it was as familiar as Charlotte and he would ever get with one another.

"Actually, I'm calling…I was wondering…." Immediately he felt foolish, unwilling to admit what he wanted. It was midnight and he was calling around, asking after his ex-wife, for god sake.

"Come on, spit it out," Charlotte said. "Whoever she is, she's not here. But I'm not doing anything tonight." She laughed sharply, an eruption that sounded more like a hiccup.

Heat rose in Donald's face. He had never understood how someone with Catherine's artistic sensibilities could befriend a woman as coarse as Charlotte.

He drew a breath. "Would you happen to know where Catherine is?"

"My guess would be she's snug in her bed," Charlotte said.

"Look, Charlotte, the deal is she's not home tonight. Holly called me a bit ago, and the kids don't know where she is." He could hear again other background voices on Charlotte's end, a male and then a female, loud in merriment, but unintelligible. "I thought there was a chance she might be at your place, or maybe you had talked with her tonight."

"Uh-uh, I haven't talked to her since three or four days ago," Charlotte said. "I have a few friends over this evening, but she's definitely not one of them. Not her type." Charlotte chuckled.

"No ideas then?" he said evenly, irritated that he had to draw everything out of her.

"Well, she's had a lot on her mind lately," Charlotte said. "She may just have been feeling housebound and needed to get out for a while. Tomorrow's her big day."

"Yes, I know," he said. He was thankful that his daughter had reminded him.

"So she hasn't been exactly herself, you know?" Charlotte said. "I'll admit, I've been really worried about her lately, too," Charlotte said.

Donald leapt on the intimation. "Oh? What about?"

"The same things. That asshole divorcing her. And then the art department guy who fired her."

Once more Donald felt ignorant. "What 'art department guy?'" He heard a peal of female laughter beyond Charlotte.

"You know. The guy who was Cat's boss. Chairman of the art department at the college, whatshisname."

"Oh. Her boss," Donald said.

Catherine had taught art part-time at Platte City State College for as many years as she had been out of college with her art degree from Lincoln, the year after she'd married Donald. But last August, she told Donald that she'd been laid off from the college before the start of the new academic year because the school reportedly was undergoing budget reductions due to state cuts to higher education. But her department head had told her it would no doubt be temporary and she'd be called back early next year as soon as the budget problem was resolved internally.

"Another horse's ass," Charlotte scoffed. "Him and his chickenshit restraining orders."

"What are you talking about?" Donald said. "What restraining orders?"

"You don't know?" Charlotte said. And in an obscenity-laced diatribe, she unloaded on Donald the lamentable story of her best friend's "recent antics" at Platte City State College. She insisted that she knew and Donald must know that Catherine's firing was just bullshit, right? "So when her asshole husband tells her he can't live with her anymore, she's suddenly left without an income to feed her family and she freaks. What the fuck!" Charlotte wanted to know. "Suddenly, she decides she's not going to let her dickhead boss off so easy for firing her. She wants her job back, and so she decides to hold his feet to the fire to prove cause. Problem is, she's been showing up at the guy's office and calling him at his home to get him to give her an honest reason for firing her, and so he takes out a restraining order on her for harassment. She's banned from going near him. She can't even go on her own campus anymore. Can you believe that?"

Donald was dumbfounded. What was Charlotte talking about? Restraining order? Harassment? Suddenly, he did not want to hear any more. He would not listen to dirt dished by someone the likes of Charlotte Sparta about the woman he believed he still understood intimately.

"So, anyway she's got a lot on her mind, and if she's not home, then she's probably out somewhere." There was a pause, and then she snorted. "Boy, that's fucking brilliant logic, isn't it?"

"Thanks for filling me in," Donald cut in. "If you hear from her… Well, never mind."

"I know you still care about her. That's really nice," Charlotte said.

When he'd ended the call, he sat on the edge of his bed and gazed through the window on the snow blowing past. Where had he been not to have heard any of this before? Nothing from Catherine or even from his girls about any problems she was having at the college. He couldn't comprehend Charlotte's exaggerated indictment of Catherine as a woman who could be charged with harassment; but if any of it were true then this episode tonight of leaving the house in the middle of a storm without a word to the girls may not be the first sign of another emotional crisis of the caliber that had put her in the hospital after their son's death.

He tried recalling earlier images of that diffident young woman he'd met at a dinner at William and Charlotte's one Christmas while she was home from college in her last year at the University in Lincoln. She was Catherine Koterba then, and she'd known Charlotte since grade school in Corinth. She did not fit his notion of someone from that part of Platte City where people depended on their street smarts to see them through their childhood and adolescence.

Donald knew all about the mean neighborhoods along the river and rail yards, the blue-collar ethic of the people she'd been raised among. He had, by then, come to know several men from Corinth, firefighters under his command as a newly minted captain of a PCFD engine company: their suspicion of people who were born to money, their contempt for unearned privilege of any kind. His brother, William, had married Charlotte Jansky, after all, because he claimed he was drawn to her "sauciness" and her own disrespect for educated, cultured people—qualities that William seemed bent on denying in himself while holding to the family's wealth and position in the community won by their grandfather and father, who had grown Sparta & Sons Enterprises "by the sweat of their brow" to its place among the Fortune 500. William defended Charlotte then as having "native intelligence," but it was evident to Donald, and he was certain to their father, that William was a Sparta son with an inflamed libido, who even in their adolescence had been drawn by the gonads to girls of liberal character.

Catherine was not cut from the same burlap as Charlotte, not from the outset, not later. She'd never had that rough, bawdy humor or confidence about her own sexuality with which Charlotte had disarmed William. That first night Donald had met her, when she was introduced by Charlotte as an old friend from East High School, he thought Charlotte and William were kidding him. This quiet, unassuming woman did not match the temperament of an East High girl like Charlotte. There had been something refined about her, something pale and aristocratic in her bearing that had drawn Donald's attention from that very first dinner at his brother's house. Thin, with delicate wrists, wide innocent eyes, long chestnut hair, she was quiet and thoughtful, an intelligent girl, at that time still studying art and art history at the University. This was a woman who, three months later when they had taken a trip together to Colorado to ski, told him she had a "mystical experience" on the mountaintop in which she saw images of their life together, their children yet to be conceived. The snow was falling that day too, in dry, fine flakes that floated straight down, and she told him that she was blessed with a mind that could imagine things to come for the people she loved—good or bad. He had not been alarmed by that or found it in any way uncharacteristic of her imaginative way of seeing life. This was a woman who he sensed was capable of having mystical experiences.

Of course, he hadn't learned until much later how often she had them or what other images may have haunted her that could bring Donald's own life and their marriage to such sorry straits.

46

Chapter 6

"Hello! Is there anyone down there? Hello!"

When Catherine opened her eyes, her mind rose to a surface of light, and the air above her had shed its depthless black shroud. Flashes of yellow and white confused her, and for an instant she thought she'd damaged her eyes. Until she heard the rumble of an engine, the sound of a short-wave radio somewhere on the road above. Then the voice calling again. A man's voice.

"Hello! Can anyone hear me? Is anyone down there?"

She was stretched on her back, her chest and shoulders wedged in the window of her car, torso craned painfully backward by the downward weight of her head and arms. She squinched her eyes against the sobering shock of the wet snow falling on her face. She raised an arm from the snow, wobbling a slack wave.

"Here!" she called, her voice impaired by her weakness. "Down here."

"Okay! Okay! Hang on. I'm coming."

A crunch and swoosh of snow, a muffled, "God damnit!" and the bulk of a man slid feet-first on his side before he stopped alongside her.

Catherine tried to bring her torso parallel with her body, raising her arms to grasp the edges of the window sash, but her fingers were too numb and her stomach muscles too weak to support her body. As she was about to let go and pendulum backward again, the man raised himself to his knees in the banked snow and caught her shoulders in his hands, holding her upright.

"Jesus!" he gasped. He sounded put out to Catherine's ear. Was he angry with her for having made him fall down the slope?

"I'm stuck," she said.

"Are you all right?"

"I think so," she said. "But I'm stuck here. I can't get out or back in."

"Jesus," the man said again. He slipped his hands through her armpits and locked his fingers together across her chest, his wrists over the slick fabric of her parka pressing into her breasts. But she was supported now, her upper torso against his chest, her head cradled in his shoulder against his own ear-flapped cap.

"Does anything hurt? Your back? Your neck? What about your legs?" To each question Catherine repeated "No."

"Okay then. I'm going to try to ease you the rest of the way out. Tuck your shoulders in, hunch them like you're shrugging, and I think there's room if I pull. I'll go slow. Ready?"

And surprisingly, with not much effort at all, Catherine felt herself slide through the open window, the sill pressing along her spine, her hips slipping through as her legs straightened out of their fetal crouch in the front seat until she was free from the car and falling backwards in the man's arms as he caved under her weight. He sank back in the snow, a reclined seat for Catherine's freed body.

They remained still for a time, she in his lap, his arms still around her, and she inhaled deeply, feeling relief as the cold air rushed into her lungs.

He released his hold on her. "I'll call for a squad."

She rolled off his lap and grabbed the window of the car to pull herself to her feet. "No! I'm all right. I'm not hurt, I don't think," Catherine said. "I'm just cold."

"You sure? I can get a squad."

"No, really. Please. I have to get home to my children."

"I was lucky to see you," he said, rising up to his feet now, placing a hand on the roof of the car to support himself as he stood splay-legged on the slope.

"I don't know what happened, exactly," she said. "One minute I was on the road, and then my car just seemed to skate off to the left and the next thing I knew…it was like a toboggan ride."

"And you're sure you're not hurt?"

"I don't think so. No. I'm pretty sure I'm okay." She looked down at herself, brushed the snow off the front of her coat. Then she realized with a rush of heated embarrassment, she was in her light dress she had thrown on when she left the house. And now it was soaked and clinging to her thighs.

"If you could just help me a bit to get up the slope. I only have sandals on…"

He looked down at her feet covered now calf-deep in snow.

"What kind of a way is that to dress for winter?"

"It wasn't winter when I got dressed this morning. I wasn't expecting to have to climb out of a ditch in a foot of snow," she said. Her lips trembled and her teeth had begun to chatter.

"Okay. Wait a second, and I'll give you a hand up the slope." Moving her away from the door of the car and directing her to lean for support against the rear fender, he grabbed the handle on the passenger door and yanked the door open, freeing it from its latch as he raised it up and propped it with his arm.

48

Then, with a little hop-step, he drove himself into the open front seat far enough to reach for something near the driver's side. Catherine looked on with astonishment at how easily he had been able to do what she, with all her strength, could not accomplish from the inside, trying to get out.

She heard him grunt with effort, and then the headlights went dark and he was squirming backward, pushing the door open far enough to let him wiggle and squirm until he was standing firmly in the snow again. The door hung open on its own for a moment longer, then under its own weight, dropped shut with a thump like a freezer chest lid.

"Here, you'll want these," he said, and reached toward her with a clenched mittened hand from which hung the door opener key fob and her car and house keys.

"Oh my god," was all Catherine could manage. She took the keys and jammed them in a pocket of her jacket with the swiftness of someone who had just snatched back a wallet from the hands of a thief.

He proffered his hand again, and she took it in hers. His grip was strong in hers, and he tugged her upward away from the car. He had her by the elbow now and a hand on the small of her back, pushing, urging her up the embankment. Her flat-soled sandals would not gain purchase on the uphill slope, and her feet skated in place like a dancer doing a moonwalk.

"When we get back up top, I can call the sheriff. They'll make a report, call a tow truck, give you a ride home. The whole nine yards."

"No. I'll call when I get home. I live just down the road. In Westgate. I'll call for a tow truck or someone, but I have to get home. My kids are there alone. I was just going to check on someone…Maybe, can't you give me a ride if you're going that way?"

"They won't let me take on no riders or go out of my route when I'm plowing. That's the rules. I could be fired." He was pushing her from behind to stop her backward slide, a shoulder and half his chest pressed against her back.

They had reached the lip of the embankment, and she was looking at the big orange county plow like the one that had almost run her off the road in town earlier. Its diesel engine rumbled with an oily clatter like pebbles in a rock tumbler.

"It's alright," she said. "I can walk from here, I think."

"I can't believe I saw you when I did," the man said again, turning to look back down the embankment at her car, a dim hulk in the dark. "You're far enough down there, if I hadn't been looking that way…I just caught your skid marks in my lights and then I saw the shine from your headlights down there. I coulda missed it altogether if I was looking to the other side of the road."

The snowfall had stopped sometime during her struggle to free herself from the car, but there was wind blowing along the road, stirring up eddies of ground snow that stung her face like icy sandpaper. Catherine was aware she was really shivering now. Her icy dress was frozen to her skin below the short hem of her parka.

The snowplow driver, in heavy woolen coat and leather mittens, must have noticed too. He looked her over, and Catherine saw his brow furrow and eyes narrow when he saw how the thin cloth was molded to her thighs.

"Look," he said. "I could maybe take you up to your street. This isn't a usual kind of situation here. I'm heading into Westgate later anyways...."

"Thank you. You're very kind," Catherine said, the words sounding to her with the familiarity of a litany.

"Up you go then," he said and helped her onto the high running board then into the passenger seat, a hand clamping her arm at her armpit and the other planted on the flex of her buttock, pushing her to climb up on her own.

Riding in the passenger seat beside the driver of the huge truck, Catherine surrendered to the cold in her bones. The fading adrenalin and blowing dry heat from the vents inside the cab brought a soporific drowsiness on her, and she was only half aware that the snowplow driver was talking to her, asking questions she had no energy to answer, cajoling her mildly for getting herself into such a predicament, then offering advice on what she should do when she got home. It wasn't until the truck made a right hand turn off 98th Street and through the brick-pillared entrance to Westgate, her housing complex, that she realized the driver was plowing his way up her street to her home.

At first, when she entered her living room, she could only stare blankly about, deciding what she was going to do next. She was still cold and bone weary, but now that she was home again, she had stopped trembling.

When she'd turned her head, surveying the room, she saw the stairs going up. *The girls.*

The lights were on in Donna's room. She found her daughter lying on her back in the bed, still fully clothed in what she was wearing when Catherine had sent her to her room. Her arms had wrapped her pillow to her chest, but her face seemed placid and pure in sleep. The half-moons of her eyeballs beneath her velvet lids rolled over the landscape of a dream, and her eyelashes fluttered once. At nearly nine, she was still immune to the poison of prolonged resentment. Her hurts, when they occurred, were intense eruptions, but she had not learned yet how to hold a grudge for more than it took to turn her attention elsewhere.

Catherine knew it was difficult for her daughters to comprehend why things kept changing as they did; harder even than for herself. In such a short span of years they had lost their brother, then their father left their home, and now they were losing their stepfather, as well. It was certainly more confusing for Donna, for whom rational reasons for such things were still blurred handles swirling just beyond her reach. Yet, in a way, it was easier for her, Catherine hoped, because her younger daughter could still accept without real cynicism the contrary ways of adults. She had not turned four yet when Donny was killed; she was only five when Catherine and Donald were divorced. She had just turned six when Catherine married Steven. Now, not three years later, her mother was alone again. But Donna continued to deal with it all, and Catherine hoped the strength of her character had not yet been permanently injured by the world to the degree that she feared her own safe voyage through it.

Catherine decided not to wake her. What harm if she slept in her clothes? Quietly, she pulled a quilt from the hall closet and laid it over the girl, then shut out the light.

Down the hall one room, Holly lay tangled in a rat's nest of bedclothes, the legs of her flannel boxers twisted up above her slender thighs. She was fifteen now and she'd changed dramatically over the past two years. With her first period, the first buds of breasts and rounding of hips last winter, she had become quieter, less sure of herself socially—something critical lost with whatever the gain. It was Holly Catherine worried about. Holly who was forced to learn at an age older than her sister at the time of her brother's death that childhood offered no protection against permanent loss.

When is the moment? she wondered. *When do they first taste the fruit?* How precise was the split between faith and knowledge? If only a mother could know that moment and snatch them back the instant before they fell from that plateau of wonder and mystery where nothing is pretense and no lie exists.

In her own bedroom, Catherine stripped out of her wet clothing and into warming flannel pajamas and robe. For the first time since she left home, she noticed the time by the bedside table alarm clock: 5:30 in the morning! She had left the house at 10:30 last night.

Dear god, where have I been? Was she that long in her car? In the snow? Her memory could not account for the hours. She had thought it all less than an hour, maybe, to Steven's apartment and back in the storm. How long had it been until the plowman found her?

She needed to clear her head. She had to get herself and her day on track. She'd lost control and now if she were to survive this terrible day, she had to take it back under her control.

In the bathroom, she ran a sink of warm water, and held a soaked washcloth to her face. Then another to the back of her neck. What next? *The car.*

She retreated downstairs to the living room and the rolltop desk in a corner by the couch where she kept her address book and Donald's business card file box with the number of a towing company, 24/7 Towing Services, he had filed among the other business names and addresses of those who could help with the practical affairs of owning a home.

On the whiteboard next to the wall phone in the kitchen, she found herself staring at the message Holly had scrawled in red marker: "*Mom—Call Dad as soon as you come home. Where are you?*" The immediate thought that came to her was, *And who wants to know!*

In an upper corner of the board was Steven's block-letter exhortation: *Don't Wait Until Tomorrow: DO IT—TODAY!* Obediently, she drew up the step stool chair and sat down with the phone receiver in her hand.

Donald answered on the second ring.

"Hi. It's me," she said. "I hope I didn't wake you up."

"I was awake. I've been awake." He sounded weary. Wary. "Where are you? Are you alright?"

She looked at the clock over the oven range. It was 6:00 a.m.

"I'm home. I'm fine. There was a message on the board from Holly that I should call you."

She heard him take a breath. "Yes," he said. "She called me last night. Around midnight. She said you had left the house in the storm and she wasn't sure where you were."

"Uh huh, she wrote me this note on the board that you'd called," she said, and rushed on, "I would have returned your call earlier but I was afraid you might be asleep already by the time I could call." Immediately the lie sounded lame to her, who was not given to lying.

"I was up late. In fact, I haven't slept yet," Donald said. "When did you get back?" His voice sounded both tight with annoyance and breathy with relief.

She hesitated. Then, "I'm not sure. Much later than I meant it to be."

"Oh?"

She was determined now that she wouldn't tell him anything more definite. She was silent to confirm it.

"It was snowing pretty heavily—the radio said we had eight inches last night," he said. "Your car handled it alright?"

"That's why I didn't get home until late," she said.

"What happened? Everything all right?" His voice was settled now, in the way she remembered it when he questioned her actions.

"It will be shortly," she said. She heard him draw another breath and blow it out slowly through his nose in that affectation he adopted sometimes to show his displeasure when he expected an explanation for something she or one of the children had done. Or a confession. "I misjudged the weather, is all, and I went out to…I had to go check on something for today. The girls were already asleep and I wasn't going to be gone long—and I wasn't long either—wouldn't have been if the car hadn't slipped off the road on my way home and got stuck in the snow."

His response surprised her. "Oh! So you got it out alright, then?"

"No. It's still stuck," she said. "I'm waiting now for the tow truck to come and take me back to where the car is and pull it out."

"You're still stuck?"

"In the snow. The car slipped off the side of the road—" She could see it there in her memory still, tilted almost completely on its side, held up by a levee of packed snow it had plowed up on its slide down into the gully.

"Where?"

"Not far from here. On Ninety-eighth Street—or *off* Ninety-eighth Street now." Reflexively she chuckled with that nervous little laugh that came like a hiccup when she caught something she'd said that was not literally what she meant.

"So, how did you get home?"

"A snowplow came by. The snowplow driver drove me to our house. It's a long story, Donald." She was becoming irritable. She was telling him more than she intended. It was not his business. She was capable of handling her inconveniences herself.

"I've got time," he said.

"Well, I don't. I'm exhausted and I'm waiting for the truck to come pull my car out."

"You should have called me. I could have come and pulled you out with my truck last night."

"I didn't have my cell phone with me, and it was so late when I got home…Anyway, aren't you at work?"

"No. I just finished my rotation days off. I go back on shift this morning."

Her tone became firmer. "Well, thank you, but I've got it handled. I just need to have it pulled back on the road this morning."

"I'm glad you're alright, then. Holly was worried." Donald said. "And so was I."

"They were both fine when I left," Catherine said. "They were asleep in bed. They still are. I didn't know I would be that long when I left."

"I'm sure," Donald agreed quickly. "But Holly said that you weren't feeling well, that you had a migraine headache or whatever they are that triggers…well, your distress. She may have thought…who knows. But she was worried that you were out so late in terrible weather."

"Is there something wrong, Donald?" she said.

"No," he said. Then he laughed softly. "*I* was worried about you, too. That's all."

She didn't know what more to say. Dead air hung between them as still as the bottom of an ocean.

"Look, I know what day this is for you, Cathy. I know it's going to be stressful. Are you going to be all right?" Again she heard him breathing. "Is there anything I can do to help?"

She couldn't answer him at first.

"Cathy?"

"It's all right," she said. Her voice had gone suddenly fluid. She cleared her throat. "I mean, it's only a divorce hearing, after all. Cut and dried, my lawyer says." She laughed tartly.

"I've never attended one," he said.

His presence at their hearing had not been needed because he was not contesting her wish to leave him. He had told her later that he was happy he did not have to sit through it to hear his wife tell the judge their marriage had become "irretrievably broken."

"You didn't miss anything," she said to him now. She laughed again and drew back her breath in a harsh moist snuffling in her nose. She realized that without intention, she was near tears. "I'm becoming an authority on the subject."

"Well, I just wanted to tell you I'm sorry it didn't work out for you," Donald said. "Although I have to confess that I'm not unhappy to see you rid of him."

At that moment, she believed he felt that for her, and she almost spoke up to defend Steven.

"Ooh God," she said, caving. "I am so-o tired. I haven't had any sleep either, and I have things I have to get done before this afternoon."

"It's all right," he said. "Too many things sometimes hit us at once."

"Hah!" she said explosively, surprising him. "Tell me about it." But then, just as quickly, she was plaintive. "I'm so screwed up right now. God, I think I must really be crazy, Donald. I really think I'm losing it again."

"You're not, Catherine. No, you're just tired," he said firmly. "This is all very exhausting, I'm sure."

"It's feels like before," she said with an edge of desperation. "My head...all night I've had these terrible *things* going on in my head."

"Now listen, all you need is some rest," Donald said. "When do you have to be anywhere today?"

"I don't know...one o'clock is when I'm supposed to be in court."

"Well, you have time, then, to just lie down. Lie down and don't think a thought. Don't think about anything at all."

"Oh right. Where have I heard that before? Like all my life."

"I just meant let your mind rest," he said.

"I can't *rest*. How can I rest? I shut my eyes and these *creatures* start playing in my head, or I feel my face split open—"

"All right, now, just stop it!" he said adamantly.

She knew she was alarming him with that kind of talk. Her bizarre way of describing her symptoms were figures of speech for her anxiety, Steven had told her; but she knew they were living figures that no one other than she could understand.

Donald was talking faster now. "You've got to take hold of yourself, Cathy. You don't want to frighten the girls. Pull yourself together; you're a strong, intelligent woman. You know what these episodes are. You know how to calm yourself."

"Was it this hard for you?" she asked, cutting in, surprising herself—the question itself.

"Was what hard?" She heard the edge back on his tone.

"Divorce. Was it this hard on you?"

"In more ways than you can imagine," he said.

"Well, anyhow, I'm sorry." When he didn't reply, she said, "I guess I'll let you go to work. But thank you, Donald."

"For what?"

"Just for…well, for thinking of me. I feel a bit better already."

"Everything will be all right again," he said. "Just tell yourself you'll be through it in a little while, and then you'll be free of your mistakes to start a new life. And…well, you can call me if you need someone to help with the girls."

When she'd hung up, Catherine stood before the sliding door to the backyard patio and looked out at the light of dawn seeping into the night. *Take care of yourself*, Donald had advised her. *Everything will be all right again.* But her mind would not quiet itself. It throbbed with activity, like the transformer on the power pole next door behind the Aisenbergs' house, alive with that hum of idling power that sometimes she could hear on summer nights with her window open.

Think of things immediate, in front of you. Be aware only of the moment, her therapist had coached her. Be aware of what? The pain in her head? Just the pain?

She went back to the kitchen to make coffee and call for a tow truck. She dialed the number on the business card from Donald's index card box. "It'll be a while, maybe an hour before we can get to you this morning," the woman dispatcher apologized. "I hope you don't have to be anywhere soon."

Chapter 7

Steven woke to sunlight coming through a shadeless window that only a moment before was blackened by night. For a time, he lay very still; only his eyes moved to search out a familiar referent that could explain away the threat of all this light.

It took a few moments before he recognized the yellow and green daisy pattern on the percale sheets and pillowslip. These were not his sheets absorbing the rank musk of his body. But then his mind was jolted awake in a shock of recognition: this was not his bed. It was the bed of Saundra Bourcek, his student from American Literature class with whom he had gamboled and rutted on this same field of daisies only a short time ago under the cover of darkness, lulled by the sound of the wind prowling about outside the house and the sandy hiss of snow gusting against the window screens. Only, it was no longer dark. He rolled upright and peered out the window above the headboard. And it wasn't snowing any longer.

Waking up in a state of displacement was not new to him. He'd experienced it a number of times in the past three months, in his own bed, in his own apartment. Often when he awoke, he felt as if only a moment had passed between closing his eyes and opening them again, and that he'd been cheated out of the revitalization of rest. It was a symptom of his growing fatigue and mental lassitude he'd begun to feel since marrying Catherine. His doctor, a young internal medicine specialist, recommended he see a therapist, but Steven was not going up that path. Catherine saw a therapist. He did not want to put himself in that camp, although he'd begun to worry he could be heading for something serious if he didn't take charge of his life again. His leaving her had been the first big step toward that goal.

For now, however, more disconcerting to him was the realization that Saundra Bourcek was not in her bed with her overnight guest, lying with him in the revealing light of her adultery. He was alone in the bedroom. The door was closed, but somewhere not too far beyond its flimsy protection, he heard muffled voices—a woman's, a child's, another child's—the clinking of metal on ceramic, all signs, he knew with an uneasiness approaching alarm, of the progress of someone else's morning rites. He was a burglar caught by the return of the family, a second story man trapped on the second story.

Across the room were two sliding-door closets side by side, each door slid open to reveal half its contents: in one, bright blouses and dresses and jeans above a shoe caddie with paired blue and white and beige shoes; in the other, plaid shirts, a brown suit, tan and green trousers hung in file like a platoon of effigies to remind him he was also in the bedroom of Jack Bourcek. He listened again, straining to hear if he could detect among the several pitches and timbres of voices below that deeper *fee-fi-foe-fum* rumble of his certain doom.

At the foot of the bed, his own pants and shirt were draped limply over the edge. A single black sock clung like a flat leech to the bedspread. In desperate summons to his body to be active, he lunged, groping for his clothes, and the quick movement sent pants and shirt over the precipice to complete their drop to the floor. When he crawled to the end of the bed and reached over the edge to reclaim them, the bedroom door opened and Saundra swept in, wearing her bathrobe and slippers, her dark red hair still sleep-tangled.

She grinned when she saw his dilemma.

"Jesus, Saundra, it's daylight!" he whispered, his morning voice a hoarse croak.

She held her finger to her lips and closed the door behind herself. "I know," she said quietly. "The kids are up having breakfast." In daylight, her face seemed faded, puffy about the eyes. But she was smiling at Steven, a conspirator in a daring adventure in which he no longer wanted to take part. There was something secure and intimate in her smile that caused him greater uneasiness. "You are a sight," she said with affection.

He sat back on the bed and made an attempt to pull a fold of bedspread over his thighs. "Why didn't you wake me up?"

"Why did you go to sleep?"

"I didn't mean to."

"I didn't either." She joined him on the bed and put her arms around him, kissing him. He could taste the night's decay in the hollow cave of their joined mouths.

"I'm sorry, lover," Saundra said, breaking from him. "I went to sleep when you got up to pee, and I didn't know anything until Chrissy came in this morning to get me up."

"Oh my god. Your *daughter* came in here?" He pulled away from her and flopped backward on the bed. "Then they know I'm here?"

She leaned over him. Her robe parted and he saw she was still naked underneath, her breasts softly asway.

"I don't think so," she said. "She was still half asleep, and I got right up the minute she opened the door. If she saw anything, she probably thought it was her dad. You were covered up enough so she wouldn't have seen the difference."

"Oh, of course not," he said. Recalling the picture of Jack Bourcek he had seen in the display of family photos on a triangular wall shelf in a corner of her living room, he ticked off the dissimilarities. "I have dark hair, he has light. I'm clean-shaven, he has a mustache. I'm here, he's away on a trip in his big purple Kenworth. Hard to tell the difference." He turned his face aside and drew a deep breath, exhaling in resignation. "What the hell."

She chuckled. "To a little girl, you're just a lump in bed beside Mommy. Anyway, she didn't ask if Daddy was home. She must not have noticed."

"I've got to leave, Saundra," Steven replied, looking back at her. "It's daylight already."

"It's only seven-fifteen." She smiled. "Who are you? Count Dracula?"

"I've got a lot to do this morning. I have to be in court by one."

"Well, sure; but that's hours away, still." She lowered herself beside him now and stretched out along his body. "A bit nervous, are you?"

"No," he said. Then he grimaced at his own deception. "Actually, yes. More than a bit."

"Oh, Steven," she cooed. "You poor baby." He tried to sit up, but she held her hand on his shoulder, pinning him down. "Don't worry about it. It'll work out all right."

He relented under the steady pressure of her hand. "I know it'll be all right. I just didn't expect to still be here so late, is all. I need to shower, shave, get dressed yet…"

"What'll happen in court? What's a divorce hearing like?"

"Like a marriage ceremony in reverse. The judge looks over the papers, says 'Omni-omni, domini-domini, presto-change-o, you're single again,' and everyone goes home free." He smiled to reassure her. And himself.

"That's not what they used to do on *Divorce Court*. Don't people fight over money and custody of kids and things? I know my mom and dad did when they split up."

He explained to her that their attorneys had pretty much worked everything out beforehand, and they'd signed an agreement. At least, he had.

"My lawyer says that Catherine did too, although I haven't seen her signature on anything." He leaned in and kissed her forehead. "If you're going to be home later, I'll call and fill you in on the whole thing then."

"Sure," she said. "I'll be home. I've got nothing else to do today, except get the kids to school. Jack will be out of town until Sunday. Why don't you come back here tonight for a little post-divorce therapy?" Her voice was suddenly smoky, her imitation of Lauren Bacall, Steven imagined. "A little P D T for my P E T?"

He looked at her face. She had not washed since before last night: streaks of mascara trailed from the corners of her eyes, and flakes of green eyeliner curled like reptilian scales from her upper lids. Something in her morning blowziness, the image of sexual decadence in her dishabille, aroused him. "That sounds very attractive." He tousled her hair once and sat up. "But I've got to end one complication before I can get involved in another."

"I'm not so complicated." She took his head in her hands and drew his face to her lips. Then they were tumbling backwards, her body on his. His hand slid beneath her robe, along the skin of her back, and traced the curve of her buttocks. Her legs sprang wantonly apart to accommodate him, and his resistance faltered beneath the reassurance she offered in this new bit of recklessness. Then, in another instant, she had risen above him and mounted him, and she began posting in the saddle of his groin to the uneven gait of their lovemaking.

Afterwards, they lay squeezed together, her leg thrown over his hips. He could hear still the clear morning voices of her children downstairs in another part of the house.

"This is way too risky for us, for me and for you, too," he said quietly.

"I know," she replied. The index finger of her right hand spun little spaghetti curlicues in his chest hair. "It's all different in daylight, isn't it?"

"Yes, that. But, it's being here, in your house," he said. "It's not our place to be. It's yours and your children's. And your husband's."

"That's funny," she said. "All night long I just thought of us."

In the morning he was always blunt, and after the depletions of sex, he was generally truthful. It was his experience that the woman set the ground rules in these situations—which was why, he supposed, he was initially grateful when a lover claimed to know better than him what he needed from her. But he always felt it necessary to make clear just what his own expectations were.

"We shouldn't hold any illusions that way. What's ours is just this time together, and I've overstayed it as it is."

"You'll come back tonight, won't you?" she asked.

There was a nebula of possessiveness he sensed around her, and with his desire for her abated again for a time, he didn't need complications that held no good future. She was married, he was soon to be unmarried. There was no room in his mind to think of anything beyond those two facts.

"I don't think that would be wise," he said. "What if he comes home early? Drives on through and gets back early. Hasn't he ever done that?"

"Sometimes. In the early days, when we were younger and he still cared for me, he would do that sometimes. Come back early and surprise me," Saundra said. "But not for years now. He doesn't care so much for me anymore; just for the idea of me, as a wife and the kids' mother. If he walked right in on us now, I doubt it would bother him all that much. He'd just trade me in for a new wife, like he would his truck if it needed too much maintenance."

"He's a husband," Steven said. "Whether he still loves you or not, believe me, it would bother him. He's a truck driver. Truck drivers think about things like the loyalty of their wives when they're alone at night on the highways. Or so I've heard."

"You don't know much about Jack," she said lightly. "If he thinks about anything, it's how far he can stretch his fuel before the next fill up or about the tight little ass on the waitress at the last truck stop. He won't be home early. Don't borrow trouble."

Her boldness grated now. If she had lost all caution in the flush of confidence their little affair gave her, nothing but trouble would come of it. Then he would have to deal with the trouble. That's what history and literature had taught Steven. "Your children are home. You don't want to risk screwing up their lives."

"I wouldn't do that, and you know it," she said. "I'm mostly just teasing you because you seem so paranoid all of a sudden."

He squeezed the soft flesh of her inner thigh, playful but reproving. She clamped her legs, trapping his hand from moving between them.

"Not paranoid," he said. "Cautious."

She took hold of his wrist and pulled his hand away from her. Rolling onto him again, she held herself up on stiffened arms planted on either side of his chest, and she looked down at him through a tumble of hair. "Are we just having a casual affair, then?"

"What do you think?"

She smiled, a tightlipped smile. "I'm just the student, remember? You wrote the syllabus. So, what are the objectives of this course, Professor Harper?"

He understood she only meant to needle him, but her sudden invoking of their other relationship unleashed qualms of self-doubt. "The objectives right now are to get me out of here and on my way home to change," he said.

"God, you're really an uptight person," she said with exasperation. It was the second time she'd said it. The first was last night when he had come scratching at her back door in the dark, in the snow, like a fugitive. He had left his car two blocks down the street in a strip mall parking lot so as not to be seen by the neighbors. Now she was telling him, "You must be a very hard person for a woman to love."

"Love is difficult enough for anyone to manage, whether he's *uptight* or *laid back*," Steven said, ridiculing her slang. It was presumptuous of her to confuse the coupling of their bodies with an invitation to invade his psyche. He didn't want to leave himself in her hands any longer. He had given over to her enough management of the situation. "Look, Saundra—"

"*Sandy.* Can't you call me Sandy?" she said. "Whenever you say *Saun*-dra, you sound like my parents about to scold me." She frowned. "It sounds so bloody Victorian."

"All right," he said. "But, Sandy, my pet, I do have to leave right now. Really. Please understand."

She blew a breath of air through pursed lips. "All right, go," she said. "It's your funeral."

He began reaching again to collect his clothes, found his briefs under the sheets at the foot of the bed, along with his other sock.

"It's safer right now if you wait here for a bit," she conceded. "I have to get the kids ready for school yet. I'll just keep my bedroom door shut and they won't come near you. Then after we leave—which'll be around eight-thirty or so—you can just stroll out the door big as life and no one will be the wiser."

"No. I'm not hiding in here until you're gone." He cranked his head back toward the window and saw nothing but daylight through the panes of glass. "Is there even going to be school, after last night?"

"Yes. Parochial school, anyway. We Catholics would never miss a day of school, even if it were the Second Coming. So okay, just wait a bit more until I go downstairs, I'll keep the kids busy in the kitchen and you can go out through the garage. But if you stay, you can shower and shave if you want—Jack's got some of those plastic travel razors in a drawer in his bathroom somewhere—and you'll be all fresh for the day when you leave."

Her invitation to use her husband's razor brought a sudden dark thrill. But her disloyalty—that in his absence she would be so free with her husband's possessions, she would not protect even his intimate personal presence—soured him.

"Get dressed," he said to her. "When you go back down to the kitchen, I'll take it from there."

She shrugged and climbed out of bed.

She rummaged the closet for her clothes, draping a dark green dress over her arm, selecting a pair of green shoes from the caddie. Finally, she pulled fresh underthings from a drawer and draped them over the dress on her arm.

She came back to his side of the bed and leaned to kiss him. He held her head briefly between his hands as their lips touched.

"Will you call me later?" she asked.

"I'll try."

"You said you would. You said you'd call me and fill me in on what happened."

"Then I'll call you," he said, although he no longer meant to. "I'm not sure what the timetable for all this is—how long it will actually take. And then I need to get into the office for a while. I'll call you this evening when I get home."

"Call me from your office."

He understood what she was asking. She wanted his reassurance that this had been more to him than just a dalliance. That old disclosure of vulnerability: yes, but will you love me in the morning? Here Saundra stood now, her clothes over her arm, her bathrobe split open like a burst seed pod, displaying breasts, navel, pubis in the apathetic posture of an anatomy mannequin, comfortable now with him after their second time they'd spent a night together, as if they had known each other beyond all pretense for years. Yet, each time he was warmed to tenderness by the courage and humility it must take a lover to shed her modesty in a heap with her clothes and offer herself to his fevered desire in sexual intimacy. He had always admired any woman who found him desirable enough to share her body with him.

"It's different for a woman," Catherine had told him once, very early in their relationship when they had engaged in one of their furtive couplings in his locked office and she had not put her jeans back on for several minutes after he had already buttoned, zipped, and belted himself safely into his own clothes. He had asked—only curious—if she didn't feel a bit self-conscious displaying herself in front of him that way when he had already readjusted his fig leaf, as he put it.

She'd replied, "Once you've permitted a man—your doctor, your boyfriend, your husband—to poke around inside your body with steel instruments or cold fingers or sex organs, modesty seems pointless, don't you think? It's not a matter of modesty, it's trust. Most women trust the good intentions of a man as a condition of surrendering her modesty. And I trust you, Steven."

To Saundra, who was waiting for his answer, Steven said, "I'll call you just as soon as I can."

"I can call you, if you want," she said. It sounded both suggestion and warning.

"Well, that'll be difficult. I have an unlisted telephone number."

"You do? What for? You get obscene phone calls from women?"

He chuckled. "I wish. Well, sort of. I got it to keep Catherine from hassling me. She's…well, *excitable* when she's upset. And she's been upset a lot since we split." He drew a breath and released a small sigh. "Sometimes she gets these over the top attacks of anxiety and needs lots of reassurance. When I first moved out, she'd call in the middle of the night, or come over to my apartment and wake me up. So I got a new unlisted phone number. And a cell phone."

"Well, I won't tell her what it is," Saundra pressed. "What's the matter, don't you trust me?"

"That's not the point," he said. "The point of an unlisted number is that it's not publicly available."

"I'm hardly the public," she said.

"No, my pet, that you're not."

And what did it matter? he thought. He'd already caved and given Catherine the new number to his cell phone anyway, because he found it was easier to listen to her crazy talk on the phone than to have her come to his apartment door, buzzing to be let in. Surrendering to Saundra now, as he had surrendered to most women in his life, he said, "Do you have something to write on?"

This seemed to mollify her. She dropped her clothes on the bed and turned to her bureau where she rummaged through several jewelry boxes and cluttered trays of stuff on top until she came up with a bank pen and a business card from a hair salon—*New Waves Images*. "Here, you can write on the back of this." She handed him pen and card. When he wrote the number and handed it back, she looked at it, and nodded. Then she added something of her own and, with a wicked smile, held the card out for him to see. Above his number she'd written:

For wild time!
Call Professor Steven Harper
4205 Taylor
558-7285

And below the number he'd printed there, she'd added, "*Gives Great c-Lit!*"

He smiled. "Why, how sweet of you."

She slipped an edge of the card under a replicated Trimline phone on the bedside table and lowered her eyelids in a suggestive way. "Now you'll know when I call you tonight that I'm calling from my bed."

She gathered up her clothes in her arms again and kissed him once more. After she'd left the bedroom to dress in the bathroom, Steven quickly put on his own clothes then sat on the bed to wait. He could hear water running, and the image of her before the mirror burnishing her skin with the washcloth, dimly moved him toward tenderness even as the fog of a postcoital gloom settled on him.

He reconsidered Saundra's offer of her husband's razor. If he could get even that portion of his own morning ablutions taken care of, it would be one less thing for him to have to do getting ready for court.

In the small bathroom, he opened the mirrored medicine cabinet above the sink and found Jack Bourcek's can of Foamy, and in a cabinet drawer beneath the sink, a new Bic razor in an opened ten-pack. It occurred to him, as he lathered his face, disguising himself behind the white beard of foam, how little anyone really knows about the inner lives of the people they live with, and how much of the glue that bonds a couple in marriage is concocted out of the unfathomable and whimsical elements of an individual's chemistry. It was all chemistry, he'd read in a *Psychology Today* article. Love, happiness, despondency, dissatisfaction, disassociation. The chemistry of infatuation and euphoria, of boredom and betrayal. A stew of hormones, amino acids, sugars, carbohydrates, proteins, fats, metals, and minerals. For all anyone actually understood, it could be that if Prozac were administered like communion wafers with the wedding vows, love might never fade.

Shaving, Steven watched the razor reveal his face in swaths from beneath the mask of lather. *Behold the cleaver, behold the disjoiner, the dissolver*, he thought as each stroke of the blade uncovered a new swatch of clean skin. *Behold the freeman.*

Only he was not free yet.

Chapter 8

Station 5 was a one-story brick building that sat at the top of a small rise off Cedar Street at 63rd in Midtown. Across the front, three aluminum and glass overhead garage doors sealed off the bays of the fire apparatus floor, and a broad concrete drive sloped down to the street. On the east side of the building was a small parking lot for the cars of the men on duty, and a shrub-lined sidewalk connected the lot to the personnel door into the rear of the building. At one time, barely fifteen years ago, all the land Station 5 sat on had been farmland, the rise no more than a small hillock in the gentle roll of the tilled fields. Now it was in the middle of a residential and shopping mall area in the west central part of Platte City.

When Donald drove into the parking lot, it was already 7:15 a.m., fifteen minutes into the beginning of C-Shift's workday. Normally, he would have been "in house" by 0630 to check with the A-Shift captain of Engine 55 for Equipment Attention notations, log entries of any fire calls, and any notices, orders, or new SOP's that had come down from Headquarters in Donald's absence. But he was late today because of Catherine's phone call and the delay it had caused him getting ready for work, his morning routine thrown off its normal rhythm by his inability to keep his mind focused.

He wished Catherine hadn't called him. He wished he had not insisted that Holly leave her a message that may have seemed like a command to her mother. Perhaps it would have been better for him not to know what was going on with Catherine than to hear it from her.

The parking lot behind the fire station was full of cars. His reserved stall as House Captain was occupied by a pickup, and all the other white-lined stalls in the lot were filled as well. It took him a moment, while he angled for a spot in the snow-covered grass just beyond the tarmac, to realize that some of the men from A-Shift had not left the station yet.

All the way to the door he stepped in large puddles of melting snow. Rivulets of water guttered down the concrete walk and onto the front apron, washing into Cedar Street below. Donald could feel the day warming to a normal spring temperature. He suspected most of the standing snow would be gone by nightfall.

Donald stepped inside the door to the apparatus floor to check the log sheets of fire calls from the previous shift. The two trucks—Aerial 53 and Engine 55—sat silently on dry concrete; their battery trickle-charger cables and airbrake hoses dangled like IV tubes from electrical outlets in the ceiling. There was no evidence that anything had moved during the storm last night. He thumbed the pages of log sheets in a three-ring binder on the alarm desk, found the last entry which was two days ago from B-Shift: "Smoke in kitchen of Dairy Queen. Overheated fryer. No damage." Closing the book, he went to his locker in the row of open cubicles along the near wall, and he grabbed his bunker gear—Nomex coat and pants, helmet and boots—to hang in another cage on the wheeled ready rack on the apparatus floor alongside the engine. His captain's space on the rack was the first in line and vacant, ready for him. He was surprised to find that the one open cage remaining of the six was also filled with turnout gear, and when he checked, he found that the Nomex coat on its hook was brand new, and across the back was the printed name *GALLANT*. His initial reaction was annoyance that someone had assumed the new arrival was already set up to ride Engine 55 right away.

He had just turned to look around the floor when he heard a noise from the opposite side of Engine 55—the scuff of a shoe on gritty concrete, the clank of a metal cabinet door on the truck's side closing—and he walked around the front to investigate. In the alley between 55 and Aerial 53, he saw his new firefighter.

She was studying the contents of an open cabinet below the hose bed of 55, her back to him as she stood alongside the fire engine. What Donald saw first was a tall slender figure with a ramrod back and level shoulder line, the dark blue dress uniform starched and tailor-fit, the creases in shirtsleeve and trousers still crisp. Her uniform hat sat squarely on her head, and out of the little inverted-V space between the cloth fabric of the cap and the elastic sizing strap, a stubby ponytail of brown hair protruded like a whiskbroom.

"Are you finding everything you need?" he said.

Tentatively, she looked back over her shoulder, but when she saw the gray shirt of an officer, she almost did a military about-face to confront him.

"Captain Sparta?"

She extended her hand and he shook it. Her own hand was slender, but she had a strong grip—tendons, pronounced and taut. "Deborah Gallant," she said.

"Don Sparta. Welcome to Fifty-Five," he said, neither cordially nor reserved.

Her high cheekbones, full lower lip, and almond-shaped eyes with dark lashes made her compelling to look at. Instantly he thought, *Damn!*

She seemed a bit nervous, he could tell, the nervousness appearing as a glint of resistance in her eyes, a sharp point of light in each deep brown iris. But her eyes shifted from one side to the other, infinitesimally small darting movements covered by the blink of her eyelids. One second she was focusing on Donald. The next, she was looking just slightly over his shoulder. Not shifty-eyed, it was more like a shell game in which the pupils of her eyes were the elusive peas. Donald found himself reacting with tension of his own. Her little spritz of ponytail sticking out of the back of her uniform cap seemed suddenly absurd to him, an irregularity in her otherwise orthodox uniformed correctness.

Deborah Gallant stood in an attitude of respectful attention, waiting.

"Well, good to have you on board," Donald replied. "Looks like you've already found your spot on the ready rack," he said.

She looked at him oddly, a perplexed frown on her face. "Should I have waited?" she said, then shrugged.

He avoided answering. "Have you had a chance to look around the rest of the station, yet, meet all the crew?"

"I stuck my head in the dayroom, but I didn't really meet anybody yet. Except, I met one of them, I think. An older guy. Wesson?" Deborah said. "He showed me where to hang my bunker gear."

Donald smiled, relaxing. "Charlie Wesson. You can't get into the station without meeting him. Charlie's the one retiring at the end of the month. You're replacing him. Big boots to fill, as the saying goes."

She nodded her head. Her eyes looked somewhere in the vicinity of his ankles. "I'll do my best."

"Things are pretty quiet in this house," Donald said. "I think we logged maybe two hundred calls all last year. You'll have time to ease your way into the routines and get to know the apparatus."

"No problem," Deborah said.

"Okay, then," Donald said. "Follow me, I'll introduce you to the crew of Engine Fifty-Five C-Shift, then we'll check out your quarters."

When he and Deborah Gallant entered the dayroom, Donald found it full of men. All of C-Shift Engine 55 and Aerial 53, and almost everyone from the previous shift, A-Shift, were sitting on metal chairs at two long folding tables, or in the few arm chairs and two Naugahyde couches in front of the television. The TV was tuned to *Good Morning, America,* as it was each day, but today the sound was muted. With their coffee cups in front of them, the men were engaged in conversation, but their talk seemed restrained, their mood obscure.

They were all waiting, it was evident. They were all pretending to ignore the presence of the two in the doorway. And all of them, Donald saw right away, were wearing their dress uniform caps. Even Mike Krupa, the C-Shift captain on Aerial 53, and George Manning, the A-Shift captain of Engine 55, were in their white-crowned dress hats.

Donald's immediate reaction was embarrassment. It was some form of protest, he was sure, but he didn't immediately understand it.

"I didn't see any black-and-white bunting on the house out front," he said to the group in general. A few looked his way then deliberately turned their attention back again to the TV or to the conversation of those around them.

Only George Manning, the A-Shift captain of 55, bit. "What for? Did someone die?"

"You tell me. Apparently, everyone's dressed for a funeral here. Did someone die?"

Gene Metzger, Donald's driver on Engine 55, spoke up first. "Well, *something* sure is dead, all right."

Donald hadn't expected a reply to what he meant as a rhetorical question. "And what's that, Gene?" Donald said.

Metzger, who was in his early twenties and was normally not very outgoing, reddened. He looked at Donald with the injured expression of someone who has been betrayed: haughty and sullen, at the same time. "How about tradition?"

"Tradition," Donald repeated. "What about it?" But he already understood now where this was headed.

Metzger looked around at the others, many of whom were grinning at him. He turned back to Donald but did not look at him directly any longer. "Nothing. Just tradition...*pride* in a tradition seems like it might be dead. Anyways, ain't this proper uniform?" He tapped the bill of his hat.

Donald understood then that they were dressed to mock Deborah Gallant's innocent formality and fresh-off-the rack blue uniform. He judged by the jauntiness with which some of them had placed the hats on their heads, and by the powdery dust on the bills of a few, that they hadn't been worn in months for any formal occasions. No doubt, they had hastily conceived the practical joke only minutes earlier. Someone had tipped them off—Charlie Wesson, maybe?—that she had come to work in a new dress uniform. He recalled Chief Thorp's stern warning to "see to it there's no flak...no bitching."

"All right, people, if I could have your attention for a moment," Donald said raising his voice. His growing irritation was amplified in the timbre of unaccustomed authority. "This is Cadet Deborah Gallant. She's the newest member of Engine Fifty-Five. Where are the other C-Shift members of the company?" he said, looking around the room, pretending not to see all of his crew. "Stand up, you guys. Now."

Charlie Wesson, then Al Czernecky, and finally Gene Metzger, all rose in their places. Donald named them off, indicating each one for Deborah Gallant, and waiting until he got some sort of response from them. Most of the other men in the room used the opportunity to turn their attention squarely on her.

Only Charlie Wesson said anything when he was introduced, "I think we had the pleasure earlier."

One of the A-Shift Aerial 53 crewmembers responded abruptly, "You're pretty damned quick, aren't ya, Grandpa?" The restraint on all of them broke in the crass laughter that followed.

"Does she cook?" someone else said.

"God, I hope so. Get some decent food around here, for a change," Al Czernecky replied.

Donald could sense Deborah Gallant's rigidness beside him. He caught Metzger's eye, then Czernecky's, and glared at each of them in turn, making sure they saw his warning.

He looked at his watch. It was a few minutes to eight. "Is there any particular reason why A-Shift is putting in overtime today?" he asked, cutting through the sudden gabble of jibes and titters. As if it were his cue, George Manning, Donald's A-Shift counterpart, stood up.

"Nope. We was just leaving," he said. "Thought we'd just wait a minute extra to meet the new firefighter." He walked forward and thrust his hand out to Gallant. "George Manning. Cap'n Manners to those who show respect for age and intelligence."

She returned his handshake. "Sir," she acknowledged with a curt nod of her head. She was not going to let herself be ruffled, and Donald was grateful.

With their captain out the door, the other off-duty men of Aerial 53 and Engine 55 stood up slowly, gulped their remaining coffee, and ambled toward the exit.

Donald sucked back his remaining irritation, deliberately calming himself. Because he was captain of the station house also—a responsibility which fell to him only because he was officer of the engine company—he said now, "All right, people, I noticed when I came in this morning, the apparatus floor is gritty from sand. Since you have so much energy to burn, all of you will clean the apparatus floor. I mean *clean* it. The floor degreased, scrubbed, brushed— whatever it takes until it's spotless and passes inspection."

Charlie Wesson chuckled. Mike Krupa, Aerial 53 captain, moved away from his crew of truckmen and sidled up to Don as if to back him up.

"Come on, Don," Gene Metzger said. "We didn't dirty it. Probably A- or B-Shift didn't clean up after a call."

"So you'll clean up for them," Donald said. "I want all the grease spots off the floor and the diesel smoke off the walls. It's long overdue."

"Aw, come on. This wasn't nothin'," Metzger replied. He took his dress blues cap off. "Just having a bit of fun with the rookie." Then Metzger grinned. It was a puckish smile intended, perhaps, to soften Donald. But it seemed to him so outrageously insincere, an attempt to con him, Donald could feel the distance rush between them like a canyon forming.

"No, I'll tell you what this is," he said from his rim of the canyon. "This is my station house. And I like a clean station house. We're going to be having visitors coming in from the press, I'm told, so this isn't a request, this is an order. I know it's been a while since you've heard one—or maybe you only read about them in training classes—but I'm telling you now, so you can recognize it; this is a goddamned order."

Metzger's grin had vanished, his face blooming red. "Yes, *sir-rr*," he replied, curling his lip. The others looked incredulous for a moment; but one by one, Donald saw their faces register sullen understanding: Donald Sparta was playing officer.

"That include the rookie?" Czernecky asked, nodding toward Deborah Gallant.

With no less iciness, Donald said, "That includes everyone. But I have to complete checking in our newest member of Fifty-Five before you have the privilege of welcoming her into our crew." He looked at them for a moment, scanning their faces to register his resolve. No one said a word, and under their resentful silence, he turned to Deborah. "Let's go see what's been done about your cot," he said.

She flashed a quick smile he couldn't quite read, and he felt himself flush.

Back up the hall from the dayroom, Donald turned in with Deborah to the common bunkroom for the crews. All the beds for the engine company were positioned in the room just as they had been a week ago when C-Shift had gone on rotation days off. Their olive wool blankets were tucked with military tautness where the A-Shift crew had made them up for the day. There were three along the far wall and two more across from those, on the wall nearest the door. The only addition was a paneled curtain on wheeled metal frames, folded and propped now against the end wall across from the foot of the third bed on the opposite side of the aisle. It was the sort of temporary divider used to separate the hospital beds of patients needing an appearance of privacy while they're being examined. It was clear to Donald that whoever from City

Maintenance had delivered the screen had left him the responsibility of deciding how to set it up.

"Well, there it is," he said to Deborah Gallant, almost apologetically. "It doesn't look like much—"

"It's a bunk room," she said. "No problem."

"That's good," he said. He pulled the screen away from the wall and looked it over. It was three narrow panels wide—enough perhaps to separate her bed from the one next to it but not enough to block the view of someone lying in the bed across the aisle on the opposite wall. There would be the awkwardness, then, of setting it up. How should they go about it? Put it in place each night the crew was on duty, and then fold it up again in the morning when the new shift came on? He'd expected something bolted to the floor, a fabric-paneled divider like the ones that walled off cubicles in those big open office buildings. "Damn it," he said. "Nobody ever gets it right in city government."

"It's okay," Deborah Gallant said. "I'm not going to need it."

"You'll need it, alright," he said firmly.

"I bunk in my coveralls," she said.

"Really?" Donald thought smugly of the disillusionment of those among his men who may have entertained fantasies of women's underwear and bare skin. "Even so," he said, smiling, "*They'll* probably want the privacy. They can be a pretty raunchy bunch sometimes."

"I can get down with the worst of them," she said, then added quickly, "When it comes to being raunchy, I mean. I was brought up with six brothers. My two older brothers are in fire service, too. Omaha and Kansas City. I'm no *prin*-cess." The way she said the word—enunciated with sudden primness—made Donald think of Catherine: for some reason, the word perfectly suited the character of his ex-wife that leapt to his mind and vanished again just as rapidly.

"I think for now, until everyone gets adjusted to the crew change, and the publicity—I mean, there are going to be questions from outside, from the press, and the public and whatnot about accommodations—anyway, I think it would be best for now to put the screen between your bed and the others."

"Sir, I think—" she began, dipping her head self-consciously before looking him in the face again. "Actually, I know that I don't want to have to hassle with something like this each time I go to bed. I mean, I would feel…*humiliated* to have to do that."

"I trust they told you you're probably going to be the center of attention for a while, both inside and outside the department," he said.

"I hope not," she said.

"Well, it's inevitable," he said. "I've been warned, there'll be media people wanting to talk to you. They're supposed to be cleared through the Chief's office first. I don't know whether that means you'll have to talk to them or not. I don't know yet what choices we have."

"Why do they bother?" she said. "They've already been after me enough—and Tammi, too—while we were in training." Tammi was the other one, Donald recalled. The one whose first assignment was Chief's Aide.

"You're news."

"There's been women in other fire departments for a long time. Nothing newsworthy about that."

That was true enough. Omaha had taken on four, and almost every volunteer department in the state had turned to female fire and medical squad personnel in towns where the populations were aging and young men were leaving to find work in other states and in the cities. But Platte City was none of those places. Change of any sort took its sweet time getting here in the rural northern part of the state.

"I've been around fire stations since I was a girl. My dad is a District Chief on the Lincoln FD. He's the reason I became a firefighter."

"Your father is a District Chief?" Donald said. "Wait a minute! Are you talking about Bud Gallant?"

"Yes. He's my dad."

"I know him! I've been out in Grand Island at the State Fire Academy with him several times over the years for *refurbishment*, we used to call it." He made air quotes with his fingers. "He was a captain then. Like me."

"That's him," Deborah said, her voice more animated now. "He's why I applied to Platte City when your job listing came up. I've wanted to do what he does for like always—be a smoke eater." She cracked a smile then.

Donald shook his head, amazed.

"I'm glad you know my dad," she said. "It makes me feel like we've already met, somehow."

"I'm dumbfounded. I've seen pictures of you as a little girl he showed me. Back when you *were* a little girl." He chuckled, then suddenly looked away toward the row of lockers. "You were my son's age back then—ten years old, I remember."

"Is your son a firefighter too?"

He felt the instantaneous hollowing of his gut and he drew away from answering her. "No. But I remember what your dad said about you, even then; he thought you'd be a 'corker' of a firefighter one day."

She grinned. "That's me. A corker," she said. "Whatever that means." Her face became composed again. "Anyway, really I mean it about being behind a hospital curtain from the rest of my company. I would feel mortified to be the only one to have to hide behind a curtain at night like I had some disease, or something. I can do just fine sleeping in my coveralls, and I can give back as much as I get from the guys, too."

"All right, then," Donald said, nodding his head. "That settles that. For now, I'll respect what you want, unless I hear otherwise."

"Thank you, sir," she said.

"Look, it's all right to call me Don. Or Cap, some of them call me."

She acknowledged him with a nod. "Captain."

"Right now, why don't you grab your coveralls and maybe go down and use the visitors' bathroom to change into your work clothes, then join your crew out on the apparatus floor. You need anything, my office is just down the hall," he said.

"No prob," she said. "Thanks."

There was nothing more he could do at this point except turn young Gallant loose with the rest of the crew and see if she were able to make her own way. She seemed capable and strong enough to suffer their ignorance.

He left her and retreated to his room to sort out what he would do next. His was a narrow rectangular room, as spare as a monk's cell. It was both his sleeping quarters and his office, and he shared it with the engine company captains of two other shifts. In consequence, it was not a room he could personalize. It was just big enough to accommodate a cot, a desk and file cabinet, and three metal lockers for the personal effects of each of the occupants. The one privilege it afforded him was its own closet-sized bathroom with a shower, stool, and sink.

Beyond his room, he could hear the voices of his men echoing now from the tall concrete apparatus floor, their intelligibility muffled by the walls and their distance away from him, but human all the same.

He sat down at the little metal desk to begin sorting through the accumulated leavings of six days of memos and notes from Central Headquarters and the other shift captains from A and B shifts, his gaze moving from the list of notes, to the thick loose-leaf binder of standing orders and operating procedures, to the red telephone on the wall above the desk. He could hear them out on the apparatus floor, their voices incessant and more jovial. It was the first time in years he had given punitive work to his men, and their instant rejection of him made him seethe.

Donald realized now that for more years than he could recall, he had let them manipulate him into a fabricated equality which, until a few minutes ago, he himself had come to believe existed. Because a captain bunked in the station house and worked alongside his crew on the fire line, just like any other firefighter, it often seemed that his authority derived from them also: he outranked them because they agreed to allow him the privilege.

He heard the door open at the end of the narrow hall outside the apparatus floor, the voices momentarily louder above the hissing of water under pressure hitting the concrete floor; then the door closed again. Probably Gallant going to join in the housecleaning detail.

He stared up at the acoustical tile in the ceiling, at the round metal cover over the recessed alarm speaker above his desk, and he considered for a minute how long he had yet to live if he achieved his normal life expectancy and how short that time really was when considered against the unfulfilled ambitions of his forty-four years. He was already beyond dead center of his productive life and felt stuck between the points of entrance and exit in the bowel-smooth funnel of a slow whirlpool of time.

When he'd first graduated from the university with his newly discovered fascination for fire service translated into a degree in Fire Technology, he'd felt an ambition to rise toward greater responsibility in his profession. He had developed his basic technical education in the practical skills of fire suppression and readily passed the tests to move up from Private to Engineer to become a Captain in the PSFD in four years. With the birth of Donald Junior, he even entertained the possibility that his son might one day follow—even surpass—his father's fervency to master the technologies to harness the destructive excesses of fire. Another Sparta and Sons enterprise? Now the unexpected appearance in his engine company of Deborah Gallant, who had been inspired by her own father's dedication to his calling and followed in his professional wake, only brought up the repressed memories from the long-submerged wreckage of Donald's initial hopes for what his son might have become.

When it all exploded in the single thunderbolt instant of Donny's death—the result of the sort of unpredictable accident he had so often responded to when it was someone else's devastating loss—it cracked open the thin shell of his self-confidence. Any future he had dared imagine for himself and his family disappeared within an emotional fog. Following Catherine's foundering and their subsequent divorce, Donald had been taking his life, as well as his job, a shift at a time.

Chapter 9

There were two other customers in the donut shop at the far end—two men in business suits, having their morning coffee before the drive into town, Steven guessed. The counter girl was just now refilling their mugs and talking at a lively clip. Steven took a stool at the end of the counter closest to the door.

The girl had eyed him when he entered and looked at him again as she talked. She had long blond hair in an arched ponytail of that incredible sun-bleached appearance of white gold that always got his attention. As he watched her watching him, she raised her hand in a little two-fingered gesture that signaled she'd be right there to wait on him. He thought then she looked familiar, that he knew her from somewhere else. Her crisp peach-colored dress and maroon bib apron didn't tell him anything, because it was not her uniform that was familiar, it was something about her body, her squared back and slim hips and, he could see from his vantage point at the end looking down the counter, her long legs below the short hemline of the dress. Presently, she turned away from the two men and came toward him with a big smile for him—"Hey, Mr. Harper!"—and he recalled then who she was. Her name was Valerie. Valerie Caine. She'd been one of his students in a composition class two years ago. Only, her hair was a natural yellow then.

"What are you doing in this part of town?"

"Visiting a friend," he said.

"On a morning like this?" She stood squarely before him now, the fingers of one hand slipped into a pocket of her bib apron, the fingertips of her other hand lightly touching the countertop like a spider on slender legs. There was a jagged blaze of powdered sugar on the apron across her belly.

"Yeah, and I'm regretting it now," he said. "But it was something I couldn't avoid."

She reached under the counter and set in front of him a tall white coffee mug with a maroon handle. "What would you like?"

"I think a bear claw, if you have one. Or a cinnamon roll," he said. "And coffee, of course."

She brought him a huge snail shell curl of sugar-glazed pastry and poured his cup full from a stainless-steel decanter. The aromas of warm dough and freshly brewed coffee triggered Steven's hunger, and he breathed in deeply. "Mmm."

"Isn't that just the greatest smell?" Valerie said.

"Died and gone to heaven," Steven replied. He poked at the glazing on the roll and touched his finger to his tongue. "However, the calories will send me to hell."

She laughed brightly, giving her ponytail a twitch. Her smile was full of white teeth, and her throat was long and delicately corded when she canted back her head in laughter. He imagined his lips suddenly at the hollow between her clavicles, his nose breathing the fragrance beneath the open collar of her blouse. Instantly, he killed the thought.

Her attention was suddenly taken by the two men down at the end of the counter. One of them was holding up an empty mug, waggling it at her.

"Be back in a bit," she said. She leaned toward him; her voice lowered confidentially: "Would you like to look at the morning paper with your coffee?"

"Sure," he said.

She moved the opposite way up the counter toward the cash register and picked a folded copy of the morning Lincoln *Journal Star* off the top of the glass bakery case and dropped it in front of him on her way back down to refill the cups of the two men. *A nice girl*, Steven thought.

The front-page headlines were about the storm—*Surprise Blizzard Buries Spring*—with photos of plows and drifted-over bushes and cars stalled in the streets. Mostly the images were from Lincoln, not Platte City, taken sometime yesterday evening. Steven skipped through the national news, scanning the pages rapidly for any headline that might catch his interest. Finding nothing, he stopped at the Arts & Entertainment section, where a large center-page picture of three female dancers in catlike black leotards and white and blackface makeup grabbed his attention. The photo had caught the three in a convoluted pose, their bodies interwoven in a twisted sculpture that made it impossible on first glance to tell whose body parts were whose—which arms went with which trunks went with which legs or heads—the whole thing an image of a six-legged, three-headed Hydra.

Perhaps because he had so recently been involved in his own kinetic intertwining, Steven found the picture of the dancers vaguely erotic, his thoughts leaping to Saundra Bourcek writhing with him in her bed. Except, what began unfolding in his mind was a picture of Jack Bourcek returning home just then to find Steven in a pretzeled embrace with his wife.

Saundra had become bolder last night, in some way encouraged by his presence in her house. He was afraid she didn't care if they were found out. He saw himself becoming the scapegoat on whom she could lay off blame for the disenchantment in her marriage. Or worse, he might become the instrument for saving her marriage, a cheap substitute for a counselor or sex therapist. In either case, he could not let himself become a surrogate for her conscience. He had enough troubles of his own resolving his marriage to Catherine. And he was more concerned by the way he had become so talkative with Saundra last night, not only answering her personal questions about his first marriage and now this one, but by her moving him to nearly confess his boyhood baptism under the narcotic of sex, feeling it grate his heart all over again with the memory of that sweet trauma and of the ephemeral girl who had inflicted it.

Twelve years old—no inkling yet that any woman might ever consider offering the intimacies of her body to him—he had been overwhelmed by the dizzying opulence of so much offered so early to his unseasoned senses. And for years following her painful dismissal of him, he had wanted nothing more than to recreate those sensations in the fission of craving ignited by the first—and only—electrified coupling of their bodies. He'd been chasing Gretchen Keel, his initiator, down the years—thirty-six years since that moment—in haunted dreams of recovering her. In his nocturnal fantasies, she always took him back, as if she had been waiting for him to find her. In all that time, even as, in waking, he derided himself for his juvenile libido, he continued to search for her in any woman who would want him. But he had yet to find her avatar.

With Catherine, Steven had let himself step across some threshold of prudence over which it was difficult to retreat safely back into the pleasures of noncommittal carnal play, as Gretchen had tried to teach him.

"That first time we made love in your apartment, it was so powerful, so scary, I thought I was going crazy," Catherine had confessed to him. "I'd never had a real orgasm until you brought me to one." It was after that illuminating experience, she insisted, that she'd had a vision: by awakening her body's desires, she was certain Steven was the one to heal her pain. In return, she would fill the need she insisted she saw in his *soul*—her word, not his belief—for someone to love him. In his mid-forties, long deadened to finding the kind of permanency he seemed to have inspired in her, he conned himself into believing that the passion he had aroused in her was a mirror into his own suppressed longing for lasting commitment to one person.

But within the first year of their living together in her house with her children, he was having night-sweat dreams of suffocation by water and entombment, until one night he had awakened in a cold sweat to realize that the woman he'd initially found seductively open to him like a Georgia O'Keefe flower had instead become the embodiment of Munch's *Scream*.

But enough! he thought. He was here in Daybreak Donuts now, safely away from Saundra's house and soon to be released from Catherine's neurotic hold on him in a snare he'd set for himself. He wanted nothing more now than to enjoy this moment's pleasure of morning coffee and a sugar-glazed cinnamon roll.

Valerie Caine was suddenly in front of him at the counter again.

"I'm going to that tomorrow night. Dance Macabre," she said when he raised his head from his blind stare at the countertop. "They're really great." She was pointing at the newspaper still open to the Arts & Entertainment page beside his coffee cup.

"Really?" he said and smiled, self-conscious. "The pretzel benders?"

She turned sideways, tilting her head at an odd angle to look at the picture from the same perspective as Steven's. He turned the newspaper crossways on the counter to accommodate her. "Huh," she said. "That is a pretty racy photo for the *Star*, isn't it?"

"Looks like they've got their noses in each other's business, all right," he said.

She gave a throaty laugh of agreement. "That's what I remember about class with you," she said. "You were always funny. Not stuffy like so many teachers who take themselves too seriously."

"Huh," he said.

"I liked that class," she said. "I got to think about things and write about things I'd never been able to express before. It was so much better than those dull 'How I Spent My Summer Vacation' kind of papers we used to have to write in high school."

"Well, I can't stand reading those any more than you can stand writing them." Steven smiled benignly, relaxing into the moment.

With her head suddenly near his while she leaned in to see the photo, Steven could smell the aroma of dough and sugar in her hair, and something else, too, a powder or perfume fragrance like lily of the valley. He drew back on his counter stool.

"So, is this a full-time job for you?" he asked.

"Nearly," she said. "Six-thirty to ten every morning except Sunday."

"How did you get here to work today? Where do you live?"

"Two streets over from here, on Castelar. I'm living at home still. I walk to work most days, and today for sure. I couldn't begin to get my car cleaned off. And then we've got school this afternoon. They never cancel classes, do they?"

"And you're interested in dance?" he asked.

"Definitely. That's my main interest." She straightened up, squaring her shoulders perceptibly. "I'm a member of Free Spirit, the modern dance company at school."

He remembered now, Valerie had written an essay on "My Body, My Instrument" that spoke about a dancer's body as an instrument for the choreographer to play upon until its movements and rhythms were imbedded in "muscle memory."

"Oh sure," Steven said. "I know about Free Spirit. My wife likes dance. Well, she likes all the arts." At mention of his wife, he thought he saw Valerie drop her eyes toward his hands on the counter.

"They're okay for Platte City. It's just an amateur company that's part of the Phys Ed program on campus," she said. "That's what I really want to do, though, is go to a school with a real dance program, like North Carolina School of the Arts or UC Irvine, somewhere like that. I'm just putting in my time here until I can apply to transfer somewhere else. Have you seen me dance before? Were you at the spring concert last year?"

"No, I didn't make that one," he said.

"The year before that?"

"I'm sure I'd remember if I'd seen *you* on stage."

"Yeah, you would," she replied without hesitation. "Anyway, we're rehearsing right now for this year's concert. I've had to be out at school every evening this week, and this afternoon, too. It's going to be a good show, some really nice original pieces of choreography by a couple of the members of the company and Mrs. Milsap, our dance teacher. And a guest choreographer from Omaha this year."

"I'd like to see that," he said to be polite.

"It's next weekend, Friday and Saturday. Wait! I think I've got some extra tickets here in my purse…just a second…." She dashed off down the counter, past the men. One leaned forward in his stool to get a better look at her backside as she swept past them and through the double doors into the bakery. The other one looked up the counter toward Steven and smiled. Steven felt a bit smug about having monopolized her attention away from them.

He bolted the rest of his cinnamon roll and chased it with coffee.

Valerie Caine burst back through the double doors to the kitchen, moving down the counter with quick little steps, grinning as she held two tickets rabbit-eared in one hand. "We're supposed to sell as many of these as we can," she said to him, "but I also get six comps, and there's only my mom and my sister who I usually give them to, so here's a couple for Friday for you and Mrs. Harper. I'd be happy if you'd come as my guests."

"Oh, well," he said. "Really, that's very nice, but—"

"Is Friday bad for you? I can get them for Saturday, too."

"No," he said. "No, it's not that. Friday would be fine." He couldn't think fast enough for an excuse in the presence of her hopeful smile as she pushed the tickets toward him, so he said, suddenly sober-voiced, "But all I need is one. There is no Mrs. Harper anymore, at least not after today there won't be."

She gave him a look of such profound dismay, her mouth slack with surprise, that he felt immediately ashamed of himself for that cheap piece of theatrics.

"Oh, I'm so sorry," she said. Her eyes glistened. With tears? For *him,* for godsakes!

"No, no, it's all right," he hastened to reassure her. "We're, um…well, it's really for the best."

"Here I was just running on and on about me," she said.

"Really, it's okay," he said. He took one of the tickets from her hand. "Thank you, I appreciate your generosity. I'd love to come see you Friday, really."

"How long ago did you…is this like recent?" she stumbled.

"Today—" and he checked his wristwatch. "We go to court this afternoon, in a few hours. And I've got to get hustling now." He slid off the stool and fished in his pants pocket for change.

"Oh, Mr. Harper," she said forlornly, "that's terrible."

"It's all right, really."

All he could find was a five-dollar bill, and he slid it across the counter at her. "No change," he said. "I've got to hustle now."

With what he imagined was a jaunty wave, he was down the counter and out the door into the parking lot before Valerie Caine could say anything more to him.

The sun was fully up now, and the parking lot was beginning to run with melting snow. As he stepped his way among puddles and rivulets, Steven felt surprisingly buoyant, almost light-hearted after the first public admission of his divorce. He unlocked his car door, ducking into the front seat just ahead of a small avalanche of snow sliding from the roof of his car. The engine had been running the whole time he was in the donut shop, and the interior of the car was warm, the windows completely clear of snow. He slipped the car in gear and spun out of the drifted-in stall onto the plowed asphalt in the lot; then turning for the exit onto 98th Street, he accelerated and felt the rest of the snow on the roof slip from its loosened moorings and slide in iceberg chunks off the back, onto the trunk, bursting along the pavement behind.

On the drive back to his apartment on Taylor, the sun was brilliant in the sky, rising at a sharp angle above the city skyline. Light splintered off the snow and glinted through the side window, pricking his eyes. Along 98th Street, water from the melt-off hid potholes in the road where winter frost heaves had buckled the macadam, and occasionally a tire found one and jolted him in his seat with the shock of its discovery. The fields alongside wore a stubble of dried cornstalks from last year's crop, like the Sunday morning whiskers on the ruined faces of downtown Division Street winos. They poked through the sagging white crust, and along the high rows, the black earth popped up here and there like moles on skin. Even with all his years here in the Midwest, occasionally, he was still astonished by the immensity of open sky and the brilliant bolus of sun you could follow all day long, from dawn until sunset, in its unobstructed trajectory from one horizon to the other. Taking in the intensity of round sky and brilliant sunlight left him woozy as seaweed.

The road on which he traveled now was in every respect a rural one, yet he was less than a quarter mile from the city limits, owing to the sawtooth way in which the city had bitten off portions of countryside annexed after developers had built subdivisions on what was only recently agricultural land. He had, in fact, passed over the dividing line between county and city twice on the same road in his trips to town when he lived out here with Catherine. The stark divisions between urban and rural landscapes was never more evident than it was driving north toward Highway 30. Two miles south of the strip mall he'd just left was Westgate.

At the broad, divided intersection of 98th and 30, the light turned red, and Steven rolled to a stop. The intersection here was disproportionately wide for the small amount of traffic it bore when the city planners first speculated on continued expansion west of the new housing tracts. For the moment, he was alone. There were no cars other than his on 98th, none on Highway 30, except for a semi-truck and trailer well east yet, lugging its way toward him.

While he waited impatiently for the traffic light to complete its mechanical cycle from red back to green, he squinted against the fixed glare of sunlight through the window. He needed to be moving again, to keep the metronome of the day's plans ticking. If he were to go through the red light, no one would be the wiser. The light would cycle red, green, yellow, red whether Steven obeyed or not, whether he was there or absent, whether night or day, clear or foul.

In his mirror, Steven glimpsed a blue car approaching from the rear, and he was relieved. There was no decision to make now. His good citizenship had been vindicated. He lost the car momentarily in the blind spot, and then it eased up alongside him and stopped. It was a mud-splashed blue Honda sedan. In the two front seats, a boy and a woman. In back, closest to him, a little girl, wearing a white knit tam, her head within the frame of the window. The boy was a head taller, his dark hair plastered wetly away from its part, the collar of a plaid shirt rising out of the crew neck of a blue sweater. His face was turned toward the woman in a dark emerald green dress, her head inclined toward him in conversation. Hers was a pleasant face, winter pale and fresh. A pretty face framed in copper red hair. Saundra Bourcek's face, all made up like the woman who last night had stoked the fires of his libido. But now, behind the glass windows of their cars, it looked like one of the framed pictures of the family ensconced on a corner wall shelf in Saundra Bourcek's living room.

She glanced past her son and saw Steven watching through his window. Instantly, she beamed a bright, surprised smile in the spirit of their chance meeting here at this same intersection. Leaning forward to see more clearly beyond the boy sitting next to her, she raised her right hand in a wiggly fingered wave, her smile opening to show her pleasure. But Steven, thrown off by this abrupt annihilation of the impersonal distance between their enclosed cars, couldn't return her smile.

The pale faces of the two children staring across at him to see who it was that had caused Mamma's attention to be diverted froze Steven with fright. His unexpected discovery of Saundra Bourcek alongside him in public daylight, her children staring at him—until this instant they had only been school portraits in a shadowbox frame on her living room wall—paralyzed any presence of mind to acknowledge her cheerfulness. His lips stretched tightly over his teeth, but he could only manage what felt like a grimace.

She waved again, grinning wider to show her teeth, and the little girl in the back-seat window smiled too. *Did they know?* Steven gave a single stiff nod of recognition, then dropped his head, pretending to look at something on his dashboard panel of instruments. When he glanced up again, Saundra Bourcek's smile had collapsed into uncertainty, and her nostrils flared with an intake of breath as she turned her head away. Steven stared back at the empty intersection. From the periphery of his vision he saw the car lurch forward and the children's faces continue their swivel back to view him. There was only an instant for them to find him through the glass and space between them before their car was beyond his, accelerating.

Automatically, he switched his foot off the brake pedal and onto the accelerator.

The traffic light was still red.

He had an instant to think, *Uh-oh, Sandy, you cheated.* Then he thought nothing more at all as his spleen opened in panic and his adrenal glands fired an electric jolt to his heart.

His eyes recorded the truck, a big gasoline transport, bearing down on the intersection with smoke pouring black from its stacks under power. Even before the air horn sounded and the smoke quit in its instant of recognition and reversal, Steven already knew. There was the blue car, the red lenses of its taillights beaming suddenly bright in alarm. The truck's air horn bellowed again, blue smoke billowed from the wheel wells of both tractor and trailer as the whole rig shuddered, bounced, angled toward the far corner of the intersection because the driver surely knew what Steven knew, what Saundra Bourcek and maybe her children now knew: all of them were trapped helplessly inside the next few moments, certain only that now they all must ride time and physical law through to their own despotic ends.

It took maybe five seconds, but each instant impressed itself on him with a minute's searing detail, branding him with all the other irretrievable moments of injury that marked his life.

The nose of the car met the center of the trailer ahead of the rear dual wheels, and its momentum propelled it under the high frame. With a grinding crash which Steven could hear even above the blaring horns, the car's roof peeled back like a convertible top leaping open to the sun, and the brake lights went abruptly dark. The trailer, under the truck's momentum, was dragged over the car, liquid suddenly gushing from a ragged wound in its belly, until the huge rear wheels, locked and smoking, mounted the side of the car and lodged in the open passenger compartment. For a moment, car and truck were wed.

Even as the car dropped over the lip of the road's shoulder into the shallow ditch on the other side, and the trailer's wheels bounced free, the trailer continued the arc it had begun to describe in blind obedience to inertial forces, but tipping now, rocking over on its side; and the tractor was pulled after it— the outboard partner in a Flying Dutchman dance—its tires screaming on the pavement. The trailer rolled on its side in the ditch like an elephant brought down, and the tractor broke loose and completed its own obligation to inertial law, sliding to an upright stop with its rear wheels off the shoulder of the road. For a time, all movement ceased, except for the liquid downpour of gasoline through the gash in the upturned belly of the trailer, and a thin wisp of smoke on the other side of the truck where the car lay obscured from Steven's sight. Road dust shaken loose from the undercarriage of the trailer hung delicately in the air above the pavement.

An insistent horn still blared steadily, and for the first time, Steven was aware that it was his own car's futile warning. His hands were locked in fists about the wheel, his thumbs rigid against the horn button. He loosened his grip and there was silence.

Abruptly, the cab door on the truck swung open and the driver leapt out, landing in a crouch on the ground, facing the trailer. He began to rise and move backward simultaneously with crab-like steps, but before he was a yard away, there was a detonating *whump* that compressed the air in Steven's ears, and a ball of orange fire bloomed swiftly, drawing a thick stem of flame after it. Through the windshield, he saw the flames roll upward, the oily pall of black smoke rise to blot out the sky, and he flung himself on his side across the front seat of the car, burying his face in his hands.

Chapter 10

Donald had already conceded to yet another day of inaction well before the two long klaxon tones squawked from the speaker in the ceiling over his head. The rasping sounds sliced his thoughts like a band saw. The dispatcher's voice from alarm headquarters downtown followed in nasal monotone. *"Engine Fifty-five, still alarm. Car fire Ninety-eighth Street and Highway Thirty. Engine Fifty-five, still alarm. Car fire…"*

He pushed away from his desk with a jolt that propelled him out the door into the hallway and along to the door that let onto the apparatus floor. He could hear the scrape and clatter of men pulling gear from the ready rack, the metallic slamming of cabinet doors on the side of Engine 55, and as he came from the hall onto the floor, his pulse had quickened and he felt the vibration in his gut from the first clamorous roar of the truck's engine revving under throttle.

He hopped two small puddles of water in his path behind Engine 55 and hurried around Charlie Wesson and Al Czernecky, who were hustling to the running board of the truck to jump up to their places in the bench seat in the rear of the cab. Deborah Gallant was already aboard, her helmet strapped to her head, one gloved hand gripping the grab bar beside the open entrance to the crew cab.

From the ready rack, Donald stepped into the leg holes of his Nomex pants and pulled them up over his hips, slipping his arms through the galluses and settling them over his shoulders. He snatched his turnout coat, stuffed his arms through the sleeves and shrugged it on, then settled his helmet on his head. With his boots in his hand, he mounted the two steps up into the seat beside Metzger.

"Go," he said.

While Donald tugged on his boots, the truck rolled through the open bay door of the station and into a brilliant, cloudless morning. The sudden light stunned his eyes. Blinking against momentary sun blindness, he searched the floorboard with his right foot until he found the round nub of the siren switch. He tromped hard, and the hysteria of the big chrome Q2 siren rose in his ears, clearing the last numbness from his body's cavities as the wail resonated through his sinuses. As if impelled by the siren's scream, the truck lunged down the short inclined ramp and turned west onto Cedar Street. Donald plucked the radio microphone from its clip on the dashboard and keyed it.

"Engine Fifty-five in service, enroute car fire Ninety-eight and Highway Thirty."

"Clear, Fifty-five. Time zero-eight fifty-seven." The reply crackled from the radio speaker against the descending wail of the siren and the accelerating cackle of the diesel engine. *"Also, Fifty-five, be advised that we're uncertain at this time if this is in the city or the county. Cambridge Rural is also enroute."*

Donald knew the intersection where they were headed. It was a mile and a half from his old home, Catherine's and his girls' home in Westgate. It was one of several places in his district where city and county jurisdictions bisected a street: if the fire were on the east side of the center line of 98th Street bisecting Highway 30, it would be his call; if it were on the west side, it would belong to the Cambridge Rural Fire Department, a volunteer company from the little town ten miles west of Platte City. For someone like Gene Metzger, who was running the truck up through its gears with the dexterous precision of his youth, a borderline call simply brought out the competitive impulse to see which department—paid or volunteer—could get first water on the fire. The officers who had to fill out the reports could worry about boundaries.

As they moved up Cedar Street toward 72nd, water from the melted snow sprayed out from under the front fenders, shooting a muddy plume off each side of the truck. Donald eased back in his seat and resettled his helmet on his head, tugging the strap tight beneath his chin. For the first time in several days, he felt almost himself again. He looked sidelong at Metzger. The young man's face was impassive, fixed in concentration as he drove, but Donald could detect in the profile a knotting of muscle behind the jaw that told him Gene was still sulking over this morning's reprimand.

"Turned out a beautiful day, didn't it?" Donald said. As if in reply, Metzger pushed the button in the center of the steering wheel, and the flat, hollow note of the truck's air horn bleated like a piercing raspberry. Donald punched the siren button with his foot, holding it down until the wail leveled out to an earsplitting scream. Metzger glowered at him and hit the horn again, holding it until the two sounds commingled with such intensity that Donald could feel the truck vibrate under his feet. He let his foot off the siren, and Metzger pulled his hand away from the horn.

The traffic was light on Cedar, and the truck rode the center of the street to accommodate curbing cars. As they approached the intersection of Cedar and 72nd, the traffic light turned from green to red, and Metzger geared the truck smoothly down. Siren and air horn blew earnestly now, and Donald could see the startled faces of the drivers closest to him—the momentary confusion, then grim resignation of those at the cross street forced to stop on a green light, distracted in their momentum by the caterwauling truck as it bullied its way past them. At 72nd Street, they turned north toward Highway 30.

Metzger saw it first. "Jesus Christ," was all he said and pointed toward the northwest. Above the rooftops of buildings, in the far distance, a cloud of black smoke mushroomed upward.

Donald picked up the microphone from the dash, but before he had time to key it, the radio speaker crackled open.

"*Engine Fifty-five, Platte City Fire.*"

"Go ahead," Donald replied.

"*Be advised, State Patrol car at the scene reports personal injury accident, a gasoline transport and automobile. The transport is overturned and on fire. Parties possibly trapped.*"

"Clear."

"*Also, Fifty-five, Patrol advises this is over county line. Cambridge Rural requests you continue in on mutual aid to Cambridge, authority Cambridge fire chief.*"

"Fifty-five clear." Donald leaned forward in his seat and turned to look at the three in the jump seat of the crew cab behind him.

"You hear that?" he said.

"Sadie, sell the barn," Charlie Wesson growled. But Donald could see a gleam of excitement in his rheumy eyes. The helmeted heads of Czernecky and Gallant peered out the open doorway of the cab to see if they could detect the smoke. Donald pointed out the window at the black plume, but Wesson was already grinning and pointing for the others to look where his finger aimed. Donald knew what it was the older man was experiencing right now—the adrenaline that made everything seem immediate and vibrant, charging the body with both fear and exhilaration in which anything was a possibility and options were blind. He was feeling it himself again, and at that moment, if he had paused long enough to consider it, he would not for the life of him have been able to express why he had been despondent earlier.

He turned forward again but looked back through the interior mirror to see if he could gauge Gallant's reaction to her first fire call with the company. Her head, on an even plane with Wesson's, seemed smaller, and her narrow face was shadowed by the visor of the helmet. Her new yellow Nomex coat, next to Wesson's and Czernecky's older, grimier gear, was like a bright caution light.

From 72nd Street, they turned west onto Highway 30, and Metzger pushed the accelerator to the floorboards. Out in the open on the wider road, away from most of the interference of houses, they could not only see the smoke, they saw the orange and yellow flames boiling up the black column of the cloud.

A half mile from the fire, two sheriff's cars flew by them on the outside lane, their electronic sirens yelping like dogs on a near scent. Ahead of them, Donald could see cars and a few trucks stalled in the middle of the westbound lane or nosed into the median and along the shoulder of the road, unable to continue past the fire.

"First spot that looks good, cut across the median and we'll go up the eastbound lane and nail the first hydrant that side on 98th," Donald said.

Metzger nodded and slowed the truck, easing over next to the snowy median strip. A single alert tone pealed suddenly over the radio speaker. "*Airport One, Special Duty. Mutual aid to Cambridge Rural, Ninety-eighth Street and Highway Thirty, a gasoline transport. Airport One, special duty….*"

"Shit," Metzger said. "Airport's fifteen miles from here. They'll be a half hour getting out."

"Well, we'll just have to keep it going for them until they do," Donald said.

Metzger eased the front wheels, then the back, off the shoulder and angled the truck down the snow-covered grass slope of the median. The engine roared under the power of low gear, spinning its rear duals as it climbed back out of the bottom of the median and up the opposite incline, rocking while it lumbered through the slippery grass. On the pavement again, they rolled westward, past the snarl of cars in the opposite lanes, until they reached the intersection. Donald grabbed the microphone from the panel.

"Engine Fifty-five on location. Gasoline transport fully involved."

"*Engine Fifty-five reports gasoline transport fully involved. Time zero-nine-o-six.*"

Donald opened the door of the cab and swung out to size up the scene. The trailer of the transport lay on its side in a shallow drainage ditch just to the northwest of the intersection, the jackknifed tractor several yards from it, angled back toward the east. The entire tank was a fountain of fiery fuel that boiled from ruptured seams torn outward from the vapor explosions in the early stages of the fire. The tires had already burned clean from the wheels of the trailer, and now the tractor was afire also from the flow of flaming gasoline around it. The drainage ditch was containing most of the spill yet, but fire still flowed across 98th Street to the opposite side, where the tarmac on Highway 30 bubbled beneath the flames.

"Nail the nearest hydrant on Ninety-eighth you find," Donald said to Metzger. "Gate the other side of the hydrant so Cambridge can tie into the same plug. Lay back a four-inch feeder line to the intersection."

Donald grabbed his coat and leapt down from the truck, giving Metzger last second instructions to gate the hydrant outlet on the opposite side from where 55's hose would connect to allow another engine access to the same hydrant. Metzger made his turn on 98th and the truck roared off southward, leaving Donald in the middle of the intersection. Even from this distance, he could feel the heat sharply on his face and neck. The sound of the fire was like the rumble of a continuous freight train.

A state patrolman trotted up to him from the median west of the intersection. He was young and his eyes looked wild. "There's a man on the ground there by the edge of the road," he shouted above the noise of the fire. As the patrolman pointed, Donald saw what he had already noted before but had passed off as a piece of rubber from the truck's tire or debris from the tank itself. In the open triangle formed by the trailer and jackknifed tractor, he recognized now the scorched and curled figure of a man on the blackened ground just out of reach of the lapping flames but not far enough beyond the intense heat to have withstood it alive. Donald nodded and buckled up his coat.

"They said there was a car involved, too," he said. "Is there a car?"

"On the other side of the trailer," the patrolman said. "But it's covered in flames. When the trailer rolled, its ports must have sprung open. The gas is blowing out of there like beer outta the neck of a bottle."

Engine 55 was returning north, nearing the intersection, a single line of four-inch hose paying out of its bed and onto the pavement behind.

"We're going to lay hose across this lane," Donald said. "Any chance of shutting down traffic coming from the west? And diverting traffic back south on Ninety-eighth Street, maybe at Beaumont Avenue?"

"It's supposed to be blocked already at a Hundred-and-Second and routed north or south. A sheriff's deputy was going to take care of Ninety-eighth Street at Beaumont."

"How about that car over there?" Donald gestured toward a dark bronze Taurus he'd noticed for the first time, parked just off the road where Engine 55 now entered onto Highway 30.

"He's a witness. I've got to deal with him yet, soon as things get in hand here," the patrolman said.

"Okay. Time to go to work," Donald said.

For the next few minutes, they operated by the book. Donald directed Metzger to spot the truck on the pavement nearest the median, out of reach of the worst of the heat but close enough to lay handlines to the fire. Metzger set the engine's pump in gear. While he reconnected the line from the hydrant to an intake valve in the pump panel, Donald, Charlie Wesson, and Deborah Gallant unloaded three five-gallon cans of protein foam from a side cabinet, along with the special foam nozzle that would siphon the concentrate from the cans and mix it with the water coming through the hose to form a viscous blanket of white suppressant. Czernecky had remained at the hydrant, hooking up the hose from that end to one of the discharge valves on the hydrant and connecting a gated valve to the other so a second line could be added after the hydrant had been turned on. It was training-ground stuff, rote procedure, like an athlete's warm-up routine, and Donald felt the assurance that always came to him when there was harmony in action. The burning gasoline trailer was a tactical problem to solve with fire suppression technology and firefighting skills.

That Donald's pleasure in the consonance of movement, the orchestration of familiar practice, had derived from death of the most violent sort had not touched him yet. A piece of truck tire, a twist of charred metal, a human corpse: they were equally part of the furnishings of the set right now. Just like a mannequin in the training tower downtown, the body was a consideration before the attack on the flames only when you pretended there was hope. Or worse, if you permitted yourself to project the image of your own burning flesh into the wreckage of the lifeless.

Wesson took the nozzle and a loop of slack hose from the inch-and-a-half line laid in the cross-mounted hose bed just to the rear of the cab, and he ran with it diagonally across the intersection, the line slipping out of its bed with a corduroy whisper of canvas against canvas. Deborah Gallant followed behind him with a heavy five-gallon can of foam, cranking her torso sideways as she ran with little scuffing steps. Donald picked up a second can of foam by its slim wire handle and set off after Wesson and Gallant. The dead weight of the container cut into his fingers and dragged his shoulder down, and he marveled at what his new firefighter had accepted without hesitation.

The first Cambridge fire trucks were screaming down on the intersection from the west when Donald signaled Metzger to charge the foam line. The limp line jerked alive, inflating under a column of water rapidly pushing air ahead of it, bouncing and twisting along its length as it tried to straighten itself against the force of the water moving through it. There was a loud, sputtering *whoosh* as the water burst from the tip of the nozzle, and shortly after, the first white foam spumed like waffle batter.

For the next few minutes, Donald's attention was focused on what was immediately before them. With a rapid sweeping motion, Charlie Wesson spread the foam over the flames in the road, angling them closer to the corner of the intersection where the tanker lay. Deborah Gallant was bent slightly behind him, bearing the weight of the charged hose line in the crook of her left arm. With her right hand, she dragged the five gallon can into which had been thrust an eductor tube to draw the foam concentrate up to the nozzle. Like an umpire, Donald crouched behind and to the side of Gallant, watching for a rupture of flame through the spreading blanket of foam or the creeping of fire from the sides trying to slip back behind them. It was evident quickly they would not stand up under the intense heat for long. Even with Charlie and Deborah in front of him, partially shielding him, he felt waves of heat sear his face and neck. Within the Nomex fiber coat, his arms and chest were already feeling the heat. He knew the punishment the old man was taking up front, and Deborah Gallant right at his back. Yet the only sign they gave was when Charlie turned his leather helmet around to use the broader rear brim as a visor over his face, and Deborah lowered her head more.

"Mother of God, I've died and gone to hell," Wesson suddenly shouted.

"Come on, Charlie, back off a bit. Back it out of here," Donald said. He was watching Gallant, too, watching her wilt behind Wesson, drawing her shoulders higher toward her ears, rounding her back under the heat and the weight of the charged line in her left hand. Suddenly, she stooped for a moment, and Donald thought she was going down. He made a move toward her. But in the next moment, she'd brought her left shoulder under the hose line and was rising again, adjusting it to the crook of her neck and shoulder.

"Let's back off a bit," Donald called again.

"Hell no, we'll lose it," Wesson rasped. "I'm okay. You go ahead and back up, if you want." It was a challenge, Wesson's old-timer's moxie Donald had seen him use time and again on younger firefighters in the heat of a blaze. Wesson glanced back over his shoulder at Gallant for a moment. "You need to back off?"

"I'm with you," she said.

Dimly, Donald was aware of great activity nearby to his left. Above the roar of the fire and his own pounding pulse, there was a tinny blare of radio transmissions over the public address speakers of Cambridge fire trucks, the shouts of men, the wail of more sirens approaching. He knew somewhere within all that noise and confusion, Casey Hall, the Cambridge fire chief, was trying to direct his volunteers into some semblance of an organized attack.

Czernecky was suddenly by their side, the third can of foam in hand.

"Get back to the truck and pull us a second line," Donald said. "Get a water curtain on us before we're baked."

"You got it," Czernecky said, and he was gone again.

They were nearly on their knees, duckwalking in a low crouch to get below as much of the heat as they could. They were perhaps only a hundred feet from the tank now. Donald saw it through a haze of tears as his eyes wept to cool themselves. Surrounded by a billowing curtain of orange and yellow flame, the gray hulk of the trailer lay as still as a foundered ship at the bottom of a sea. Behind all the flame, it loomed darkly potent and sinister. He was finding it harder to get his breath, his tolerance for the heat rapidly disintegrating. He shifted his eyes from the tanker and they found the body of the truck driver near the edge of the road. From this angle, there was no question now. He lay on his back with his legs drawn up to his chest, his arms partly over his face, open-handed, as if to ward off the sky. The brain's last signal to the muscles had frozen him into a grotesque statuary toppled by the scorching winds of his death. A wave of dizziness narrowed Donald's vision, and the air turned gray for a moment. He nearly fell.

The foam from the nozzle began to sputter and break up under an increased volume of water as the first can of concentrate was sucked dry. Donald popped the top on the opening of the second with a small spanner wrench from his coat pocket, and Gallant yanked the eduction tube from the empty can and jammed it into the fresh one that Donald set beside her. Wesson inched forward some more, sweeping foam before him.

He was about to summon what breath he had to order Wesson and Gallant to back out, when the first cold shower of water rained over his back. He twisted his body toward it, letting it drench his face and neck. A shimmering helix of water sparkled in the sunlight, ringed about by a hazy aura of rainbow. Behind it, Czernecky's towering form seemed opaque and distorted, as if the water and the man were part of the same emanation.

When Donald turned back again, he could see tendrils of steam rising from Wesson's and Gallant's helmets and shoulders. In a moment Czernecky was alongside them, the nozzle of his line set for a full fog pattern that shot the water out in a shallow conical sheet like a showerhead, and the four of them huddled behind the cool curtain it created between them and the flames.

"Don't stick the goddamned thing in my face, I'm fightin' fire here," Wesson said.

Before they had advanced the line another ten feet, they were joined suddenly by three firemen from Cambridge, lugging cans of foam. "Captain Sparta here?" one of them asked.

"The ugly one." Czernecky nodded toward Donald.

"Chief Hall sent us to help on your lines. Wants to know if you'd meet him at the command truck."

"Ooh, the *command* truck," Czernecky mocked.

Donald stood up, grateful for the relief. "Sure, where is it?"

"Over there. It's that panel truck," the fireman said.

Donald looked at Deborah Gallant once more, checking. She was bent intently to her work behind Charlie Wesson, her face weeping with water now from the fog nozzle, and he was struck with an uncustomary surge of tenderness by the sight of the curls of wet hair plastered over her ear. Her ponytail drooped like a dead flower down her neck.

"Charlie, you're in charge of the lines here. Don't get anybody hurt."

"Just some singed eyebrows," Wesson replied.

Away from the fireline, Donald was surprised to see how quickly the landscape had altered. Three of Cambridge's fire trucks were already on location—an engine, a rescue squad van, and the chief's panel truck—with a fourth, another engine, just laying line across the intersection from the hydrant on 98th where Engine 55 had laid in.

Casey Hall stood by the open door of the panel truck, a portable radio in one hand.

"Good, I thought this was your shift," he said when he saw Donald.

"Yeah, well, I knew you'd be here when I heard a mutual aid call go out for Airport One," Donald said.

"That ain't the half of it," Casey said, grinning. "I've got three other departments coming with all the foam they can spare." Hall had the reputation for overkill. People who knew him agreed he wouldn't hesitate to call up the State Forestry slurry bomber for a small weed fire, if he thought it would make a more spectacular show of power. "Better to have too much coming and cancel it, than to get caught with your shorts down," he dismissed his critics.

"I left two guys back at the station loading the rest of our foam in the utility truck. We've got about a dozen cans altogether. They should be right behind us. How about you?" Casey asked Donald.

"Three, and we've nearly shot two already."

"Well, Wheeling and Ute Rural will be along in a bit. I know Wheeling's got eight, 'cause I sold it to 'em to use on their bulk tanks in town." Hall worked as a sales rep for a fire equipment distributor out of Omaha. "We'll get a two-and-a-half-inch line set up here in a minute and maybe knock some of the heat out of it."

"We've got one fatality, Casey, possibly more," Donald said. "There's a car somewhere on the other side of the tanker."

"Figured there had to be," Casey said. "Let's go take a closer look."

Casey walked ahead of Donald, the young man big and limber, with a shambling gait like a polar bear in his tall rubber boots and dirty white chief's coat. They skirted the fire line, stepping over hose and sploshing through water in the street from leaking couplings, angling to get around the perimeter of the fire and north on 98th to see what things looked like on the other side.

As they passed behind Engine 55's crew, Donald watched the three of them at work behind Czernecky's water curtain, laying out an even, thick swamp of foam ahead of them. Deborah Gallant was hunkered down now behind Charlie, her helmet turned around to the front like his so the wide part of the brim shielded her from the heat and provided a long visor over her face for the water to roll off like rain. Her bright yellow coat was the only thing that gave away she was someone new. But watching her right then, Donald figured someone who didn't know might assume only that she had got a new coat because maybe the old one had been worn beyond rejuvenation. He felt immense pride in his crew at that moment, and he was already calculating that any concern people had that Deborah Gallant might not to be able to pull her own weight was soon going to be academic. The three of them, Al, Deborah, and Charlie, had advanced on the fire a good twenty feet from where they had set up their initial attack, and already the flames were being swept away from the tractor and pushed back to the tank.

Just north of the intersection, on 98th Street at the east end of the fire, Donald could see down the length of the trailer, where it lay rolled half over. The covers on both its ports had blown open, and fire spewed from the tank in twin columns that boiled back up over the cylinder of the tank and twisted into a single bloom of flame roiling in orange and black fury. And where the fire poured down heaviest before curling back up, like a basin receiving liquid flame from an urn, sat the roofless car. At least, it looked like the shape of a car, although at the particular angle the trailer was dipped and the way the flames boiled around in a vortex, it was hard to distinguish anything clearly inside the fire.

"Sweet Jesus," Casey said, in a near-reverent tone, voicing the awesome aspect of the fire that Donald felt, too.

"About all we can do with what we've got is contain it," Donald said. "Airport One is going to have to put it out."

"When I was in the Navy, I fought a big shipboard fire, once," Casey said. "You can do a lot with water, if you use it right."

"What's the point? This isn't going anywhere, as long as we keep it in the ditch."

"I get bored easy," Casey said. "I didn't come all the way out here to stand with a thumb up my ass."

"It's your fire," Donald said. "What do you want us to do?"

"You're doing it. Keep your guys working that side with foam. We're setting up a second line to help and we'll use all the foam there is between us.

Meanwhile…" and he pulled a portable radio from the pocket of his coat, "I'm going to set up Wheeling and our second unit with two-and-a-half-inch water lines on this end and the backside and try to cool some of it down with fog. Be good practice for the guys." And he keyed the mike on the portable and began calling for more equipment.

Chapter 11

Driving north on 98th Street on their way to the girls' Aunt Charlotte in town, Catherine slowed the car to crawl past the spot where she had gone off the road. In the daylight, the snow-angel swath of compacted snow where the car had slid sidelong did not appear as far off the road as it had seemed to her in the dense dark last night. She was intensely thankful there had been no damage done to the body of the car, not even on the side that had suffered the weight of the banked snow plowed up against the driver's door in its downward slide toward the gully below.

"It was all ice underneath," she tried to excuse herself, speaking to herself as much as to Holly and Donna in the back seat. "I could hardly see where I was with the wind blowing the snow on the windshield." The girls were silent as they looked at the scene in slow passing, and Catherine could only wonder what they thought.

Earlier, when she had returned to the house with her car after the tow truck had winched it from its entrapment in the snow, she had confessed what Holly already knew, that she had left them last night to go to Steven's apartment for a "discussion" about the hearing today, and her car had slid off the road on her way back home. She apologized for leaving them; but they were so sound asleep when she had to leave, she said, and she had thought it would only take an hour at most—

"What did you talk about?" Holly had asked abruptly, doubt in her voice.

"Nothing. He wasn't home," Catherine said, her own tone a warning not to push it further. She'd turned away from them then to get ready for the long day ahead.

A half mile farther at the intersection of Beaumont Avenue, a sheriff's car, with lights ablaze on the roof, was blocking 98th going north. "What now?" Catherine said.

Looking beyond the car northward, she saw a cloud of black smoke rising above the horizon and curling westward. At the direction of the sheriff's deputy wind-milling an arm and pointing with the other to intersecting Beaumont Avenue, she slowed and nosed the car toward the main entrance into Beaumont

Heights. She stopped the car alongside the deputy and powered her window down.

"What's happened?" she asked.

The deputy leaned down to see in. "Highways closed. A bad accident," he said.

"What's burning?"

"Gasoline."

"Oh dear. Is anyone hurt?"

By now, the girls were looking northward as well at the smoke. From her rearview mirror, Catherine watched Holly lean across the back seat to see out past Donna's head.

"I don't know, ma'am. Just keep moving, please. You can get out on Highway 30 by turning left when you get to Castelar."

"Yes, I know. I live in the neighborhood. Thank you."

She drove into Beaumont Heights and past the Beaumont Village strip mall with its half dozen little shops: Maxwell Cleaners, where Catherine used to bring the dress clothes she wore to the College on teaching days, and DayBreak Donut, and the several other little shops along the strip. Past the Village, the street became the main artery through the Beaumont Heights housing development, deserted this morning of cars on the move, and just one or two homeowners out blowing the melting snow from their drives. The only other moving vehicle she came upon was a big purple diesel truck with twin chrome exhaust pipes rising on either side behind the cab and a chrome front grill, tall and oval like a startled mouth. She pulled to the curb on her side to allow it to pass on, but just beyond her, it pulled up to the curb on the opposite side, stopping in front of one of the homes there.

"Yuck, what a gacky color purple," Holly said, the only words either of her children had spoken since they left the house.

"I like it," Donna replied.

"You would," Holly said.

And then they were quiet again.

By the time she reached Charlotte's huge house in Fairview, the city's gold coast neighborhood of landed wealthy business owners and bankers, Catherine had decided she could not face spending any time with Charlotte before the hearing. She was already worn down by the night's frenetic events; the thought of Charlotte's buzzsaw voice pressing her for dirt, pressuring her with spinning squirrel-cage advice, already made her feel enervated and defensive at once.

While Charlotte's daughter, Tricia, met them at the huge front door and instantly whisked Holly away to "show you something totally rad," Catherine

98

begged off Charlotte's pressured invitation to come in for "coffee and sisterly counsel."

"I have to go back home to get some things together and dress for the hearing. I don't want to look like I don't have myself together," she said. "I promise, I'll stay for a while when I come back to pick up the girls. I'll have something to talk about then, I'm sure."

"You don't have to dress up any more than you are," Charlotte said. "It's not a wedding, it's a divorce hearing. Actually, you should look more dowdy and destitute to get the judge's sympathy."

"I am dowdy and destitute," Catherine said.

With time yet to kill before she had to be anywhere, but no real plan for what to do before 1:00 p.m., Catherine drove the twelve blocks back out of Fairview and down Center Street to Buzzy's Diner, a popular hangout for students and downtown workers in the Haymarket District of the city. Buzzy's was a facsimile of one of those roadside diners popular in the '40s and '50s, with a gleaming, white-tile-and-stainless-steel facade. They served coffee in white ceramic mugs with pale green rings around the rims, and the waitresses wore white, starched dresses with green piping on the collar and their first names stitched in green thread across a breast pocket.

Catherine sat alone in a booth across from the short-order counter with its line of revolving toadstool seats. The young waitress who came to her table knew her. She had been in Catherine's beginning drawing class, and she seemed excited about waiting on her now. The name stitched across her pocket read, *Tiffany.*

"Are you still taking classes?" Catherine asked her.

"Oh, gosh yes. I've got another forty hours for my degree," the girl said. "At the rate I'm going, geez, it'll probably be Two Thousand Twenty when I graduate. I've gotta work full time. I have a baby and a car to support."

She kept eyeing Catherine while she talked, as if she were seeing something different or odd about her. Trying to figure out what her former teacher was doing here by herself at this time of the morning, Catherine guessed.

"But hands down, yours was one of the best classes I've had out there." The girl smiled sweetly.

Catherine returned the smile, but at that moment, her heart wasn't in it.

"I'm in the Business School, and Art was just an elective I took. But I'd sure take another course from you if I had the money and the time in my schedule."

Catherine could feel herself blushing, pleased at the timing of the girl's praise. "Thank you, Tiffany."

"Your husband is Dr. Harper, isn't he?"

"Yes," Catherine said.

"I took English from him. He's good too. Funny, in a weird sort of way, you know what I mean?" The girl blushed. "I don't mean *he's* weird, just his humor. He was good to me, gave me a B-plus."

She knew Tiffany was only trying to be complimentary, but the fact that she had brought up Steven at all caused Catherine to look away momentarily.

Tiffany poured more coffee from a glass carafe. "Enjoy your meal," she said, even though Catherine had ordered nothing else. She hurried away.

"There you are, then," Catherine said quietly to herself, as if she had just proven a point to Steven. Or her chairman, Martin Stuart. Her students remembered her. She was a good teacher.

She turned her face to the window and was dismayed to see in her reflection the dark hollows beneath her eyes and parenthetical crevices around her mouth. She grabbed her coffee cup and held onto it, her hands shaking. With no clear image of what lay ahead, it seemed to her that her life could well be like this from now on: sitting alone in booths of diners looking out the window at the normal commerce of the world passing by while she tried to understand how she got there and what she was supposed to do next.

When she left Buzzy's, Catherine headed west on Center Street away from the Gold Coast section of the old city, her view tunneled by the office buildings around and ahead of her. She passed the familiar landmarks along Platte City's main thoroughfare—the Riverton Building, the Sheraton Inn, Younkers downtown store—and entered the stream of cars flowing around her, carried along in their current with no thought to what she was doing to keep moving with them, her mind again on Steven.

In the lane next to her, a car inched alongside and pulled ahead, going a few miles per hour faster than Catherine's little Escort. It was a silver-gray Japanese car of some sort, with an old woman in the passenger seat. The woman's weathered face, safe and inscrutable in its years, looked blankly out at Catherine through the window of her door. Catherine was nearing the southern edge of the Platte City State College campus at 56th and Center. It used to be her favorite part of town, the place where she had always felt necessary and secure. For an instant she couldn't breathe in the quake of a grief that rocked her, and in the next second she had turned into the bypass lane at the next light and was waiting for the green arrow that would let her complete her turn across Center and onto the frontage road around the campus.

Steven had classes on Friday mornings, she knew. Hopefully, he would be in his office before class. If she could just see him, talk to him for even a minute….

The campus comprised a dozen old brick buildings and a small forest of trees, an island of greenery in what was now the center of the city. At a break in the trees, her view opened onto a wide expanse of lawn that rose up a gentle slope to the crest of a knoll where sat a huge U-shaped building like the Sphinx. Carson Hall, the Arts and Sciences building. It was the oldest building on campus. It was Catherine's favorite building in all of Platte City. It was where she had her office when she taught in the Art Department there and where Steven still officed. Years ago, she had made a silkscreen print of Carson Hall and the campus in its fall colors, drawn from across the street in Memorial Park. It had been in the gallery showing of her work on campus, and in the early days when she was a student yet in his class, Steven had bought it to "brighten the walls of my hermitage," he'd told her. When he had moved in with her after their wedding, he brought it with him and it hung in the family room next to another of her popular prints of Memorial Park in winter with children sledding down its front slope. When he had left her two months ago, he had not taken his print with him, and now it was stacked again with others in one of the wide print drawers in her attic studio over the garage.

At this time on a Friday morning, the campus was only moderately full. End of week classes were not popular with students; many held jobs in town and commuted to campus, and yesterday's snowstorm would have given them reason to stay home. A few cars were leaving campus along the frontage road, and the parking lots were sparsely occupied. She passed by one of the little red Nissan trucks with the Campus Security emblem on its door, but she didn't recognize the young officer behind the wheel, and he paid no notice of her. If it had been one of the others—the one she called the Tartar with his ridiculous Manchurian mustache—if he'd been the one, he'd have called some sort of red alert and had her treed and surrounded by now. The last time he'd discovered her on campus she had just left her car to go to the University Theater box office and pick up tickets for *Antigone*. He came up from behind her and grabbed her by the arm—actually held onto her arm!—and marched her back to her car, where he'd taken a razor blade scraper from one of the pouches on his gun belt and ceremoniously scraped the college faculty parking sticker off the windshield of her car. "Listen to me, and listen carefully," he'd said with a great air of authority, "We now have orders from the Director of Campus Security to detain you and call the city police to have you arrested for trespassing. Do you understand? You've been banned from this campus unless you have official business or are enrolled as a student."

"No," she had said stubbornly. "I don't understand any of this."

Nonetheless, she had driven away, shaken by the fierceness with which the Tartar had threatened her.

Catherine pulled into the faculty parking lot at one end of the Arts and Sciences building. Immediately, she recognized Martin Stuart's car in his reserved department chair's stall. She felt alert and defiant in enemy territory that not so long ago had been the sinecure and animus for her creativity.

She wheeled her Escort down the lot to a more distant empty slot and pulled in. There were two cars now between hers and his, blocking the sightline.

She had not come to see him—*harass* him as the restraining order accused her—so she couldn't be arrested for defying the order, could she? She was there to see her husband on "official business." He was still her husband, and she had a right to be with him.

Steven's office was in a warren of boxy little enclosures on one side of a hallway along the east wing of the building. The English Department had more faculty and office allotments than any other discipline because it served every student in the college through required freshman composition courses. This was one of Steven's biggest complaints about teaching here: no one was exempt from instructing at least one composition course a term, even if they held a doctoral degree and had reached tenure in the department.

On her way down the long hall, Catherine slowed and looked through the windowed doors to the classrooms in case he was in one of them, teaching his morning class at this hour. Each of the rooms was sparsely populated with students, captives to the lone faculty member at the head of the room lecturing. In one room, an animated young woman in slacks and sweater paced behind the desk with hands and arms in balletic motion as she conducted some point she was illustrating. Her students were laughing in delight at her antics. Catherine paused to watch a moment, feeling a twist of heart recalling her own exuberance to communicate to her students her passion for her art. She turned away.

The next room down was darkened, a handwritten message posted on the door:

Professor Harper can not meet with class today. Please continue the assignment from Wednesday.

Confused, she hurried now down the rest of the way, crossing to the other side of the hallway to pass the faculty office doors. The anteroom door to Steven's office was locked, and there was no answer to her knocking. She stood for a time staring at the darkened window in the door. The cryptic message, "...*can not meet his class today*..." ran through her mind. What did that mean? Was he ill? Was he maybe as despondent as she was and could not teach today?

She nearly ran back down the hall with her mind heedless in thought to where she was even going. She had passed by the elevator to the first floor before she found herself at the complete opposite end of the building, in the wing where the Department of Art and Art History and her old office resided. *Can not meet? Will not meet?* What did that mean?

She was outside the alcove of the Department office before she recognized where her roiling thoughts had taken her.

She saw past the entryway that the desk in the tiny reception alcove was vacant. Susan, Martin Stuart's gatekeeper secretary, was not there!

The door to his office was closed. Relieved but disappointed, Catherine imagined that he was absent now, as well. Nevertheless, she passed by Susan's desk and rapped gently on his door. There was no sound from within. She rapped again.

She heard a scraping of chair legs on wood floor, and her heart quickened.

When the door opened, Martin was displaying an expectant smile. But in the next moment, when it seemed to register on him whose face it was that was looking back at him—Catherine tried smiling as best she could—his reaction was electric. He jolted backward a step and jerked his head to the side as if he were ducking something thrown at him. His eyes grew wide over the flat edges of his reading glasses, his lips taut in alarm. Finally, his countenance sagged, and his whole face clouded. He took his glasses off in a brushing motion of his hand, like someone sweeping at a fly buzzing too close to his face.

"Catherine Harper, what on God's earth are you doing here?" It was the voice of someone disciplining his dog. He seemed both angry and, oddly to her, frightened.

Catherine, out of her own anxiety, wanted to assure him he had no reason to fear her. "I'm sorry, I know I'm not supposed to be here," she said quietly. "I just need to talk to someone for a minute."

"No! Go away now! Leave here this instant!"

Bad dog, she thought. She could never understand why, when a man wanted to dismiss her, he responded to her out of a cavern of apprehension, the way he might shy from a rabid animal or a street thug. Steven, Martin, even Donald when he came to the house to take the girls for a weekend—what did they see in her that confounded them?

"Please, Martin. Just for a minute? Just to explain something, so maybe you won't need to be angry with me?" But she didn't have an inkling what there was she wanted to explain to him. It was she who needed an explanation. Why his attitude toward her had changed so drastically, why he closed all the doors on her that were open to her not so many months ago.

"Just leave, before it's worse on you," he said. He shook his head in disbelief. "Now you've put me in a position to have to report this to the police."

"But why do you have to report it?" she said. "Actually I came to campus looking for Steven in his office and—."

"No, I have to report this," he repeated.

"But why? We're two adults just talking to one another," she pleaded.

"Because you won't leave me alone. Because now you're in violation of a very specific restraining order."

"But I haven't done anything that I need to be restrained from. That's what I want to understand. I'm not going to hurt you," she said. She smiled in what she hoped was reassuring. "I just need someone to show a little compassion today."

"You need help, Catherine. That's what you need. Get some counseling, won't you please?"

"I've had counseling," she said. "It doesn't do a thing for how I'm treated by other people. I don't know what I've done that seems to upset everyone, but talking to a counselor doesn't help anything."

"That's not my problem," Martin said.

"I was a good faculty member in this department. You were my friend once, or so I thought. You were kind to me once. Why all this unkindness now?"

"This goes well beyond the limits of friendship, wouldn't you say?"

She felt the heat rise in her face. "Who's making you do this?"

"There's nothing more I have to say. I did what the Provost ordered me and all the other department heads to do—not just to you, to whole departments—for *budgetary exigencies*," he said, as if that abstraction were indeed the problem, and not his personal choice of who was laid off and who remained. "It was out of my hands."

"But that's what I don't understand. Why was it out of your hands? What happened that made all these other people take control of your life so suddenly? Just tell me what I did wrong that would make you suddenly turn on me."

"Because…. Okay, you want to know what I think?" Martin said fiercely. "Just look at yourself. You've lost yourself, your self-confidence. You've lost your *dignity*. After you went…after your *illness*, you weren't the same person who taught here before. I'm sorry, but you weren't. And all your bizarre behavior after we let you go—*we had to*—only confirmed it was the right decision to make."

"My husband has left me. I've lost my job when I was at the best in my teaching career. I can't do my art any longer. I can't even get myself to lift a paintbrush. Everyone treats me like a pariah. I might be willing to accept it's something I've done if someone could just explain it to me."

"You call yourself a pariah? Well, Catherine, you've made yourself a pariah. I told you that I would consider taking you back when this budget business was resolved, but you wouldn't go away gracefully. Now, I'm not going to discuss it any further."

She felt heat behind her eyes. "Just for *talking* to you, Martin?" she wheedled. "What's the harm in that?"

He looked at her for a moment, the sternness in his expression softening, and she thought, through the blur, she saw a glimmer of the old compassion that had made her welcome his friendship. But then, the steel went back in his eye, and in that instant, he shut the door in her face. She stood staring dumbly at the little brass plate at eye level on the wood:

Martin Stuart, Chair
Department of Art and Art History
Welcome.

She thought she heard a chair or some piece of furniture in his office slam to the floor. Then momentary quiet, until she heard his muffled voice through the wall between them: "This is Martin Stuart, Chairman of Art and Art History. I want to report a disturbance...."

In the next instant, Catherine was in flight, running out of the office anteroom and down the hall to the elevator.

When she got back to her car, she was breathing in large gasps. She found her key where she had left it, foolishly, in the ignition, and she turned the engine over. But she sat for a time, catching her breath, slowing her racing thoughts, trying to calm her anguish.

A rapping on her side window startled her, and she shied back as she looked up to see a bearded face grinning in at her.

"Mrs. Harper?"

The face was wreathed with long, stringy brown hair, as anachronistic as the olive Army fatigue jacket its owner wore. It took her a moment to recognize he was one of Steven's students who had also been in Catherine's art history class five years ago. Rodney or Rocky or something. She turned off the engine and rolled her window down.

"Sorry," the young man said. "Didn't mean to scare you."

"No, no," Catherine said. "Well, just for a second, when you first knocked. How are you?" What was his name? She was always so good with names. She just couldn't think straight anymore!

"Great. I thought it was you. Your hair..." he said and smiled.

Richard. Richard Cooper, she remembered now. A thoughtful young man who read everything he could on the Sixties, because he had been born in the Eighties and was convinced the Golden Age of America happened before his birth.

"Thank you. And how about you? You've graduated now, haven't you?"

He laughed self-consciously. "Not yet. By the end of this summer, I hope. I just finished signing up for summer session, my last two courses."

"Well great," Catherine said. "Not long then."

"If you're looking for your husband, he's not in his office. I was just by there to drop off a paper for his Am Lit class," he said.

"No," she said quietly. "I was just going to pick up something at the Art Department office." She was not comfortable with lying. "But I've changed my mind." She started her car again, and Richard straightened up, pushing away from the window. He adjusted the camel-humped weight of a bulging book bag by its shoulder strap.

"Which way are you going?" she asked abruptly. "Can I give you a ride?"

He looked doubtful for a moment, then smiled. "Well…if you're headed west, I'm going to the Crossroads." The Crossroads was a shopping mall right on Catherine's way to her house. She felt almost grateful for the convenience of being able to accommodate him.

"Sure, hop in."

The young man unslung his backpack and crossed in front of her car to the passenger door. As he opened it, a red Campus Security truck wheeled into the lot and angled across two empty rows of stalls to cut behind Catherine's car. The truck stopped with a sandy scratch of tires on pavement. Richard Cooper hesitated, the book bag on the front seat of Catherine's car, his left foot on the doorsill, and turned to see what was the matter.

Catherine, who had seen the truck out of the corner of her eye and had turned her head to watch it coming at her, sat with both hands clutching the steering wheel, anger and fear thrashing within her. "Oh, this is so stupid," she said in dismay.

The officer driving was the same one she'd seen earlier, but now the Tartar was with him in the passenger seat. The Tartar jumped out and came to her door.

"Shut your engine off," he said to her.

"Why? I'm just leaving," Catherine said.

"Shut it off. You're not going anywhere until the Platte City police get here."

"Well, I'm sorry, but I have to get home. My children are home alone and expecting me."

"You've been warned about coming onto campus," he said and hiked up his sagging equipment belt. "You've been warned about accosting Dr. Stuart. Now we're arresting you for criminal trespass."

"Look, dude," Richard suddenly spoke up, "Wait a minute, she's hasn't done anything here. She came to pick me up and give me a ride."

"Who are you?" the officer said.

"Cooper. Richard Cooper. I'm a student here, a senior."

"And she came here just to pick *you* up from school?" The man's voice was scornful with disbelief.

"I asked her to, dude. She just now pulled in here and I came out of the Admin Building and we were about to boogie outta here so I can get to work and pay all that good tuition they're charging me in there. What's she done so bad in just stopping for a second to pick me up?"

"For one thing, she's—" He looked down at Catherine again. "You're parked in a reserved faculty stall."

"She's not parked, man," Richard Cooper said. "She's *standing*. She never even shut off her engine. And what's the beef with that, anyway? It's a Friday and no one's hardly here." He made a gesture with his hand, pointing out the empty stalls in the parking lot. "I mean the dude who's stall this is, he's not even on campus."

"These stalls are reserved. That's twenty-four hours a day, three hundred sixty-five days a year. And she's—" He looked back at Catherine. "You're no longer allowed on campus anyway, and you know it." She did not reply. She was trying to look as recalcitrant as she could. She was amazed and grateful that Richard Cooper would lie that way for her.

"Well then let us outta here, man," Richard Cooper said. "She just came in to pick me up and turn around and head out. Simple as that. There's no law against coming in and turning around on public property. She's just a visitor."

"You wait right here," the officer said to Catherine.

Catherine kept silent.

The man went back to the truck and picked up a walkie-talkie off the seat. The younger officer had stepped out and was watching the whole thing, leaning on the hood of the truck. Catherine could hear the Tartar speak, but could not catch what he said. She heard the staticky crackle of a reply from the radio. More talk, more static.

Richard Cooper slid into the seat beside her and closed the passenger door. He looked at her and grinned. "Geez, what did you do, anyway? Threaten to blow up the science building?"

She was watching the two men standing outside the truck behind her.

"Don't worry," he said. "They can't do anything."

"They don't know that," she said. "They've sent some pretty legal-looking letters to me."

"Whew! What did you do?" Richard Cooper repeated. "I've never heard of anything like this before. Did you ignore some parking tickets, or what?"

"No, not even that bad," she said.

"Your husband's a respected professor on this campus. How they gonna keep his wife from coming here? You've got a right."

Catherine continued watching the activity behind her in her mirror. The young officer suddenly got behind the wheel of the truck again, and the Tartar was coming toward her side of the car. She looked for handcuffs among all the equipment on his belt, but she saw nothing and his hands were empty, as well. The truck pulled ahead far enough to clear the way behind her.

The Tartar leaned in toward the window, his face close enough to hers that she had to pull her head away to focus on him.

"Now you take this car and yourself and you get out of here right now," he said. "Don't even pause until you get out onto Center Street."

To Richard he said, "And from now on, if you require a ride of this individual, you have her pick you up at the curb out on Center or at the bus stop across the street."

"Well, now, I'll tell you what—" Richard started, but Catherine had the car in gear and was already backing out of the stall.

"Thank you," she said to the Tartar.

Then he tried to appeal to her: "Why don't you just go away? Doctor Stuart is a well-respected and decent man, a pillar of the community. Why don't you leave the poor man alone?"

She backed straight past the rear end of the security truck and then cranked the wheel of her car to arc it out into the lot. When she shifted to drive, the Escort leapt forward and out the exit onto the frontage road.

A pillar of the community! Catherine thought. A pillar of the community! And she was what? Bird droppings on the pillar? The humor of the image brought a tremor of relief to her taut nerves, and she felt momentarily clear, almost balanced. Steven had taught her the emotional defense of humor. When your emotions were overwhelmed, your sensibilities in revulsion, it was often humor that could save you from going over the brink.

"Those jerks didn't have a leg to stand on, and they knew it," Richard Cooper said. "How can you keep someone off public property who isn't doing anything wrong?"

"They can," she said. "People in authority can do anything they want, really, and it doesn't have to make sense."

"I hear you," Richard said. "But this is the new millennium. You can sue the ass off 'em. You ought to tell your husband about this first thing. Let him go kick some administrative butt out there. If anyone can do it, he can."

"I don't have a husband anymore," Catherine said flatly.

Richard Cooper looked at her, perplexed. Then suddenly his jaw dropped and he smacked his forehead with his palm.

"Soon, anyway," Catherine said. "Today, officially, as a matter of fact."

"God," Richard said and laid his head back on the headrest above his seat. "Open mouth, insert foot. I'm real sorry."

Catherine smiled. "It's all right. It's not exactly big news to most people. Anyway, I want to thank you for helping me out. That was very nice, and you really did save my bacon, I'm sure."

Richard blew a breath through pursed lips. "Well, at least I feel a bit better now. That explains a lot."

"What does?" Catherine asked.

"That you guys got divorced and all. I don't have to feel like I'm having to keep some dark secret. I've never been good at that, ever since I can remember."

"What secret? That we're separated?"

"No, that Mr. Harper has been seeing other women. Students. Well, one student in my lit class, anyway." He was turning red suddenly under Catherine's gaze. "Just a couple times maybe…like, on occasion after class, or whatever. I mean, I'd hate to think I might betray someone I respect. But the truth is, I'm lousy about keeping secrets."

"Well," Catherine said, trying to swallow back the jagged stone tearing at her esophagus, "well…I wouldn't worry about it. It's no secret to me."

Chapter 12

Paralyzed in shock, Steven had collapsed across the front seat of his car in a dead faint. In fact, he believed for a time that he was truly dead, feeling himself rise like ash on the winds of heat and bone-shuddering concussions from the apocalypse outside. And he was mindful that his life had ended at its most untimely moment.

But shortly, he was no longer dead. He was excruciatingly alive again and looking up through the windshield of his car, like a skylight above him, through which he could see once more the volcanic column of fire, could hear the freight train rumble of its breathing. His mind registered only the pictures and sounds and smells around him.

For a time after, there was such a riot of noise and activity that it seemed as if he had happened by chance upon some tragedy already well in progress, so quickly had trucks, cars, people on the run converged about him, drawn by the thick thunderhead of smoke that rose over the orange and black fireball. Through some mystery of communication that escaped him, he watched the mob of people and vehicles separate themselves into their constituencies: firemen, policemen, spectators. Quite slowly the firemen had advanced with water and viscous white foam on the flames, swept them back from the road, back from the truck, back to the tank of the trailer where they had poured out as if the cargo it carried were fire all along. Finally, another fire truck arrived, a box-shaped yellow behemoth with a cannon-like nozzle mounted on the roof of the cab, and it fired a ropy salvo of foam onto the flames until they were smothered in a swamp of steaming gray lather.

In all that time—how long? Steven's car clock read 9:58 a.m., but he could not recall when it had all begun—no one had paid him any notice. A policeman, before the first fire trucks arrived, had told him to move his car off the road and wait until he could return for a statement. But no one had spoken to him since, and he had not seen the policeman again, could not recognize him among the small platoon of uniformed clones who had appeared on the scene in their white cars with elaborate escutcheons of eagles or buffaloes decaled on their front doors, and red and blue lights blazing from rooftop chrome bars.

Now the firemen were busy disconnecting the hose lines, and rolling them up in doughnut coils. Steven sat in the front seat of his car, his legs out the open door and his feet on the ground. Water from the leaking coupling of a fire hose a few yards away ran along the edge of the road and over the toes of his shoes. Among the men fighting the fire, he thought he had recognized Catherine's ex-husband Donald Sparta, registering the fact of his presence as a given, without any emotional connection beyond a feeling of the appropriateness of the man's presence. During all the commotion, the firemen had mostly had their backs to him while they attended to the mayhem before them. Since the arrival of the big fire truck from the Platte City Airport, he had lost sight of Sparta, who had disappeared somewhere on the other side of the trailer. The trailer looked like half a hatched egg, the shell of some prehistoric raptor that had flown now, leaving behind its monstrous womb sinking beneath the surface of a viscous swamp.

He could not stop trembling, although he was no longer fearful for his own safety. The police had begun to move the traffic again, a car at a time, waving them on across the median and up the eastbound lane of the highway. He envied those who passed by, their lives set in motion again after the delay. He was unable to do the same: having seen the beginning, he was compelled now to the end.

With deliberate effort, Steven overcame the torpor of waiting and stood up. Outside the car, he stepped through the rivulets of water at his feet and over two hoses until he was near the dry crown of the road. He made his way slowly across the intersection to the far side, where he attached himself for a moment to a gawk of spectators who had crossed the highway for a closer look at the steaming wreckage. They watched silently as the body of the truck driver, covered with a blanket, was loaded onto the stretcher of an ambulance. The acrid smell of burnt rubber and gasoline fumes from the swampy water in the drainage ditch was overwhelming, and Steven's stomach lurched.

With more exertion than he'd anticipated, he jumped the narrow ditch. His muscles felt sodden, and his right leg almost buckled when he came down on it. Someone shouted, "Hey you!" but he didn't look back to see if it meant him.

On the other side of the semi, a small cluster of firemen stood on either side of the burned-out shell of an open car resting a few feet beyond the trailer. Steven made his way to them, slogging through the swampy ground. A fireman in a sooty white helmet and coat leaned on his forearms on top of the driver's door, peering in. Across his back the stenciled legend *Hall* in black letters looked at first, through the smear of grime, to read *Hell*.

A brown-shirted sheriff's deputy was looking into the rear of the car. Next to him in a yellow coat with a silvered name stripe across the back was Sparta.

"Until we get an engine number or find what might be left of the front license plate—if it had one at all—" he was saying to the deputy.

"Well, I imagine somebody's husband or wife will be reported overdue home eventually, and we'll have the answer," the deputy said. He straightened up and saw Steven standing behind them. "Is there something you want?" he said curtly.

"There were three people," Steven said. Sparta and the deputy turned to regard him. The man named Hall in the white coat straightened up from where he was bent into the front seat of the car.

"I saw it happen," Steven said, hearing his own voice in his ears, but thinking it could be someone else talking, a detached reporter. "I witnessed it."

"I know you, don't I?" Sparta said.

"Yes," Steven said. "In a manner of speaking."

"You know him?" the deputy asked Sparta.

"Yes, I think so," Sparta replied. He stepped away from the car and stood at Steven's side. "Harper, right?"

Steven nodded. "There were three people, a woman and two children," he said.

"Yeah, I guess we've never met face to face before," Sparta said, frowning as he looked Steven in the eye.

"Three? Three people in the car?" the deputy asked.

"Yes. A woman and a boy and a little girl."

"Shit," the fireman in the white coat said. Steven winced under the force of the invective, uncertain whether the man had directed it at the news or him.

The fireman looked into the car's front seat again. "Well, that's all there is now."

Sparta turned and he and the deputy edged closer, following the fireman's finger to where it pointed down. Steven would go no closer, but from where he stood, looking between the men, he saw nothing but bare, blued metal and nuggets of fused glass. The back seat was as bare as the front. Everything that could burn had. For a moment, he thought they must have escaped, and he felt a sliver of relief. Then, as the fireman in the white coat squatted, and the other two edged away from the opening, Steven saw on the floor, beneath the steering column, the blackened rack of ribs.

His mind slammed shut the last door on his feelings. "There were three," he repeated.

The deputy, standing beside him, said, "You don't, by any chance…I don't suppose there's a chance in hell that you might know who they were, is there?"

What Steven saw now on the floor of the car was charred beyond individual distinctions. No stretch of imagination could bring him to associate this obscene object with the image in his mind of the woman with the winter-pale face in the green dress and her two children, their heads turned toward him. It was only an image from memory now. It had nothing to do with what he saw here.

"No," he said. He put himself suddenly back in his own car before it all happened. When he was looking through his driver side window into the window of the car next to him. "Just a woman wearing a green dress, her children. The children...." Suddenly his voice tripped. "A boy and a girl all dressed up...." Then he couldn't speak, something brittle cracking within him like glass. He rocked unsteadily on his feet.

"Can you describe the car? Do you remember the license number, even a few digits?"

"Not the license. I never really saw it. The car was blue, a Honda I think." He turned to Donald who was staring impassively now at him, not really looking at him but through him, as if he were invisible or a window to something beyond. Steven couldn't finish his thought. His mind latched onto another notion, and his voice changed to match a sudden resolve. "You know it's so strange, but for a minute—just an instant, really—before she pulled away from the stop light, she looked at me as though she recognized me, and I thought maybe it *was* someone I know."

"You think so? It was really someone you knew?" the deputy asked.

His mind was elastic with indecision. If he told them anything more, if he gave them the information they needed—

"No. I don't think so," Steven replied. "I didn't really recognize her, but then she drove away before I could really get a good look at her. "

"Maybe coincidence?" Sparta said.

"It was just a feeling I had that she thought she knew me, and if I'd had another second before she jumped the light and drove off, maybe I might have recognized her."

The deputy said, "The light was red?"

"Yes. We were both stopped there for it," Steven said.

"And when she pulled away, into the intersection, it was a red light?"

"Yes," Steven said. "She drove out into the path of the truck."

"She didn't try to stop?"

"Yes, but it was too late. And he tried to stop, too—" Steven vaguely described with his finger the arc the truck had made, and he pointed to the turned-over wreck.

"Well, look, I need you go over to that sheriff's car over there and talk to the sergeant. He's handling the accident report," the deputy said. He pointed to a police car with a bronze image of a bison inset in a shield on its door.

Steven looked once more toward the inside of the burned-out car, on the passenger side, but he could see nothing more than metal and glass. What more could he report with certainty, after all? His speculation that the woman was his student, that she had recognized him, that he had refused to acknowledge her...? Or that moment's enduring image of a girl in a white knit hat, a boy with slicked-up hair in a blue sweater, a woman in an emerald green dress. And an acknowledgment between them only of their common waiting at a stop light on the edge of the city. He alone held the image of their last living moment in his mind. How did one report that terrible burden?

Suddenly, Donald Sparta said to him, "Sorry we met for the first time in a situation like this."

"Yes, it's ironic," Steven said.

Sparta frowned. "I'm not sure I'd call it irony," he said. "Anyway, you can go now. I believe you have somewhere to be this afternoon. Another wreck to witness?"

Steven stiffened. The comment was like a slap, and he felt it in an icy burn on his face and throat. He would have responded but the sarcasm that rose like bile in his throat had no substance. He was, for the first time, at a loss for words. "Thank you," he said weakly and turned away.

When he had slogged his way back out onto 98th Street, he saw the sheriff's car the deputy had indicated, parked on the edge of the road north of the intersection. A sergeant, wearing his western uniform hat, stood beside the car talking uncomfortably at the lens of a television news camera held on the shoulder of a man with battery packs belted around his waist. A woman in maroon slacks and a print blouse stood beside the sheriff, holding a microphone between them, her face knit in counterfeit interest. Beside the cameraman stood another person, a woman, wearing the yellow canvas coat of the Platte City Fire Department. She held her helmet in her hands, like someone waiting respectfully for the national anthem to end, and her hair was wet and corkscrewed about her head, the splayed ends of a ponytail stuck to the collar of her ungainly coat. On the back of the coat was stenciled in black the name *Gallant*. The irony of the name soured him; he was feeling not the least bit gallant.

He veered away and crossed the intersection, following the route he had come from when he had first left his car, drawn like a penitent to the sacrificial altar.

Back inside the sealed safety of his car, he began to tremble uncontrollably, his body chilled to his core. When he'd started the engine, switched on the heater, and put the shift in Drive, a state patrolman suddenly crossed the intersection with one hand up to stop him, the other holding a big clipboard.

"Just a minute, sir," he said.

Steven rolled down the window.

"I need information yet from you," he said through the side window, his voice both stern and somehow apologetic.

"I already did. Give information, I mean. A policeman over there." He pointed through his windshield, indicating the other side of the road where the hulk of the gas transport lay. His hand was shaking badly.

"Yes, but this is a state report," trooper said and held up the clipboard for Steven to see. He bent his head and peered in at Steven's trembling shoulder and arms. "May I come around and sit in your car, or would you like to come to my vehicle?"

"Come sit here, if you must," Steven said. The trooper rounded the front of the car and got into the passenger seat beside him. "Please, I'm still very upset and need to get home. Will this take very long?"

"No, sir. Just some questions for my report, and then you're free to go."

Steven nodded in resignation, and turned off the car's engine.

"Now, why don't you tell me everything you saw from the beginning."

Steven told it all again, slowly so the trooper could write it down, repeating words or phrases when the man couldn't keep up in his slow scrawl. His wait at the light at the empty intersection. The approach of the blue Honda. The woman and two children in the car, their approximate ages. He hesitated, picturing the scene when the trooper asked if he could describe the three occupants of the car. He was struggling with whether or not to tell the trooper whose faces had looked at him. What it would mean to disclose he knew the *victims*.

Finally, he said, "It all happened very quickly. The car pulled up and stopped for a moment. Then it just started off again, drove right out into the intersection. I thought the light must have turned green and almost went ahead myself. But it hadn't and there was this gasoline truck coming pretty fast down the highway right there."

The patrolman was writing furiously. "How fast would you say the truck was going?"

He couldn't say for sure. Not faster than the speed limit, maybe, but fast enough to make it obvious he wasn't going to hesitate going through the intersection—just driving the way you do when you have a green light and a clear road ahead.

The patrolman wrote some more, then flipped the page on the clipboard and pulled a blank sheet from underneath the form and repositioned it on top. "I need to get all of this," he said. "Now, as clearly as you can, can you describe the accident itself? Where did the truck hit the car? How did the two vehicles end up after the crash? I'll draw a diagram here, and you tell me if it's right."

So, Steven tried to recall each detail of the accident, superimposing on the inert blackened hull of the tank across the street the picture in his mind of the deadly dance of the two vehicles.

"So, you say Vehicle Number One initially struck Vehicle Number Two about midway between the rear duals of the tractor and the rear quads of the trailer?" the trooper said, drawing a diagram which reduced the whole thing to arrows denoting motion and direction, and rectangles labeled "V1" and "V2" to signify the truck and the car. And detached from the arrows and rectangles in the center, Steven saw the little box labeled "V3" stuck motionless and directionless in the lower right portion of the wide cross the deputy had drawn to show the intersection of the two roads. His car, frozen like himself, struck dumb as dirt and useless and craven in its safety at the mouth of the intersection.

"Yes," he replied.

When he had caught up in his graphic depiction of the scene of the accident, the trooper said, "Now, is there anything else you noticed that might help us get a better idea of what happened?"

The woman looked at him across the space between their cars. Her face was pale and freshly made up, and she was smiling happily. For the last moment in their lives, she occupied the same time and space and shared history with Steven.

"No," Steven said. "No, there's nothing else."

"All right, then. I just need your full name, and your address and a phone number we can reach you at if we have any other questions."

Steven's stomach clenched when he gave his identity to the trooper.

The trooper thanked him and slipped out of the car. As he shut the door, he said, "You have a safe drive home, now."

Steven slid the car away from the curbside and waited at the intersection until another policeman directing traffic blew his whistle and pointed Steven's car across Highway 30, north on 98th Street. When he passed by the wreck once more, the TV reporter in her maroon slacks was interviewing the female firefighter, and Catherine's ex-husband, Donald Sparta, had disappeared again, somewhere back into the steamy rubble.

Part II
Friday Afternoon

Chapter 13

After lunch in the stationhouse, Donald's crew and the men from Aerial 53 sat at the two long tables in the center of the room. They drank coffee or pop and talked about the fire. Deborah Gallant was among them. She joined the table with Czernecky and Metzger and Donald, and she listened to them talk, laughed at their jokes, nodded her head appropriately to support Wesson's or Metzger's descriptions of the action at 98th and Highway 30. Donald already sensed this was going to be one of those memorable fires that would become catalogued in the lore of these firefighters' careers. *The Highway 30 Fire*. Like the others, they passed on in their apocryphal tales of the firehouse: *The Beacon Warehouse Fire. The Branding Iron Hotel Fire. The Playmor Bowling Alleys Fire.* It was in the hard-edged excitement in their voices. It was in the way they interrupted each other in the telling of some moment or incident to insist no, no, it happened this way not that way.

The noon news on the television had featured coverage of the accident. The opening shots showed a wide view of the fire, with the crew from 55 in the center of the scene. Charlie Wesson, his back humped over the hose line, was sweeping a thick batter of white foam in an arc toward the roiling Halloween-orange flames. Right up behind him on the hoseline was Deborah Gallant, and beyond her, the young Cambridge volunteer who had relieved Donald on the line. Close beside them was Czernecky and the other volunteers with the second inch-and-a-half line fogging them with cooling water.

While the reporter provided a voice-over account of the sketchy details surrounding the accident at that point, the camera showed other shots of fire trucks arriving from surrounding towns and the attack on the fire by Airport One, the big rig used for aircraft fires. A relatively new truck in the PCFD arsenal, this was the first time it had been in service for anything more than training exercises.

Donald only spotted himself once in any of the collage of momentary scenes. It was during the time after the fire had been suppressed when he was inspecting the burned-out car with Casey Hall and a Marchant County deputy sheriff. It was not a close-up, and probably he would not have been recognized by anyone who knew him, unless he were to point out his distant, fleeting image with his back turned to the camera. But something else caught his eye in the wide-angle shot. In the background to the left, seeming to come out of the sea of foam from behind the burned-out hulk of the trailer, there appeared in outline the stooped figure of a man laboring toward the three of them at the side of the car. He was so curved and dimly defined that, at first, Donald thought it might be something that had become detached from the debris itself, a spindrift curlicue of foam perhaps. But it continued deliberately toward the car, and just as it came to a hesitant stop behind the figure that Donald had identified as himself, before the camera cut to another shot of the news reporter interviewing one of the sheriff's deputies, he recognized Catherine's ex-husband Steven Harper. The man, slinking like a wraith out from the grave of the fire scene, caused Donald in that instant of recognition to feel his own body sag under its own recently dispirited weight.

Deborah Gallant got up to refill her coffee cup from the big urn on the pass-through countertop between the kitchen and the day room. "Here, Cadet, get me another, too, would ya?" Charlie Wesson waggled his empty cup as she passed by his chair.

"Sure," she replied. She grabbed the cup without breaking stride.

When she returned with Wesson's full cup and set it carefully on the table beside him, one by one, the others downed their coffee and repeated, "Here, me too, Cadet. While you're up." Deborah dispassionately obliged, traversing back and forth from the tables to the coffee urn as unflinchingly as a truck stop waitress. Donald snuffed out his annoyance at this latest test. There was, after all, a tradition in the fire service of older members haranguing new members, lording their seniority over the rookies. It was usually good-natured and lasted only a month or so before it was abandoned and the tyro was accepted as "a regular guy."

Because their spirits were high following such a big fire, they seemed more cohesive. Engine company and truck company members mingled at the two long tables in the dayroom, as they usually did when things were running smoothly, when events followed the normal course of stationhouse routine. Donald had observed how a working fire drew that out in them, brought them together in a way nothing else about their lives could. Their real synergy as an engine company was exhibited on the fire lines. There was in the marrow of fire something that connected all of them. The connection, Donald liked to believe, didn't exist simply because they were all in the same profession, like ironworkers or doctors or longshoremen. They were firefighters because each of them was bonded in some metaphysical fashion to fire. In primitive times, they might have been the keepers of the flame in ways that were both practical and mystical. But there were less altruistic aspects of solidarity among firefighters, as well. These were similar to what held soldiers together in military combat units: people who would have little to do with one another outside the time they had to spend together on duty were nonetheless like family for the periods of time they were engaged in a hazardous undertaking. It had to do with daily being dependent upon another for your safety, with the necessary trust you had to have in the ability and willingness of another person to put himself in harm's way for your survival. And it was reciprocal because you felt an unquestioned responsibility toward someone other than yourself. It was stronger often than family bonds. In some instances stronger than blood. He hoped they were feeling some of that now for Deborah Gallant after her first trial by fire.

Donald was startled when she suddenly appeared at his side. "Another cup for you, Captain?"

"No. No, thank you," he said quickly. "I'm done." That wasn't true. He was ready for more coffee. But now that he'd lied, he couldn't recant.

She smiled at him, something enigmatic that he could not read, and leaned nearer to speak quietly near his ear. "If I can be excused, I'd like to shower and change my uniform. Is there going to be a problem with that?"

"Of course not," he said to her. Then he realized, with a pang of guilt, that she hadn't showered and changed earlier when the rest of the crew had after cleaning up the dirty hose. Both companies shared a common bathroom with three toilet stalls, two urinals, and an open shower bay with four showerheads. Only the captains' rooms had private showers and toilets. As Deborah turned to go, Donald stopped her by tugging the elbow of her coveralls. "For now, use the one in my quarters. I'm going to have to get a ruling from downtown on how they want to handle this. That's one of the things they didn't tell me about." The District Chief's memorandum which accompanied the new duty roster last Friday had stated only that the new firefighter was to use the visitor's rest room, which held only a toilet and sink. But there had been nothing said about showers.

"Thanks. Excuse me," Deborah said, and headed for the door.

Down the hall from the dayroom, the house pay phone was ringing.

"Why don'tcha get that, Cadet, while you're up," Charlie Wesson said.

Deborah paused in the doorway, looking back and smiling. "And if it's for you, are you in?"

"No. I've gone home for the day," Wesson replied.

When Deborah had left the room, Wesson turned to Donald and winked. "So what are you gonna do if she clogs up your drain with hair?"

Donald shook his head. "Call a plumber from Maintenance. They can put it on the list with all the other things that need fixing around here."

The telephone call was for Donald. "A woman," was all Deborah reported when she stuck her head back in the door. Donald rose from his chair and followed her down the hall. He picked up the dangling phone receiver from the box on the wall as Deborah entered his bedroom across the way and closed the door behind her.

It was Connie Towers, the secretary from the Chief's office downtown. "You didn't answer your office phone, so I gave you a ring on the house phone," she said cheerfully.

"Sorry, I was having a late lunch."

"Then are you all cleaned up from your last call?"

"Sure," Donald said curtly. "What's up?"

"There are some people coming down from Channel Five news—um, let's see…Ann Baxter and a camera guy, I guess. They want to talk to Little Miss Susie Q, your new fireman."

At another time, Donald would have laughed at Connie's brassy humor. She had worked in the Chief's office for over twenty-five years and three different administrations, and she was not one to put on airs. But right now, all Donald could think was, if he'd been the one to refer to Deborah Gallant like that, he could be subject to disciplinary action. He said to Connie Towers, "When are they due here? She's, ah…indisposed at the moment."

"Wasn't that her who answered the phone?"

"Yes, but—"

"Well, you better *dispose* her pretty damned quick, Sport. I don't know when they'll get there, but they left here ten minutes ago, with The Man's blessings." The Man was Chief Bouton.

"Okay. Do you know what this is about?" He looked across the hall at his closed bedroom door. Inside, Deborah Gallant would be taking her shower.

"Whatever they want it to be about. 'How's your first-day-on-the-job' questions, I imagine. 'How's it feel to be the only woman living with all those gorgeous men?'"

"Jesus, Connie. I sure as hell hope not!" Donald said.

"Don't worry. Ann Baxter's an airhead. Everything upbeat and sweetie-sweet, if you've ever seen the kind of stuff she reports on."

"Oh, fine. That sure sets my mind at ease," Donald said.

"Take heart, it's just beginning, Sport. There's a station from Lincoln that wants to come up and do an interview, and I imagine there'll be some others soon, some newspaper reporters and disk jockeys and who knows what other cheap-thrill mongers. Chief thinks it's all good press for PCFD. Budget requests to the mayor are coming up in a month."

Donald blew a breath through pursed lips. "Okay. Anything else?"

"Not yet. But when there is, you'll be hearing from me."

"Thanks," he said.

When he'd hung up, he sat down in the metal folding chair beside the phone and wondered what he was supposed to do next. Was he expected to be in on the interview, too? Give them a special room to use? Maybe chaperone his new cadet like some talent manager. It wouldn't do for Deborah Gallant to get all the attention while the rest of his crew, who had just demonstrated what real firefighting was all about, were ignored. That was sure to split open the tentative stitches that had only begun to bind them as a unit this morning.

In a few minutes, the door to Donald's room opened, and Deborah Gallant emerged in her blue uniform, her hair stringy wet from the shower. She carried her folded drab coveralls tucked under her right arm, and a towel draped over her shoulder.

She smiled shyly at him, then lowered her eyes as she slipped by where he sat leaning his chair into the wall next to the phone box. Seeing her suddenly like that took him by surprise. "Wait a second," he said. She stopped and turned to look back at him, and the image of her in dress blues, her hair hanging lank and glistening wet as seaweed down her neck and over her ears, and the bundle of work clothes hugged now to her chest, drove from Donald's mind what it was he needed to say to her. All he knew was he wanted to behold her a moment longer to take in the reality of his new firefighter and Engine 55 crew member.

He drew himself upright and stood, feeling suddenly ungainly before her. She looked at him expectantly.

"I need to tell you—" and he remembered the urgency of the impending invasion by the TV news people. But seeing her waiting dutifully where he'd stopped her, he thought he'd say something encouraging first. "I'll try to get this *situation* about the shower straightened out soon. I'm sure they have a plan in mind already. I mean, they must have given it some thought…. Anyway, you can continue to use the facilities in my room when I'm not in there, until something more permanent is worked out."

"Thanks," she said. "I don't want to put you out."

"No, not at all," he said, and added quickly, "It's not your fault, in any case. Everything was supposed to be taken care of by the City Maintenance. I don't really think they're quite ready yet for what a co-ed fire department involves."

"Well, I don't need things much different from anyone else. But I guess open showers would be a problem." She did not smile when she said it, and he wasn't sure if she were trying to be humorous.

He smiled for her. "Yes," he said.

She waited for him to say something more, but he could think of nothing to fill the silence.

"Well," she said finally.

He pointed suddenly toward the end of the corridor near the vestibule to the outside door. "Also, the call I received was from the Chief's office. You have to get ready to meet the press."

She looked blankly at him for a moment, then alarm came to her eyes. "Who?"

"Channel Five is sending over a news team to interview you, and—" he shrugged—"you're supposed to answer their questions, I guess."

She looked down at herself then, at the bundle of dirty clothes she still clutched to her chest, and—Donald noticed for the first time—her bare feet. "Oh crap," she said. "I can't...are these TV people? With cameras?"

Donald smiled at her panic, and he felt his own tension ease a bit. "Just one more thing," he said, and she turned so quickly about-face that it made a squeak on the tile floor.

"I thought you handled yourself really well on the fireline this morning. Really, I was impressed."

"Thanks," she said, smiling. "I appreciate hearing that."

"And I apologize for the stuff in the dayroom earlier today. The guys do that sort of thing to rookies."

The phone in his office across the hall began to ring.

"I don't mind," she said bluntly. "Well, I did mind about this morning, I guess, but I don't now. We were warned about this sort of thing."

"Warned?" Donald said.

The phone rang again.

"Yeah. They said there would be some guys who wouldn't take to a woman in the same company, no matter what."

"Who warned you?" Donald asked.

"A woman in Personnel. And Chief Bouton."

"Really? What, if I may ask, did they tell you exactly?"

She shrugged. "They said we can either ignore it, or if it gets too bad, we can file a grievance. Actually, Chief Bouton said I should call his office if I had any trouble."

"The Chief said that? He told you to call him personally?" Donald struggled to suppress his sudden anger. The phone continued to ring.

She eyed the door to his office nervously. "He just said we could call his office, I think he meant."

"We? You and...Tabby, is it?"

"Tammi. Tammi Whitmore, yes." Deborah was watching him anxiously now, nodding her head as she spoke.

"When was this?"

"Two weeks ago, when we graduated from Academy. He called us into his office—"

"Called you in *together* or just you?" Donald interrupted.

"The two of us." She'd begun to frown, perplexed. "Was that wrong?"

Donald looked away for an instant, took a deep breath. When he looked back at her, he saw nothing in her face to show—what? That she was going to make trouble for him? That she was there for some ulterior political reasons that were meant all along to make a public issue of sexist attitudes in the fire service?

And the phone was still ringing.

"No, it wasn't wrong. Of course it wasn't." He edged toward the door to his room. "I mean, the Chief calls you in, you have to go. I'm just surprised he'd give you total privilege to go directly to his office without first going through your captain and district chief like everyone else."

She nodded again. As he stepped to his office door, she began to back up the hallway toward the company sleeping quarters.

"So what do you intend to do?" he asked bluntly.

"My job."

For the seventh time the phone rang. "Well, I'd like to talk to you some more. But I've got to answer this." He raised a finger and wagged it as ducked into his office. "Hang on a second more."

"Yes, sir."

He picked up the phone, expecting Connie Towers again with a message or directive or heads-up from Chief Bouton's office. "Sparta."

It was Casey Hall from Cambridge VFD.

"What has Rubber Maid legs, a Michelin tire middle, and carries American Tourister under its eyes?" Casey said without introduction.

Donald turned to Deborah and rolled his eyes. "I give up," Donald replied.

"A forty-five-year-old Platte City fire captain." Hall exploded in laughter, rich and full-throated. "I made it up. Pretty good for a farm kid, huh?"

"Jesus," was all Donald could come up with.

"What a coincidence, he's the head of my church, too," Hall said, and roared again.

"Listen can you hold a second, Case? I'm just finishing something here." He cupped the receiver of the phone in his palm and looked out the door at Deborah. "Just one thing more," he said to her. She looked down, then back up at him in a blink, her expression unsettled. "All I want to say is, I really hope you'll talk to me first, if you get to feeling unfairly dealt with."

"Of course I will, no sweat," she said. Then she smiled. "Tammi doesn't have to worry about going through the chain of command, though. When she's got a gripe against the people she works with, who can she complain to?"

At first Donald didn't get what she was saying. Then, he remembered that Tammi—Maureen O'Hara, as Connie Towers called her—was Bouten's driver. He chuckled. "I guess to the mayor."

"No kidding."

When Deborah had disappeared down the hall, Donald turned back to the phone. "So, do you have anything yet about what the coroner may have found?" He figured Hall had not called him at the station just to kid him about his age. Something was always up with Casey, some piece of news or gossip, some iron newly poked in the fire of his undisciplined ambition.

"Actually, I called to ask you the same question," Hall replied.

"You could have saved yourself the dime," Donald said.

"Well, the coroner's got the bones we found on the floor under the steering wheel, and there were some other bone fragments we sifted from the debris on the passenger side floor, too. But without dental work, he says he's not going to find anything conclusive. We're pretty certain the car was a Honda, and we tore the engine compartment apart with the Jaws of Life and did get a motor number on the block to work from. The State Patrol's running that down, and we should know soon who owned it. We got everything we need on the trucker."

"That's a lot more than I knew last," Donald said.

"Not about the people in the car, though, except for what your ex's husband gave us."

"Well, that's a police problem now, I guess," Donald said.

"That's why I like being a fireman. You get in on all the action, and you don't have to worry about nitpicky paperwork after. Although fire investigation is pretty interesting stuff."

"I suppose," Donald said. He had taken a course in arson investigation when he'd been newly made captain, and he had found it such an exacting and tedious science that he knew it would take someone with a plodding, patient personality to be good at it. It was like any investigative work: hours of labor could go into looking at something as small as a grain of sand, and all it might amount to was eliminating it as something relevant to the case.

"Let me know when you have something new," Donald said.

"Ditto," Casey replied.

When he'd hung up, Donald pulled the chair out from his desk and sat heavily into it. Events were accelerating much too fast for him right now, and once again he felt singled out and beleaguered. Deborah's unintentional revelation had aroused his suspicions. It was unprecedented that a probationary firefighter would be given permission to circumvent the chain of command and report directly to the Chief. That was not just courting trouble from someone who might misuse the privilege through inexperience or immaturity, but it was inviting accusations of reverse discrimination from the men and a possible suit from the union. Ultimately, it was terribly unfair to Donald himself. He had been given the responsibility for integrating Deborah Gallant into his company and into the fire department without any guidance on how he was to handle unforeseen mixed gender problems and the inevitable public scrutiny. That was either a gross oversight by the City, or it was an intentional way of setting him up to become the scapegoat for any failures. Whichever the case, things were moving much too fast, and he was having to face again the disheartening gut feeling of how bad he was at making the kinds of crucial decisions that protected the lives of the people around him.

Chapter 14

It was 1:35 in the afternoon, and no one had turned on the lights yet inside the courtroom. Catherine was seated at a long table near the judge's bench, watching Steven stand with his back to her before one of the tall windows overlooking the front courtyard of the building. The light outside pressed flat against the windows, and within the cavernous room, the air seemed gray and spectral. Such bleak illumination and flat shadows were all wrong to Catherine's painter's eye. Steven's silhouette against the center window, as he stood looking out, seemed stamped from sheet metal, like the ornate ceiling of the courtroom.

She was talking to him, telling him about her terrible night. "It was one of the worst nights of my life. I didn't sleep a wink all night." When Steven didn't reply, she raised her voice to be heard. "I had awful premonitions. There were those steel bands again around my head, squeezing me until I thought my skull would crack. And then this hand—I'm certain it was *your* hand, Steven. I know it was. It came right out of the center of my head and reached toward something. You were reaching for someone." She tried pointing to the spot on her head, spreading the hair on her scalp there to reveal the exact point at the frontal lobe of her skull where she had seen and felt the hand stretching. But Steven wasn't paying attention to her. His silhouette against the light from the window was almost black in the dimness of the unlit room, like a cutout police target.

"Look," he said brusquely, addressing the windowpanes, "I don't want to talk right now." His voice faded to a pleading groan. "I can't listen to all that right now. I don't have an ounce of strength or ability to help you." He kept his back to her, staring out the window, his hands pressed flat on the broad sill.

"I'm just saying I had a bad night," Catherine replied. Then she recalled what Richard Cooper had told her. "But this morning things are much clearer."

"Well, good, because I had a shitty morning too. A devastating morning." When Catherine didn't reply, waiting, he finally turned to face her. "In fact, I could be having second thoughts about"—his hand made a sweeping gesture to include the whole room—"all of this."

Taken aback, she studied his face to see if he was being sarcastic; but he stared back at her, his features expressionless in the way he always looked at people when he was gauging their reactions to something he'd posed while showing nothing of his own feelings. She felt a flare of irritation. "You're having second thoughts? What happened? Didn't she want to sleep with you?" But her own sarcasm stung her with its bitterness.

"What's that supposed to mean?" he said.

She shook her head and shrugged, immediately cautious not to go too far and expose her vulnerability. Her emotions teetered between anger and apprehension. "I was just wondering if you were maybe out last night with the girl one of your students told me you've been...*cozy* with lately."

"What the hell, Catherine. What the fucking hell. Who told you a lie like that? I wasn't *out* with anyone. I was indoors the whole night. There was a blizzard, in case you hadn't noticed."

She jerked her head up to face him. "Oh, I was aware of the blizzard. And aware that you weren't home *indoors* when I needed to talk to you—" her hand swept the room before her, imitating his earlier gesture—"about *all of this*."

Steven scowled. Then she saw his expression change to uncertainty, and she plunged on. "You weren't home last night. So who were you with?" Her heart was pounding now.

He recovered instantly, his eyes once more cold as glass. "How would you know if I was home or not?"

"I tried to get hold of you—"

"I wasn't answering my phone," he said.

"No, you sure weren't because I was at your apartment last night, and you were gone," she said behind a rush of exhilaration at catching him out. "Why do you have to lie to me? What's the point of it if you believe you're already gone?"

His lips were tight with that rubber band tension she knew so well.

"So, where were you when I needed you? I was scared to death," she rushed on, unable to stop herself. "All I wanted was for you to give me a little assurance when I needed it to help me get through all this. But you couldn't even wait one last night before shacking up with someone else."

Steven glanced quickly around, then back at her. "It's none of your business where I was, Cathy. My life is mine again, and if you'd wake up and look at yourself positively, you'd see your life is yours again, too."

"Well then, so what did you mean when you said you were having second thoughts?" she said. "What were your second thoughts, then?"

He leaned across the expanse of the wide table at her and snapped his fingers rudely in her face. "I'm *done*." His own face was strained, reddening, and it seemed to Catherine as if he could actually be fighting back tears.

"Oh, Steven, why don't you come sit down? I can't *see* you in this light," she said. She looked up at the ceiling, at the darkened globes of the light fixtures hanging on their tubular stems from the pressed-metal ceiling. "Why don't they turn on some light, for god sake?"

He leaned in toward her again, and then pulled out a chair and sat rigidly down across from where she sat. The plane of polished wood between them was as broad as an island, she thought.

"Don't you recognize this place?" she said. "This is the same courtroom we were married in! The same *room*, and he's the same man who married us."

"I know that," he said. Steven stared at the closed door to the judge's chambers. "What the hell are they doing in there, anyway? How bright is it to leave two people in a divorce suit sitting alone in a courtroom?" The muscles along his jaw were tight cords beneath his skin

Catherine laughed abruptly. "They must think we're civilized," she said. "But, hey, let's teach them a lesson. Why don't we sneak out? Wouldn't they be surprised when they came in to pick our bones and found we'd flown the coop?"

Steven's forehead furrowed, his eyebrows turning up like two caterpillars rising to a leaf.

"What? Not a good idea?" she said.

"No, it's not that," he said. "I just don't really know what the fuck anything is about that's happening right now. Everything seems so…inconsequential right now."

Then suddenly he was telling her about an accident, at an intersection near where they—near where she—lived in Westmont. A woman, two children, all killed right in front of his eyes.

"Oh, Steven," she said with real sympathy. "No wonder. No wonder, you poor man. You were there?"

"I saw it all happen."

"I saw it, too. The girls and I saw the smoke. The police wouldn't let us go up 98th to the highway.

"I mean, I *witnessed* it. They just vanished in flames, evaporated from sight. And I can still see them right at the instant they disappeared. I was the last living person to watch them vanish." He looked distant to her, not here in this room but somewhere else, wherever he had witnessed this terrible event, and this time there were real tears like crystal lenses gleaming in his eyes.

"Who was it, do you know?"

He shook his head. The police had asked him the same question, he told her. The firemen, too. Did she know her ex-husband was at the scene? That they had talked? Then he described the gory aftermath of the fire, how he had seen the car beneath the rolled-over tanker, had heard the men talk about what few remains they had been able to find. He had seen the evidence of all that was left on the floor beneath the steering wheel.

She did not have a moment to ask the real question that had come to her like a buoy of hope: what was he doing near Westmont? Had he been coming to see her? Was he really having second thoughts? But, he was totally self-absorbed now, and tears were spilling openly while he shook his head over and over again in disbelief or denial. She had never seen him so distraught, and her heart ached for him.

Then in the next moment, while Steven fought to regain his composure, the door from the judge's chambers opened and the duo of lawyers emerged.

Hurriedly, Catherine leaned across the table reaching out to touch Steven's hands. "Are you so sure you don't want to be married to me anymore?" she whispered.

Avoiding hers, he spread his hands on the table in front of him like the blackjack dealers she'd seen in Las Vegas standing before their spread cards waiting for someone to sit down and play. And then he was present again, pulling out the chair next to him for his attorney to sit.

It was John DiMarino, Steven's attorney, who arrived first at the table—a short, black-haired man with an unctuous bass voice. Catherine found him totally repulsive, even in the way he hurried across the room and sat down, putting his hand on Steven's shoulder. The way he whispered close to Steven's ear, his oily head turned to avoid making eye contact with Catherine while, she knew certainly, he was talking about her, poisoning her husband's mind toward her. DiMarino made her think of all the spiteful names for attorneys she'd been taught by her father: shyster, ambulance chaser, bloodsucker.

Her own attorney, Sally Melvin Green, stalked past where Steven and DiMarino sat huddled, without so much as a sideways glance at them. She was a stout, dour woman in a severe gray suit. Earlier, Catherine had intercepted her in the rotunda of the courthouse, under the dome, as she was entering the building. Catherine had arrived in time to make sure she caught Sally before she got to the courtroom.

"I have grave misgivings about all this," she'd told her attorney. "I've given this an awful lot of thought, and I'm sure I don't want to go through with it, after all. Not today, anyway." It was her last stab at assertiveness, taking charge of her life, as friends and counselors had so frequently advised her.

Sally had stared scornfully at her, then dismissed her. "It's too late for that now. We've been too long getting this to court as it is. Look, Catherine, I can't deal with your capriciousness. I'll take myself off your case, if you insist, and walk out of here right now."

"Yes," Catherine had said, "yes, that's fine, I understand. You're off the case. Thank you for your help, and I'm sorry to be such a bother!"

"Well, I have to advise you, you can't just dismiss me and think you've dismissed the hearing. Your husband is the petitioner in this action which means that he can continue the proceedings with or without you. And unless he has agreed to drop his petition, there will be a divorce here today, my dear. So you may as well let me see this through with you to protect your interests."

Catherine already knew this, of course. It was the way her divorce from Donald had gone. He had not attended the hearing because of—what?—his conciliatory nature? At the time she had been relieved, he had not been there to hear her assert her claim of an irretrievable breakdown of their marriage. So she had relented and followed Sally meekly into the elevator and up to the courtroom level.

Now, Sally drew up a chair next to hers and, with a great show of exasperation, plopped a thick folder of papers tabbed *Steven Harper vs. Catherine*. "Your husband will be the only one taking the stand. You will not have to say anything," she said flatly.

The sudden re-opening of the door to the judge's chambers simultaneously chased a chill up Catherine's spine and clinched a hot knot in her stomach. Both sensations swept over her in the swiftness of Judge Moravic's entrance striding down the room to the high bench.

Catherine was a beat or two behind everyone else, rising numbly to her feet when Sally Melvin Green plucked at her sleeve, then sitting down again after everyone else was reseated, collapsing, really, under her own weight. The only thought she could muster repeated itself in her head: *Uh-oh, I'm going to get it now.* She felt the same trembling and nausea she experienced as a child when she tried to make herself small and invisible in a house resonating with her father's booming wrath and the shrill, harpy cries of her mother.

For the next several minutes, while she was aware of voices speaking in somber, monotonic cadences, she scarcely heard anything they said. Sally, closest to her, responded at one point, "We are, your honor." Seeing Judge Moravic, stone-faced, in his black robe like a bird of prey mounted behind his judge's bench, had stunned Catherine's thoughts.

The first time she had seen him he had seemed jaunty and dapper, in good spirits as he met them in the rotunda on a sunny Friday afternoon, chatting amiably while they rode the elevator up to his fourth-floor courtroom—a white-haired man dressed in a three-piece tan suit, about to perform the pleasant ceremony of marriage for two people in love.

He had ushered her, Steven, her two girls, and Charlotte, their "witness" to the ceremony, into the courtroom with a courtly sweep of his arm. The room was vacant, no sign of the trial that had recently been held there. With its 19th Century high, polished bench, witness box, and attorneys' tables, all separated from the rows of straight-backed gallery chairs by a low railing, the setting struck Catherine as unreal as an empty theater, as anachronistic as a museum exhibit.

Before he actually performed the litany of the civil ceremony—the "Do you, Steven…Do you, Catherine" call and response, Catherine was anxious to hear—Judge Moravic delivered to them a solemn homily on the significance of the marriage contract. "Among civilized peoples," he told them, "the uniting of a man and a woman in marriage is the very foundation of a society's ability to survive. The vows that you will take constitute the most elemental and solemn contract between human beings. In those times and in those societies where the marriage vows are agreed to lightly, or without conviction, *all* cooperative endeavors and loyalties among their peoples are proportionately weakened or fail. The commitment of love, respect, and loyalty between two individuals is the center of concentric circles of family, community, and nation. If the center does not hold, then, in their order, so will the other contiguous rings of civilization disintegrate."

Like chastened children, Catherine and Steven had held tightly to one another's hands while they repeated their pledges. After the judge's official pronouncement of their union, Steven had slipped his arm around Catherine's waist and kissed her on the temple.

Before they left, Charlotte had taken a "wedding photo" with Judge Moravic standing between Catherine and Steven on his one side, and Holly and Donna on his other for a record of the happy occasion.

"It was strange, but I felt somehow privileged," Catherine said to Steven when they compared their impressions later that day. "It was as if we'd been singled out from everyone else in Platte City, to have an entire courtroom in the Marchant County Courthouse reserved just for us."

Steven agreed only that it was strange. His own reaction was tempered with his usual note of irony. "It seemed odd to be married by a man who regularly sits in judgment on the miseries of the socially mal-attuned. It lent to what should be a simple contract between two people the onus of a binding arbitration, like a sentence. Don't you think?"

But if Catherine feared now a lecture from the judge because they were fewer than three years later before him to dissolve the union to which he had bound them, she had nothing to worry about. It was immediately evident by his cool, businesslike demeanor that Moravic in black gown was different from Moravic in tan suit. In fact, he gave no indication at all that he recognized her or Steven, and Catherine was a bit disappointed.

Shortly, Steven was directed to take a seat in a mahogany captain's chair in the raised witness dock beside the judge's bench. Catherine thought he appeared nervous as he crossed by her table. His face was rigid and his mouth was pinched, the way he got when he was angry or scared. And suddenly he seemed thinner to her eye now—his sports jacket loose on him, as if he'd shrunk away from its fit or it was a thrift store compromise on his size. The idea that he may have actually lost weight because of anxiety or grief gave Catherine a measure of satisfaction.

John DiMarino stood to one side of the witness dock asking Steven a series of rhetorical questions.

"Is your present address Forty-two-oh-five Taylor Street, Apartment Six?

"And you have resided there since September of last year?

"In the period of your marriage to Catherine Harper, did you both seek to resolve differences that existed between you in the conduct of the marriage?

"Are you convinced that irreconcilable differences still exist between you and Mrs. Harper?

"And are you further convinced the marriage is irretrievably broken by virtue of these irreconcilable differences?"

Steven's answers were uniformly monosyllabic: Yes. Yes. Yes. The incantatory quality of it seemed to Catherine preface to something else. This was just some sort of opening invocation, as ritual as catechism or confession. Judge Moravic did not even appear to be listening. He was turning printed pages of paper, like someone reviewing the text of his speech, preparing to go to the podium next.

Through it all, Catherine waited to be called on. She waited for the human part to begin. She could not believe that Sally Melvin Green would not call her to the stand where she would be permitted to speak her side of their marriage.

It was Catherine's experience, exemplified by what was happening to her at the moment, that in matters that were crucial to her desires, people whom she counted on treated her as if she were an unreasoning child. As if she were someone who didn't know her own mind.

Her parents had kept her cloistered at home when she wasn't in school. She was not permitted to date before she was sixteen. This was for her own good. When she went to college it was against her mother's wishes. For her own good, she should have got a civil service job. Or a good secretarial job. Even though she paid her own way through school from her job as a medical secretary for a clinic of urologists, her father argued against her quitting there when she graduated with her first degree in art. Her desire to pursue art was frivolous, self-indulgent. The word her father had used was "selfish." He'd said, "You can't make a decent living painting pictures. That's the road to welfare, unless you're a Norman Rockwell, which you're not."

Only her marriage to Donald Sparta had received any approval from her father, and only then because Donald was a son of the man who owned one of the largest construction companies in the Midwest. But, Catherine couldn't even handle that right. Twelve years invested, and then she divorced him! What on earth, her mother demanded to know, could a man with Donald's sort of pedigree do, short of beating her daily and leaving scars to prove it, that could bring her to leave him? Was she still holding him somehow responsible for the death of their son? "You've got to let the past go, Catherine," her mother said. "You can't blame the man for an accident simply because he wasn't there to prevent it." Catherine's stubborn answer, to her own astonishment, had been repeatedly, "He doesn't love me any longer. He loves his job more than me or our children. And I can't live with someone whose love doesn't inspire me."

It was the wrong answer to give someone who lived in a two-bedroom bungalow in Corinth. It was not the appropriate answer to give to aging parents who'd lived all their own married lives in the same tiny house, raised two children of an angry man and complaining woman, and were waiting on fixed income for their time to run out. Catherine's divorce from Donald was the final profligate act of estrangement from her own family and past.

"The conditions of the settlement seem conscionable," Judge Moravic was saying now. "The home remains with the respondent and her children, and a temporary support settlement of eight hundred dollars a month for two years payable to respondent by petitioner is equitable. Personal possessions and furnishings the petitioner brought into the marriage to be retained by him. I am therefore granting petitioner's request for dissolution of this marriage and so order it entered in Docket 819, page…." He fumbled momentarily through the papers in front of him. "Whatever the page number is," he said, finally. "District Court of Marchant County." He looked down at Steven. "You may step down."

While Steven made his way back to the table where DiMarino was gathering his own file of papers together, Judge Moravic rose to his feet, and Sally Melvin Green rose to hers. "Have a good day," the judge said, and as quickly as he entered the courtroom, he was gone.

Sally Melvin Green took Catherine's limp hand in hers and pumped it once. "Now, that wasn't so tough, was it?" she said. "You're a free woman again. Make the best of it." Catherine smiled because Sally was smiling at her, but she knew that something had either gone by her or else was coming toward her yet. In either case, her mind would not take in all of it.

Almost before Catherine had become aware of it, the courtroom was empty. The judge had swept back into his chambers like one of those carved figures on an old German clock, and the attorneys were just entering the elevator together across the lobby. Steven had disappeared. Catherine lingered behind in the dim and cavernous room, taking a last look-around as if to seal the details for her own dismal memories, or to fix an impression of shadow-and-light texture for some future painting she might call "An American Courtroom."

The doors on the elevator were closing behind Sally Melvin Green and DiMarino, but Catherine saw they were the only occupants of the car, animated in good-natured conversation with one another. *Bloodsuckers*, she thought, and hurried out to find Steven.

She peered over the rail to the stairwell below, caught sight of the top of his head disappearing around a bend two flights below, and started down the stairs after him. "Steven!" she called, her voice reverberating in the hollow tower of the stairwell. The percussive rap of her shoes on the marble slabs of the steps and the throbbing of her pulse in her ears conspired to drown away any acknowledgment he might have given. "Steven!"

She made the turn onto the second landing—she nearly ran out of one of her shoes: the modern Cinderella chasing after her prince, he the one in flight against the tolling of the midnight hour—and she saw him waiting on the next landing, a palm over the knob of a baluster post, looking without expression back up at her.

She slowed for the last flight down to him, collecting herself. But she thought she must look the way she felt: anxious, almost panicky again.

"Well," she said bravely, "how was that? Some fun, huh?"

Steven did not reply. He turned and continued down the stairs as she drew alongside.

"How about buying your ex-wife a drink, for old time's sake," she said.

Steven looked at his watch. "It's only two o'clock."

"Too early, huh? Well, how about a cup of coffee, then? I'll buy."

"I don't know, Catherine. I need to get back home. I have things to do," he said.

"Hot date waiting?" She regretted it immediately, not so much the impropriety of the remark but what it gave away about her. The thought that this was what his freedom might mean to him was already a source of grinding pain to her.

Steven didn't answer, and the ambiguity of his silence made it worse.

The stairs gave onto the main lobby, the floor of which was taken up with a huge mosaic of pioneer images—an ox-drawn covered wagon, shocks of wheat, an Indian on his pony, a bison, a fur trapper leaning on his long rifle—the images skewered by the tips of inlaid brass spokes which radiated out from a brass hub that circumscribed the seal of the county. The entire mosaic had always seemed to Catherine emblematic of the character of Platte City: meticulous, painstaking craftsmanship had gone into creating the most insipid artwork. As she and Steven crossed the lobby, she noticed a line of people had formed over the image of the fur trapper, queuing up at the municipal court window to pay traffic fines.

"So what about it then?" she said to Steven. "You want to go for coffee, or what? You'll still be divorced afterward."

"Jesus, Catherine. Let it go, will you?"

He had hit the bar on the revolving door, and she stopped abruptly as the glass panel of the next door wedged him away from her. She caught the third panel as it spun by and pushed her way around. As she exited onto wide, stone steps leading down to the sidewalk, she saw that Steven had already reached the bottom and was hurrying off, leaving her at the top of the courthouse steps, the hem of her white dress flapping like a flag of surrender in the spring breeze.

Chapter 15

When he'd left the courthouse, Steven had driven to the College hoping to find refuge in the windowless cell of his campus office on the third floor of the Arts and Humanities building. He was not ready yet to retreat into the solitude of his apartment.

He'd closed and locked his office door. He hadn't even turned on the overhead fluorescent light. Only a green-shaded banker's lamp on his desk illuminated the area immediately around him. From the main corridor outside the anteroom, the muffled sounds of other office staff closing down for the weekend drifted to his ears. There was the hollow clunk of a door closing at the north end of the wing, the rise and fall of voices passing like a sudden wind. Within his department's suite of offices, Steven was the only English faculty member left this late on a Friday afternoon.

Bunkered into this stuffy cubical, hiding out, he was painfully aware that he had no one to turn to for help or succor. The images of the accident, the fire, the faces of the children played themselves over in his head like a repeating slide show. There was no one to share his story with, to open up and lighten the weight of his mind's burden of guilt.

In twenty-two years in Platte City, he had not made a single close friend, male or female. He wasn't a bowler, a golfer, a sports follower of any ilk that would put him in the company of other men. He didn't gamble, he didn't drink in bars. The only couples he'd known were those whose friendship Catherine had cultivated when she was still teaching in the Art and Art History Department. With their marriage on the rocks, so were the flimsy social alliances they'd both made within it. And now that their marriage officially dissolved, he no longer had even her to confide in.

It was all supposed to be for their mutual pleasure, wasn't it? That was the dictum of the one who still haunted him in dreams. He had thought that might include marriage, that it might be possible he and his first wife Janice, even without the miscarried pregnancy, could be more than two people in rut with each other. But when that inevitably failed, he had let pass all those years without any desire to test the complexities of marriage again. Until Catherine.

It was her certainty they were meant to be together, that their lives would be better—*healed* is the word she used—if they were married to each other. He had wanted to believe that. She was different, yes? Well spoken, imaginative, artistically talented—which wasn't too difficult, he supposed, in this unimaginative community in the rural heart of the heartland. He had let himself be persuaded, in order to keep the fervency of her awakened libido alive, that they both suffered some emotional malaise that living together would cure.

He should have sat down over a beer with her ex-husband before he married her. There was a man who would have known what Steven was in for.

He knew there would be hiccups in adjustment; he was not naïve about moving in with a ready-made family not his own. He had assumed there would be opportunity to integrate himself into the life that had existed in their house before him. However, the bald truth was, this was not his family—Catherine and her kids. From the beginning, he couldn't shake the feeling that he was on loan there, a stand-in. Family-sitting. A stuntman, doubling for the star in the dangerous chase scene. He was living some other man's life in his absence, and he couldn't wait for that one to return and claim it back. He'd become as detached from his own life's flow as an oxbow lake from the river that was once its source.

Then, at some turning point—if he cared to think hard enough about it, he might have recalled there was a specific moment—he found himself wanting the end to come. He fell into a moroseness of spirit, a funk that deadened what little was left of his desire for Catherine and blurred his memory of the times that were once pleasurable when she was the woman he had met in his writing class who flattered him with her body because he had complimented her work. The one he knew when it was still fun to know her. It was all for fun, his muse had impressed on him. Never confuse the pleasures of the body with those of the heart, she'd warned. *Carpe diem, Stevie.*

The door to the outside hall opened, and he heard the rattle and bump of the janitor's cart being wheeled into the anteroom with its cargo of buckets, mops, sprays, and rags. When the janitor paused just in front of his closed door, Steven cleared his throat a couple of times to announce his presence.

There was a light knock on the office door—two small raps on the opaque pane of glass in the center of the top half of the door—and almost immediately following, Steven heard a key being applied to the lock.

The door opened inward and the janitor—a woman, not a man—an ebony-skinned, rotund woman wearing the light tan uniform shirt and chocolate brown trousers of the maintenance employees, looked in at him. "Oh!" she said. "'Scuse me, I didn't think nobody was here." Her voice was powerful, but as modulated and mellifluous as a radio announcer's.

"Come in," Steven said. "It's all right, I'm just finishing up."

"I just found this slipped in the door outside—says your name on it." She handed a stapled sheaf of papers to him.

He took it and saw it was from one of his American Lit students, Richard Cooper. "Thank you," he said. "One of my students turning in a late paper."

The janitor nodded. "Isn' that the way with 'em? Day late and a dollar short, most of 'em." She laughed at her joke.

"Do you wish me to leave while you tidy up?" Steven asked.

"No, no, s'all right. I'm just emp'nyin' wastebaskets for now," she said. "Don't disturb yourself. Go right ahead. You go right a-head." She grabbed the round gray metal basket from beside Steven's desk, and she was out the door with it before Steven had a chance to respond.

He glanced back at the paper in his hand. Cooper was one of his better students, but slovenly in his discipline. Now Steven would need to teach him a lesson for his tardiness by lowering his grade.

The janitor returned with the empty wastebasket. "You go right ahead," she said to him again, putting the can, like an offertory vessel, down beside his desk. "I wouldn'ta bothered you, except I gots the chance to be outta here early today. My little girl's in the hospital."

"Sorry to hear it," Steven said. He placed Cooper's paper precisely on top of an unread stack of newsletters and textbook flyers on his desk.

The janitor picked up the telephone receiver from its cradle and began wiping it with a cloth. "Yah, she went in las' night with real heavy bleeding," she said.

Steven saw a child lying in the street, her dress covered with blood. "That's terrible," he said. "And they wouldn't let you off work to be with her?"

"Oh yeah," she said. "If I finishes up here before reg'lar time, I'll be leavin' early."

She set the phone back on its cradle. "That your fambly?" she asked, indicating a picture at the back of his desk. It was a picture of him and Catherine and her two girls and the judge who'd married them, taken at the wedding by Charlotte Sparta. He had put the photograph there the week after they were married, framed in leather like the cover of a valuable first edition book, to prove to Catherine that she had replaced all others in his life. There it sat on public display in his office, declaring to whoever entered this space— particularly for any woman by whom Catherine might feel threatened—that Steven was off limits, unavailable, happily married. The model husband and step-father.

"Yes," Steven said. He picked up the frame and looked at the photograph momentarily, as if he were confirming the fact. He offered it to her, and she took it in her hand and studied it a moment, nodding her head.

"That's nice," the woman said, handing it back. "And those children. I seen it there before when I clean around your desk. It's nice to have a picture of your fambly at work. I don't see too many that do no more."

"Well..." Steven said.

"Some of the women teachers and a *lot* of the sec'taries, they keep their husbands and kids at the office. But the men don't do it that much. It's nice to see you care."

Steven felt embarrassed. "I never thought of it that way," he said. He took the picture from her and set it at the back of the desk. "I'd better get out of your way, so you can finish up and go see your daughter."

"You go right ahead," she said. "Don't let me get in your way." She turned to the door, taking a swipe with her cloth at the seat of the empty side chair next to his desk, running the cloth over the top of the file cabinet by the door.

"I hope your little girl gets well soon," Steven said.

"Oh, she's doin' purty good. Doin better, anyways. She had a miscarry, lost a baby."

"Oh," Steven said. His image of the child's body in the street, the bloody dress, vanished.

"Well, I'm sure it'll be all right, she's young yet. She can try again," Steven said reassuringly, hoping to end the conversation. "Sometimes it takes more than once."

"Don't know about that, or not. My daughter's seventeen. She maybe can't have another one; she had so much trouble with this. She's lost two others in two years, too."

Steven flushed. "Oh dear," he said. "Well...."

She nodded and turned to her cart in the middle of the anteroom floor. "You have yourself a good one," she said over her shoulder and shut his door again.

The janitor was just opening the door to the next office down the line when Steven rose from his desk to leave. He took the wedding picture from his desk and tucked it under his arm. In the hall, he leaned around the cleaning cart in his way, almost lunging back to close the door behind him.

Two flights down the stairs on the first floor, he slowed his pace through the central corridor of the building. Now that he'd been ferreted out of his office, he was considering where he would go next. He thought of going to a bar, the way other men did when they needed the insights or obliterations of alcohol; but he dismissed the idea immediately. The image of himself sitting alone, staring down his own solemn image in the mirror across the bar, or cornered in the shadows of a booth with a glass of gin in front of him, seemed patently cliché, even for his present frame of mind.

Ahead of him up the hall, the double doors to the college theater suddenly clattered open, and the high warble of girlish laughter rang against the empty stone walls as three young women in rabbit gray leotards and leg warmers burst out and spun like wind-driven leaves across the atrium lobby to a water cooler.

"Did too, Lisa."

"Didn't."

"Too. Saw ya. And so did Mark."

"You fat liar."

And more laughter from two of them while the third bent to the bubbler, reaching behind with a hand to stretch the leg-band of her leotard back down over the crescent moon of her right buttock. The two waiting slapped playfully at each other's arms.

The occurrence had momentarily taken his breath—startled him to a near stop by the suddenness of all that gaiety and movement exploding into the lobby, the sight of the leotards stretched like skin over their slight forms. In the next moment, he identified the one bending over the water bubbler by her white-blond hair.

When Steven was nearly on them, the girl at the fountain stood up and turned, running the back of her hand across her mouth to catch the over splash of water on her lips, and she noticed him cross out of the narrower neck of the hallway into the light of the rotunda.

"Hello, Valerie," Steven said.

She finished swallowing a mouthful of water, a pronounced undulation of her throat as she craned her neck quickly to get it down. "Hi, Mr. Harper," she replied, smiling as if she were pleasantly surprised to see him.

"What's up?" he said.

"Oh, just rehearsal." She looked down at herself, holding her arms out from her sides like penguin flippers, as if to confirm by her outfit that she spoke accurately. All three young women, Steven noticed, were barefooted.

Closer to her now, he could see the glistening of sweat on Valerie's forehead. The strands of blond hair around her temples were wet and stringy. On the shiny pearl-gray leotard were darker gray Rorschach blots: a butterfly between her small, wide-set breasts, a sunburst around her navel. Her cheeks were flushed and there was a strawberry bloom of heat at the base of her throat.

"Is it a good one, then?" he asked. "Is the show shaping up all right?"

"Coming together great," she said. She had detached herself from the other two girls and come toward him, stopping before him in the middle of the atrium, in the big circle of natural light beneath the skylight dome. She looked up at him, a quizzical smile on her face.

"And how about you?" she said tentatively. "Did…you know, did everything turn out all right?"

At first he looked at her with uncertainty, and then he recalled in the next instant that he had mentioned his court appointment to her earlier this morning. In fact, he'd told her he probably wouldn't even be in school today. "Well, everything went as scheduled, which I guess means successfully. I decided to come out here, after all, since I couldn't stand going home alone just yet."

"That's so sad," she said. "What will you do now?"

"Well, that's a good question. Let me think," he said, lightly. "What shall I do with all my free time now?" He made a show of looking at his watch and in the gesture raised the wedding portrait in his right hand. "Let's see, it's quarter past three, so…." Valerie noticed what he held, and as he lowered his hand, she stopped it with hers, looking momentarily at the picture. Her eyes went tragic for him, just as they had earlier in the donut shop, and he felt that little rush of warmth the first magnet of attraction always gave him.

"Actually, I'll head home and freshen up and then probably go out to dinner. I seemed to have worked up an appetite with all the stress today." As he spoke, he tried unsuccessfully to slide the picture into his jacket pocket, but the frame was too large.

"Yeah, me too," she said. "A four-hour rehearsal, and I'll be starved. We've got another two hours to go."

He gave up on the picture and simply held it at his side again. "So, what does a dancer eat when she's in rehearsal?"

"Oh ho!" she said, as if he'd just said the magic word. "You name it. Pizza, spaghetti, loads of carbs. Salad is what I should have, and I do eat lots of veggies. I eat like a bird, though."

One of the other girls had bent to the water bubbler now, and the second one, of darker complexion, stood next to her, watching Steven and Valerie. She reminded him of a girl long ago, in high school—Carol Pistillo—who had the same dusky skin. This girl was short-waisted with round, parenthetical hips. She seemed to Steven on the verge of laughter.

Valerie caught Steven staring over her shoulder and turned to look back at her friends. "I'll catch up to you guys in minute, okay?"

They nodded, hesitated a moment, and the girl who had been at the water bubbler tittered.

"This is Mr. Harper, you guys. My English teacher," she said. She turned back to Steven and wrinkled her nose. "This is Lisa and Natalie."

Reminded again of his age and position, he drew himself a bit more erect and smiled at the two girls. "*Merde*," he called to them.

"Thank you," one replied. The two set off across the atrium to the main doors of the theater. "See ya, Val," the darker girl said in a coquettish drawl.

"You're here for another two hours, did you say?"

"Actually, probably until five o'clock. We've got a lot of stuff to work out, still."

"So, how about a bite to eat when you're done?" Steven said, looking again at Valerie's face. "I mean, if you're ready for something to eat by then."

"Are you kidding? I'm always ready to eat."

"Well, I'm sort of at loose ends right now. I'd really like some company for dinner tonight—oh!" he interrupted himself at his obvious oversight. "Are you expected home to eat?"

"No, no," she said quickly. "All I have to do is call my mom and tell her I'm eating out tonight. I do all the time. I just live with my mom 'cause it's cheaper than paying rent right now, but I don't have to report in, or anything like that." She grinned. "I'm old enough to take care of myself now. And my mother…well, she goes out with her boyfriend a lot, anyway."

"Well, then," Steven said. "Would you like to have dinner with me?"

"You bet. I'll be done by five-thirty. Then all I gotta do is go down to the dressing rooms and change—well, *shower* and change, but I don't take very long, usually—so, if you want to like meet me…where?"

"Here? I'll meet you right here, say at six?"

"Cool. I'll be here."

"In the meantime, think about where you'd like to go," he said.

"Anywhere's fine. I'll leave it up to you," she said. "See ya."

She headed back toward the same double doors into the theater, and Steven watched her move away from him, her upper thighs tautly muscular. A dark caterpillar of sweat crawled up the base of her spine. He was suddenly grateful for the unexpected distraction Valerie provided. Once again it bore in on him how exquisite it was to feel new energy in such serendipitous encounters, how it melted away unhappiness in the flush of surprise. Even if, in the end, unhappiness inevitably returned.

Chapter 16

When the news crew from Channel 5 arrived at the station house—a short, pale woman, wearing a white spring dress and navy-blue jacket, and a bearded man in jeans and denim jacket carrying a huge portable TV camera—Donald and Deborah Gallant were out on the apparatus floor, waiting. The woman introduced herself with a one-pump handshake for each of them.

"Ann Baxter, Five-Alive News," she said. "I appreciate your taking time for us from your busy schedule."

Ann Baxter smiled ingratiatingly at Deborah Gallant, as if she were a missionary come to convert. "What our viewers would like, naturally, would be to see Debbie in action as a fireman doing her job. But I guess we won't be that fortunate. So, maybe we might be able to set something up?" What she wanted was a shot of Deborah on the tailboard of Engine 55, with the other members of the company on board in full gear, going out the door of the station with red lights flashing and siren blaring as if they were going to a fire. Donald stammered for excuses, unable to say definitely yes, he would pull the men out for the staged shot, but unable, as well, to find a reason not to cooperate. "Our firefighters don't ride on the tailboards any longer, so it wouldn't be permissible or accurate," was all he could come up with.

Ann Baxter compromised and posed Deborah in front of the pump panel on the driver's side of the truck so that the light from the camera gleamed in the chrome-capped fittings and valve handles. "What was that first call as a Platte City firefighter like for you?" she wanted to know.

"I was a bit nervous at first," Deborah said quietly, "but when we got there, I was too busy to think much about anything except the fire." She did not know what to do with her hands, and she squinted self-consciously into the light atop the camera. She tried standing at parade rest, with her hands clasped behind her. Her eyes exhibited that tic she had first shown Donald of shifting, blinking, shifting again without looking directly at the camera or her inquisitor.

"Your very first call involved a fatality. I imagine that's got to be a firefighter's worst moment, no matter of how many calls you've made. What were your feelings when you realized there were deaths?"

"I felt bad, naturally; but there wasn't anything we could do to help those people. It was pretty much decided before we even left the station."

Ann Baxter stood for a moment with an insipid smile on her face, nodding her head as if in agreement, and when it became evident to her that Deborah was not going to elaborate, she pulled the microphone back to her own mouth. "Knowing that you were the first woman on the fire line in the history of Platte City, did you feel any extra burden on your shoulders?" Deborah was already shaking her head no to the question, and Ann Baxter plunged on, "Did you feel you were representing other women who might wish to follow you into the profession?"

"No," Deborah said.

"How about working alongside men who have more experience? Did you find it more difficult as a woman than you expected it to be?"

"No," Deborah said.

Ann Baxter smiled again, and then lowered her microphone and said to her cameraman, "Okay, hold it, Tony. Cut." The red eye of the camera's recording light went dark. "Am I making you nervous?" she asked Deborah.

"No," Deborah said. "I just am."

"Well, what would you like to talk about? How would it help you to conduct this interview?"

"What do you want?" Deborah said.

"Our viewers would be interested in knowing why you became a firefighter."

"Okay," Deborah said.

"Can I ask you that?" Ann said.

"Sure."

Deborah answered in the same terse fashion, her responses clipped and almost monotone. Donald could see the tension in the lines around her mouth, and the nervous glint in her eyes. She had become a firefighter, she told Ann Baxter, for the same reasons anyone else did: it was a "worthwhile profession" where one could make a difference in the lives of others. When Baxter pushed her to explain why this profession, which had for so long been considered the choice of men only, Deborah simply shrugged. "Why not?"

"Well, the nature of the work," Ann Baxter pursued. "I've talked with those in the profession who say the work is very strenuous, it requires great explosions of brute strength at unpredictable times, and physical stamina for extended periods of time. In other words, the sort of muscular activity that many would say is better suited to males. How do you respond to that?"

Donald was surprised at how prepared the interviewer was to articulate the litany of arguments used over the years to keep women out of line service in fire departments. She had done her homework; she wasn't the "airhead" as Connie Townsend had dismissed her. But the question didn't seem to faze Deborah Gallant.

"My boyfriend's an assistant weight coach for the University of Nebraska football and wrestling teams. He trained me. Strength is not always in sheer muscle mass, but how you use the muscles you have."

Donald chuckled. *A weight coach. It would figure.* That's what he had seen in her build when he first observed her earlier—the look of the gymnast or weightlifter.

Next, Ann Baxter turned to Donald, to get his views on Deborah as a new firefighter in his company. She suggested some footage of Deborah coming down off the back of the truck, perhaps with Donald teaching her some things about fighting fires. Just as Deborah had, Donald declined staging any shots that would make them feel foolish. In the end, Baxter opted for his standing at the alarm desk near the front overhead door of the No. 1 bay. Sunlight through the bay door windows sliced in and caught the side of Donald's face.

When the camera began shooting again, Ann Baxter introduced Donald as Deborah Gallant's "superior officer."

"Captain, what did you think when you heard your company had been chosen for the first female firefighter in Platte City's history?"

Donald caught the intent of the question and sidestepped it. "I never viewed it as having been 'chosen,' in the sense that Engine Fifty-five was singled out from all the other companies. I was notified by a new duty roster that Private Gallant was the replacement for a member of our company who will be retiring the end of this month."

"Any *private* feelings of your own," Ann Baxter said, seizing on the pun, "about the replacement being a woman?"

"None at all," Donald said flatly.

"I imagine you've had an opportunity now to observe Private Gallant at a fire, any thoughts on how she did on her first day out?"

Donald said, "She took a lot of punishment from the heat of a very hot fuel fire, and she handled it as well as anyone else out there."

Suddenly, from off-camera, behind Aerial 53, Charlie Wesson's rasping voice spoke out loud enough, Donald was certain, to be caught by the microphone: "She covered my ass real fine. She's a corker." There was an explosion of laughter from others, and Donald realized that a number of the men had come onto the floor and were watching the interview from behind the ladder truck.

Ann Baxter lowered her microphone and said to her cameraman, "That ought to be plenty, Tony. Let's wrap it up out front of the station."

When Baxter and her cameraman had packed up and left, Donald retreated to his office. He was debating whether or not to call Connie Towers downtown to inform her he was miffed by the tenor of the interview but Deborah Gallant suddenly appeared at his open door and peeked in.

"How'd I do?" she asked simply.

"Did just fine," Donald said. "She asked some loaded questions and some stupid ones, too, I thought."

Deborah nodded. She held a magazine in her hand, and he noted she'd taken off her boots and was back in bare feet.

"I was told by the Chief's secretary that she'd be more upbeat," Donald went on, "but I think she saw her opportunity to be Channel Five's Nicole Wallace in this."

"I don't know. I don't watch Channel Five," Deborah said. "But thanks for saying I did okay at the fire."

"Well, you did," Donald replied. "Even with all of the confusion around here today, I think everything's going to shake out smoothly in no time, and everyone will forget there was any question about whether or not you're going to fit into the job."

"God, I sure hope so," she said.

"What's the reading for today?" he asked, nodding toward the rolled-up magazine in her hand.

She looked down and then back. "Just *Cosmo*. I was gonna do some reading down in my bunk."

"Ah, yes, *Cosmopolitan,*" he said. "My ex-wife used to read that, too. Full of cogent articles on how to find a man, keep a man, get rid of a man."

"You're not married?"

"No longer," Donald said. "Occupational hazard of being a firefighter. Too much time away from home, too little to talk about when you are at home. And…too many times not there when your family needs you most."

"Do you think that's true?" she said. "Don't you think marriages can succeed if you're in this job?"

Donald realized his flippancy and relented. "Sure, I do. Most of them do. I'm just generalizing out of my own experience. Actually, I read somewhere there are more divorces among policemen than anywhere else in public service."

She was leaning against the doorjamb now, looking down at him in his chair at his desk. Donald saw something almost coquettish in the angling of her body against the frame, and he looked away.

"So, your boyfriend lives in Lincoln?" he asked.

"Yes," she said.

"And what about you?"

"I have an apartment here," she said.

"Huh. Doesn't that put a strain on your relationship?"

"It hasn't yet, but I think it probably might, eventually. At least, for him," she said.

"He doesn't like the idea?"

"He's not too happy about it, no. He wants me to be closer to him."

"Why don't you do it, then?"

"Because the job is here, not in Lincoln."

Donald smiled. "Oh. Well, that makes sense. I don't mean to grill you; I just like to know how serious my people are about their work."

"No problem," she said. "I know you're not asking like everyone else, anyway. You know, the ones who really want me to admit I made a mistake. They think I'm just in it to make some kind of feminist statement."

"Pain in the ass, huh?" Donald said.

"Yes. I mean, why did Charlie Wesson want to be a firefighter? Why did whatshisname, Metzger, want to be one? Or you?"

He understood the frustration she was feeling. But she could not have been entirely innocent of what would follow her decision to challenge a system so historically stacked against her. "I'll tell you why some men do," he said in a consoling tone. "It's a way to give their lives some importance where it might not have in another blue-collar job. It's because it *is* a blue-collar job that they can still call a *profession*. They are respected for what they do, and it doesn't require a great deal of formal education, only a strong heart and strong back. Then again, with some of them it's the feeling of importance they get in wearing a uniform. And of course, for some there's the realization of a boyhood hero fantasy come true: I want to be a jet pilot, I want to be an astronaut, I want to be a fireman."

"What about you?" she said.

"Ah," he said. He looked at her and weighed whether or not to pursue the question seriously. At the same time, it occurred to him he did not know if he had a serious answer to the question he'd kept from asking himself, had been unable to answer for his father, his brother, his wife in any way satisfactory to them either. He chose a middle ground. "Partly, for me, it was a way of freeing myself from my father's expectations for me, and I couldn't see my way clear to running away and joining the carnival." When he saw her nodding her head, he snorted ironically. "No, that's not it. I don't know. I don't like chaos. I don't like destruction. I like an orderly world, and this job is a way of snatching order out of the jaws of chaos in a manner that you can *see* the results. There's something about fighting a fire—any kind, all kinds, big, small, weed fire, house fire, or one like today—where I still get great satisfaction out of staring down something so fierce and mean, and then beating it back to cinders."

She nodded more vigorously this time, as if he had said the right thing. As if he were the one being tested.

"There are those in my family, however, who think I'm bona fide crazy," he said. "My father sent me to college to become a construction engineer and join my brother in the family business when I graduated. I was supposed to be constructing high rise office buildings and big bridges over highways and rivers, and college classroom buildings like some of those right here on the Platte City State College campus. He had big plans that both his boys would be part of Sparta & Sons Enterprises. I disappointed him when I got hooked on Fire Technology courses in college and switched majors without telling him."

Deborah looked surprised. "Are you...? Is your family *the* Sparta Enterprises?"

"The same," he said. "Although, in my father's view, I'm the least enterprising member of the family." He smiled, but he felt the barb in his own admission.

"Wow," she said. "I guess I'm lucky. I grew up a stationhouse brat. I took Fire Tech classes at the University of Nebraska in Omaha. My dad is all behind what I do. It's my boyfriend, Cal; he says I'm going to get myself killed. And he thinks I'm a troublemaker." She took a breath, as if from a sudden rush of excitement their professional kinship seemed to have caused. "Anyway, I'm sorry your dad doesn't like what you are."

"It was a long time ago," Donald said. "Water under one of his bridges."

Perhaps it was the sincerity of her passion that struck him, or the chord she unintentionally struck in his own requiem for the separations of fathers and sons; but now he wanted to know more about Deborah Gallant. She had uncorked that memory of the earlier Donald Sparta—before Catherine, before his son Donny Jr.—when he was newly embarked on his career as a firefighter, and he first knew Bud Gallant when they were both novitiates as line officers in training courses for higher administration, and Bud had a daughter named Debbie who then, at ten years old, knew she wanted to be like her father. It was this period in time, when his life was all new beginnings of his own conceiving, that he felt in the defiant zeal of Deborah Gallant a rush of nostalgia. "You know, I would like to see your dad again. It's been so long, but I still remember the time I spent with him."

"Oh, he'd love to see you, I'm positive. He was happy when he found out I was assigned to your Engine Company."

And before he could think about it, he said, "I'd like to talk with you more about all this. Would you maybe like to go for dinner when we're off duty tomorrow night?"

"Sure. I'd love to. If that's okay."

Instantly he regretted it. *What the hell am I doing?* Backpedaling, he said, "Only, maybe you've planned to go home to Lincoln tomorrow. You'll want to spend your time off with your boyfriend."

"No, I'm not going anywhere."

"No?" he said. He thought he heard disappointment in her tone, that she understood he was hedging his invitation.

"Not 'til my next rotation off. I want to get used to things here first," she said.

All Donald foresaw now were even more complications to his life; but he said, "Well fine, dinner it is then. But now I've got some more business to attend to."

He began thumbing through the few papers left out on his desk.

"No prob. Thanks, Captain. I'm outta here," she said, and with a toodle-oo wave of her fingers, she vanished from his door as suddenly as she had appeared.

Chapter 17

It was a magnificent house, really—a brick and wood Tudor design with high gables and leaded glass windows. It sat back from the street across a huge expanse of lawn shaded by maples and elms and flanked by two of the tallest blue spruce Catherine had ever seen in the city. An iron fence enclosed the property, and she entered through an arched gateway and along a circular brick drive to the front door. William Sparta, Charlotte's ex-husband, had bought it for them when she was awaiting their first child. It was a house one would expect a Sparta to own, and sometimes Catherine tasted envy like something sour on the back of her tongue. It wasn't the money or the size of the house she envied so much as the security it all seemed to offer, a child's feeling of safety in a place of comfort that could nurture the imagination.

Charlotte answered the door, wearing jeans and a red sweatshirt with flaking white lettering, GO BIG RED NEBRASKA, in a circle around a white appliquéd football with a red "#1" in its center.

"Donna is in the kitchen having some cookies with Buddy; Holly and Trish are upstairs in Trish's room plotting mutiny; and I'm recovering still from the effects of self-administered poison." Her voice had that husky quality, the mellow burr that Catherine always associated with cigarettes and liquor: a voice like her father's.

They entered the twilight of darkly burnished hardwoods and brocade tapestries and textured walls painted in earthy colors, soft on the heart. Catherine had always admired Charlotte's untutored tastes in furnishings that had drawn out the refinement of the old house.

Charlotte had gone to work right after they'd both graduated from high school. She worked as a receptionist for Sparta & Sons Enterprises, her first and last "real job." That was when the company still kept its headquarters in Platte City. Now they were in Omaha, with satellite offices in Minneapolis and Denver. "William married me, and they had to close the place down. Couldn't run it without me," she used to joke early in her marriage when she and William still seemed happy together.

In the living room, Charlotte had already set out a tray with a silver coffee urn and china cups. Catherine could see that she had made her face up and brushed her black hair to its usual luster and wave, and she moved with the same bird-like quickness as always. The hangover she had claimed earlier was mostly an affectation, Catherine concluded.

"All right, no bullshit now. How'd it go?" Charlotte said.

"It was…well, it was *surreal*." She tried to sound off-handed, but she felt as transparent as a teenager might who was trying to fool her mother about whether or not she was having sex.

"So…?" Charlotte persisted.

"I'm a free woman, I guess," Catherine said. She couldn't find the right tone for humor. The notion was still so foreign to her, as if she was hearing it about herself from someone else.

"Congratulations," Charlotte said. "How does it feel?"

Catherine shrugged. "I don't like it; but I can't do anything about it now."

"This was a blessing," Charlotte said. "You were in an impossible situation and you ended it. I'm proud of you."

"No, he ended it. I don't feel very proud right now."

Charlotte poured them both a cup of coffee from the urn. "You did the right thing. Now you can get back to doing the things that gave you happiness before all that shit came down on your head. You won't have anyone to distract you, except your children, who are certainly not a problem."

"I can't help it," Catherine said. "I have this wretched feeling I've done something dire and irrevocable."

"I should hope it's irrevocable."

"That's not what I mean."

Charlotte took a cigarette from a wooden box on the table before her, tapping the filter against the top. When she'd lit it, she raised her head slightly, regarding Catherine through the veil of smoke she let curl from her mouth and nose. "Tell me everything."

Catherine took a breath and swallowed back a knot in her throat. She didn't want to cry, but now the strain of it all had caught up with her once again. She cupped her face to keep it from splitting apart and spilling her anger, her fear into her hands. "I've done something really stupid. I just know it. I'm going to be in trouble," she said, her voice sepulchral within the cave of her fingers.

Charlotte crowded up to her on the couch, cradling her. "All right. It's all right." She produced from somewhere a cloth hankie and Catherine used it, dabbing her eyes until she was quiet again.

"I can't seem to stop myself, even when it's obvious he doesn't want to talk to me."

"Steven?" Charlotte asked.

"Yes, him too. Which is what started it—his cold absence from me before the hearing. And now Martin Stuart. I only wanted to talk to him. I need to be working again. I need to be back in the classroom with students who want me."

"Whoa! Wait a minute," Charlotte said. "I don't think we ought to be doing this."

"Doing what?" Catherine said.

"Drinking coffee." Charlotte indicated with a little erasing motion of her hands over the coffee urn and cups on the table before them. "This isn't a Sunday-morning-over-coffee chat. This is a brandy heart-to-heart we're working up to here." She got up and put her hand to her forehead in the manner of someone trying to remember where she had mislaid her gloves. "Don't tell me any more of this just yet. You wait a minute; I'll be right back."

"No, I don't want anything to drink, thank you," Catherine said quickly. "I couldn't handle any alcohol today."

"Well, I'm not going to handle this very well without it. I'll bring you a glass in case, but this kid is definitely going to have a drink."

While Catherine waited for Charlotte to return, Donna and Buddy, Charlotte's younger son, came in from the back of the house, a stack of cookies like sand dollars in their hands.

"Where have you *been*?" Donna said.

Catherine quickly wiped at her eyes and tried to sound cheerful. "Did you have fun? Did you behave yourself?"

"Yes. But where've you been so long?" Donna said again.

Charlotte swept back in with a bottle in one hand and two slim liqueur glasses in the other. "Buddy, go take Donna to your room now and leave Mommy and Aunt Cathy to talk a bit, okay?"

"*Ge-eez,*" Donna lamented.

"Come on, Donna-Bonna," Buddy said. He took her hand and tugged her away from Catherine.

Charlotte set the glasses on the coffee table. "Are you going to have some with me or not?" she asked Catherine in the same parental tone of voice. She uncorked the bottle of brandy.

"I guess so. Just one," Catherine said.

Charlotte poured the amber liquid to the brim of each glass, then set the bottle down on the table. "*Skol.*" She handed Catherine a glass of brandy.

They each sipped from their drinks simultaneously and were silent, as if reflecting on something they'd just agreed to. Catherine felt the warm vapors scour her nostrils.

Then abruptly, Charlotte said, "So what kind of trouble do you think you're in?"

Catherine took a deep breath, trying to decide where to begin. At the beginning, she thought, just to see if she knew for herself how to unravel the confusing events.

Soon, she was pouring it all out, everything from the night before when her mind was filled with nightmare images, to her the crazy rest of last night, leaving the house in the middle of the snowstorm to go to Steven's; the accident, trapped in her car, being rescued by a man in a snowplow. "It was so humiliating. I was stuck in the window of my car. I could have died there!"

"Oh my god! *Cather-ine!*"

But that wasn't the worst, Catherine confessed. It was not finding Steven at work this morning and then ending up at Martin Stuart's door to plead for his compassion, until he slammed his door in her face and called security.

"It was all so bizarre," she said, still amazed at herself, because she felt shame, too. She drained her glass and turned away, embarrassed. "It was due to not finding Steven home that made me react like that. It was the night before we were to be *divorced*, and he was with another woman."

"How do you know he was out with someone else?"

"I just *know* things," Catherine insisted. "He had told me himself that, before he met me, there was always another woman. He told me that. It's how he found me, looking for someone that he'd lost, or hadn't found. Some fantasy girl from his childhood!. Until me! Until me, he said."

And it was the same for her, she had to admit. He had brought her for the first time into a union of her body and her spirit in a way she'd never experienced, and she believed—no, she *knew*—they were meant to find each other at just that nadir in their lives.

"Wow, the sex was that good, huh?" Charlotte broke into a laugh that turned into a coughing spasm.

"I'm not defending him," Charlotte said, recovering from her hawking fit. "I'm just trying to figure out how you are so certain that he's shacking up with someone else."

"Ever since we've been separated, I've seen it in his eyes, and he gets so defensive when I ask. Even today in the courtroom, while we were waiting for the judge and the lawyers to come in and carve up our lives, I told him that I went to see him last night but he wasn't home. He got so *furious.*"

"He's a jerk. But dear girl, you don't have a right to his private life anymore. He could have twenty women at once, and you have no say about it anymore. You can't even hold him to book as a parent of the girls. So, why, for god sake, do you want to go torture yourself?"

"Because, I get scared, and then I get so *pissed*." Catherine said. "Because they've taken away any right I ever had to *my* life. None of this was what I brought on myself. I didn't want to leave teaching—a profession I'm very good at—but I can't even go back and talk to anyone about it. Martin Stuart doesn't want to talk, so presto! he has all these security goons and court order legal mumbo-jumbo to keep me away from even talking to him. I never wanted to be divorced, but because Steven wants a divorce—bingo!—waltzes right through divorce court like I wasn't even there!"

"That's how divorce laws work in America any longer," Charlotte said firmly, although her voice was softer now. "He's done you a favor. You don't have to be concerned any longer who he may be with, what he's up to now. You are free of him."

"It doesn't make any sense. Just once—one time only, is all I ask—I'd like to get my way in something."

Charlotte reached for another cigarette and lit it. "Well, you did, once," she said.

"When, I'd like to know?"

Charlotte sucked in the first smoke and exhaled it in twin plumes through her nostrils. "With Don. You got your way when you divorced him. He didn't want to be divorced, either, as I remember."

"Why do you bring that up?" Catherine replied.

Charlotte shook her head. "You just said you never got your way against men. Donald was a guy who seemed pretty steady and everyone thought you guys were a good match."

"He changed," Catherine replied. "He was different when I first knew him. He was bright and intelligent and defiant of the right things, or so I thought. Then he became. . .I don't know...*dreary*. The whole marriage became so dreary and mundane, our lives running on separate tracks until there was nothing left of it after we lost Donny."

"They're always different when we first meet them," Charlotte said. "Maybe they see us differently, too, than what we become later."

"When you introduced me to Donald, I thought here was a man who was intelligent, good looking, had good health and came from a good background, had a college education. All pluses. Here was a man, I thought, who would be a suitable father for my children. He even had the right moral values: he wasn't impressed by power, he wasn't impressed by money, even though he came from it. These were virtues, and I thought all the waiting I had done had proven me right. Maybe I wasn't going to live on Country Club Road, but one day I would be a teacher, an artist, and he'd be Platte City's fire chief, and my children would know a respectable life as distanced as possible from the coarseness I grew up in. And I believed it would work that way because I had done everything right to make it happen. But when all of my plans and belief in a moral order couldn't prevent that terrible thing happening to my little boy, I guess that's when I understood how lifeless my marriage really was. I'd never in my life experienced real romance or done anything unconventional or daring. Not until Steven came along."

Charlotte looked at her oddly for a moment, expectantly.

"Donald didn't have a clue why I was really leaving him. I didn't know how to explain it to him properly then. He thought it was all because I was upset with him about Donny's death."

"Well, wasn't that it?" Charlotte said. "Wasn't that why you ended up in the hospital?"

"That's what blew things apart for me. But that wasn't all of it." Catherine said and picked up her glass. She waggled to show Charlotte it was empty, and Charlotte was quick to refill it. "If he hadn't been off chasing other people's misfortunes, he might have been there to do something when Donny needed him." She put her hand up to hold off Charlotte's anticipated response, but Charlotte only drew on her cigarette and released a slow stream of smoke. "I divorced Donald, finally, because his life didn't include me. I was what I was: The Fireman's Wife. Donald was what he was: a man living out some little boy fantasy of being a fireman. His career was his alone, and he kept it all to himself. His family was separate from his professional life. On the other hand, I actually believed that as a teacher and an artist, I would be in a society where men and women were equal and my professional life and personal life could easily intermingle with anyone else's."

"Hah!" Charlotte said.

"Hah! is right," Catherine replied. "Dumb me."

"Nobody's calling you dumb," Charlotte said.

"No, they call me worse," Catherine said. "Anyway, that was years ago, and marrying Steven proved me wrong once again—and *finally*." She reached resolutely for her glass of brandy, but her hand trembled the liquid in the glass when she raised it to her lips, and the brandy slipped like oil over her fingers.

Charlotte said, "What are we going to do about all this self-destructive behavior? People are worried about you, Cat Girl. I'm worried about you. Donald's worried about you."

"Why do you think Donald's worried about me?"

"Well, he called last night," Charlotte said.

"He called *you?* What did he want?"

"You. He was worried when he couldn't find you home last night."

"But why did he call you?" Catherine asked, immediately discomposed.

"Well, dearie, he thinks I'm your warden or housemother, I guess," Charlotte rasped. "Who knows? He thinks you and I hang out with each other and dump on the Spartas for entertainment."

In spite of herself, Catherine laughed ruefully. But now she was upset with Donald, as well, that he would call Charlotte and not tell her about it when she spoke to him this morning. For a time after they had talked on the phone, she had been feeling kindly toward him for caring about what was happening to her. But now?

"So, what did you tell him, then?" she said.

"Nothing. I told him you were probably screwing your brains out to celebrate."

"Charlotte!"

Charlotte exploded with laughter again. "Oh. Oh, please," she said between hoarse pops of air.

Catherine could hear Charlotte pretending to catch her breath, and the charade of good humor only made her feel more alone.

Catherine's daughter Holly suddenly burst into the living room, with Charlotte's daughter and Donna just behind her.

"So can we, Mom?" Holly asked.

Catherine looked at her, smiling uncertainly. "Can you what?"

"Stay for dinner tonight. Didn't Aunt Charly tell you?" Holly looked at Charlotte for help, then back again.

"We haven't had time to get around to it yet, sweetheart," Charlotte said.

"So, can we?" Holly asked again.

"Well, I don't know. You've been here all day."

"Trish's having some other kids too, and they're gonna sleep over, a slumber party."

"Oh, so it's a *slumber party*," Catherine said.

"Oh, come on, Mom," Charlotte said. "A slumber party! You remember those. And Trish doesn't get to see enough of her cousin."

"And Donna wants to stay, too?" Catherine said, looking at her daughter.

Donna nodded. "Better fun than at our house," she said. "They're having a *real* supper."

"All right, I guess you both deserve a night of fun," Catherine said. "Thank you, Aunt Charly."

"Thanks, Mom," Holly said. Then she put a curious look on her face. "Is everything okay? Are you like, you know...all *unmarried* now?"

"Yes, I am. How does that make you feel?"

"No biggie," Holly said. "It's not like it's any surprise."

Catherine nodded. "I guess not. No surprises there, all right."

For a while longer, she and Charlotte talked over even more brandy, and Catherine became giddy and warm, her troubles somehow nearly manageable once more. But finally, she could no longer avoid her own need to get back home and let everything she'd experienced wash over and out of her in the quietness of her own house.

"You're welcome to stay for dinner, too," Charlotte coaxed. "And all night if you want. The distraction could do you good."

"I really just need to go home and collapse in bed," Charlotte said. "But thanks so much. I'm sorry we've taken up so much of your time."

"Time's all I have," Charlotte said. "I like to spend it lavishly."

On the way home, Catherine looked out through the windshield at the enormous dome of unbroken sky and level horizon to the west. She was taken with the cleanness of it all, the illusion of something fixed and permanent as a painting into which the imagination followed the eye and refreshed itself. She felt the power of its geometry for a moment, the tranquil sensation of herself ethereal.

She took a different route home, north off Highway 30, to avoid the intersection with 98th. She imagined all the debris still there, and she didn't want to see it. Fifteen minutes later, she was back in the comfortable nest of her neighborhood. Once again, she was exhausted, the brief rejuvenation of the brandy having worn off, leaving a sudden hunger for sleep.

As she approached her house, she saw it, but it didn't register immediately through her great weariness. Not until she'd actually made the turn into her driveway and had to confront the problem of how she would park her car with the other one blocking the way, did she note the configuration of placards and lights on the body and roof of a Platte City Police car.

Already she was thinking of how she might express her indignation for the violation of her independence that all this craziness Martin Stuart was causing her.

Chapter 18

It was shortly after dinner, and Donald was out on the apparatus floor when Gene Metzger stuck his head in the door and called out, "House phone, Cap."

"Who is it?" Donald replied.

"Your ex-wife," Metzger said. "And she sounds real upset."

Out in the hall, Donald picked up the receiver dangling by its cord from the phone box. On the other end of the line, Catherine's voice pleaded with him, "Donald, I'm in trouble. I need your help."

"What is it, Cathy? Where are you?"

"I've been *arrested*! I'm down in the *police* station, and they're going to lock me up because I don't have the cash with me to post my bail," she cried. "Why are they doing this? What have I done that's so awful they would treat me this way?"

"I don't know what you're talking about. Tell me what's happened, Catherine." On the wall on each side of the telephone box, there were phone numbers scrawled in pencil and ink. The city phone directory sat on a chair beneath, its cover tattooed with numbers, as well.

"I've been arrested is what's happened, Donald. A policeman was waiting in my driveway when I came home from court this afternoon and right there, view of the entire neighborhood, he put *handcuffs* on me and took me to jail like a common criminal."

"But why?" he asked. He could not picture Catherine in handcuffs. Had something happened at her divorce hearing? Had she shot the son of a bitch? "What did you do?"

"I didn't *do* anything," she said with grand indignation.

Donald hesitated, then reframed his question patiently. "What did they say they were arresting you for?"

"Oh, it's so stupid. They say I'm harassing someone. *Harassing!* Like I'm shouting him down at public meetings, or threatening his life, or something. It's so stupid and childish."

Donald instantly felt relief. The alarm in Catherine's voice was translated in his mind by the hodgepodge of ciphers scrawled everywhere before him on the wall, and he saw himself in league with all of the others who felt the impotent frustration of trying to tend the needs of those outside while they were imprisoned here for twenty-four hours at a stretch. Wives and girlfriends called with requests, parents and children took ill, fenders were dented, water pipes burst, and the men on duty took down numbers to call, offered advice or admonition by phone, helpless until the end of their shift to do any more unless the order came down from division to release a man from duty on an emergency.

"Is this the guy out at the college?" Donald asked.

"Yes," she said. "Can you help me, Donald? I have to get out of here. They wouldn't let me go in and get money from the house."

"What about the girls?" he asked.

"They're staying over at Charlotte's house tonight, thank God."

"The cop just took you right there in the driveway?" Donald said.

"Yes! I told you, he just put handcuffs on me and told me I was going to jail."

"So tell me what you want me to do," Donald said.

"I want you to get me out of here! Can you come down and give them forty dollars to get me out? I'll pay you back as soon as I get home."

"I can't just leave the station, Catherine. I'm not off duty until seven in the morning."

"I know that. I just need you to take an hour—a *half* hour off—and come pay them their blood money."

Donald said, "Okay. I'll see if I can get one of the off-duty guys to go down."

"Why not *you,* Donald? Why can't you help me yourself?" she keened in his ear.

"I'll do what I can, Catherine. I'll call the district chief, but I don't think this qualifies as an emergency—bailing your ex-wife out of jail." His own frustration was mounting, the insistence in her pleas sharpened by the anger in her voice.

"This *is* an emergency! You can't just leave me here all weekend, I've got to get home. I have children to take care of. *Your* children, so this *is* an emergency."

"That didn't seem to bother you last night when you left them alone half the night," Donald said, giving over to his own indignation. "I can't believe you'd let yourself get involved in something like this, for god sake."

"Forget it. I'm sorry I asked. I didn't mean to interrupt your important work; just go back to watching television or sweeping up the floors or sitting on your *ass* waiting for something more important to happen."

Donald did not say anything.

"I don't believe this is happening," she said. "I can't believe you're doing this again. You're *never* there when your family needs you!"

"Catherine—"

The line snapped dead.

For a time, Donald stood before the phone box, gripping the receiver as if it were the head of a snake. The dial tone hummed like an insect, and finally, he hung the receiver back on its hook. He went into his office and slammed the door shut, then picked up his own phone and tapped out the four-digit extension for Kyle Thorpe, his district chief. Someone else answered. Chief Thorpe was "out in the territory," Donald was informed. The territory was District 5, with its three fire stations in the central part of the city.

"When's he due back?" Donald asked.

"Hard to say. Maybe an hour, hour-and-a-half."

Donald hung up. He could try calling Thorpe over the radio, but he didn't want his conversation to go out over the air. He drew in his breath and let it out, his hands over his face, trying to ward off the swarm of stinging emotions and find the one dominant feeling, the one clear thought, that would show him what he was to do. Finally, he dialed the Assistant Chief in his Station 1 headquarters downtown. He got Connie Towers, who received calls for all the brass.

"How did your little rookie's debut go with the press?" Connie asked him.

"Actually it went pretty well," Donald said. "She did just fine."

"Well, it don't surprise me," Connie said. "She's the weightlifter, right?"

"Yeah. How'd you know?"

"Honey, I know everything. That's why I'm here running things."

"Well, I need to talk to Assistant Chief Fleming. Do you know if he's available?" Donald said.

"If he ain't in the john, I'll ring you through," Connie said, and immediately he was on hold.

It was Merle Fleming who answered next, and Donald felt a hitch of anxiety at the surly edge to Fleming's voice. "What do you want, Captain?" Fleming was a man in his fifties, a hard-nosed officer with a chip on his shoulder for people he thought might know more than he—which, so far as Donald could tell, included anyone with better than a high school diploma. Donald thought him a stupid man, which made his relationship with him even tenser than with other brass, because he was sure Fleming was just smart enough to know Donald's feelings toward him.

"I need a favor, Chief," Donald said. "I need an hour to take care of some personal business outside the station."

"This have anything to do with Gallant?" Fleming said, a quick note of concern in his tone.

"No, sir. This is a…well, kind of a personal emergency," Donald said.

"What kind of emergency?"

Donald felt himself flush with annoyance. He did not want to explain anything to this cretin that would give him something to hold over him. Still…. "My ex-wife…she's gotten herself in some trouble, and I need to go down to central police station and sign some papers or something."

"Sign 'em tomorrow, why don't you?" Fleming said.

"Well, sir, that will be too late. I have to do it shortly, or else it will be too late and things will be…well, complicated more."

"You have to do it *shortly*, huh?" Fleming said, mocking him. "What's going on, Sparta? Tell me what the problem is, and we'll see what we can do about it."

Donald drew in his breath and held it a second, both to control his temper and to give himself a moment to choose his reply.

"She's been arrested. I'm not even sure what the specific charges are, but she wants me to come down and post some sort of bond for her, because they didn't give her an opportunity to get any money before she was taken downtown."

"Well," Fleming said, "isn't that the shits." Donald could detect the smile in the Assistant Chief's voice. There was a pause while, apparently, he waited for Donald to elaborate, because the next thing Fleming said was, "So?"

"Well, so I'd like permission to do that, sir."

"Off the top of my head, I can't see how I can permit it. That's not an emergency, Captain. What is it, DUI? Shoplifting? What?"

"Sir, my kids are at home alone," Donald lied. "If I don't post bond, she won't be able to get home maybe until Monday—"

"So post bond. Call a damned bondsman and send him down there. That's simple enough," Fleming said. "See what I mean? This isn't a bona fide emergency here. There are options. Call a friend. Call a neighbor. This is more like routine business than an emergency."

Donald could sense Fleming gloating behind the receiver, proud of himself for having intelligence enough to come up with a string of alternatives. And they *were* logical; the man was right about the nature of the problem and its solutions. He couldn't tell Fleming that he had to do this himself, in person, to prove something to Catherine.

"I'm sorry about this, I know how frustrating it is being stuck at the station when someone wants us," Fleming said, sounding paternal. "But that's the nature of the game we chose to play in, don't you see? We have to be ready to help out the rest of the good citizens in our community when they need us, too."

"Yes, sir," Donald said.

"Well, anything else I can do for you?"

"No, sir," Donald said.

"Good. Nice talking to you." And Fleming hung up.

He had blown it. He should have known. If he had only gotten Kyle Thorpe right off, Donald probably would have been given permission to leave the station for an hour of personal business. Now that he had been denied by someone at Fire Department Headquarters, he had no recourse. And he had blown it with Catherine. Again. "You're *never* there when your family needs you!"—her accusation lacerating the emotional scar from five years ago now.

There had been only the one time he'd ever been released from duty for a family emergency.

It was about the same time in the afternoon as today—around four o'clock—and he'd been relieved right off the fire line by Kyle Thorpe, who was a battalion chief then.

Donald had made a three-alarm fire that afternoon at Playmor Bowling Alleys in his alarm district, and the call had initially come in as a smell-smoke-see-no-fire alarm. But Engine 55 and Aerial 53 had no sooner cleared the doors of the station and hit the street when the status was upgraded to two alarms. Engine 55 had been the first unit in on the fire, eight blocks from the station at the Cedarcrest Shopping Center, and flames from burning lacquers and waxes on the alleys were already rolling out the entrance doors. Donald himself had called for a third alarm, even before the battalion chief had arrived from his home station at Engine 42's house on 68th and Franklin. There was so much incendiary material and open space in a bowling alley, it was like a warehouse when one got going. Polyurethane and waxed coatings on the hardwood lanes became liquid rivers of fire; acoustic ceiling tiles and plastic bowling balls melted and rose in tar-black clouds of toxic smoke.

It was during the clamor of setting up the initial attack on the fire—Czernecky, Wesson, and Donald on a two-and-a-half-inch line fogging through a blown-out front window of the lounge, Metzger on the mounted water cannon atop the truck's hosebed, sweeping the roofline while Aerial 53's truckmen vented the roof with their axes and power saw to let the superheated air and toxic smoke escape—that Donald missed hearing another alarm come in over the truck's radio, this one a rescue call for Medic 40 to the scene of an automobile-pedestrian accident in the six hundred block of North 101st Street four miles away. "*Child struck by car*," the dispatcher reported.

Twenty minutes later, when there were two aerials and five pumpers working the fire and Donald and his men had been redirected by the district chief to hump their line through the shopping center's central mall and work the fire through the main doors to the alleys, he was unaware of Medic 40's status call to the dispatcher—*"en route County Hospital with one male patient, ten years of age, lacerations and contusions of head and torso, possible fractured skull, compound fracture of right femur. Respiration shallow, pulse irregular, BP ninety-eight over seventy-eight. Code Three"*—the code number signifying life-threatening injury.

Then forty minutes later, while Donald was inside the Eleventh Frame Lounge, his face masked and a replenished air tank on his back, crawling with a flashlight on his hands and knees through the rubble while two crews with inch-and-a-half handlines mopped up the hot spots, Medic 40, taking a diversionary route on its way back to its own station, pulled up in the parking lot outside long enough for the squad captain to locate and confer with the battalion chief.

They found Donald a few minutes later. The chief had sent in another firefighter, who had called Donald's name from the doorway off the central mall into the steamy, blackened interior of the alleys. Wesson heard him, tapped Donald on the shoulder and relieved him at his task, the old man dropping to his hands and knees, nosing like a Basset hound among the ruins.

"Chief wants to see you outside," the firefighter, a kid named Bennett from Aerial 33, reported and hurried back out through the acrid stench of smoke still holding to the ceilings of the mall.

"There's been an accident, Don," his battalion chief, Kyle Thorpe, had said. "The guys from Medic Forty just took your son to the hospital. He was riding his bike and was hit by a car over on North Hundred-First Street."

Donald had not comprehended at first. In the middle of the parking lot with all the apparatus of his profession set up like artillery, diesel engines rattling, pumps whining, the PA speakers on the trucks amplifying the voices of the captains with walkie-talkies inside the building, the responses of pump operators and the central station dispatcher outside, and with smoke and steam still rising from the ventilated roof and empty windows—Donald could not comprehend what Chief Thorpe was saying about his son's bicycle and a car in a quiet residential area so far away from all this commotion.

"You're relieved here. I'll have someone take you back to your station, and you can go on into the hospital from there," the chief said.

"What happened? How bad is it?" Donald asked finally.

"He was hit by a car, apparently. On his bike. The captain from Medic Forty that took him into County say he's got a head injury, broken femur, maybe some internals. They took him in Code Three." Each inclusion of another detail, each small fact of procedure, brought into focus for Donald the reality of that other emergency call in another part of the district that involved his own family. He shucked his air tank and mask.

He was driven back to his stationhouse by the chief's driver, and he'd called the hospital emergency room. He was told his son was in surgery. The desk nurse did not have a current report of his condition. Was Mrs. Sparta there? he wanted to know. He was assured she was, somewhere on the third floor in the surgery waiting area, did he want her paged? No, he said, he would be along shortly.

Donald knew what he looked like right then, the black and white panda-faced markings defining where his mask had been and where the rim of his helmet met the back of his neck and along his forehead, the exposed skin grimy, the insides of his ears flaked with soot. And the stink of wet smoke and burned plastic in his hair, in his sweaty clothes. He could not go into an antiseptic and orderly hospital looking like he did. A few more minutes to put himself in order, so that he could meet head on this newest challenge in a succession of challenges that, in his agitated state of mind, remained connected to the fire call he was currently on: he'd been relieved from his duty on the line, but not from the scheme of the events that had been set in motion from the moment he'd left the station aboard Engine 55 and was still a part of the adrenaline reaction that he'd been experiencing all along.

Donald showered, put on his street clothes, and with his hair still wet, he bolted from the station to his pickup truck parked in the side lot. By the time he reached the hospital, an hour and forty-five minutes had elapsed since the initial alarm for Medic Forty had gone out over the air from the dispatcher's desk. This was important to him later. He had checked with the 911 center, had pieced together the events during that period while his son's life was ebbing on the operating table—what he had been doing at the moment, why he was not any quicker in getting to his wife's side at the hospital—because that hour and forty-five minutes became, in the course of time, the cane wielded to punish him again and again.

At the hospital he found Catherine sitting in an alcove outside the double doors leading to the surgery suite. He was shocked by the sight of her. Her blouse and the lap of her slacks were stiff with blood, and the whites of her eyes were fiery from tears. She was no longer crying, however. "You're too late," she said. Her voice was hard and rusty as iron. "He was asking for you while he was still conscious. The whole time he kept asking, 'Where's Dad? Is Dad coming?'"

"What do you mean 'too late'?"

"Our son is dead, Donald." The pronouncement was too harsh even for her to utter in hurting him. She sucked in her breath with an involuntary shudder and let it escape again in an animal sound of incalculable anguish.

"What do you mean?" Donald repeated lamely. What *he* meant was, he was here now, he had arrived. It couldn't possibly be over before he'd weighed the choices, made some further decisions, could it?

"I was with him. I held him in my arms until the rescue squad came, and all he could think of was you. And all you could think of was you."

"I was at a fire, they came and got me. As soon as I heard…. What happened, for godsake?" Donald said.

Catherine let him know. For over an hour she waited for him to join her so he could combine his strength with hers to keep their son alive. Their son had died even while she was on the waiting room telephone trying to contact Donald. "Where *were* you?" she accused him. "It would have made a difference if you'd been here. It would have! He was alive when they brought him in. He was talking to me. He asked for you, and you didn't come. There was plenty of time for you to get here."

"I was at a fire, I said. I came as soon as they told me," he said.

"Look at you!" she cried, pointing at him.

He looked. He understood then what she was saying. He had gone back to the station to clean up, to change his clothes. She sat there in the hospital waiting room, her own clothes carmine with Donny's blood.

From the doctor, Donald had heard the medical explanation. Before there was anything that might be done to relieve the problem, his son's brain had swelled beyond the capacity of his fractured skull to confine it, and he was hemorrhaging not only in his head, but also, as they discovered, from his spleen, which had been ruptured, as well. The force of the blow by the bumper, the way he had landed on his head when he had been thrown up and over the trunk of the car—they were sorry, they'd done all they were humanly capable of doing with injuries so severe and time so short.

From his daughter Holly, he had learned later the circumstances, heard her description of the two of them racing down One-Hundred-First Street two blocks from their house, Donny in the lead and looking back to see how great the distance was between them; and of the big Cadillac backing steadily out of its driveway, an old man at the wheel, his old wife beside him, their car reaching the end of their driveway at the precise moment that Donny jumped the curb with his prized Huffy banana bike and landed on the sidewalk in an acrobatic stunt he had pulled over and over on their own sidewalk in front of the house; and of the way he had collided with the back corner of the car, his pratfall separation from the bike which crumpled under the back wheel while he body-surfed across the trunk, up the back window, and tumbled head-over-heels onto the concrete intersection of driveway and sidewalk on the other side.

Donald had gone through all the details in his mind to determine if things might have been different; but he could not find any way by which his presence could have changed what happened to his son. And even in the two days which followed, before the funeral, when Catherine had permitted him to hold her in his arms—she was silent during all that time—he still could not find a single moment in that entire chain of moments when he might have made a difference, except he could have stood in front of her to shield her in some way from the direct assault of the surgeon's pronouncement when he came out of that operating room to tell her that there was nothing more he could do. She might have been spared the wait alone in that little alcove room next to surgery wondering how in the world she could possibly endure such monstrous information while Donald was taking a shower.

Now he sat helplessly holding the telephone considering who next to call to go help free her from jail because he himself was once again powerless to act. He decided Charlotte would be the most logical to step in. She was almost family still, and she knew about Catherine's escapades, maybe knew by now that Catherine had been arrested. If he could avoid calling a bondsman, he would. But, when no one answered at Charlotte's—he let her phone ring over to voice mail twice before conceding she was not home—he was at a loss where next to turn. He did not want to involve anyone he worked with for obvious personal reasons. For lack of anyone else he could think of, he called Casey Hall's home in Cambridge. But it was Casey's wife Jessie who answered, and she informed him Casey wasn't home. "He's still chasing around after information on that fire this morning."

"Well, tell him I called, and I'll try to catch up with him some other time."

"What did you need?"

"Oh, just a favor. I'm stuck here in the station and I needed someone to run an errand for me."

"I've got nothing to do till supper, what do you need?"

"No, it's all the way into Platte City," Donald said, but he was already thinking that if Jessie didn't do it, he wasn't going to find anyone else.

"Well, now, I need to get out. I'm sick of being in the house. That snowstorm depressed me something fierce and I'd like to get out of here and go shopping."

"Well...," he said, "if you really wouldn't mind." He explained to her the predicament Catherine was in, and what Fleming had told him when he'd tried to go off duty for an hour.

"Shoot, that's no problem. I don't think I've ever been in a police station in all the time I've lived here. It ought to be interesting."

"I really appreciate this," Donald said. "I'm concerned about her, is all."

"Sure you are. You're not convincing anyone that you're not still attached to that woman."

When he hung up, he leaned against the wall for a bit, thinking about what Jessie had said. He hadn't thought she knew him well enough to even have any opinion of his emotional life. He saw Jessie very infrequently and usually at gatherings with lots of other people, firefighters mostly, and he had not been married to Catherine now for almost five years. He had arrived some time ago at the watershed in his love for her, he believed: he cared for her yet, but he had become more and more uninvolved. He carried both of these emotional attitudes simultaneously. There were days like today when something akin to his old need for her flared again like a fresh rash; and there were many more days when he knew only that he had loved her once but couldn't for the life of him remember what that was really like. Only, there had been no one to fill the void left by her absence.

On the wall next to the phone, he located the number Catherine had given him and he had written down for the police department jail.

"Mackey. Holding." The officer who answered had one of those abrasive voices of someone older who had abused his throat for years with alcohol and tobacco smoke.

Once again, Donald wasn't sure what to say. "Yes, this Donald Sparta. I'm a captain on Engine Company Fifty-five, Platte City Fire."

"What can I do for you, Captain?" the officer said.

"You're holding a woman down there, a Catherine Harper, I think?"

"Harper? Yeah. Long dark hair, sorta moony-eyed woman?" the officer said.

Donald smiled. "That's her. Anyway, there's someone coming down, a friend, to post her bond, and I just wanted to know if you could tell her for me."

"She knows."

"She does?"

"Yeah, she talked to him already."

"That was me she talked to," he said, thinking Mackey must be referring to the call she'd just made to him. "But the person coming down is a friend."

"What'd you say your name was?" Mackey asked.

"Sparta. Donald Sparta."

"No, it wasn't you. You were earlier. This is her husband. He's coming down to post bond and take her home."

"Oh," Donald replied. "Well then…."

"Won't hurt none to have two people coming, though. She needs to get outta here real bad." He chuckled. "I'll tell ya, partner, this has not been a beneficial experience for her. She's about to come unglued."

He managed to thank the man and hang up. Now he did not know what to do. Even as he was dialing Casey Hall's number again, he knew he'd have to apologize to both of them for the wild goose chase, when he was already embarrassed at having again revealed to outsiders how ill-managed his personal life had become. *Damn it, damn it, damn it,* he berated himself with each ring of the phone that went unanswered.

Back in his room, while everyone was watching the 5:00 p.m. local news to catch them up on any new information and to see themselves once more in the footage of the morning fire, Donald dropped on the bed with his uniform still on, trying only to hasten this day into extinction. Through the walls he was aware of the continual murmuring white noise of the television and the voices of the men in the day room. Nearer at hand, it was the occasional static crackling of a keyed mike and the droning voice of the dispatcher coming from the scanning monitor on his bedside table, which he left on at low volume to hear what was going on in the rest of the City. Around 5:30 p.m., Engine 15 and Aerial 13 from the downtown station went into service on a fire in a stack of wooden pallets at one of the warehouses out by the airport. Engine 25 responded, as well.

Then, from the next door down the hall came the sounds of water running in the pipes as Mike Krupa, captain of Aerial 53, got ready to shower. For Krupa, it was another night, another notch in the long tally-stick of duty shifts that would stretch uninterrupted to his retirement. Donald wondered sometimes how Mike found it bearable. Donald accepted his own ennui as a consequence of choices he'd made to be where he was; the limits on his ambitions were his own devising. He was good at what he did; in general, he loved what he did. He had just become lazy at it in the past few years. But now, in the events that had unfolded today, he understood all that would have to change if he was to make it through even another year on the department. He could not much longer ignore what he had done to himself. Unlike Mike Krupa, Donald could master whatever book knowledge he needed, and it seemed, from this vantage point in his life, it was an insult to Krupa for him not to do it. An insult, as well, to people like Charlie Wesson, who never rose beyond the lowest rank but were among the best hose men or ladder men in the department; and to young Metzger and Deborah Gallant, the new order of firefighters who needed a new breed of line officers to break ranks with the old guard before they were burned out by their redundancies. If the events of the day had pointed up anything, it was that he could no longer ignore what he was supposed to do at this point in his career: test for Battalion Chief and apply for the opening with the next retirement of a chief. Or get out.

Lying on his cot, stranded on some sandbar in the river between wakefulness and sleep, he heard the sound of someone scuffing softly down the hall toward the visitor's bathroom. Deborah Gallant would be preparing for her first night bunking in as a member of Engine 55. He recalled now that he had impulsively asked her to go to dinner with him on their evening off duty. And she had accepted, even when he tried to retract his offer. He thought about what lay ahead for them: the awkwardness of their conversation, getting to know one another away from the station; the difference in experience and age. That he should have found thinking about her even the least pleasurable meant he was already in danger of making a disastrous mistake for both their careers. He could not ignore that, either. He would have to resolve it when he was awake and refreshed and was thinking clearly. Like an officer.

Part III
Friday Night / Saturday Morning

Chapter 19

At the Platte City police station, Steven presented himself to a desk sergeant in the lobby. The lobby was little bigger than a doctor's waiting room—against one open wall, a short Formica-topped counter; opposite, a row of four straight-backed chairs with vinyl-padded seats. At the counter was the duty sergeant who handled the public. He sat on a bar stool in front of a computer monitor. Behind him was a desk with a bank of phones and above that a shelf on the concrete block wall with five closed-circuit TV monitors picturing various hallways and the front door through which Steven had just entered. This counter was the barrier between the outside and the subterranean recesses of the building that were hinted at in the bleak views of tunneled hallways on the screens. The whole place filled him with dread, and for an instant he felt trapped, thinking Catherine's phone call for help may have been a ploy to lure him down to his own imprisonment. "I'm here to bail out Catherine Harper?" he said, his inflection at the end rising to a question.

"Post bond," the sergeant replied, turning to a computer keyboard just below the countertop.

"Beg your pardon?" Steven said.

"No bail's been set," the sergeant said. "You're just posting an appearance bond so the *lay-dy* can go home and come back Monday to go before the judge and plead a citation." He drew out the word "lady" in a hesitation of sarcasm.

"How much?" Steven said.

"Just looking here," the sergeant replied. He clicked some keys on the keyboard and squinted at the screen of the monitor mounted on the countertop. He tapped another key. "Should be forty dollars, if there's no other hold on her." He squinted at the screen. "Yep, forty dollars and she's all yours."

Steven paid—drawing out the cash slowly from his wallet—a twenty, a ten, a five, five ones. The sergeant wrote out a receipt and rang up someone on one of the phones at the desk behind him. "Bring up Catherine Harper. She's being released." He looked up at Steven when he'd hung up. "She'll be up in a minute. Go ahead and take a seat."

Steven retreated obediently to one of the four chairs against the opposite wall. The absence of anyone else in the lobby only fed his anxiety. He looked at the white receipt paper in his hand. He'd never purchased someone's freedom before.

When she'd called him a half-hour ago, he'd just arrived back home to wait out the time before he had to return to school to pick up Valerie Caine for dinner. The evening newspaper had been delivered and was lying in the hall outside his door. The front page had a big color photo of a fireball blooming above a burning truck, the headline below: Death Count Uncertain in Fiery Crash.

He'd drawn the curtains over the windows, left the lights off, except for a single table lamp next to his chair, and settled in with the paper on his lap. In the picture, the firemen were dwarfed by the fire, but Steven could still make out the name on the back of the coat of the man in the foreground of the shot. SPARTA. Catherine's first husband was crouched behind two other men on a water line, like an umpire waiting for the pitch. Great dramatic irony, he'd thought, that on the day of her second divorce, Catherine's first husband should be facing a moment out of Dante's *Inferno*.

He had just begun to read the accompanying article when the telephone in the kitchen rang. When he'd picked up, it was Catherine shrilling at him on the other end.

"Steven, thank God you're home. Please, this is really important. Please, oh please, I need your help."

When he had quieted her a bit, she told him about her arrest, the policeman at her door, Martin Stuart's betrayal. *Ah, Martin Stuart,* he'd thought. *That was it, then.*

"Please, Steven, come and get me, and then I promise I'll leave you alone."

Here was an opportunity to show good will, he thought. "All right, Catherine. I'll be there as soon as I can."

"Bring cash, Steven," she said. "They don't take checks or cards."

A stout woman with tight dark curls and rimless glasses suddenly pushed open the entrance door and rushed into the room, past Steven in his chair against the wall, and up to the window where the sergeant was still seated at his computer. She stood impatiently, waiting for him to look up.

"I'm here to post bond for Catherine Harper?" she said when he finally looked over the countertop at her.

Steven focused on them.

The sergeant looked at her with a quizzical smile. "She's already spoken for."

"I'm sorry?" the woman said.

176

"That fellow over there has already posted her bond. She's on her way up."

The woman turned and looked at Steven. "But her ex-husband sent me to take her home. She supposedly called him, but he was on duty and couldn't leave."

Steven rose and came across the narrow lobby. "Hi. I'm Steven Harper. Her ex-husband. It was me she called to bail her out. Who are you?"

"Oh!" The woman looked confused. Her deep brown eyes, magnified behind her glasses, appeared like the snouts of two dazed mice. She turned back to the sergeant. "Her ex-husband. Donald Sparta. He's a captain on the Platte City FD; he called me because Catherine had called him to come get her."

"And you are?" the sergeant said.

"Jessie Hall. I'm Casey Hall's wife. Fire Chief of Cambridge? We've known Donald and Catherine for years." She seemed totally flustered now. "Used to know Catherine, anyway."

Immediately Steven sensed opportunity. He could release himself from his mission, let this woman take Catherine home and be relieved of any emotional aftermath that was sure to arise if he drove her back to their—to *her* house. But in the same moment he relented. It would not look good to have his ex-wife rescued by some emissary of her former ex-husband. It was a territorial obligation he believed was his to discharge. "Ah, well," he said. "She must have called all her ex-husbands. Covering her bases, I would guess."

Jessie Hall shook her head, perplexed. "Okay. I see, I think. You must be her...husband? Steven Harper?"

"Her ex-husband," he said, and delighted in the look she gave him. "Most recent ex. Brand new, officially today ex. So, I drew the short straw as the rookie."

Jessie Hall frowned and drew a deep breath, as if contemplating. "Well, I guess it's okay, then." She turned to the sergeant. "So she's being freed, yes?"

"Yes, ma'am," the sergeant said, a smirk twisting his lips. "As we speak."

"Okay. I'm sorry for the confusion," she said. She nodded at Steven. "It was nice meeting you. I guess."

"Likewise," he said.

"Say hi to her for me," she said as she started for the door. Her head down, she pulled the door open and disappeared into the outer hall.

"Well, that was interesting," the sergeant said. "Hope you're the right guy she's expecting."

In one of the TV monitors above the desk behind the sergeant, Steven saw movement—a greenish-gray top view of what looked like Catherine's image passing beneath the surveillance camera in company of a light-haired woman in uniform.

At the moment the sergeant stamped a paper on the countertop with a gavel-like rap, Catherine emerged from another steel-clad door beside the counter and made straight for Steven. The female officer followed behind, but stopped at the desk to confer with the sergeant.

Steven smiled at the sight of her. Her hair was disheveled, her face drawn and tight.

"Is that it, then?" Steven said.

"Yes, let's get out of here."

In the car, driving toward Catherine's house, he said, "So who's Jessie Hall?"

"What?"

"Jessie Hall. A friend, I gather, of Don."

He related the scene in the lobby of the jail, the woman who had come at the behest of her ex-husband Donald. "You asked him to help?"

"Yes," she said. "But he couldn't leave his fire station. He said he couldn't do anything for me. He was just going to let me rot there in jail. Let his children starve alone at home. Then I called my former sister-in-law, but she wasn't home. So, you see, I didn't just automatically turn to you. You *were* my last resort."

Steven laughed ironically. "I can see the experience hasn't dulled your knack for hyperbole."

Catherine glared out the window.

"So what was it like, rotting in jail?"

"What an awful, awful experience. I can't believe people can be so humiliating."

"What happened? Torture? Cockroaches and rats in the cells? Did they put you in a lineup and shine bright lights in your eyes?"

"Worse," she said. At the police station, she'd been fingerprinted and had her picture taken with a number hanging from her neck. She held her hands up and showed Steven tracings of ink yet in the pads of her fingertips. "I'm going to be a woman with a record. A *rap* sheet. I'll never get a job now."

She was silent a moment. Then she looked at him with imploring eyes. "They *strip*-searched me, Steven. This fat, dyke woman cop took me into a little room right off the main hall, with a window right in the door, and made me take all my clothes off—*everything*!—and then she made me bend over and…well, *spread* myself open, the cheeks of my ass, and she even searched me *there*!"

Steven tried to envision the moment. "No kidding? How did she search you? I mean—"

"With her fingers!" Catherine said disgustedly. "She put on a rubber glove and poked in my vagina and then stuck a finger right up my rectum."

He couldn't help laughing. "Find anything?"

"It wasn't funny!" she said. "I was so outraged. I told her at first I wasn't going to submit to any of it, not even taking my clothes off, that I wasn't some dangerous criminal or drug dealer. She kept saying it was policy, *standard procedure* for anyone who was being arrested and detained in a cell overnight, just like handcuffing me to bring me down to the police station was *regulations*. And I said, 'Well, you're just going to have to alter your procedure, I'm not planning to stay overnight in any case.' And she said, 'No matter, sweetie, it has to be done, and if you continue to be uncooperative, I'll have to call in a couple of other uniformed officers'—and she meant *men*— suit myself but she was going to conduct her little search."

"All this for harassment?" Steven said.

"Isn't it the stupidest thing you've ever heard of? Why do they want to persecute me?" Catherine said.

"Who?"

"Everyone. The police, the campus cops, Martin Stuart."

"Nobody's persecuting you."

"Well, what would you call it, then?"

"People protecting themselves from someone who refuses to leave them alone when they don't wish to continue a relationship with her."

"Well, they have an overactive way of doing it. Why do they want to put me in jail for something as harmless as wanting to talk and clear up some miscommunication between two intelligent people?"

Put just that way, there was no real comeback, as far as Steven could see. "Hmm. Well, maybe he doesn't see it that way. Especially when you've been told more than once he doesn't want to talk any longer about hypothetical miscommunications."

She looked sidelong at him, and then out the window on her side of the car. "All he would have to do is tell me he was wrong to fire me and promise to take me back on in the Fall. But now it's criminally wrong for me to go anywhere near him." She seemed to be speaking more to herself now than to Steven. "I only wanted to clear up this misunderstanding he has about my intentions."

"Evidently he doesn't need it cleared up."

"I just don't know why so many men can get away with harassing women, and a woman can't do the same."

Steven said, "Obviously you don't keep up with the news. Women are suing men right and left for harassment in the workplace. It's *the* big sport right now."

"Damned few are successful."

Steven let it go, hoping she would stay quiet long enough for him to get her home and drop her off. Coming to get her out of jail had been a bad idea. Now they were very close to one of those explosive moments that had made marriage to her like crossing a mined harbor in a bomb-laden freighter. How many tons of emotional cargo already lay at the bottom of those two and a half years!

"Actually," she said, and chuckled suddenly, "things might be equaling out more."

Steven nodded but didn't speak.

"When I was in the police car on the way down to the station, there were two calls that came over the policeman's radio in his car. They weren't for the guy who was driving me downtown, they were for someone else. One of them, the man who tells the cars where they're supposed to go, says, 'Car Thirty-four'—or whatever number it was, I forget now—and then he gives this address on Pine Street—Fifty-three-oh-four Pine Street'—and says, 'See a Rhonda. Man in the house refusing to leave.' And I thought, yeah, see if they throw him in jail. But then, not five minutes later, just before we got downtown, another call went out for a different police car to go to some address in Corinth, and the voice says, 'See a Mark. Woman refusing to leave.' Can you imagine that? In Corinth, a man calling the police to get rid of a woman who won't leave his house? The policeman driving me said he hears a lot of 'woman refusing to leave' calls lately. But usually the person has left before the police even get there. I got this really sad image of these two lonely people being rejected by someone they loved, and I thought, wouldn't it be nice if the man-refusing-to-leave could be introduced to the woman-refusing-to-leave, as a sort of a public service to help lonely people find each other."

Steven laughed in spite of himself. That was one of the charming things about Catherine: her quixotic humor that always warmed him.

When they reached Catherine's house, Steven pulled into the driveway and stopped in the center between the two garage doors. He did not take his hands off the steering wheel. He noted the house would need painting again this year, and the junipers on the terrace by the front door needed to be trimmed down.

"Don't you want to come in for some coffee?" Catherine asked.

"No, I have to get back home," he said. He looked at his watch.

"Hot date waiting?"

"I'll see you later," he said.

"Will you?" she asked. She was smiling, but her smile was tight. His nerves drew taut.

"Sorry. A figure of speech. I need to get home," he said. "It's been an exhausting day for me, too." He was becoming testy now, always the consequence of his anxiety fencing with her over her incursions into his private life. Why did she press to know things she didn't want to know? And why did he always seem to concede eventually and tell her?

"Well, I need to get your money for you. Come in while I write you a check," she said. He felt relieved that she'd relented so quickly. "Or would you rather have it in cash?"

"No, that's fine," Steven said. "Don't worry about it. Consider it—" He wasn't sure what to say. He wanted to be on his way. Even the sight of her house from the outside was making him claustrophobic, depressed in an obscure way. "Too many bad vibes," his students would say. Inside that front door was the burial ground for a part of his past he was anxious to distance himself from. Didn't she feel it, too? That house had been the site of a lot of misery for her, as well, and he wondered how she could stay there. A fresh start in a new setting might be just the thing to cure her. "Consider it severance pay," he said. But by the way she winced and pinched in her lips, he could see that had been the wrong thing to say, even lightly.

"I intend to pay you back," she said. "I would have had it with me if that policeman had just let me go inside to get it before he took me away."

"Why couldn't he?"

"More *procedure*. The man who arrested me, actually he was very sympathetic. He kept apologizing for having to treat me that way." She described for him the scene in her driveway, how she was required to lean against the police car while he patted her sides and hips. "You could tell he felt stupid doing it. He was courteous the whole time. I was so embarrassed I couldn't stop crying."

She opened the door and got out but kept her hand on the frame as she leaned back in. "Thank you for your trouble. I really appreciate it."

"When you called, I was just reading in the paper about the fire this morning. Your ex-husband's picture was on the front page."

"Which ex-husband?" Catherine said.

Steven ignored her jibe. "Anyway, he looked too busy to be bailing you out of jail."

"That was hours before. He probably didn't have another thing to do all day, after that. He just wanted to let me stew, probably."

His father used to say that, too, of people whom he thought were responsible for their own troubles: *let them stew in their own juices.* "Well,

181

now don't worry about what's going to happen," he said. "I can't imagine a judge will do anything more than dismiss the complaint, or at most slap you on the wrist with a warning not to go near Martin again."

"That's not what I'm worried about," Catherine said. "I'm worried about facing my kids now. I mean, here I'm going to have to explain to them why their mother is a criminal."

"You're not a criminal," Steven said. He smiled. "A miscreant. Tell them their mother is a miscreant. They'll probably think that's cool."

"Well, now, will you wait here while I go get your money—?"

"Mail it to me, if you want. I want to get home." He began to inch the car backward down the drive.

"Okay," she said. She shut his car door and stood back a step, leaning forward slightly to smile at him through the window.

Without his intending it, he squeaked the back tires on the concrete drive as the car leapt backward. He smiled apologetically when he turned into the street, gave a quick wave, and drove off while she stood in the middle of the drive watching after him.

It was after 7:00 p.m. by the time Steven and Valerie Caine were sitting in a snug booth at Michelangelo's—a downtown restaurant—where they were enjoying spaghetti and salad, with warm garlic bread and Chianti.

"This is really great wine," she said after her first sip.

He smiled. "Chianti's a very sociable wine."

"I like red wines more than I like white," she said. "Which is just the opposite of my friends. Most of the girls I know like white wines. But they're too sweet for me. Reds are warmer, don't you think?"

"Another glass?" he offered.

Over dinner, she told him all about herself. He conceded one of the blessings of youth was that its history was short and could be readily related in a single sitting. But he envied her for all she had yet to experience, and the mettle she possessed to take it on.

She told him how she had been raised by her mother, who divorced her father for "messing around with another woman" when Valerie was seven years old.

"I saw what it did to my mom. I thought she was really going to die over it. I don't think I'd ever seen her cry as much as she did the first year he wasn't living there. I decided that was never going to happen to me, you know?"

Steven assured her he knew. "But every relationship has its final day," he said. "People leave us or we have to leave them and move on."

182

"I hear that, all right." Suddenly, her eyebrows knit and her eyes shone tragically. "I feel so sorry for *you*," she said. "I can only imagine how bad a divorce must be, seeing what it did to my mother."

"Have you ever broken up with someone?" he asked.

"Oh sure, lots of times. But it wasn't really breaking up. Not for me, anyway. Well, except for one time, the first time I really cared about someone. That hurt, I guess, because it was the first time, and everything. It was sort of sad, in one way, but sort of sweet in another."

Steven picked up his fork and stabbed at an olive among the remnants of the antipasto. "When was that?"

"When I was thirteen. I had a crush on my best friend Rebecca Cowper's older brother."

"Ah, a crush on someone older," Steven said, nodding his head at a circumstance he understood fully. He popped the olive into his mouth.

"They lived near us in Beaumont. Rebecca and me were ballet freaks and hung with each other constantly for about two years taking dance. I must've spent half my life over at their house, and like I said, I got this crush on her older brother Brad and he really liked me, too. So I guess we were boyfriend-girlfriend; at least I liked to think we were. Poor Brad kept getting in trouble in school, so his parents decided they'd send him to Missouri to this military school there, to give him some discipline. God, I've read what they do to normal little boys to make some sort of stiff-backed robots out of them. They say more kids get screwed up in those places, turning them into nerds or perverts at boarding schools. Especially military ones."

He watched her mouth as she spoke, the lips animated and lambent, revealing flashes of her white teeth, the pink tip of her tongue.

"I couldn't agree more," he said. "Military academies are factories for Philistines."

"Yeah," she said. "Anyway, it was about two-three days before he was leaving to go away, and I was real sad, and he was, too. I was up in his bedroom helping him pack some things, and his folks were gone, and Becky was with her own boyfriend way downstairs in the rec room shooting pool—and that's when I lost it.... Well, you know what I mean. That was my very first time."

Steven thought she was trying to tell him something about her emotions, about losing her composure over brawny Brad's departure. "I'm sorry," he said.

"Oh, no. Don't be sorry. I wanted to do it. It was just that we'd never done anything yet, hardly even petted. And we were in his room and his bed was loaded with his clothes all folded up by his mother. I can't even remember now how we got down to it, but we did, right there on top of his nice neat piles of

T-shirts and shirts and pants and stuff, and I thought, 'Well, we might not see each other again for a long time, so it's okay.' We didn't even know if we were doing it right, or anything, and I couldn't feel much. It was over for him real quick. When it was done, I went down the hall to the bathroom to go pee and there was blood! And I said 'Wow, I'm not a virgin anymore!'"

Steven didn't know how to respond. While she had been talking about her encounter his eyes grazed her face, her throat and the hollow between her clavicles, those bones as prominent as a small horse collar on her thin body. "Good for you," was the best he could come up with. *"Finally!"*

She grinned at his sardonic response.

"And you were how old again?"

"I was thirteen. Eighth grade."

"Thirteen years old?"

"Yeah, in eighth grade, middle school," Valerie repeated. "Like back then we thought if you hadn't lost your cherry by the time you're fifteen, you were out of it, you know?"

"Well, you made it under the wire," Steven said. He was once again surprised by the openness of young people to discuss their most intimate experiences. The events of their lives seemed somehow detached from their emotional knowledge of them, even during the high drama of adolescence, when, he remembered, his own feelings lay along the surface of his skin, shimmery like the tentacles of sea anemones. Valerie's emotionless account of her deflowering sorely evoked his own first experience, how it continued to fester in his subconscious, even to this day in his life.

"So then, young Bradley went away to reform school?" he pursued.

"Bradford. To military academy. We never saw each other again. With him, I think it was like, you know, out of sight, out of mind. Anyway, I wrote to him a few times, but he never wrote back. I only remember it because he was my first time, but I don't remember anything much about what I felt about it. Does that make sense?"

"Eminently," he said. "That's what's so unique about human beings: we either bury our earliest injuries in our minds as emotional miscarriages, or we cling to them until we've fantasized them into alternate replacements for ourselves."

Valerie Caine frowned a moment, thinking. "That's cool," she said.

He looked at her in a clearer light, this young girl. It *was* cool, he thought. It had come to him just then, like tearing a bandage from a wound, opening it to the air.

But then Valerie Caine said, "Now though, I only think about it like it happened to someone else, not me."

When they'd finished their meal, he drove her back to her car parked yet at the College. As he sat with the motor running, his car next to her old red Pinto, she put her hand on the door handle.

"Well," she said.

"Thank you for your company," he said. "I appreciate it. I really needed a pleasant distraction."

She leaned toward him and left her face in the space between the front seats for just the breath of time it took him to make a decision—had she planned it?—before he dipped his own head to kiss her lightly on her forehead. When she pulled back, she flashed a puzzled smile, as if to say, "Is that it, then?"

She settled away from him, her hand still on door handle. "I'm free for the rest of the night."

There was just a beat of hesitation, that habitual rush of effervescence like nitroglycerin to the heart, before he said, "Not this evening. Maybe another time when I'd be better company."

"I'd like that," she said. "A lot."

In the next moment, she was out the door of his car, and he waited for her to open her own car door to get in behind the wheel and start the engine. When she was safely inside, she looked again at him through the window in her door, but her face behind the window was pale and featureless. In its place he saw the image of the orange and searing white thunderhead of fire bloom in his mind, obliterating Valerie Caine from his sight as she drove off.

Back in his apartment, Steven went straight to the kitchen to make himself a drink. He had no whiskey, just wine and maybe a third of a bottle gin. He rummaged the refrigerator for tonic water to soften the sharpness of the alcohol, but there was none there. He had finished it off last night, he recalled, before he'd driven to Saundra Bourcek's house because he could not be alone with himself. So now he poured three fingers of gin straight into a water glass. He was desperate to short circuit the million synapses buzzing like forked lightning across his brain, searching to connect a single thread of logic through the tangle of harsh events he had suffered this day.

He felt cloyed by his dinner, and his stomach had begun talking back to him. The food had been rich and stress did nothing to help his digestion. But he was also troubled by the evening's most recent and serendipitous moment when Valerie Caine had wanted to kiss him goodnight and he had resisted. Hers was the sort of unexpected magnetic act that would have made its innocence arousing if he had let it. But during dinner, listening to her story of her first act of sex at a child's age, committed as much out of curiosity—*for the fun, Stevie,* Gretchen had encouraged him—as to prove to herself that she was willing to abandon her childhood for the boy to take away the pain of his leaving. Listening to her account, Steven had felt a revulsion in his gut—not for her, for her innocent gift, but for himself and the insatiable emptiness of his need.

Now he hoped the gin might burn away all other interferences of the day in order to free his mind to reimagine it in a cleaner version of himself. But when he sat in his chair in front of the darkened television set in his living room and took a first swallow, the hot bite of the gin into the soft tissues of his throat was instantly repellent. He set the glass aside on the door-panel coffee table in front of him and leaned back in his chair, closing his eyes. Against the black screen of his eyelids, he summoned the clear image of Saundra Bourcek and her children in her blue car drawing up next to him, saw again the radiant delight in her smile at recognizing his presence next to her, watched the conspiratorial wave of her fingers acknowledging the coincidence of their being stopped at the precise same time by the same red light at the broad intersection of an empty crossroads. What would it have cost him, after all— what could it have possibly hurt if, simply out of gratitude for their night together, he had waved back? What could it have affected in both their lives if he had shown his face to her and her children and...*smiled?* Then all of them could have driven off through the inevitable green light to fulfill their separate commitments to others on a warm spring day.

Last night, Saundra Bourcek had awakened his repressed memory of the summer he was twelve years old; and this evening at dinner, Valerie Caine, unpretentiously confident in expressing her body's pleasure, and unrestrained by anything that might thwart her desire to celebrate herself in dance, had refloated the memory among the flotsam of the wrecked lives that had been tossed on the red tide of his betrayals.

Chapter 20

It was the summer his mother was hospitalized with a bronchopneumonia that settled over her lungs like a thick fog, cocooning her in an oxygen tent.

Steven's father had hired an eighteen-year-old high school girl, Gretchen Keel, to do light housework, cook the evening meal before he arrived home from his work or from visiting Steven's mother in the hospital. More importantly, Gretchen was to look after Steven during the day, since he was out of school for the summer and too young still to be left to his own devices. It was an opportunity for her to earn some money toward tuition and books at Boston University come fall.

She was pretty, Steven thought right from the first, and when she came to his house every day, she was dressed in smart summer clothes—white shorts and crisp blouses with the collars turned up behind or skirts that swirled around her sandal-strapped ankles. She had a straight back and shoulders that pushed her breasts against her blouses, and her legs were tapered and drumhead tight as a Rockette's. She was smart, too, and funny, and she called him "kiddo" or "sport." The diminutives seemed warm, with no hint of sarcasm.

"Hey, kiddo, what's cookin'?" she'd say when she arrived in the morning, just before Steven's father left for work.

"Cold cereal," Steven would say, and she'd reward him with a laugh and a playful jab in the arm with her fingers.

That summer, when his mother was hospitalized, it was his father who made the breakfasts—corn flakes and grapefruit, mostly; scrambled eggs and bacon on the weekend—before leaving for work at his office in Boston. Gretchen made lunch and dinner before she went home for the evening.

She did the housework in the mornings while Steven biked over to the Country Club for tennis lessons. He hated tennis. He thought it was a sweaty game, played by stuck-up kids in his parents' snotty club where you were always on your best behavior or they'd call your home. But he could not defy his mother, and the lessons were her idea. And he did like the smell of the early morning sun on the clay courts and the tock-tock tune of a good volley by more experienced players in the adjacent courts. In any event, she insisted, "Boys need physical activity to develop coordination and use up their excess energy." He came to understand later, in high school biology class, that excess energy meant high levels of testosterone during adolescence. His mother had been watchful on his behalf for the pitfalls he would encounter in his teens, although she was never direct with him about what to look out for. He was only eleven when she warned him, "Don't you be one of those foolish boys who pins a girl because he's too lazy or shy to date. Play the field. Go out with lots of girls while you have the chance, and you'll always be popular."

On hot June and July afternoons, Gretchen often took him swimming at Turner Pond, a tepid and algae-laden puddle of water with a small public beach and shallow swimming area fenced off by a cork-beaded rope floating between metal posts. It was the place where some of Steven's friends from school went to hang out and "mess around" after a morning of scrub baseball, pickup basketball, or in his case, tennis lessons.

It was in her bathing suit that she awakened what Steven much later came to describe metaphorically as a blunt-nosed shark nosing about in the depths of his groin.

At Turner Pond, Gretchen would spread towels on the sand and anchor them with a straw bag containing suntan lotion, a portable radio, a paperback book, a couple of apples and bottles of Coca Cola.

She'd oil up with Coppertone lotion, going over and over her elastic flesh until the cream was all absorbed, leaving a moist sheen. She had only one bathing suit, a sky-blue nylon affair that molded to her like a rubber glove and displayed the major spheres of her body.

She'd settle onto the towel and take out a paperback book, which she never got to read because shortly she'd be surrounded by boys she knew from high school. They'd begin a nonstop session of flirtatious conversation while Steven went to goof off with his buddies—his "playmates," Gretchen called them— out on a plank-and-barrel raft in deeper water just beyond the bobbing rope. As he roughhoused with his friend Robert Crowley—who was in his class in school—and whoever else had shown up for the afternoon, playing king of the raft or cannonballing each other in the water, he was aware of Gretchen on the beach and the older boys sniffing around her.

"She's choice stuff," Robert Crowley declared one day while the two of them sat on the edge of the raft, taking a breather. "You seen anything yet?"

"Like what?"

"You know. Does she take baths and everything at your house?"

"Don't be stupid," Steven said. "She's only there during the day to do cleaning and stuff."

"Yeah, but doesn't she ever have to go pee or nothin'?"

"So what? What do you think, I peek through the keyhole?"

"Sure. I would," Robert said. "She's choice."

Because she had been hired to "look after him," Steven grew jealous of her time with the older boys. He certainly didn't need a babysitter, but she didn't have to abandon him to his friends, either. Whenever he observed Gretchen on her beach towel, she was reclined with elbows spread like outriggers and her head cocked back to get sunlight on her throat. Two or three older boys lay beside her, casually plucking leaf bits or pebbles from the sand and flicking them away while they talked. He envied their closeness to her, smelling the tanning lotion on her warm skin. Their eyes, he knew, grazed her body from behind their sunglasses.

It wasn't that she never paid attention to him. When it was just the two of them, at the house or in the car, she could be quite friendly. She sometimes, while making a point in conversation, patted his hand when she was sitting near him; or she slugged him in the arm playfully when he wised off. She talked to him about everything from hot rods to college, and she knew more than he did about lots of things.

"You're real lucky," she said to him once. "You've got money and a big house and your father drives a Chrysler."

"I can't help it," he said, thinking it was a bad thing she was pointing out about him. "I don't have any money. I don't even get an allowance."

"You don't need an allowance. Your parents can afford things. And you're good looking. You're going to be a real lady killer one day."

That floored him, her thinking he was good-looking enough to be attractive to girls. And she wasn't all joking when she said it, either, the way she did with him a lot of the time. Sometimes a look came across her face, like she'd lost something and had just now remembered she didn't have it anymore. That was the way she looked at him when she told him he was really lucky. It made him feel somehow older, closer to her age. He began noting the mannerisms of the older boys with whom she spent time at the beach, their particular way of swaggering without being childish about it like his friends. Sometimes, as they stretched on the sand beside Gretchen, they showed the cool arrogance of cats preening themselves. And Gretchen paid side-glancing attention to them.

Gretchen continued to come each morning to do the house cleaning and to look after Steven while his father went to work. And in the evenings before he returned home, his father would visit Steven's mother in the hospital. Each Sunday, he took Steven to visit also.

His mother lay on her back inside a strange, clear plastic tent that covered her head and torso—an oxygen tent, they called it—and while she could talk, her voice was clipped and her mind didn't seem engaged with what she said.

For the most part, Steven sat in a chair in a corner of the room while his father sat at the side of her bed and stroked one of her hands beneath the vinyl covering. Everywhere there were warning placards: NO SMOKING! HIGHLY FLAMMABLE! He thought of his mother as vaporous, explosive. A single spark, an inflammatory word, might ignite her.

One Sunday in early July, when he and his father went to the hospital, his father said to Steven before they entered her room, "They said she seems to be much better. She wants to talk to you."

He stood at the bedside, staring at his mother through the crinkled plastic tent, and her face smiled out at him.

"Are you behaving?" she said. "I know you are."

He nodded.

"Is Gretchen taking good care of you and daddy?"

He nodded again.

"I miss you."

"I miss you, too, Mom," he said. He meant it. She was the bellwether for his behavior, directing him toward some fruitful future that she had mapped out in her mind for him.

She motioned him to take her hand underneath the tent. Her fingers felt very cold in his. "You're going into Junior High School this fall, a whole new adventure for you. Lots of new friends, boys and girls. Study hard. Pick your friends carefully. Don't tie yourself down to any one girlfriend. You'll have plenty of time later for that after your education."

"I won't, Mom," he said, but he found her advice vague and set toward some life he could not even begin to envision.

Back home, his father was in the best spirits he'd seen him for weeks. They listened to music together on the record player—Strauss waltzes, and part of the New World Symphony—and Steven didn't complain. He went to bed happy.

He was asleep when his father received the telephone call from the hospital: his wife had gone into sudden cardiac arrest and they had lost her.

Though Gretchen remained her same spirited self, Steven lost most of his own spirit. He took his cue from his father, who rose every morning heavy-hearted, arrived home every evening the same way, and was generally quiet all through the night. Steven continued to go to his tennis lessons at the Country Club. He tried to find purpose in them, as he knew his mother would want him to do. It was for his good, after all. It was to help him make the right kind of friends. It was to help him use up his excess energy. He could have skipped a lesson or two, could have quit, even, and his father wouldn't have been the wiser. But it seemed important to him now to honor his mother, who, he believed for the first time, had done so much, had sacrificed so much for him and his father.

In the afternoons at Turner Pond, he had trouble being with his noisier "playmates," and he spent more time with Gretchen on the sand, even when the older boys made snide references to his age and jokingly offered him money to "buzz off." But Gretchen defended him. "He can stay, if he wants. It's not hurting you," she said. "Stevie and I are buddies, aren't we, kiddo?"

Then one day, Gretchen said to him, "Let's go somewhere else today. I know another place to swim. It's better than Turner Pond."

"How come we're going somewhere new?" he asked, once they were in her car.

"Because it's a better place," she said. "And 'cause I didn't want to be alone with those goons. I can't stand them."

"Me either," Steven said, pleased she felt the way he did about her admirers. "How come we haven't gone to this other place before?"

"I thought you liked Turner Pond."

"It's okay," he said. "I've never been anywhere else."

The new place she took him turned out to be an abandoned granite quarry six miles out of town, at the end of a dirt road through some woods in the country. Because he had never been there before, and Gretchen had driven him in her car away from what was familiar to him, he imagined it was almost like being on a date with her.

The quarry was filled with spring water, cold and black as night from the impenetrable depth of the abandoned rock crater. On the surface of the water, the trees and sky and clouds were reflected brilliantly, as if in a dark mirror.

He was surprised to find other kids there—about a dozen of them, mostly teenagers—although none of them were from his part of town. Gretchen seemed to know a few of them, got along easily with them, which made Steven feel even more isolated without anyone he knew from among his own friends. Still, he liked the quarry more than Turner because of the long ride alone with Gretchen to get there.

They set their towels out on a flat area of rock at the highest point along the rim of the quarry—a spot where the rock jutted out over the water in an arrow-shaped formation, which Gretchen said everyone called The Anvil.

Maybe because she was the most recent arrival at the quarry that day, or maybe because they just knew she was a good sport, Gretchen was soon singled out by the other guys to dunk and cannonball and horse around with. She suffered good-naturedly the indignities of the boys. She shrieked when they threw her off The Anvil to the water twenty feet below, then cannonballed near her as she bobbed along the surface in their wakes. She endured, like a trusting puppy, their slap-splash fights, blinking her eyes and pinching her nose while she thrashed in circles away from each plume of water in the circular gauntlet that would suddenly form around her. Sometimes she simply disappeared underwater, arching momentarily like a blue-skinned porpoise and slipping beneath the spray. The boys would stop and tread water, their heads dipped to peer beneath the surface for a glimpse of her blue bathing suit.

Steven did not participate. Instead, he swam just conspicuously enough away from the rest to dramatize his separateness. He did not see the difference between this place and Turner Pond, as far as her attentions were concerned. He was solitary, an outsider, so he spent the first half hour swimming alone underwater, surfacing like an otter for air and then gliding beneath the surface to meld his gloominess with the twilight green reaches of sunlight from the surface where it began to fade into the impenetrable blackness of the deepest part of the quarry. He courted his primordial fear of things unseen below light, kicking downward against the water's pressure into the black. Finally, near exhaustion, he crawled out onto a flat rim of granite and climbed up the ledge to the top of The Anvil where they had left their towels, and he lay on his stomach, cradling his head in his arms.

He dozed in the warmth and at one point, must have slept, because when he next opened his eyes, he was looking at the white curve of girl thighs and an exposed crescent of buttocks where the flesh swelled beyond the elastic pinch of the bottom of her bathing suit. He looked up into Gretchen's face, and from within the black depths of his sulk, his heart swam to the sunlit surface. She sat next him, leaning back on her stiffened arms, her head tilted up to the sun. Her hair hung in thick black strands below her shoulders. The down on her arms and thighs glistened with moisture.

"Did they finally give up pestering you?" he asked.

She opened her eyes, looked down upon him with a placid expression. "It's all in fun," she said. She swung half around, facing him, drew her legs up and, closing her eyes to the sun, leaned back once again on stiffened arms. At the level of his eyes, he was looking at the narrow panel of fabric that covered her privates. Still wet from her swim, the material was translucent, so that against the forward strain of her trunk, he could see the mat of dark curls, pressing. The plumpness was like a perfect nest in the fork of her limbs. He looked quickly back to her face; it was composed and guileless, showing no awareness of what she was arousing in him. Without thought or volition, he became erect.

At that moment, she opened her eyes and gazed at him. And when he saw that Gretchen observed the change his bathing suit could not hide, he rolled away from her, to conceal himself.

"It's all right," she said.

"What?" he said.

"I see you," she said. She reached over and pulled at his shoulder, trying to rock him back. He resisted, shrugging her hand off. "Are you thinking sexy thoughts?"

He was mortified. "No! I'm not thinking anything."

"Well, don't be embarrassed."

"I can't help it." He felt himself redden more.

"It's all right. I think that's cool, how that happens to boys," she said.

He looked back at her. "What's so cool about it?" He had already wilted under his embarrassment.

"The mystery of it," she said. "How it all works, the way bodies seem to speak to one another even when we don't think about it sometimes. Don't you think it's remarkable?"

He shrugged. It was his body they were talking about. "It's stupid. I just wake up that way, sometimes."

"Only you didn't just wake up that way," she said. "I know, because I've been watching you sleep. You woke up and you looked at me, *then* you got a hard-on."

"I wasn't looking at you. I didn't see anything," he said, his voice almost a whine. "I mean, I didn't think anything dirty about you."

"I didn't say you did. I just asked."

He looked away and grabbed his towel, draping it over his thighs.

"Have you ever fooled around with a girl?"

He hesitated answering. Should he lie or tell the truth? "Sure. I mean…you know, not a lot."

"You will," she said. "And then you'll know what I mean. All sorts of cool things happen to your body, lots of warm feelings and sensations. Like you're on a big, wonderful Ferris wheel, along for the ride."

He knew about the sensations on a Ferris wheel: the long belly-heavy ride up, and then the moment of over the top, where you were suspended in air before the centrifugal force lifted you up, before that tingling, freefall rush in your groin as you plummeted down the other side.

"When are we going to go home?" he asked. He realized that most of the other kids had left already. There were only four left, two boys and two girls, on the rocks on the other side of the quarry.

"One more dip in the water," Gretchen said.

"I don't want to," he said.

"Do you really want to go home?" she said.

He thought of what was there. "No," he said.

"Come on, then. Last one in...." She stood up and held her hand out to him, and in the fleeting moment when he could have resisted, when he might have done the childish thing his friends would do, refusing her out of awkwardness, he reached out to her, instead, and took her hand and let her pull him closer to her.

"There's no looking back," she said, and ran with him the few steps to the rim of The Anvil and leapt out over the edge. Still holding her hand, he noted during their fall toward the water twenty feet below that she screamed and held her nose with her other hand, like a girl, just before he squinched his eyes shut, and they plunged feet first into the chill dark water. In an instant, the world was muffled in silence, except for the distant cavernous *plosh* their implosion made above them and the hiss of bubbles all around.

Once in the water, he opened his eyes immediately, and as their descent slowed and then suspended, she turned toward him, letting go his hand to put both of hers on his waist as they started up in an underwater ballet of body against body, holding onto each other through lift and spin. Her face was white as dough near his, and her cheeks were puffed while perfectly round bubbles of air rolled from the corners of her mouth. Her hair drifted about them like seaweed, touching his shoulders.

When they surfaced, their faces were only inches apart, and she held onto his waist with one hand while she brushed the hair from her eyes and pinched water from her nose. His own hands were on the shelf of her rump, along the sweet curve of her lower back, and as she moved against him, he sensed the pressure of her breasts like soft tennis balls against his chest.

They swam to shore and hauled themselves out on the flat rock shelf, and they climbed back to the top of The Anvil and lay out on their towels side-by-side in the afternoon sun. They were the only ones left at the quarry. Steven could hear the last four making their way up the road to the clearing.

"Feeling better, sport?" she asked.

"Uh huh," he replied, although his teeth were chattering slightly and gooseflesh rose on his arms and legs as the water evaporated on his skin.

Then she did a remarkable thing. She reached out and touched his arm nearest her with her fingertips, and she idly stroked the downy hair there, sending currents along the nerves below his skin. Eventually, her hand rested on top of his. He lay very still. Soon her fingers were working their way between his, and they were holding hands. They lay like that for a time, and Steven felt the cold disappearing from his skin under the heat his heartbeat was radiating within him.

When she spoke, her voice was quiet but held a breathy edge of tenseness. "Do you like poems?"

He shrugged. "Not much." Then, afraid she might be disappointed by that, he said, "I used to like some of the poems my mother read to me when I was a little kid. But I haven't read too many myself, except a couple of dumb ones for school. I like stories."

"Yes," she said, "stories, too. Poems and stories can tell us lots about the way we feel. I mean about feelings a lot of people have but don't know that others feel the same way."

"Like what?" he said.

"Oh, I don't know. How we feel about dying. How we feel about love and about being sad or happy. Things like that. Last year, in my Senior English class at school, we read a poem by an English writer, Robert Herrick. It was about telling young people to—you know—do it while they still are young. He tries to tell us to take advantage of the moment while we're young, because we may never have the chance again. There's one line I love: 'That age is best which is the first, when youth and blood are warmer.' I think about that a lot. Isn't it cool?"

He frowned. "What does it mean?" He rolled his head toward her. She was lying on her back, her other arm under her head, and her breasts rose and fell as she breathed. From his eye level, they were like a breathtaking mountain range, dropping dramatically from their summit to the valley of her belly.

"Our teacher called it a 'carpe diem' poem. You know what that means?" He shook his head. He could not take his eyes from her. "It's Latin. Like the ancient Romans spoke. It sort of means doing something because it feels good now. Doing what you know you want to do, before it's too late and you miss the chance." She looked at him, her eyebrows arched in a questioning way, waiting, he supposed, for him to acknowledge he understood. He rolled his head away from her and again he nodded. And suddenly she rolled on her side and rose up on her arm, her face hovering over him, and she took his chin in her hand that had been holding his and tilted his head so his eyes met hers. When she had captured his gaze, she bent down to him and kissed him on the lips. The hand that had held his chin steady now took one of his and put it on the cool fabric of her bathing suit, flattening his palm against her belly. While she continued to nibble at his lips with soft grazing kisses, she slid his hand up and cupped it over her breast, squeezing his fingers into the round, sponge of flesh. "Seize the day," she whispered.

She moved his hand all around, over both breasts, and his fingers took on their own life beneath hers. They tried to move to the top of her suit, to grope under toward her bare skin, but the suit was too tight across the top.

"Let me do it for you, Stevie." She drew her hands up to each shoulder and slipped away the shoulder straps and peeled the front down to her waist. Then

195

with a teasing smile, she leaned forward on stiffened arms until her breasts ballooned down above his chest. "Go ahead," she urged him. "Touch them if you want."

He did. Tentatively at first, then, when she rocked her shoulders gently, making her breasts sway, he captured them in his palms and held them, squeezing fitfully. One of her hands reached down between them and found his crotch, captured his hard-on through the fabric and rubbed him.

"Take your trunks off," she said. "Let me see you, too."

He hesitated, until she stood up suddenly and slid her bathing suit the rest of the way off, where it dropped like a snake's shed skin at her feet. He could see the imprint of it on her body yet against the borders of tanned skin, and at the nadir of all that white skin, the dark hair of her sex, the first he'd seen on any girl, except for pictures in Robert Crowley's father's *Penthouse* magazines.

"Now you," she said.

He slipped his trunks off his hips and legs. He couldn't resist her, his pounding heart and the rush of lust fired by what his eyes drank in of Gretchen's nude body.

"God, you are beautiful," she whispered, kneeling down beside him.

He was confounded that she found him attractive—his skinny body, his first little strands of pubic hair—amazed and frightened and tremendously aroused.

"Oh, Stevie, it'll be so-oo nice, I promise you."

He laughed, a self-conscious snort.

"Think of it: this is your first time. My first time was so-o incredible. Think how proud you're going to feel later that you've done it with an older girl."

"I guess," he said. "Only—"

"Shh!" She put a finger to his lips and leaned against him, the weight of her body shifting, as she lifted a thigh over him and straddled him, her eyes lizard-lidded. He felt a hand on his prick, moving it around between her legs.

"Can you feel me, Stevie?" she sighed. "Feel how open and wet for your hardness." But her skin was dry, except where he could feel himself somehow inside her now. There it seemed very slippery, as if water had gotten inside her while they swam, and was just now coming out.

Then there was too much for him to feel all at once, too much offered up to his senses, to his amazed and wild eyes and dry lips and greedy hands, as Gretchen began to move on him, her face thrown back and grimacing in some kind of private pain. He couldn't sort it all out. He wanted her to stop, or slow down; he wanted to touch her everywhere at once. But oh…oh…there was that prickly current of tickling electricity that happened each time he masturbated.

And Gretchen bounced and bounced on him; her back arched and her breasts jiggled wildly. He was trapped beneath her as she pinned his shoulders to the rock with her hands and his pelvis with her cantering hips. Then came that paroxysm that held him powerless in a ball of excitement, fear, anger, all as a single emotion that erupted from his throat in a boyish growl while Gretchen continued to rise up and down on him, unaware of his presence. Shortly her head drooped, covering his face with her hair.

"Oh, Stevie, isn't it so-o incredible?" she sighed. And she stretched out languidly on him, her full body the length of his, her breasts crushed into the side of his head as he turned his face away to breathe through the cove of her armpit.

For the next week, he was in a constant state of arousal for her, waiting for the next time she would teach him his next lesson. He was excruciatingly aware of her presence in the house while she went about the housework. The curves and thrusting angles of her body—trying to remember the texture and touch of this part, or that one, out of the whirl of those few minutes he'd had to take her all in—how her breasts at one moment seemed to fill her blouse as she leaned over the vacuum cleaner wand, then diminished, settling altogether differently when she straightened up again. She was just as friendly to him as formerly, calling him "kiddo" and "sport," winking at him or jabbing his arm, but there was no hint from her acknowledging what had happened. His complete ignorance of sexual protocol left him bankrupt of any idea what he was expected to do next. She had been so courageous, he thought, against his fear and awkwardness, that he knew it must be up to him to say something.

Finally, one day he asked, "Can we go to The Anvil again today?"

She took his meaning right away, and shook her head. "No."

He felt a hot stone in his belly, and heat rose in his face. "How come?"

"That was a one-time adventure," she said, "because I think you're very special and I wanted to show you in a special way. It was meant to be light and fun and, you know, to show my affection for you. I know it's been real hard for you to lose your mom, and not have anyone around to talk to, or anything. My dad died two years ago, and I miss him very much."

When he could not answer her, she said, "But now that you know how good it can be, there'll be another girl. Lots of other girls. And you'll want to have fun with all of them, too, and they will want to make love with you, just you wait and see. You know, you are so lucky. I have three brothers, and I know what boys at your age have fantasies about. But now you don't have to wonder anymore."

"But don't you love me?" he asked, because he believed he loved her.

"You don't have to be in love to make love," she said. "It's just a wonderful thing to do with someone when you want to make each other feel good. It's all fun and good feelings, and it can take away the hurt, Stevie."

He did not understand what she was saying, but in some way, he could not have expressed just then, he sensed she was right. She was a fantasy become real. And he wondered, as well, how he would ever get even with her for what she'd done by denying him.

By the end of the summer, Steven's father had found a full-time housekeeper, a woman older even than his mother had been, who could come in every day all during the school year. On Gretchen's last day, his father thanked her profusely for looking after the house and his son, and he gave her an envelope with a check. "Something extra," he said, "for your college plans."

She thanked him with tears in her eyes and told him how sorry she was for his loss. Then she hugged Steven goodbye, holding him extra tight. "Take care of yourself, kiddo," she said, and whispered in his ear, "*Carpe diem.*"

Now exhausted, sitting hunch-backed in his chair like an old man under the weight of emotional rubble that had imploded disastrously in a single day, he heard Gretchen Keel speaking to him the lie that had so long been his opiate: "It's all fun and good feelings to take away the hurt, Stevie."

It took what was left of his energy just to heave himself up from the chair and struggle down the hall to his bedroom. Shucking everything except his boxer shorts in a heap on the floor, he crumpled onto the bed and steamrollered under the events of the day he could no longer outrun; he fell into a sleep as black as the depths of The Anvil's waters.

In what seemed only a moment, he was jolted back to consciousness by the shrill ringing of the telephone on the table beside his bed. The clock radio showed he had been asleep an hour already. In his waking stupor, he groped the phone out of its cradle, believing he was required to answer.

It was Catherine's voice in his ear. "Hi, it's me."

He was silent at first.

"Are you awake?" she asked.

"No," he said. "What is it you want?"

"Nothing." She paused. "It's what you want. Can I come over for a while?"

Steven propped himself up on his elbow, alert for signs of disorientation in her voice. "Why?"

"I can't sleep. I need to talk to someone. Actually, I have a proposition to make you," she said. "Is anyone else there?"

"Of course not. Cathy, I'm in bed," he groaned. "I'm exhausted, it's been a long and emotionally taxing day for everyone."

"Don't even get out of bed. That's part of my proposition."

"What is?"

"I was thinking…closure. What we need—both of us need—is closure, so that I…*we* can continue on with our lives. I need you to help me with closure."

"How can I possibly help you? I'm part of the problem," he said.

"How about if I come over and go to bed with you and have you make love to me? Do what you do best."

"Oh, Catherine," Steven groaned again. "What are you talking about?" It was there now, that quality to her voice that he associated with her delusions. Her mouth was dry, her saliva so thick that her glottal consonants clicked like an inexperienced public speaker's. She was trying to sound light and careless in her speech, but her voice was timorous and childlike.

"Why not? It sounds good to me," she said.

"That's not what you need at all."

"It's not just for me. It's for you, really. I want to give you this gift, and then—"

"Catherine! My God, that's the last thing I can handle right now." He nearly confessed, out of sudden spite, that he had already turned down a better offer tonight.

"It'll be the last time, I promise you." Her voice was the child's again. "If not for you, then for me. For old times, you know? There's all this ritual of sex in getting married; don't you think there should be sex involved in getting divorced, too? You're fucked when you marry, fucked when you part?"

"Go to bed, get some sleep. You must be exhausted," Steven pleaded.

"What's the matter? Give too much at the office today already?" she replied, but there was that tightening of her voice when she was suspicious.

"Catherine, I don't believe you even know what you're saying."

"I do know what I'm saying," she insisted. "I've been to sleep. I woke up, and it was suddenly very clear to me. I'm losing my power to create, Steven. I'm losing my imagination, and I won't get it back once it's gone. I can't paint anymore. But it came to me that if we make love now, then I won't lose my imagination forever. I'll transfer it to you. Don't you see? You'll have what you need to make you complete—my romantic imagination, your love of language. I can give you this last gift, the powers of my creativity, if we make love before I lose them completely."

This was just the sort of hair-brained mystical psychobabble that always put him on edge whenever anyone talked "powers" of creativity in dreams and visions. "Destiny and doom talk," he called it. And Catherine was susceptible to it more than most people he knew.

He lay on the bed in the dark with his eyes closed, the phone cradled in his neck. "This is just crazy. It doesn't work that way," he said. "Imagination. Creativity. These are not *fluids* that are passed from one body to another, Cathy."

"Please? It's important to me. I promise I won't bother you after this one last time."

"This is just drunk talk. 'Last drink and then I quit' talk."

"I'm not drunk. And I'm not quitting," she said.

On the nightstand beside him, the green numerals of the clock—the only source of light in the bedroom—read 11:45 p.m. "It's almost midnight, for godsakes. Get to sleep, you'll think differently in the morning."

"I'll sleep even better if I'm well fucked," she said.

Steven sighed deeply. He tried another tack. "I'll tell you what," he said. "You call your therapist tomorrow and get her to tell me it's all right, that it's good for your therapy, and I'll service you all you want. But you get her to tell me that, okay?"

"No. It'll be too late tomorrow. It has to be now. I can feel my imaginative powers flowing out of me through my eyes and my mouth and my…my *cunt,* Steven. My imagination is flowing out of my cunt, and you can capture it, right through your thick, hard *cock.*"

A laugh erupted from his chest like a hiccup at her attempt to arouse him with dirty talk. The words were totally foreign to her way of speaking, and the triteness with which she emphasized them was not so much erotic as artless. "There's a metaphor," he said. "My cock as a straw to suck out your creative spirit."

"Yes!" she said seriously. "My spirit, my imagination, it's all the same. And we can connect with each other through your penis and my vagina, and we'll complete each other the way we did when we first made love."

"Jesus," he said. "I don't think even D.H. Lawrence would have thought of it that way."

"I'll come over in a minute, Steven. You can have me any way you want."

In spite of himself, he found her attempt to be erotic mildly arousing for him. She was childlike in her wanting, and he felt a terrible power in that. But he said, "I can't talk about this anymore tonight. I have to sleep, Cathy. Try your vibrator. You'll feel better in the morning."

"You're my vibrator," she said. "I'll see you in a bit."

"Don't you dare," he said. "Go to sleep. Let yourself heal now." But she had hung up already.

He reached over blindly in the dark and fumbled with the receiver base until he found the cradle to couple with the phone.

It was the cicada chirring of the door buzzer that woke him again. The sound was coming from the intercom in the kitchen, and it bleated with an intermittent but nagging insistence that brought him upright in bed. "Shit," he muttered when he realized what it was. He rubbed his face with a downward sweep of his hand and looked at the clock. It was past midnight.

The buzzer quit all at once, and Steven raised up on his forearms, propping himself half upright while he cleared his head. He had no idea how long she had been trying to summon him awake before he finally heard the sound in his sleep. The buzzing began again. She would not quit, he knew. He could not ignore the noise.

Turning on lights as he went, Steven made his way to the intercom panel on the wall in the kitchen. It was useless to engage her on the intercom. She would continue to push the button for him to buzz her in, as she had done in the past when they were first separated. He pushed the security lock button and heard the muffled electric rattle of the front entrance lock disengaging.

As he waited for her by the door to his apartment, he thought about what he might say to keep her from coming beyond the threshold. But even while he stood there, trying to concoct that one final argument to convince her that their lives were changed irrevocably now, the lizard in his brain was stirring with narrowed eyes. He felt the familiar tongue-flicks of arousal that happened every time he was certain he was going to make love to a woman. By the time he heard her hesitant knock on his door, he was nearly erect. He opened the door to her without a word of protest.

Instead of Catherine, he faced a stranger. A man in a dress western shirt and jeans. His face was bristled with spiky new growth, and his eyes were blasted by red streaks that seemed to spill into inflamed lower lids. There was something dead in his eyes, unblinking, and for a second it seemed to Steven he'd seen the man before.

"Professor Steven Harper?" His voice was softly hoarse.

"Yes," Steven replied. Haunted. That's what he saw in the man's face. The dull light of someone possessed.

The man's gaze moved down Steven's body, as if taking his measure, before he looked back up into Steven's own eyes.

"Can I help you?" Steven asked, even as his hand flattened on the back of the door to push it shut.

"Do you know who I am?"

"No, I'm sorry, I don't."

"Well, I've never met you either, but I know who you are. Let me give you my card." The man handed him a white business card. Steven looked at him, questioning, then at the face of the card. In black script letters it presented *New*

Waves Salon, Styles to a Hair's Breadth. There was an open line drawing of a woman's face framed by a flip-up hairdo. He turned the card over and saw his own name and telephone number there, and the legend Saundra had penned that morning: *Gives Great c-Lit!*

"I'm sorry, I don't understand—" Except he did.

"I'm the guy whose family you took."

He looked back at the man, and even as he was closing the door on him, Steven saw the other hand move, rise, level something at him—*what is that?*—and the explosion hit him like a fist in his chest, and he sprawled backwards onto his living room floor. He thought only, *No! It's not over yet.*

There was a second detonation, not as loud as the first, dampened by the ringing in his head. This time he felt nothing.

Chapter 21

Donald wasn't sure if he was asleep, or if he hadn't slept at all, when the alert tone from the monitor on the wall of his room brought him upright on his cot. In his train caller's voice, the fire dispatcher announced: *"Medic Ten, Engine Fifty-five, rescue call, Four-two-oh-five Taylor, the Carlton Arms, Apartment Six, a shooting. Medic Ten, Engine Fifty-five rescue call, Forty-two-oh-five Taylor—"*

Donald listened again to the address, and his initial astonishment numbed rather than quickened any sense of urgency he might have had. 4205 Taylor. The adjoining fire district. Why were they calling for Engine 55?

When he swung his feet over the side of his bed and sat up, he realized what the dispatcher had reported. A shooting? He could hear the scramble of footsteps in the hall outside, the door onto the apparatus floor thudding open and closed as hands slapped its metal skin. He was out his own door before he was even aware of his haste.

On the apparatus floor, he grabbed his boots and bunker coat from the ready rack by the truck just as Gene Metzger fired up the engine of 55 with a rattling roar, and the overhead bay door rolled upward along its tracks. As Donald swung up into the seat of the truck, the radio crackled again, and it was the voice of the squad captain competing with background sounds of the ambulance's engine and the rising wail of its siren: *"Medic Ten in service, Forty-two-oh-five Taylor, Carlton Arms, Apartment Six."*

The dispatcher replied, *"Clear, Medic Ten, time zero-zero-forty-five."*

Donald craned his neck to look in back and see if everyone was aboard. He counted three heads in the gloom of the crew cabin. "Go," he said to Metzger, and the truck growled out of the station and down the ramp onto Cedar Street. He plucked the microphone from its clip and put them in service.

"What are we doing on this call?" he asked Metzger.

"Engine Fifteen is still out on that warehouse fire near the airport," Metzger replied. "We're next in."

"Oh sure," Donald said. "I heard that call earlier."

From 63rd and Cedar Street to 42nd and Taylor Street, where the Carlton Arms apartments were, it was a ten-minute run east. Once they were on Cedar, Donald's familiarity with the landmarks along the route normally would have guided him like radio signals. Without thought he knew where Metzger could speed up, where they must slow down to accommodate the changing topography. At Buckley's BP Station on 61st and Center the road narrowed abruptly to one lane on his side for three blocks of street repair; at Ponderosa Steakhouse and Aquarius Liquors, Metzger needed to be in the lane closest to the center stripe to avoid a series of closely spaced chuckholes which had opened up over the winter and were not patched yet. Buckley's BP, Aquarius, Burger King, Pat & Mike's Pizza, Midtown Furniture. He knew the names, he knew what each place was, but in a moment of disequilibrium, he felt as if he were entering somewhere unknown.

There were at least a half dozen police cars along the circular drive up to the front entrance of the Carlton Arms. Below the stone steps to the front door, Medic 10 sat idling with its beacons pulsing and its back doors open.

He thought, *So this is it*, and a stillness spread through him as everything came into sharp three-dimensional focus. Within the calm center of his chest, beneath his beating heart, he sensed what he was heading into was what he had been waiting for all day, poisoning his mood.

Almost before Metzger had set the brakes and the others climbed down from the crew cab, Donald was out of the door and down to the ground, leaving his boots and coat in the cab. He hurried up a flagstone path to the steps. Inside the foyer of the building, painted arrows on the wall with numerals indicating apartment numbers directed him down a short hall to a wing on the north end. Two uniformed police officers stood at the opened door to Apartment 6, and around them, a cluster of residents stood in the hall craning for a view inside.

Donald stepped between the two officers and through the door into the apartment's living room. He stood for a moment, trying to get his bearings while Czernecky and Deborah Gallant filed in behind him. It was a small living room, made even smaller by the number of men in it. In the center space between the living room and a dining el, a cluster of paramedics and policemen huddled in a prayer-meeting tableau around something on the floor mostly hidden from his view. At first, he could not recognize what he was looking at—a pile of laundry, a spill of liver-colored pudding? Surely, not what it was, what in the next instant he had to admit to his consciousness from years of personal detachment at the scenes of emergencies: a bloodied, nearly nude body of a man. All this blitzed his mind in a second, until his heart, having stood still, began beating once again.

One of the paramedics was untangling a clear plastic tube and bag of intravenous fluid. The other paramedic, in gray shirt—Ed Bourke, the captain of Medic 10—held a field telephone to his ear, listening to instructions from the emergency ward at County Hospital.

Donald, feeling both intruder and intruded upon, edged his way through the outer ring, slipping between two policemen, who gave him only a brief sidelong glance before turning their shoulders like turnstile gates to let him through. Beside the paramedic administering the intravenous liquid was a rolling stretcher, its wheels collapsed to floor level.

Donald squatted to look over Ed Bourke's shoulder. A flash bulb lit the room, and then another, as a man in civilian clothes leaned in to get pictures. Donald could see clearly now that the man on the floor was alive yet. His nose and mouth were covered by a green neoprene respirator mask, and the respirator control valve clicked with each breath of oxygen it delivered, fogging the mask with vapor. The face that showed around the mask was hideously swollen and bruised, the eyes occluded by bloody apples of swollen tissue covering them. The hair on his head was matted with blood.

"What going on?" he asked Ed Bourke, his first utterance since he'd arrived.

Bourke placed his hand over the mouthpiece of the field telephone and shook his head. "It's a real mess. The guy's been shot twice, a flail wound in his chest, another in his stomach. And looks like someone pounded on him, as well."

"What do you want us to do?" Donald asked.

"Help load him out, is all I need right now. Maybe you could do me a favor and start collecting what history you can for the report—name, age, etcetera."

"No problem," Donald said, relieved to have a direction. He turned to Czernecky and Gallant. "Just stand-by for now. Help carry him out when they're ready."

"Looks like he sure pissed somebody off," Czernecky said.

Deborah stared fixedly at the form that was the center of attention. Her face was pale, and her eyes shone darkly.

"You okay?" Donald asked quietly.

She looked up momentarily. "Yeah, no problem." Her voice was barely audible. Then a bit louder, "The poor guy. He looks like a truck ran over him."

"A truck woulda been kinder," a young police officer said.

Donald turned to him. "Who's running the investigation?"

"Down the hall, bedroom on the right," the young officer replied. "Detective Gates. He's talking to a witness there."

"Mark Gates?" He'd known Gates, a police sergeant from the detective bureau, since high school, when they'd played basketball together for two years on the Platte City High team that still held the all-time record for consecutive losses.

The officer nodded. "Sergeant Gates."

At the end of the hallway to the rear of the apartment, Donald stopped at an open bedroom door and looked in. He spotted Mark Gates in his trademark brown western-cut jacket and white shirt, a maroon bolo tie with silver steerhorn slide dangling from his neck. He stood against a chest of drawers against the near wall, going over some notes on a pad. Nearby a female police officer sat on the end of the bed, writing on a clipboard.

In the middle of the bed, her legs folded yoga-style and her head bent so her hair nearly concealed her face, sat Catherine. She was wearing a brown camelhair coat, open wide, and beneath it a white satin nightgown. She looked exhausted, sunk back into herself like a deflated ball. There was blood—was that blood?—on the sleeves of her coat and soaked in the basin of her gowned lap.

"Cathy?" he said, stunned to find her at the scene of one of his calls.

When she saw him, Catherine scrambled from the bed to embrace him. "Oh, Donald…"

"What are you doing here?"

He stepped to the side of the bed and held her by the shoulders, at arm's length to look her up and down. She leaned into him to bury her face in his chest. But she seemed without strength, and he held her at bay for a moment.

"Steven," she said. "He's…oh, dear God."

"Steven?" Donald said. He tried looking into Catherine's face. "That's your husband out there?" She nodded her head vigorously against the hollow of his neck and shoulder.

"How did it happen? Who did this to him?" Donald said. He did not dare think of possibilities right then.

"Ex-*cuse* me," the female officer said, looking first at Donald then at Gates.

Gates hitched at his beltless pants and shifted from one foot to the other. The brass tips of his bolo tie clicked together with each abrupt move. "Hey, Don. Give us a few minutes here, will you please?" he said. "We just need to get some more information from Mrs. Harper, and then you can talk to her all you want."

"But what's going on?" Donald said.

"Katie…." Gates turned to the other officer and nodded toward Catherine and Donald. The officer got off the bed and reached for Catherine.

"Come on, Ms. Harper. Just a bit more, please." She took gentle hold on one of Catherine's arms and turned her body to come between Donald and Catherine.

"Don, can you come with me for a second, while Officer Milton talks with Mrs. Harper?"

"Why is all this happening?" Catherine said meekly.

"What the hell?" Donald said again, glaring at Gates.

"Come on with me." Gates drew Donald back into the hall and to an adjoining room. It was another bedroom, but furnished like an office—two walls of books on brick and composite wood shelves, a big desk with a computer, a corkboard shingled with notes and papers on the wall above the desk.

"That's my ex-wife," Donald said.

"I know who it is, Don," Gates said, smiling ironically. "Geez, I was at your wedding."

"So what's the deal?" Donald asked.

The deal was, Mark Gates explained with the sort of measured patience of people who know they have the upper hand, they had Catherine's husband lying critically wounded by gunshot on his own living room floor; they had Catherine, who made the initial call to police from the kitchen phone, claiming she'd discovered Harper shot when she came over three-quarters of an hour ago "already dressed, she said, in just a nightgown and car coat." They had, as yet, no suspect or motive and no witness, except for several of the neighbors who said they heard two gunshots shortly before Catherine made her call to the police. "Oh, and we have this," he said, dipping into his jacket pocket and extracting a white business card in a sandwich baggie. Donald took it and looked it over. There was a printed endorsement for a beauty salon on one side, and on the other, scrawled in penned ink, was the legend:

For wild time!
call Professor Steven Harper
4205 Taylor
558-7285
Gives great c-Lit!

"What does this mean?" he asked.

"That's what we'd like to know," Mark Gates said. "It was lying on the victim's stomach."

"Are you even possibly thinking that Catherine had something to do with the shooting?"

"I'm not thinking anything at this point," Gates replied. "I'm only asking questions, trying to piece things together. All I want to say is, your wife—your ex-wife—is pretty stressed out right now, and I don't want to take her down to the police station to interview her if I can get enough done right here while the details are fresh in her mind. All I'm sayin' is, don't confuse or distract her while we're trying to do our thing here."

"All right," Donald said. "Do you have any ideas?"

"Oh, I got ideas," Gates said. He pinched his nostrils, then wiped his nose vigorously back and forth with his finger. "I got plenty of ideas. That's the problem."

Donald supposed there was some routine pattern to the questions Gates needed to follow with Catherine, but he did not believe his old classmate was much of an investigator. In high school, he'd always been slow when it came to seeing the world around him with any real understanding.

"I'll get back to my end of business," Donald said. "Let me tell you, though, Catherine is incapable of dishonesty. You can take what she tells you to the bank."

"I never thought different," Gates replied.

Donald got from Gates what information he had on Steven Harper to give to Bourke for his log sheet and report, and he returned to the living room. Harper still lay in the same position on the floor. The blood that had soaked through a large gauze bandage on his bare chest was congealing in waffled clots, and the respirator in its case beside him clicked and wheezed asthmatically. The paramedics were administering plasma and some clear liquid in another plastic bag—perhaps a Ringer's solution. Donald wasn't sure. He had never worked the medical squads, and he admired those who put in the hundreds of hours extra time and training to become paramedics.

"Is he breathing on his own?" he asked.

"Barely," Bourke said. "We've got him as stable as we're going to. We're about ready to transport."

Bourke and one of his paramedics slid a hardboard under Harper and strapped him down. Donald and Czernecky helped lift the board onto the rolling stretcher, and they wheeled it out into the hallway and down to the front lobby of the building. Deborah Gallant carried the respirator case alongside the stretcher, and a paramedic held two plastic bags of fluids aloft to ensure a constant drip through their umbilical tubes into the needles taped to Harper's arms.

When they'd loaded the stretcher into the back of Medic 10 and had seen it off down the drive to the street, Donald said to his crew, "I'll be a few minutes more. Standby here."

"Well, don't be too long, I gotta take a leak," Charlie Wesson said gruffly. He had not come with them into the apartment, remaining, instead, with Gene Metzger at the truck to have a cigarette.

Back inside, Donald found Mark Gates with Catherine in the front room now. Catherine stood by the couch, her hands forming a tent over her nose and mouth, as if she were covering a sneeze, and Gates was by the front door. "The door was still open?" he said, and Catherine nodded behind her hands. "And your husband was lying right there the whole time." He pointed to the bloody area on the carpet. She nodded again.

Donald paused at the doorway until Gates acknowledged him. "Need to make a phone call," he said.

"Go right ahead," Gates said. "Use the phone in that back bedroom. We're printing the one in the kitchen."

Donald looked at Catherine before he headed down the short hall to the back of the apartment. He could see she was crying again, the tears spilling onto her fingers as she stood looking at the place on the rug where her Harper had lain. He could imagine how it must be for her, and his inability to comfort her right then translated itself as irritation with Gates' callous way of questioning her.

"Okay, now Mrs. Harper, let's just take a few more minutes for me to make sure I've got all the events in line, here. Let's start again with when you found your husband."

She said, "I called his name and then went right to his side."

"And that's when you got the blood on your coat and nightgown?"

"After. After I called nine-one-one. I held him in my lap to raise his head. He couldn't breathe."

Down the hall in the bedroom office, he sat at the desk and dialed Kyle Thorpe's number at Station 6. A sleep-thickened voice answered the fourth ring.

"Kyle, it's Don Sparta."

"Okay, what has she done? What have they done to her?" Thorpe said.

"What has she *done*?" He thought the chief was referring to Catherine, and he couldn't conceive how Thorpe knew.

"Yes. Gallant. I hope that's the only thing you'd wake me up for in the middle of the night. What's happened with her?"

"No, look, it's not that, Kyle. I've got a real problem, a personal problem, that just came up on a call we made with Medic Ten."

He related to Thorpe the information he had so far about the shooting and Catherine's dilemma.

"So what do you need?" Thorpe asked.

"I want to stay here. I want permission...I don't know...permission to make sure she's all right, and that my kids.... This is my family, Kyle," Donald said, and in the ambivalence that admission created in him, there surfaced an apprehension of himself as impostor, too: the word "family" seemed alien to him now.

"So go ahead," Thorpe said.

"How? Just leave on my own recognizance?"

"Has this got you upset?"

"Yes, sir, of course it has."

"So, can you effectively focus on your work?"

"I don't.... I'm not sure I understand."

"See, you sound fucked up to me," Thorpe said. "You're out of there. I'm releasing you on a medical emergency leave for the duration of your shift. Appoint a temporary replacement and go home, or wherever you need to be."

Before Donald could say anything more, the phone went dead. For a moment, he did not move, his mind trying to engage itself again. On the desk in front of him was a haphazard pile of papers and brochures, and on top was another framed picture turned face down. He turned it over and discovered a photo of Catherine, Steven Harper, his girls, and a man in judicial robes, all smiling. For a moment he could not think what to do next under the stain of sadness that spread within him.

When Donald came back through the living room, he saw that Catherine was sitting on the couch, the female officer alongside her taking notes. Gates was ensconced in the lounge chair nearby. He was holding a glass with a clear liquid in it, waving it slowly back and forth under his nose.

"And you saw no one else at all?" Gates was staring directly at Catherine.

"No. Just the one man going out the front door of the building when I was coming in—he held the door for me."

"What did he look like, this man?"

"Nothing. I mean, he was just a man. He was wearing a cowboy shirt and jeans, and looked like...well, like someone who would live in a place like this."

"Another resident?" the other officer said.

"Yes. He was very polite and held the door for me when I came up the front steps."

"But nobody you knew? No one who looked familiar to you."

"No, of course not. I don't know anyone here, except Steven."

"So, when you got to your husband's apartment—after this nice man held the security door open for you—and you found him shot and were frightened there might be someone here, did you think to leave and go to someone else's door for help? Did you scream? Did you look around, check the bedrooms? I'm trying to get a clear picture here of just what you did."

"I've told you that. I just tried to rouse Steven; there was bleeding everywhere and a horrible rattling sound in his chest. I ran to the kitchen and called the rescue squad, then came back to try to help him breathe. I held him in my lap...."

Donald felt himself on the verge of interrupting, wanting to defend Catherine against Gates' jackhammer repetitive questioning. This seemed more than normal information gathering from a witness. He quashed the urge and instead slipped through the living room and out the door and down the hall to release his crew from service.

Czernecky, Wesson, and Gallant were standing at the bottom of the steps in front of the main door. The engine of the fire truck rumbled expectantly, and Gene Metzger stood on the drive beside the open cab door.

"I'm not going back to the station with the rig," he said to the three just below him on the steps. "I've just been released for the remainder of the shift. Wesson, as of now, you're in command."

"What the hell they do, fire ya?" Wesson said.

"You're not that lucky," Donald replied. "No, I'm staying here for a while longer to help out. There are some things I have to do yet."

"Well, then, can we get the hell home?" Czernecky said. "I can still get a couple more hours' sleep."

"Go on," Donald said. "We're done here."

"Yeah, and don't give me any shit for the rest of the night," Wesson said to Czernecky. "I'm not a soft touch like Sparta."

Deborah Gallant looked momentarily puzzled, but she turned and followed the other two toward the truck.

"Deborah!" Donald called.

She turned around and regarded him.

"I want to talk to you just a second," he said, and she detached herself from the others and returned to the bottom of the stairs, looking up at him where he stood at the edge of the stoop.

"Look," he began, and searched beyond her for the moment, trying to gather his thoughts. At the truck, Charlie Wesson was already climbing into the shotgun seat and Czernecky was climbing into the crew cab behind. "It's been a very long day, not at all the usual for Engine Fifty-five. And, after everything, I don't think I'm going to be able to go to dinner tomorrow evening, after all."

She regarded him without expression, simply waiting.

"It's not that I don't want to," he added quickly, "It's just that—well, to be truthful, Mrs. Harper, the woman in the living room—"

"She's your ex-wife," Deborah said, a statement rather than question which took Donald by surprise.

"Yes. How did you know?"

She shrugged. "Captain Bourke said. And the man who was shot is her husband."

"Well, that's right. Anyway, the thing is, I need to stay here a while and help out, maybe see her home. I don't know all the particulars here yet, but I may need to stay with our children for a time during all this, and—"

"I understand," she said. She smiled at him for the first time, a whimsical turn of her lips and slight tilt of her head. "Don't worry, you're not breaking a date, or anything."

"No, I don't suppose I am," he said. "But I really would like to talk to you more about some of the things we were discussing this afternoon. I truly like your attitude toward...well, actually toward lots of things, but firefighting especially. It's reminded me of some feelings of my own I'd almost forgotten."

"I'm glad," she said. She nodded toward the door behind him. "If there's anything I can do...."

"You've already done admirably today."

"I mean later. When I get off shift this morning. I can maybe help out, watch your children for you, or something."

Her offer seemed ingenuous enough, but he didn't know what to make of it, nor why his immediate impulse was to want to accept it. "That's very kind of you," he said. "But you must be exhausted, too. I'm sure you'll want time to yourself, maybe now you'll want to get back to Lincoln to see your boyfriend."

She dipped her head, smiled enigmatically.

"And if you get another call tonight," he said, pushing into the moment's silence, "Charlie's a good firefighter. The best. You won't get hurt following his lead."

"They're all good," she replied. "This is a great crew."

Donald waited at the top of the steps a minute longer, watching her cross the drive and take her place in the back of the crew cab next to Ed Czernecky, and thinking, *if she were not a member of this engine company, if only she were someone else....* But then, in the next instant, he wondered if she were someone other than a firefighter, would he feel anything that might draw his attention to her?

When Donald returned to the apartment, a uniformed officer was taping a yellow Police Department crime scene ribbon on the door. Inside, Gates had apparently finished questioning Catherine. She sat on the couch alone now, gazing down, her hands like belly-up crawfish in her lap. The woman officer sat at the Formica table, looking over her report, adding things, like a college student bent over an exam paper. Gates was somewhere else in the apartment.

"Are you done with Mrs. Harper?" Donald addressed the woman at the table.

She looked up, seemed surprised to see him still here. "Well, yes, I think so. For tonight. But check with Detective Gates."

"Where is he?"

"Back there." The woman jerked her head toward the back of the apartment.

"Cathy?" Donald turned to her. She looked up at him, her face gray with exhaustion.

"Is he going to live?" she asked in a childlike voice.

"I hope so. We'll know more later when I check in with the hospital," he said. "I'm going to see you home safely."

She nodded. "I don't think I can drive home right now."

"I'll drive you. You wait here a minute."

He headed down the hall and found Gates in the bathroom with the lab tech. The tech was still dusting the sink counter and mirror, and Gates, with a lit cigarette in his hand now, was leaning against the doorjamb, watching.

"I'm taking Mrs. Harper home now. Unless you want to grill her some more tonight," he said.

Gates looked up with an expression of mild amusement. "Not tonight. If we need to *grill* her for any more information, I'll get in touch with her tomorrow."

"Well, for my own satisfaction," Donald said, "I want to know where the hell you were going with your questions tonight. You can't possibly think she's involved in what happened, can you?"

"I don't make judgments on anyone, I just try to find things out," Gates replied.

"What do you think you'll find out from her other than what she told you?" Donald said.

"I'm not sure. But let me tell you, there are connections here, Don. All of the events she named today seem separate on their own merit; but there are connections."

"What connections?"

"Well, for starters, this afternoon Catherine Harper divorces the victim, and one of the big issues of the marriage, according to her, is infidelity. A couple hours earlier, she gets busted on breach of a restraining order for harassing another teacher at Platte City College. And this evening, she just drops by the apartment in her sexy nightgown to visit the man she's just divorced, and, lo and behold, he's been shot by person or persons unknown. If you start to connect the dots, you could begin to get some kind of picture here."

"A very primitive picture," Donald said. "You think that she came over here tonight and shot him? Where's her gun?"

"No, she didn't shoot him. Not herself. And she didn't kick the shit out of him, either. Not by herself."

"Goddamnit, Mark, this isn't an episode of *Law and Order*. This is a real-life woman who's had an extraordinary day. Show a little human sympathy, can't you? She may have lost her husband here to some hood or young punk."

"She already lost him in court today, I would have thought. But here she is at his apartment tonight. This wasn't a robbery or thrill shooting. This was a jealousy thing, I'll guarantee you."

"What makes you so sure?"

Gates patted his jacket pocket. "Well, the guy wasn't just shot, like someone caught up in a robbery; he was stomped or pummeled, either before or after he was shot. And there's the business card. The motive's in that somewhere. The handwriting on the back is a woman's, I'll bet."

"And you think Catherine wrote that?"

"Maybe, maybe not. But it's a good bet your ex-wife maybe knows who did. And for sure, Harper knows whoever shot him. I only hope he survives long enough to tell us, but I'm seldom that lucky," Gates said. "Anyways, I'm just working on all the angles I can find. And I see connections. I'll bet a month's salary everything that happened to her today ain't all coincidences. 'There's a reason for everything,' is what I've believed in all my career, and it's stood me in good stead all these years. No sense quitting on it now."

"Thanks for the wisdom of your years," Donald said curtly. "But I think I know her a bit better than you do."

"I'm sure you're right. Why don't you see she gets home and let me do my job finding out more about who done this. I'm not going to frame anyone here," Gates said. "But my advice for you is, you should maybe stay clear of her. She's not especially healthy for you to be around right now."

"I can take care of myself, thank you." Donald moved out of the way as Gates slipped by him out the bathroom door.

"I sure hope so," Gates replied. "Oh, and Don—"

Donald looked at him.

"I'm going to need her coat and nighty when you get her home...or wherever. For the blood samples. I'm going to send a cruiser back with you.

He'll wait at the house 'til she changes and take her things with him," Gates said. He patted Donald on the arm and ducked into the back bedroom.

In the hall outside the apartment, Donald took Catherine's arm and guided her toward the front door. "Why did you come here tonight?" he asked, trying not to sound reproachful.

"I don't know." She shook her head. "To say goodbye. To make it feel like it was really over, somehow."

That would be right, he thought. That would be something Catherine would want to do. "I can maybe understand that," he said. "But you didn't even get dressed?"

She didn't answer at first. Then she said, "I wasn't thinking straight. Which should come as no surprise."

"Is that what you told the police?"

"Yes."

Donald could think of no response. Although he believed her, he understood Gates' reluctance to accept the flimsiness of that as a reason.

As they walked to the lobby, Catherine leaned her head against his shoulder.

"Where are your firemen?" she asked when they were outside and she found no trucks.

"They went back in service," he replied.

"Why didn't you go back with them?"

"I got permission to stay. I thought I could help you."

Her eyes went limpid, and in the yellow glow of the front stoop lights, they seemed to swim for a moment. "Oh, Donald, that's the nicest thing anyone has said all day." She buried her face in his neck and squeezed him to her for a long moment.

He walked with her to her car, parked around the back of the apartment building. She slid into the passenger seat without any prompting.

When Donald had got behind the wheel, Catherine said, "When I change my clothes, will you take me to the hospital? I want to be there with him."

"No," Donald said. He started the car. "There's nothing you can do at the hospital that will be helpful. Also, there's a police cruiser that is supposed to follow us to collect your coat and gown when we get you home."

"Why?"

"For blood evidence."

"Evidence of *what?*"

"That it's his blood, I suppose."

"Of course it's his blood, the poor man," she said.

"They know that. But it's part of a crime scene. They need all that kind of stuff, who knows why." He glanced up and looked in the rearview mirror, saw the headlights of a cruiser parked in front illuminate suddenly.

She was quiet again, looking out the window of the door.

Donald eased the car down the long drive leading onto Taylor.

"But he's all alone. He probably doesn't even know where he is," Catherine said.

"There's not a thing you can do to help," he repeated and turned right toward the intersection with 42nd Street.

After a bit, she said, "He thinks I did this to Steven, doesn't he?"

He was surprised she was that aware right now. "Gates? I'm sure he doesn't. At least not seriously," he said. "I think he's just going down every path as a matter of procedure."

"Well, Steven will tell them I didn't hurt him."

"I'm sure. It may be a while, though, before he can tell anyone anything. He's pretty banged up."

She looked at him, and her eyes seemed dull with hopelessness. He saw that she must sense, as he did, her husband might not live. Even now he was probably dead on a table in the emergency room, Donald thought, waiting for the police coroner to release him to the county morgue. And Catherine was only taking her time to ease into the hard truth of what she had once before experienced when she had waited beyond hope for Donald to come and make things right again.

At her house, he parked the car in the driveway. "I'm going to need to get back to the station for my truck, sooner or later," he said, "but I can stay here for a while. We'll need to talk to the kids sometime tomorrow, tell them what's happened, I guess."

She groaned again. "I can't face that yet."

"Do you want me to talk to them?"

"No. I'll do it. Tomorrow's soon enough," she said. He was assured by a note of decisiveness in her voice, and he thought that she might not need him, after all.

But, as if she'd read his thoughts, she said abruptly, "You'll come in for a while, won't you?"

"If you want me to," he said.

"Please!" she replied, and reached out, taking his hand. "I'll make you some coffee, if you want. Or a drink. But don't go, not just yet."

"I'm off duty until Monday. I have plenty of time."

"You can stay as long you want," she said. "I'm really grateful you're here."

When they climbed the three steps up the terrace and opened the front door to enter the house, Donald felt for just an instant as if he were coming home. But when the police car that had followed them pulled to the curb in front of the house, he knew there was still more to come before it would all be over for the both of them.

Chapter 22

The sun was well up, the bedroom lit by daylight. Out the window beside Catherine's bed, an anvil of cloud drifted across the sky above the paintbrush tips of the poplars along the fence line of the back yard. Her body was enervated, heavy in sleep hangover, but her mind seemed alert. It was the way she felt sometimes when she was expecting something to happen, before she knew what it might be. It was the way she used to feel when she began work on a new painting.

She was surprised that she had slept soundly. She looked at the pillow beside her, the dent there yet from another head. Donald had lain there last night. In bed with her for the first time in five years. He'd held her close, his fingers spread through her hair, cradling the back of her head in his palm, and she had cried into the protective hollow his body had sculpted for her. She had cried for a long time. More than tears poured from her as she released her spirit's toxins in great, shuddering sobs. He had held onto her until she was empty, and then had they...? No. She recalled that now. Recalled nearly everything. Their quiet embrace as familial and unselfconscious as any two people accepting of the vast changes their lives had undergone over time. With Donald's arms around her, she had fallen dead asleep.

She could not hear any sounds from downstairs or the girls' rooms, and it took her another moment to remember that Holly and Donna had spent the night at Charlotte's at a "slumber party" with their cousin Trisha. Then everything else clicked back into place. Yesterday's events—the divorce hearing, her humiliation in the Platte City jail—were distant already, their limits known and finally situated in their order of time. But not last night's. Donald had helped her subdue her anguish in the moment, and she had resisted calling back the horror of events in detail. They still waited there just beyond her need to face them. Soon enough she would gingerly begin to peel back the layers of emotional detritus between what was delusion and what was real in order to save the living tissue of mind and heart.

In the bathroom, she stood under a hot shower, letting the water beat on her upturned face. She stood a long time in the water, turning slowly front to back, back to front, to feel the needling massage of the spray on her flushed skin. Everything seemed immediate and free from the weight of time. There was just this moment and the hot water awakening her muscles and scouring her skin.

In terry robe, with a towel turbaned around her head, she descended to the kitchen for coffee. The state of the kitchen was the same as she had left it. The way it had been yesterday. The day before. The soiled dishes helter-skelter in the sink, the dining table scattered with crumbs and empty glasses. All that had happened in the last two days outside this room, beyond the doors of this house, was in another world, another dream state. Only the aura of lives lived here seemed real yet. *And here I am,* she thought.

Catherine poured herself a cup of coffee, already brewed in the Mr. Coffee maker. Had Donald done that? But where was he?

There was something she had to tell her daughters, she realized, some vital knowledge about her they had to have. It was high time she began paying attention to them again. She'd been neglectful for too long in that department, and she was in danger of losing the best friends she had. The only friends right now.

With a cup of hot coffee in hand, she went to the patio door and looked out onto the deck. The grass in the back yard was flattened and wet, but it was for the most part green as spring again, and only a few places under the poplars and around the bushes by the deck rail were white. All the way down the broad boulevard of back yards below Catherine's house, the earth had taken back the snow, and spring continued in its regenerative growth.

The phone beside the whiteboard rang, and she returned to the kitchen and plucked the receiver off the wall phone on the fourth ring.

"Catherine!"

"Charlotte?" Catherine said.

"What the hell's going on?" Charlotte demanded.

"I'm having coffee," Catherine said. "How are the girls?"

"On their way home with Donald," Charlotte said. "Now, what's been going on? What the hell happened last night?"

"How are they getting home?" Catherine evaded.

"Donald. Donald came to get them a little while ago in your car. He's bringing them home. What happened last night, for chrisake?"

"Well, what did you hear about last night?"

"That Steven was shot by someone? You were there, for chrisake, you tell me. Is he really dead?"

Hearing Charlotte's harsh voice tore the curtain of uncertainty between what was real and what she still hoped might be delusion. It all returned to her with icy certainty. The phone call Donald had made to the hospital. Last night. From this same phone in the kitchen. Steven had died on the way to the hospital. Was that what he said? Steven *dead*? And she had broken down, and Donald had held her close, his arms wrapped around her, until he carried her upstairs to her bed, exhausted.

"Cat?"

"Maybe," Catherine said, her voice suddenly husky with phlegm. "That's what they told Donald." But she knew that it was true. How could he have survived? All that blood. Not a flicker of life on his face, even when she held his head in her lap and called his name. Even when he had breath still, he had already died, she knew, before they had taken him from her arms.

Under all the rubble of yesterday's confused events, there were two granite certainties: Steven was gone; and there was nothing more that could happen that would be any worse.

"Donald made it sound awfully grim," Charlotte was saying now. "He said Steven was shot by someone, and you were there with him."

"He told you that?" Catherine said. "Do Holly and Donna know?"

"No, of course not. They don't know anything. Not yet. Tell me what the hell happened, will you?"

"No. I can't. I wouldn't know where to begin."

"Anywhere. Jesus Christ on a crutch, Cat. What were you doing there?"

Catherine drew a long breath and cleared her throat. "I thought I would just go over and see him one more time. Say goodbye properly, without all the craziness that had surrounded us. I needed a time alone with him to have some closure for both of us."

"Oh, Cat...." Charlotte groaned. "What are you going to do?"

"I'll tell you what I want to do, what I want real bad." Catherine could hear Charlotte breathe a sigh in the pause between her words. In her mind she saw her mom and dad. That dinky little house in Corinth. She saw her child self under the covers in her old bedroom. *Under the eaves,* she thought, seeing that secret place in her cracker-box house where she used to hide from all the noise, the tumult of angry voices. Under the rafters in the tiny attic room, hearing rain drum the roof. "But I can't, Charly. I never could. There has never been anyone there to make things better for me. So somehow, I'm just going to have to do it for myself."

"What are you talking about? I don't understand what you're saying," Charlotte replied. "You're not going to do anything foolish, are you?"

"If I knew myself, I'd tell you," Catherine said.

When she'd hung up the phone, she returned to her bedroom to dress. She tore through the clothes in her closet and drawers—what to wear? for what eventualities should she be prepared?—until she settled on a pair of jeans and a green Platte City State College sweatshirt.

While she was combing out her hair, she heard the front door tremble open, the aluminum storm door rattle shut. Holly and Donna were home.

"Lo-a-lo!" Holly called out.

Catherine called back. "Up here."

"And I'm down here," Holly said brightly.

There was that manic edge to her voice, a taut energy from being wired by fatigue. She'd been away all night with her cousins a couple of times before, and it was the same each time she came home: she would be garrulous and silly for a time, and then suddenly she would deflate all at once and move about with a dreamy smile on her face, her heavy-lidded eyes barely focusing, until she found a place to get out of the way and crash to sleep. Catherine wondered what, if anything, Donald had told her. Worse, what Donna had heard. What way was there to put the news in any light her daughters could see clearly right now while she herself was still catching up to it all—whatever *it* was in its totality. Her head was filled with images she could not connect in a single, coherent composition yet. All of them aswirl in her mind, nothing cleanly lit. Shadow and brilliance, red and black.

Momentarily, the front door opened and closed again, and she could hear Donald's heavier step up the three stairs from the entry to the living room. "It's me," he called. "Can I come in and use the phone?" It seemed strange to her that he would ask. But there was a tentative hitch in his voice, the outsider announcing his presence to the house. In the years they'd been dealing with one another over visitations with the children, the occasions were rare when Donald had come beyond the entryway into the house. And when Steven had lived there, too, she had never invited Donald farther than the entryway.

"I'll be right down," she called back. "Have some of the coffee you made."

Catherine could hear Donna talking to him, wanting to know if he would watch television cartoons with her for a while.

"Maybe. But first, I've got to go make a telephone call and then have someone drive me to the fire station and get my truck."

When she came downstairs, Catherine found Donald sitting on the stool by the whiteboard, on the phone. Holly was at the refrigerator, bent over with her head poked inside as she rummaged the lower shelves.

"They didn't feed you?" Catherine said.

"I wasn't hungry," Holly said. She straightened up and opened the freezer compartment. "Why don't we ever have anything good to eat around here?"

"As soon as I'm employed again, we'll have snack food. Right now, it's only the basics," Catherine replied.

221

"Basics," Holly said. "You mean TV dinners, hot dogs and beans."

"Thanks a lot," Catherine said.

Holly grinned broadly. "Just *kidding*. Lighten up, Mom." She opened a cupboard and snatched out the box of crackers. "Why don't you get a job at Ralston-Purina? Francine's mom works there. She makes lots of money just taking bags of dog food off the conveyor belt and putting them into cartons."

"I may just have to, if I can't get back to teaching or find myself a decent office job," Catherine said.

"Beggars can't be choosers," Holly said.

Catherine was not sure where the sharp point in her daughter's offhanded comments were coming from: either Holly was too tired to know what she was saying, or else she was reacting to something her cousin and she may have talked about last night. She sometimes seemed resentful when she came home from Charlotte's and all the comforts of her cousin's house. Catherine remembered how defensive she herself used to feel in junior high school the few times she got together with her girlfriends for a night in houses clean and without tension, and she'd come back home in the morning sullen and resentful of her mother. Whatever the source of Holly's remarks, Catherine decided to let it slide. Truth was, ever since she'd been laid off at school, she had been too depressed to even try to get another job. That attitude would have to change. She would never be hired back to teach at Platte City State College. Holly was right, beggars definitely could not be choosers.

With a dish of crackers on a plate, Holly disappeared into the family room where Donna had already turned on the television. From the family room came the distant jabber of bird-voiced cartoons.

Mostly Donald was listening to whoever was on the other end of the line, nodding his head solemnly, his verbal acknowledgments little more than grunts. He plugged his open ear with a finger, trying to block out the sounds of his family around him. Seeing him there in the kitchen, Catherine tried to remember what it was like when they were a family. At the moment all she could retrieve were the long hours of waiting for him to come home from his 24-hour shifts, and Holly and Donny Jr. hoping to do something on weekends—a movie, roller skating—if Daddy wasn't too tired or didn't have some other project to do, was how Catherine remembered it all. It wasn't that everything changed for them in the instant of Donny's death; it was that Donny's dying exposed what had already changed long before.

From the other room, Donna suddenly shouted, "No! Leave it alone, I'm watching it."

Holly said something too low for Catherine to hear, and Donna replied, "I was here first. This is my show!"

Catherine sucked in her breath. "Hol-lee…," she crooned wearily.

"All ri-ight," Holly sang back in a two-note response.

Then Holly and Donna were calling each other names.

"Brat."

"Dorkface."

Catherine was already moving toward the family room to respond. Donald rolled his eyes at her.

"Isn't there enough animosity and violence in this world without two sisters constantly quarreling with one another?" she cried as she burst in on them. They were startled silent by her energy. "Holly, you have *got* to stop picking on your little sister, she's the only little sister you'll ever have in this world."

"But I didn't—"

"And, Donna, you had better get that chip off your shoulder. You've been bad-tempered for days now. But if you're going to be grouchy, you'd better stay out of your sister's way."

"I was staying out of her way. I was just watching my TV show, and she comes in and turns the channel over and calls me dorkface!" Donna's face was full of injury over the injustice.

In the kitchen, Donald was saying to whoever was on the line, "Then you shouldn't have any further questions of Mrs. Harper any longer, right?" He hesitated, listening, and then picked up a marker from the tray and wrote a telephone number down on the board just below the boxed reminder, DO IT TODAY! "Okay, but I don't think she has anything more to add that can help you."

He hung up the phone and turned to Catherine. "It looks like they have the man who shot your husband.*"*

"How do you know?" she said. "Who was that?"

"Mark Gates, the cop who was such a…*dorkface* last night." Donald smiled. "Anyway," he continued, lowering his voice suddenly to just above a whisper, "Gates says they've caught the shooter. Actually, he turned himself in sometime last night."

"Who? Someone who lived there?"

"According to Mark, the guy thinks your husband was, in Mark's words, 'diddlin' his wife.'"

She flushed, the heat of her humiliation automatic. "At his apartment? Was there someone at his apartment *last nigh*t?"

"Shh!" Donald warned, nodding toward the family room. "No, not then."

Something more clicked in her mind about last night when she had called Steven. Another ray of light cutting the shadows in her memory. His insistence that she not come over, even for sex. And how she had dressed in her slinkiest nightie, had come even when she thought he might not let her in. Hadn't she known he would be with another woman? Had she gone there when he so bluntly refused her, just to catch him out?

"The guy who shot him, he's a truck driver, and he came home from the road yesterday to find his wife and children had been killed in that fire on Highway 30."

"Dear God," Catherine said.

"Bouracek, Borachick or something. Jack. His wife, it turns out, was a student in one of your husband's classes."

Catherine groaned. "But how could he think Steven had something to do with the accident?"

"No, not the accident. Only coincidentally, anyway," Donald said. "Mark showed me a card last night—"

"Yes, I saw it. A business card from the same hair dressers I go to."

"Well, did you see what was written on the back? Where someone had written something pretty personal on the back, with your husband's name and telephone number—"

"You can say his name," Catherine said flatly. "*Steven.*" The way he said "your husband" each time, with a bluntness that was judgmental, stung her.

Donald smiled. "Well anyway, I imagine that when this guy Borchick...Bourcek found his whole family wiped out, and this card with your—with *Professor Steven Harper's* number and address on it—he was devastated enough to want somebody else to pay for the deaths of his wife and children."

"But it was an *accident,*" she said. "It was a terrible accident. What kind of reasoning is that?"

"No reasoning at all. Just animal pain," Donald said. "He needed catharsis, or whatever."

"But to shoot somebody, want him dead because your family died in an automobile accident? What sort of catharsis is that? I would never even think to do such a thing."

"Jealousy and despair are similar emotions. It doesn't take much of either to kindle rage."

"Why do men hate so much? Where does all their anger come from?"

"What do you mean?" Donald said.

"Their anger. At *everything.* Anger at women, at children, animals. But never at themselves."

"I'm not touching that one," Donald said. He looked at his watch. "I've got to get rolling, if we're going to get to an early movie. I need to get my truck at the station, and then go to my apartment to change."

"I can take you to the fire station, if you'll let me," she offered.

"Yes. Thanks. I was counting on it."

"What movie are you talking about?"

"Don't know yet. I kind of told the girls on the way home that if they wanted, I would take them to the movies this afternoon. To give you some time to yourself."

Later, driving to his fire station in her car, Catherine said, "How can I ever explain to them about last night? How am I going to tell them their step-father was *murdered*?"

"You don't worry about that right now," Donald said. "They don't need to know right away. It's not like he's been present in their lives recently."

"But they know I saw him yesterday. They know we just got divorced yesterday. They lived under the same roof with him, and they had a relationship with him. And they need to know I was there when he died last night."

"Look, I can talk to them, if you wish. Just give it a bit of time. In any case, they don't need to know that you were over there when he died. The police aren't pursuing any more questions where you're concerned," Donald said earnestly, putting a hand on the dashboard and inclining his head toward her.

She did not answer him. What could she say? Once again, he was wrong about handling tragedy. But for the right reasons. Probably the time had passed for her to bring it up to the girls, anyway. It wasn't a revelation she could pass off as an afterthought, something she had forgotten to mention when they had come home. And how was she going to tell them that she had been arrested yesterday and would have to face once again the legal consequences of her irrational behavior. Donna was angry already for her mother not sticking up for her against Holly. And Holly was probably still upset that her mother had left them in the snowstorm to go to Steven's apartment two nights ago. But to suppress the knowledge of what so painfully wouldn't leave her mind, and to lie that she didn't know what she already knew when they would inevitably hear the truth from someone else....

"But you told Charlotte already. She knows I was there last night," she said.

Donald leaned back in his seat. "Yeah, well that was a mistake," he said. "But she knew you were gone the night before and the kids were alone, and she asked me how you were doing." He shook his head. "It was stupid of me. I guess I thought she could be of some support to you, if things got...." He shrugged. "Anyway, I'm sorry. I don't think she'll say anything to the girls."

She pulled into Station 5 and drove around to the side where the on-duty firefighters parked their cars. She stopped behind Donald's pickup.

"Thanks," he said, reaching for the door handle.

Catherine put the car in Park. She struggled suddenly to bring her voice above a whisper. "I really thought once I could change things. I used to believe I could make things better for everyone."

"What things are you talking about?" he asked.

"Everything," she replied. "The way people treat each other, mostly. The irresponsible way people use each other. I don't have the heart anymore, Donald." She looked at him, right into his eyes looking back at her. "I feel empty of any spiritual power. I don't think I have a soul any longer. Do you suppose that's possible?" She saw the sudden worry in his expression.

"No," he said, turning his head abruptly to look out his side window. "I definitely do not think that is possible."

"No?" she said. "But if you don't have a soul, you can't feel responsible for others."

Donald looked back at her, his eyes fixed on hers. "You haven't lost any of your soul, or your goodness, Cathy. The only thing you may be guilty of is bad judgment when you act on your emotions."

She had been apologizing to him, she realized, and in doing so, she felt a tenderness. "Earlier, while I was getting dressed and trying to figure out how I was going to explain to our girls all that's happened in the last couple of days, I was thinking it could have all been different if any one of us had made even a single, small, different choice that wasn't selfish. Me, Steven, Martin Stuart could have changed all that has happened by a different act or word—the tiniest gesture of compassion or goodwill that could have sent events another way entirely. I saw it in my mind like the image of rings on the surface of a pond where the stone drops in: concentric ripples outward from the center that eventually move every bit of water in the pond."

"Connections, Mark Gates called it." He pinched the bridge of his nose and closed his eyes momentarily. "But the quickest way to get around or over a tragedy is to acknowledge that what has happened already can't be undone. This is just the way things turned out from something we may have done or left undone. What has to be different is what we do *now*. Where we go from here."

"Well, I know where I go from here," Catherine said, her mind leaping to what lay ahead. "I go to jail. I go on trial for my personal convictions. Then I go to jail. Or back to St. Joseph's."

"We'll see where you go. And if it comes to that, I'll be there with you."

"I'm going to work on the chain gang. I'm going to hell on a handcar," she said, caught up in the lilt of the language.

"No, you won't do any of that. You're not there yet," Donald said. "But now, poor Mr. Bourcek, that's another story. His moment of catharsis will cost him at least ten years in prison. Maybe more." He swung open the door and looked at her sidelong, one leg out in the parking lot, his body half turned to get out of the car. "If you want, I *will* talk to the kids about what happened," he said. "It might be easier. Think about it."

"No, I'll tell them myself," she said resolutely.

"What are you going to say?"

"I don't know yet. I don't know how to explain to them something so horrible. But I'll handle it myself when the moment presents itself."

"Well, if you do, take it slowly," he said and stepped out. "I wouldn't lay too much on them all at once. Start with what they already know, that you went to see your husband in the storm and he wasn't home, so you went last night again, and he had died. He was killed by someone who'd mistaken him for someone else."

On impulse, she said abruptly, "I'm free today. Do you want some adult company at the movies, or would you rather be with your daughters alone?"

"You kidding?" His eyes brightened. "You want to come along?"

"I don't think I've been to a movie with anyone since the silents."

"You were never silent," Donald said, grinning. "Okay, I'll see you later."

At home again, passing through the kitchen, Catherine found a drawing Donna had made on the whiteboard while she was gone. She paused to look. It was of a car, broad-nosed, with big white tires. In all the windows, Donna had drawn heads of people—a woman's, a man's, staring straight ahead, the way adults always did in a child's mind; three children peering out the large back door window, face-on with fish-eyed flat expressions. The two girls with string mop hair, and a boy with a crewcut. A family. But she could not see from anyone's faces what they might be feeling. There were no mouths, only eyes, and the eyes showed nothing in regard to each other or to what they were observing out their windows. Donna had not finished the picture yet. Or sadly, she had, Catherine thought.

She found both her daughters in the family room with the television tuned to a rerun episode of a series about adolescents stranded on an island and trying to survive in a society of their own making. *Flight 29 Down* was a show Holly liked to watch on Saturday mornings.

"You guys," Catherine broke in on their concentration, "your dad's going to be back later to take us out to a movie this afternoon."

"Yeah, he told us already," Donna said without taking her eyes off the screen.

Holly turned to look back. "Are you going too?"

"I'm going too," Catherine said. "He asked me to come along."

"How come?"

"Just because," Catherine said.

"All of us are going?" Donna said, turning now to look at Catherine with a perplexed frown on her brow.

"Why not?" Catherine said. "We haven't done anything together as a family for years."

"Is that why Dad came to pick us up this morning?" Holly asked. Catherine saw something else in her countenance that alerted her to her daughter's mind at work.

"What did he tell you about why he was there?"

"He just said you were still in bed asleep, so he came to get us," Donna cut in.

"Well, that's right. I didn't even know he had gone to get you," Catherine replied.

"But why wasn't his truck here?" Holly said.

All at once, Catherine caught in the shift of Holly's tone of voice the same edge she felt when the police sergeant who was Donald's friend questioned her about her presence in Steven's apartment.

"Well…," she said, and it came to her in a blue effusion of light behind her eyes that this was the moment. "Both of you, come sit down with me in the living room. I have something I need to tell you, and I want your attention."

Passing by the whiteboard in the kitchen, she paused to regard again the motto in the upper corner above the unfinished picture Donna had been drawing. "Do It Today," she said, as if she were seeing it for the first time. "Now, that's good advice."

"That's *old*," Donna said from behind her. "It's been there forever."

"And do you remember who put it there?" Catherine asked.

"Didn't you?"

"Does that sound like something I'd write?" she said. She plucked up the eraser on its string and squared it in her hand; then with several broad strokes, she bore down on the board, wiping it all clean.

When they had gathered on the living room couch and wingback chair, she no longer felt that pent-up anxiety she had been battling all morning. A confessional aura of calm had enfolded her. She was ready, whatever the outcome.

<<<◇>>>

www.ingramcontent.com/pod-product-compliance
Lightning Source LLC
Chambersburg PA
CBHW060916180626
46817CB00004B/1289